STAGE OF LOVE

STAGE OF LOVE

CECILY SHELBOURNE

G.P. PUTNAM'S SONS, NEW YORK

SBN: 399-12078-5

Library of Congress Cataloging in Publication Data

Shelbourne, Cecily.
   Stage of love.

   I.   Title.
PZ4.S54313St3   [PR6069.H418]   823'.9'14   77-9005

Chapter One

LOOKING ACROSS THE ROOM at the curtained bed where her sister's peaceful figure lay, Isabella felt a surge of impatience. How late Kate slept! And she never budged. She always lay in the position she took as Juliet after taking the sleeping potion, arms on her breast, flat on her back, her thick red hair round a face of perfect stillness. She didn't seem to breathe. It was a valuable gift in an actress.

Isabella longed to creep across the room, give a loud whoop and jump on her sleeping sister. But she thought better of it.

She never felt the actor's need to rebuild her energies in long hours of sleep. Every morning when the farm carts rumbled into the town she lay listening to the wheels on the cobbles, the shouts of the carters, the crack of their whips. She knew the time to expect the sweet shrill whistle of the baker's boy going by with his trays of fresh loaves. In the town outside everybody was alive and awake. How could Kate waste time asleep?

Unable to stay in bed a minute longer, Isabella climbed out. The room was bitterly cold, and in the night a glassy lay-er of ice had formed on top of the jug. When she poured out the water, cupped her hands in it and splashed her face, her cheeks burned. She dressed as quickly as she could, shivering.

The sisters were startlingly different in appearance—a stranger would never know they were related. Isabella was tall and thin, leggy, with an olive skin and very dark brown eyes. There was something Celtic in her looks. But Kate was a little thing, with a luminous white skin, wide-apart green eyes and luxuriant red hair. The single similarity between them was the shape of their short straight noses.

At the bottom of the staircase the housemaid, Milly, a sturdy thirteen-year-old, was on her knees in a cloud of dust.

"Mornin', miss."

"Good morning, Milly," said Isabella with her most casual air. She was not yet used to the family having a maidservant, although it was already a year.

She whisked into the front parlor.

Her mother, Ellen Winter, was sitting sedately at the breakfast table drinking coffee. The room was rather bare and certainly cold, although a small fire was lit. Ellen Winter was muffled in a shabby gray shawl over her plain dark dress. She was a small woman, with Isabella's olive skin, brown hair which had not yet turned gray, and an expression in her dark eyes which changed from energetic liveliness to prim disapproval. When she saw Isabella, she frowned.

"Now, why have you risen so early? You know I prefer you to rest."

"*You* are up, Mama."

"I am not an actress and don't need to keep fresh for the evening performance. Kate has more sense."

"Oh, Kate! She's so vexing, lying there looking like Juliet. One day I know I shall have to jump on her."

Ellen should have frowned again, but laughed. She liked what she called "ill-discipline," enjoyed romping bad behavior while firmly correcting it; her dark eyes always snapped with interest when her daughters quarreled. Once, when there had been a backstage fight between two actors, Ellen had stood watching attentively and cried, "Good shot!" when one actor landed a savage crack on his opponent's jaw.

She poured Isabella some coffee and looked her over. This year, 1837, all the girls were in striped muslin, and Isabella had been enchanted with the new dress her mother had made her, white striped with marigold-colored flowers. But the girl would wear it all the time.

"You should keep your clothes for occasions," remarked Ellen. "Or when the time arrives there will be nothing to wear."

Isabella ignored that, gulped her coffee and buttered some bread. Her mother continued to study her. To Ellen her children were objects of the deepest interest—she made them the best audience in the world. She never showed them her love by words and would not dream of telling them they were handsome, although she thought so.

The moment she'd finished her breakfast Isabella jumped up restlessly and went to the window. She peered out into the street, saying she was sure it would snow. Suddenly she pressed closer to the windowpane.

"Goodness! A carriage stopping here!"

"Then do not be seen looking at it."

"But Mama—"

"Come away from the window this instant. Do you wish to be thought a servant?"

At her mother's sharp voice Isabella crossly left the window, remarking that there was a coat of arms on the carriage door and wasn't *that* interesting, at least? Ellen did not deign to reply.

A moment later Milly, distinctly dusty, came into the room.

"Letter for the master, ma'am."

"You may take it to him, Milly."

"Not got the stairs finished, ma'am."

"Very well, give the letter to me," said Ellen, with a look of dignified dismissal. Milly still hung about, looking on with eyes like a clever terrier's.

"Waitin' outside still. Wants an answer, 'e said."

"Tell the *footman* to wait," said Ellen, closing her eyes.

Milly left the room, and Isabella rushed to her mother and waited while Ellen broke the heavy seal.

"What can it be? Mama, speak!"

"Isabella, don't be ridiculous," said Ellen automatically.

Reading the letter, she did not look pleased. Her face grew slightly red. She passed it to Isabella in silence.

The paper was so thick that when it was unfolded again it creaked. The letter, written in the third person, announced that it had the honor to inform Mr. Thomas Winter that Mr. Edwin Sidaway, steward to His Lordship the Earl of Bagot, wished to inquire whether Mr. Winter and his actors would consent to pay a visit to Bagot Park. Might a private performance be arranged of "some dramatic offering of suitable interest? Mr. Sidaway would do himself the honor of waiting on Mr. Winter etc. etc."

Before Isabella could exclaim, enraptured over this request, her mother said briefly she must go and see Thomas at once.

With Ellen safely out of the way, Isabella ran to the window again. Rank, possessions, the world of privilege always fascinated her. The Bagot carriage at the door was certainly worth staring at. Everything shone. The beautiful chestnut horses shifting and stamping, sending out clouds of steamy breath in the cold air; the glittering brass lamps and yellow and black coachwork of the carriage, the coachman's tall hat, the silver buttons on the footman's livery . . . half in pleasure, half in envy, Isabella sighed.

Thomas Winter was upstairs in the room he called his "sanctum," a kind of office where he kept his papers on the battered table drawn up to the window. His papers indicated Thomas's state of mind; they were in wild disarray. Untidy heaps of unanswered letters, notes he had scrawled and afterward couldn't read, bills to pay, plays to read. Thomas never admitted to being cold, and there was no fire in the small grate. He had a small shawl of his wife's draped round the shoulders of his rusty black coat and was bent at the table writing with a scratchy quill. He glanced up as his wife came into the room.

Thomas looked what he was—an actor. His face was high-cheekboned, his manner theatrical, his curling hair cut to show at its best onstage. His voice had a richness, a declamatory note. As a young man he had been handsome, with russet hair and swimming eyes, but middle age had dried and coarsened his looks and covered his cheeks with broken veins.

"Tom, do I disturb you?"

"I cannot spare any time just now, my dear."

"Scratch" went the quill.

But she still came into the room and closed the door. The air was so cold that their breathing was like smoke. It's very stubborn of Tom, she thought, to keep his sanctum as cold as the street. She went over and draped the shawl more closely round his shoulders as if he were an aging baby.

"I am afraid I have to speak to you. This letter has come. It is from the Earl of Bagot."

She waited while he read the letter, standing quietly beside him. She knew the letter would harass him, and expected the frown and the sigh.

"His Lordship has never honored me before with such a request."

"Indeed, no."

He looked at her anxiously. Everything Ellen said and did affected him.

"It might be the beginning of great things for us," he ventured, waiting for an encouraging reply.

She said nothing.

"You will be back in the gentry where you belong, my love."

Ellen merely said, "A servant is waiting for your reply."

"I shan't write it, I had better speak to him," he said, standing up so that the shawl hung off one shoulder, looking very ridiculous. She removed the shawl.

"Yes, tell him that you will call at Bagot Park. We do not want the steward coming here."

Thomas, throwing back his head as if about to make his entrance on a stage, hurried down the stairs.

The Bagot footman, a tall young man in beautiful livery with silver buttons, listened politely to Thomas's message. Had Ellen been watching she would not have liked her husband's manner to the footman; it was too friendly.

"I will inform Mr. Sidaway that you will be waiting for him," said the footman, bowing.

The carriage clattered away, leaving the street to more workaday folk, a farmer on a donkey, a man with a milk cart and some children bowling hoops.

Isabella started guiltily when the parlor doors opened and her parents came into the room.

Coming away from the window and beginning to talk to avoid being scolded, she said, "Papa, is not the news exciting? Imagine, the *Earl* has sent for you! When shall we go? What play shall we do? Mama, you always said you wanted to see inside Bagot Park!"

Thomas had sat down heavily and Ellen draped the little shawl round him again and solicitously poured him some coffee, generally behaving as if he were recovering from shock. Then she said mildly, "I'm afraid I shall not be going to Bagot Park."

Her husband and daughter looked aghast; Ellen was the center of the family and nothing was done, could be enjoyed, without her.

"But my dear—" began Thomas. She interrupted.

"No, Tom. Nothing would induce me to go."

"Mama—nobody at Bagot Park knows who you are!" exclaimed Isabella, "Of course you must come, you *know* you wish to come—"

"Isabella, your father and I want to talk. Please leave us."

Longing to stay, full of curiosity, Isabella unwillingly left the room.

She thought of listening at the door, but it was oak and

very solid. Then it occurred to her that here was an excellent excuse for waking Kate.

She ran up the stairs two at a time, burst into the dark bedroom, tugged open the curtains and rushed over to shake Kate awake.

"Go away."

"I shall not! This time you *have* to wake up! Listen to what has just happened!"

Kate, groaning, came slowly to her senses, scarcely taking in what her sister was saying. She tried to pay attention but Isabella's voice was loud and excited. Kate lay back in sleepy silence while Isabella talked on.

Different in looks, the girls' characters were always at variance, Isabella talkative, volatile and restless, her elder sister quiet, sometimes radiant, sometimes dreamy, her thoughts reflected in large, melting green eyes.

Isabella plumped herself down on the bed, and her weight hurt Kate's feet. Kate moved them.

"The parents are in the parlor now. Mama is talking and Pa has gone into a dumpish gloom. Imagine, Kate, Mama says she positively will not go with us to the Earl's house."

"Because she is related to them."

"Only twenty times removed!"

"She still can't forget she is gentry," said Kate, swallowing a yawn.

"She forgot it when she fell in love with Pa and eloped with him in a chaise from the vicarage."

"Isabella. Do stop shifting about."

"I know how Mama feels, you know," said Isabella, not listening. "She won't go to Bagot Park as a menial—the person who *mends the costumes*."

"Being in the theater is not menial."

"Pooh. Trundling from town to town is. Living on a gift of the gab and a few tattered cloaks and feathered hats. If Pa hadn't known half a hundred plays, Shakespeare and Sheridan and *The Smugggler's Bride* and Lord knows what, and if *we* hadn't danced and sung and played elves since we could walk, and if poor Mama hadn't sewn everything from Hamlet's black to Lear's rags we'd have starved."

Kate did not bother to reply. She was accustomed to her sister's disparagement of their profession, though neither their parents nor the girls themselves ever imagined they could do anything else.

Until their mother's legacy had been spent buying the North Street theater here in Market Chester, life had been a journey up and down England. Kate sometimes thought they must be the descendants of Shakespeare's players in *Hamlet* with their baskets of props and Greek tags. The girls had both been named after characters in the plays in which their parents were performing when each of their daughters were born—a favorite custom among actors. Kate and Isabella had learned to dance when they learned to walk, flitted across the stage as fairies, popped out of cardboard pies as infant blackbirds. They played the Little Princes in *Richard III* when they were six and seven years old. Thomas taught them to recite the Ten Dramatic Passions. "Joy, Grief, Fear, Anger, Pity, Scorn, Hatred, Jealousy, Wonder, Love." They learned these when other children learned nursery rhymes.

But it was a year since their father had been able to buy the North Street theater and they had come to live in this plain, pleasant little house opposite the theater. Life was different now.

"I don't know why you still grumble so about the circuits when it is months and months since we traveled," Kate said mildly. "Besides, you may look down on being an actress, but if it weren't for that you wouldn't have this *Earl's* invitation you're so excited over."

"Aren't you excited?"

Kate, her teeth chattering with cold, finally climbed out of bed in her long cambric nightgown and began to wash.

"I might be if I knew which play Papa will choose."

"We know which one *you* want. Juliet, of course."

Kate dried her hands, swathed herself in one of the family supply of old woollen shawls and sat down at the dressing table to examine her freckled face. She combed her hair. Impatiently watching her sister's leisurely movements, Isabella cried, "Of course you want to play Juliet at Bagot Park! Why not admit it?"

"Because it is the wrong play."

"Everybody loves *Romeo and Juliet*."

"Not the gentry."

"How can you talk such nonsense! What about old Lord Craven, who has his box reserved every single week when you are Juliet."

"The Bagot gentry will have been out hunting all day."

"How can you possibly know that? What do *you* know about the gentry?"

"Only that they'd sooner laugh than cry," said Kate.

Isabella couldn't help laughing. Kate, for all her mildness, was so positive, so absolutely certain of what she thought. She always knew exactly which plays she liked, which she thought worthless. She seemed to know uncannily when an actor had talent. Like Thomas, she thought of nothing but the theater. But her father's mind was full of the price of taffeta for costumes or oil for lamps, of how many tickets were sold, whether the carpenters had been paid. Kate thought of how to conquer an audience.

During the following days the family talked of the Bagot invitation until the subject was quite worn out. Thomas was flustered by the prospect. What play should he choose? What fee would be paid?

"I must decide what fee to suggest, my dear."

"Gracious, Tom. Mr. Sidaway will inform you what the Earl will pay for the evening's entertainment."

"But it might not be sufficient. Not all the gentry are open-handed," said Thomas anxiously.

"It would not be becoming to mention a fee," said Ellen.

Kate, listening, thought this very foolish but held her tongue.

It was decided that Thomas should hire a hack and ride out to Bagot Park to meet the Earl's steward, Mr. Sidaway.

Ellen, who knew her husband was nervous, helped him to dress. She brushed his coat, put in his best studs, tied his satin cravat and waited upon him as if he were preparing to attend a Coronation. She watched while he put his tall hat on at a rakish angle.

"You look very nice, Tom."

It was high praise.

He put his arms round her and they stood close for a moment, sharing each other's thoughts.

Thomas rode out of Market Chester along a country road deeply rutted by the carts which came and went daily. In wet weather the road was a sea of mud but now in the cold the mud was frozen into ridges, iron-hard and very deep. On either side stretched meadows and plowed fields white with frost. Every blade of grass, every bramble glittered.

He did not like the country, thought it lonely and melancholy and to calm his nerves tried to fix his mind on practical matters: they were worrying, too. The stage carpenters were a lazy bunch. A new actor he had just engaged, a little comic scarcely bigger than a dwarf, had been drunk the previous evening.

"Laurie Spindle nearly fell into the pit," Ellen had said this morning, pursing her lips. She despised drunkards.

The road straightened, and in the distance Thomas saw a high brick wall to the right and twin stone pillars topped with heraldic animals, half-stag, half-unicorn, clasping shields between knobbly legs.

The lodgekeeper, always on the lookout for the visitors who continually drove up or left the Park, came out of his cottage to open the gates. Thomas bowed his thanks, and felt sure the man knew to a farthing how much he'd paid to hire the horse.

The avenue between leafless trees appeared to go on for miles, and as Thomas rode through the deserted frostbound landscape he felt more and more nervous. He knew nothing of the aristocracy except what he saw in theaters—they were

arrogant, self-confident, sometimes rude. They were behold-
en to nobody for their position and their wealth.

At last the drive curved, and he saw the house in the distance. Long ago, Bagot Park had been a low, rambling Tudor place, but in the 1750's one of the Bagots had visited Italy and fallen in love with classicism. The house was given a
pillared facade, an imposing entrance, tall symmetrical windows all tacked unself-consciously on to the Elizabethan
manor. The house stood on a rise of ground with woods and
downland in the distance. The gardens, too, had been
changed, the old walled orchards and herb beds swept away
and replaced by sloping lawns, prospects, statues, vistas of
meadows set about with solitary and beautiful trees, a lake, a
bridge, ghostly in the winter mist.

As he rode nearer to the house, the doors under the portico opened and a group of gentlemen came out. At the same
moment, round the side of the house came the grooms, leading what seemed to Thomas dozens of horses. Through the
clear air he heard laughter and talk.

Something in the manner of the gentlemen, in the way
their servants waited on them, made his nerve fail. He reined
in his horse and turned to the left, riding down the side of
the house to the back.

He went under the archway into a back courtyard. Here
some maidservants stood at an open door gossiping to a cart-
er. Dogs were running about. The cheerful faces of the girls,
the village atmosphere, made him feel comfortable, and he
dismounted and went to the back door to inquire for Mr. Sidaway.

He was taken first to a small woman in dark silk who introduced herself as "Mrs. Judge, the Earl's Housekeeper," and
then accompanied by a footman on a journey through the
house. He seemed to walk miles, along corridors where servants hurried by with armfuls of linen or trays of silver, up
staircases, down more staircases. The place hummed like a
hive of bees and reminded him, in its activity, of backstage.

And as in the theater he had to go through a pass door. This one was covered in green baize, studded with brass nails, and divided the servants' quarters from the main house.

The footman knocked at a paneled door and announced, "Mr. Winter, sir."

"Ah. Winter. Good of you to make the journey. How-de-do?"

Sidaway came over to greet him.

Thomas was rather surprised at his appearance. He was not at all the way he imagined the gentleman would be. Sidaway wore a plain brown coat of coarse cloth and hobnail shoes; with his red face and white linen stock, he might have been a rich tradesman except that his voice drawled and there was something indefinably easy yet reserved in his manner.

"Please take a chair. I trust you do not find this room over-heated? Mrs. Judge has a mistaken idea that I feel the cold, and this stove is devilish fierce, but I have not the heart to tell her so."

He put Thomas at his ease.

"What size of room have you in mind for your play, sir? We have every sort of size, d'you see, big as a ballroom, small as a billiard table. Depends on the size of your audience, of course. Well, some are leavin' and some arrivin'. That's as may be. Shall we say fifty? Come and take a look at the Music Room. It might suit."

Thomas agreed respectfully. He would have agreed to acting in the larder. Sidaway took him down a huge curving staircase to a hall, marble-floored like a chessboard, with statues in niches. Thomas caught a glimpse through an open door of a group of ladies and gentlemen breakfasting. They, too, were as plainly dressed as Sidaway. He had imagined velvets.

"This is the room," said Sidaway, opening double doors. It was a high-ceilinged room, the ceiling covered with elaborate, rather absurd goddesses, clouds, cherubs, warriors. The walls were set with paintings and behind a gilded settee stood a larger-than-life-size marble Venus. A great fireplace at the end of the room, in which a fire was freshly lit, had an elaborately carved chimney piece of vine leaves, grapes and birds.

"Does it suit, do you think?" inquired Sidaway looking about. "Just tell us what to push out, eh?" He gestured at the chairs and tables, a spinet, an embroidered carpet and a bronze tiger eating a dead antelope.

Sidaway put his hands in his pockets. Thomas stood and frowningly studied the room, wearing his most officious (and harassed) expression.

"I'm lookin' forward to hearing what play we're to see. I am bound to warn you, Winter, that His Lordship dislikes to weep. Easily moved when he goes to the play. Only time in his life that happens. Ha ha!"

Ellen was waiting for him when Thomas returned home. She helped him out of his coat and shooed away Milly, firmly closing the door.

"Well?"

Thomas sat down with an exaggerated air of weariness and allowed her to fetch him a cushion.

"Mr. Sidaway was most kind."

"And?"

"A clever man, my dear, very genteel. We have been given the Music Room for the performance. A comfortably large room which in summer opens on to the garden. But of course the curtains will be closed, and Mr. Sidaway will arrange rows of chairs."

Ellen sat down facing her husband.

"Tell me about the house, Tom. Somebody said the drive is four miles long and there is a waterfall. Did you see the family? How many guests have they? The Bagots gave a ball last month and had three hundred. Describe everything. Do!" She gave him a sudden, very charming smile.

But though he liked to please her, he could not give her an impression of the sumptuous house he had visited. He had lived in the world of imagination all his life—it seemed simple for a cardboard circlet to become a king's crown. But he noticed nothing except about the theater. He told her instead about the standard oil lamps, the carpet which could be rolled up so that the players could move more easily and the number of gilt chairs and sofas for the audience.

Recovering from the excitement of the Bagot invitation, the Winter family settled to their daily occupation—acting. Thomas and his daughters played every night at his North Street theater; Thomas was also owner and manager with attendant worries. Ellen made or refurbished the costumes and worked as the prompt. The company at present were rehearsing a new piece, *The Welsh Girl*, which Thomas thought might be a success, with Kate playing the leading role.

Laurie Spindle, the newly arrived comic, also settled down. The actors liked him because he made them laugh. His manner to most of them was dry and satirical, but he developed a doglike devotion for Kate. The couple, the little man with his big long-chinned face, and the slight redheaded girl, were constantly together.

He found her one morning seated on a prop basket learning her lines for *The Welsh Girl*.

"I'll hear your lines for you, Beauty."

"You are kind, Laurie."

"Your mama does not think so. She looks on me as a drunken beast."

"You do drink rather."

"So I do. I like it."

She grinned at him disapprovingly. He had a voice with a break in it which he used in a certain way, a talent for driving a joke straight at the audience so that they caught it with both hands. When sober, his gift was remarkable: it was not inconsiderable when he was drunk.

He heard her lines for a while, then said, "What has your father decided we're to play for the nobs?"

"Sheridan, he says."

"That's a mistake, Beauty."

"But why?"

"Well, I'll tell you. Never play the gentry *to* the gentry because you'll make them laugh at you instead of with you. Simple, isn't it? Shakespeare knew it. Look at the mechanicals in *The Dream*. The Duke thought them ridiculous. What the nobs would enjoy is a little comic melodrama. *The Welsh Girl*, for instance."

Kate's large eyes grew larger.

"I see you're pleased," he said.

"Laurie, I would *love* it to be that play. But my father would never consent. And I couldn't persuade him."

"Not as you've such a thumping big part in it, you couldn't," he said, laughing. "Leave it to me, Beauty. We'll see if we can talk him into seeing a bit of sense."

Kate had no idea how he persuaded Thomas to change his mind—Thomas was a stubborn man and never listened to anybody but Ellen. But somehow the "comic melodrama" began to attract him. She heard him talking to her mother, asking her whether she agreed that the gentry might be entertained by the piece with its intrigues and disguises and mistaken identities.

"You could talk to Mr. Sidaway, Tom."

"Now, Ellen, that *is* an excellent idea."

Mr. Sidaway agreed so heartily that Thomas immediately became convinced of his own acuteness and judgment. When he announced the play to the company, Laurie looked at Kate but did not even wink.

Kate spent a diligent week before the Bagot Park visit studying and rehearsing. She never complained at late hours, was always on call, always patient, concentrated. She stood without moving when her mother pinned her into a new costume (Isabella complained and fidgeted). Kate was in the theater from morning till midnight. Sometimes when Isabella was fast asleep Kate rose very quietly and sat in the ice-cold bedroom, studying her part by candlelight.

Although she had only a small part in the play, Isabella was in a fever of excitement at the prospect of visiting a great house; she hung round her mother tiring her with questions. At what time did the gentry dine? What did the ladies wear at home? How many footmen did she suppose they had? Did each lady have one maid or two? What did one call an Earl?

When the evening came, Thomas Winter closed the theater, for the performance was to be at ten o'clock, after the Bagots and their guests had dined.

Ellen supervised the packing, bullied the theater dressers, chose the frocks her daughters would wear for supper at the Park after the play, commanded, criticized and enjoyed being in charge. Satisfied that she would not be demeaned by visiting the Bagots, her six-times-removed relations, Ellen was keenly interested in the visit.

An hour before they were due to leave Kate was waiting at the stage door for the cart which was to collect the costume baskets. The night was frosty and blazing with stars. She wrapped her cloak round her and thought with relief that the night was dry. She'd seen costumes sodden and scenery ruined by rain many times. Now she waited alone, determined to see her own costume basket safely placed in a particular corner of the cart.

As she stood under the light of an oil lamp at the stage door various men lurched down the alleyway from the inn at the street corner. The doors of the Cat & Custard Pot swung open every night and out reeled men in various stages of drunken violence or stupidity. Kate was indifferent to them. The only time she noticed and actually hated them was when they sat in the pit and shouted oaths and threw things. She knew how to dodge bottles thrown on to the stage, how to use her voice to drown hisses and shouts from the pit or the loud voices of the gentry talking in the boxes (sometimes with their backs to the stage). The theater had made her a hardy little creature.

When the cart and horses arrived, Kate called to the old

stage doorkeeper to get her father. Thomas arrived to or-
ganize the scene shifting, and two carters with backs as broad
as their own horses filled up the cart with screens, painted
flats, boxes and skips. Kate wedged her own basket safely
and made a note of exactly where it was placed so that she
herself could find it. In matters of her costumes she trusted
nobody.

"So there you are, Kate," cried Isabella, darting out of the
theater without a cloak. "Why are you waiting? It isn't nearly
time to go yet."

"Papa says the carriage will come directly."

"But the performance is not until ten!"

"We need time," was Kate's brief reply.

Their mother had made up her mind that the Winter family must have a carriage to themselves to travel to Bagot Park.
The rest of the company would have to crowd somehow into
two broughams and sit on one another's laps.

"But a carriage only for us, my dear," demurred Thomas.
"It is very extravagant."

"Remember, you *are* the owner."

When the Winters were installed in their private carriage
and the journey began, the sisters huddled together for
warmth. The carriage jolted so badly on the rutted country
road that Isabella's teeth knocked together. But every bump
and shudder of the carriage bringing her nearer to the great
house made her more excited.

"Surely we are there now, Papa?"

"Not yet."

"Bagot Park!" said Isabella, with a sigh of pleasure. "I must
remember to look at *everything*. I want to see what the family
are truly like, and the guests, and the ladies' dresses, and the
servants, and the house and—and everything. I shall describe it all to Mama tomorrow morning."

"Here we are," said her father, looking from the carriage
window. "This is the lodge. Why doesn't the driver get down,
he really should not shout like that. I am sure the lodgekeeper will not like it."

The driver was giving undignified halloos and cracking his whip for the gates to be opened.

"What country bumpkins drive hired coaches," exclaimed Thomas irritably.

"We are bumpkins, too," murmured Kate, and Isabella said loudly, "*You* can be if you like. I'm not."

To Isabella's disappointment the carriage did not drive up to the portico of the great house, where she could see lamps burning under the archway, but down the side of the house past many different-sized buildings all joined and jumbled, until they drew up at a back door in a courtyard.

Before the coachman could help her Kate jumped down. The cart of scenery and costumes had arrived and was drawn up at the open stable. She hurried over to drag out a small basket and tucked it under her arm. Then, beckoning Isabella, she walked coolly into the house.

The passage smelled of spices and lemon; there was the hot breath of cooking from two large kitchens nearby; Isabella was nervously sure the servants would come out to question them. But Kate merely shrugged and pulled her by the hand as if she had known the house all her life. She had an instinct about finding her way in theaters: the same instinct worked now.

Smiling at two housemaids who passed them, she went down a passage, then another, skirted a flight of uncarpeted back stairs and somehow found one of the green baize doors which divided the house like a frontier between countries.

Isabella, following Kate down a richly carpeted corridor with white and gold walls hung with paintings, felt oppressed. Her excitement evaporated—she wished she had never come. But Kate, unconscious of the curious eyes of a footman who walked by or of the splendor of the surroundings, turned in at the magnificent entrance hall with heroic-sized pictures lining the walls and a vast marble staircase curving upward to a gallery.

"There," said Kate. "That must be it!"

She walked straight to the open doors of the Music Room and only then looked round with interest.

Isabella followed, feeling subdued, envious and sad.

A tall young man was standing indolently by the fireplace watching the busyness of the room. The butler was in command, the chairs being arranged, the place in a turmoil. It amused him. He turned and saw two girls standing in the doorway. He could see at once that they were actresses, although he was not sure why this was so. It was true the shorter of the girls had an arresting, radiant look about her with her mass of red hair escaping from the hood of her cloak and those luminous eyes. Perhaps it was her air of confidence that made her look the actress as she stepped into the room, walked over to Sidaway and immediately engaged him in talk.

But the other girl remained in the doorway. She was not as beautiful, but he had always preferred dark women. He walked over to her.

Isabella stood adrift, taking no part in the talk and activity, the conferences of actors grouped round her father. The noisy crowded room emphasized her stillness.

The young man bowed.

"Allow me to present myself. Carteret."

"I am Isabella Winter. My father is Thomas Winter." She gave the merest curtsy.

"So you and your sister are playing for us tonight."

"I hope you will enjoy the performance," she said, almost indifferently.

She intrigued him. She was rather tall and slender, with pointed breasts and a narrow waist. Her skin had a tint of olive. He liked the beautiful oval of her face, her brown eyes and long neck. And she was serious. She had none of the playful manners of the girls he met in society. It was amusing to be treated coolly by an actress in one's own home. An actress! Everybody knew the lax morals that such a young woman must have. It was piquant to think of that.

"I have to confess I have not had the honor of visiting your father's theater and seeing you and your family upon the stage."

"You do not go to the play, Mister—"

"Carteret. The Earl is my father."

"Oh." Isabella was confused. She must be talking to a Viscount. Her manner became stiffer.

"It was my notion to ask your father if he would be good enough to give us this performance," Lord Carteret was saying in his lazy way. "It gets dull, you know, in the winter. Especially for the ladies. We hunt and shoot a good deal and they drive out and go visiting, but there are only cards in the evenings. Such a lot of evenings."

He laughed pleasantly, as if she shared with him a dismay at the evenings of winter, the interminable games of bezique and backgammon.

She thought him handsome, in a way. Not in the dramatic, deliberate way of actors who force people to admire them. He was unself-conscious, as if unaware of how he looked. He had a round face, dark hair rather straight and not thick which fell on his forehead, a mustache which did not hide a pleasure-loving mouth. His manner was extraordinarily kind and gentle.

Feeling it ungracious not to have visited the North Street theater, Lord Carteret murmured, "My family do sometimes go to the play, you know, at the Garden."

"Covent Garden. My sister's idea of paradise."

"Not yours, Miss Isabella?"

She smiled for the first time. She had looked distant and disconnected; he could not know how rare such an expression was for her. Now when she smiled her whole face changed.

She gave him a mischievous, veiled look.

"I must not say so, but the theater has never been heaven to me, My Lord. Kate would be excessively cross if she heard me confess it."

He looked at her and then, smilingly, at Kate. The young girl was surrounded by actors, carpenters and footmen. She seemed to be playing, as to the manner born, the role of duchess in a drama of high society.

Chapter Two

"Mr. Swayne, I think?" said Kate, coming up to the butler. He was standing in the Music Room, taking no part in the scurry of preparations, a broad-shouldered elderly man with white hair tinged with yellow. Two young men were in attendance ready to carry out his orders.

"Madam?"

He looked down at the small figure.

"The statue over there will have to be moved, I'm afraid, Mr. Swayne."

Kate pointed at the marble Venus, nine feet high, which dominated part of the space allotted for the actors. The Venus, naked except for a piece of drapery held in one broken hand, had stood there since her arrival sixty years ago, when the Earl's grandfather had brought the statue from Italy. He'd seen the goddess fished from the Tiber.

"That is out of the question, Madam." Mr. Swayne, perfectly courteous, was cold as the marble itself. He turned to send one of his men-in-waiting for more gilt chairs. Kate moved a little closer. She did something a person of rank would never do, put out her hand and rested it lightly on his arm. Thomas, looking at her from across the room, frowned.

He had already tried to persuade the butler to provide extra lamps: it had been like talking to a brick wall. Did Kate imagine she could succeed where he failed?

"You see, sir, it is not easy when one is an actress," murmured Kate. "That beautiful statue is a little large, you know, and I am rather small. In our profession . . . "

Modest as a daughter, she confided to the impassive old man some of the mysteries of her art.

Mr. Swayne listened in silence. Orders were then given. The Venus, upended without dignity and with one hand accusingly pointing, was borne away by four footmen.

After the removal of her rival, Kate would have enjoyed further chat with Mr. Swayne, but he wisely withdrew at the same time as the Venus. Kate's enslavement of the housekeeper was a minor matter after that. Kate had known how to conquer her own sex since she was a baby. Men fell under Kate's spell, but women wished to look after her. "They are so kind and understanding," was how Kate thought of it.

She explained to the sympathetic Mrs. Judge about such things as enough lamps and candles, the fact that the dressingrooms were a trifle crowded and so perhaps . . . ? Her father did not know whether to be pleased or angry at Kate's success.

"Kate!" sighed Isabella when the girls had been escorted to a large bedroom which overlooked the moonlit park. "This house!"

The sisters were resting together on a four-poster bed, Kate in the Juliet pose, relaxed and still.

"It is very splendid," Kate replied.

"But there are so many *things*. Even in this room. Look at the gold-framed pictures and that clock with those gilt warriors sitting by it and the vases with the birds and those screens and the chest of drawers and *six* chairs and a chaise longue and that alabaster bust. When you think how bare our rooms are at home! And in the corridors there are so many paintings one cannot fit one's hands between them. All the marbles and bronzes and tapestries—and did you see a fountain trickling into a basin full of ferns? It is so stately—so beautiful. And the flowers. Where do they come from?"

"Hothouses, I suppose."

"Have you ever seen such strange flowers? Great white scentless circular ones like plates and little yellow ones," said Isabella dreamily. "And as for servants, it is a sort of army. With the butler in command. He's the Duke of Wellington."

"Mr. Swayne is a nice man. Bella. Please let me rest."

"Did you know who I met? The Earl's son. The Viscount Carteret. Wait till I tell Mama!"

It was after ten o'clock when the Music Room began to fill with people. Thomas and his daughters, the actors and some servants who had been ordered by Mr. Swayne to help with props (much to their enjoyment) were waiting in a parlor which led into the Music Room and which tonight was being used as the backstage. Laurie Spindle, by the door, opened it a crack and whispered, "They're coming!"

There was a murmur, a rustle of dresses, the sound of voices, noises the actors knew well as an audience takes its place. But this noise was more subdued, lacking the vitality they were accustomed to. Kate, in her Act One costume in *The Welsh Girl*, feet bare, hair pinned on top of her head, wondered if it was her fancy that she could smell a mixture of scent and flowers, cigars and brandy.

Thomas drew his white gloves tight, opened the Music Room door, strode into the center of the space to be used as a stage and waited for the ladies and gentlemen to be seated. He stood erect, grizzled head thrown back. When the audience was quiet and he had the attention of the room, he made his opening address: "My Lords, Ladies. Gentlemen. We have the honor tonight to present a play for your pleasure. We cannot, of course, use all our scenery or backcloths; many of the aids to our art will be lacking. We must ask you, as Shakespeare did his audience, to employ your fancy. Help us poor actors to transform this room into a scene on the Welsh hills . . . " Isabella, listening to the speech, which was stylishly delivered, thought its tone obsequious. Why did he behave like that to these people? *She* would not do so! She looked at Kate, hoping to catch her sister's glance of mutual disapproval at their father, but Kate was in a trance. She had that actressy look, intent, withdrawn . . . Thomas stopped speaking, there was a scatter of polite applause. Kate picked up a basket of rushes and made her entrance.

Kate was always surprised when people who had never acted believed the players could scarcely see the audience, either because of the glare of lights or because of the actor's own concentration. The reverse was true. As she lightly moved through the play's disguises and absurdities, she saw the old Earl of Bagot, the young man who had spoken to Isabella and who must be the Viscount, two ladies, clearly Bagot daughters, and many other members of the brilliant audience. Acting in a drawing room had gains and losses. She preferred an audience to be close, and they were very close. She could see the old Earl slumped sideways in his chair, his face like that of a beaky gray-feathered bird. Some of the ladies quizzed her through glasses of the kind used in the Regency; to be stared at worked on her actress's spirit, and she played with more grace and strength. The ladies, glittering with diamonds and seeming with their draperies and bouquets and fans too large for the tiny gilt chairs, watched with attention. The gentlemen were more difficult to engage. They clearly preferred horses to actors, probably looked on acting as a game sometimes indulged in by the nobility for fun and forgotten the instant it was over. She had no intention of allowing them to forget *her*.

The actors were excited by the rich surroundings and the unfamiliar atmosphere and played well; Laurie Spindle made the audience laugh time and again. When the play ended, the applause was surprisingly warm. One or two of the younger gentlemen actually shouted "Hurrah!"

Kate and Isabella curtsied deeply. Thomas bowed, his hand on his heart.

The actors finally left the room, and the audience, talking and smiling and in a good humor, began to rustle away.

Isabella and Kate left the Music Room and went back upstairs to the bedroom to change. With the rest of the actors,
they had been invited to supper with the family and the
guests after the performance.

The room, their room for this evening, had been rearranged, the fire made up, fresh candles burning. A young
maid was waiting to help them to dress—she had been sent
by Mrs. Judge.

She unlaced Isabella's costume, and when Isabella sat at
the dressing table the girl began to brush her hair soothingly.
Isabella enjoyed the sensation and sat still for a while. Then
suddenly exclaimed, "Kate! Stop dreaming."

Kate, still in her apron and Welsh petticoats, was staring
into the fire. She gave a slight start and yawned. "I think I
must go home."

"But Lord Bagot has invited us to supper!"

Kate yawned again. She was very white and seemed half
asleep.

"I'm sorry. I couldn't possibly talk to people. You must
make my excuses. Thank the Earl and explain."

She stood indifferently as the maid began to help her to
take off the petticoats; every now and again she swallowed
another yawn.

When Isabella was dressed she did not say good night to
her sister but left the room angrily. She might have guessed
this would happen! When Kate collapsed after a performance there was nothing to be done. What was so horrid was
that everybody here would want to talk to Kate; *she* had
played the leading role, she was the interesting one. It was
too vexing of her, and rude, too. Isabella felt so miserably
embarrassed at the thought of telling the Earl that Kate had
gone home that she wanted to run away.

In the distance she could hear music, and as she turned a
corner at the head of the staircase she came face to face with
the tall figure of Viscount Carteret.

"Miss Isabella. I was in search of you and your sister."

"I am afraid my sister is tired and wishes to go home."

Shaken from her pretended poise, she gave him a beseeching look. She was almost on the verge of tears. How could she enjoy this evening when nobody would wish to speak to her, when the one they wanted was gone?

She did not expect any help from the elegant unknown man looking at her so attentively. It was true she asked for help by her look, but she was accustomed to actors, always selfish, and never thought men could be otherwise. She'd never met a man to whom good manners were as strong as religion.

"Would you prefer me to make your sister's excuses to the Earl?"

"Oh, Lord Carteret!"

"It will be an honor and a pleasure." The formal speech did not match his expression, which was kind and rather teasing.

He offered her his arm, and they went to the top of the stairs down which, it seemed to Isabella, they floated. Touching him—her hand lightly rested on his arm and no more—she trembled slightly. She felt weak. She looked at him from under her lashes and thought, I never knew until now that men could be beautiful.

"The Earl will perfectly understand," Lord Carteret said as they walked toward the music, "what an ordeal it has been for Miss Winter to play a part of such length. He will be glad she had the wisdom to return straight home."

Thomas Winter and Isabella were driven back to the town in the Bagot coach. During the drive she was perfectly silent, but her father did not notice. He was impatient to be home with Ellen.

He found his wife propped up in bed, wearing a little lace cap, and broad awake at three in the morning. They kissed tenderly.

"We must congratulate ourselves, my dear. I think I can say that only jockeys and prizefighters usually please the gentry the way we did tonight," he said. "This may be the first of other visits of the same kind. And in houses where the family is not—not connected with your own. You will, I hope, then consent to accompany us."

"Oh, yes," said Ellen vigorously.

"You were much missed. Nobody keeps things as well organized as you do."

Ellen agreed.

Lying side by side in the dark, they continued to talk comfortably.

"Lord Fletcher has a country seat not far from Brighton."

"And there is the Duke of Norfolk at Arundel."

Ellen was gratified by the success of the visit, not only because of the handsome fee, which relieved some of Thomas's worries, but because in the future he would not be so nervous if he had to deal with people of rank. She looked forward to hearing a description of the glory of the Bagots, those distant relatives she'd never met. Isabella loved describing adventures and always did it vividly. But the next day Isabella was irritable and gloomy by turns, sat about the house and blushed crimson every time there was a knock at the front door. Kate who finally described Bagot Park to her mother, tried to smooth things over.

"She cannot help it. Perhaps she is a little in love."

"With a Viscount?" said Ellen with a hard laugh.

Kate took her mother's unresisting hand and pressed it.

"It is not impossible. Even when I was there, and you know I did not stay for the supper, he sought her out. He was very handsome."

"I am sure."

"But Mama—"

"It is useless being sentimental with me, Kate. If Isabella thinks a man of title would look twice at her, she's out of her wits. The only reason he would pay her attention is a dangerous one. I shall tell her so."

Poor Isabella, thought Kate. It was the first time her sister had shown signs of falling in love. She scarcely talked, slept badly, ate almost nothing. When Kate spoke to her, she snapped back.

Isabella knew she was behaving badly and did not seem able to help it. She was like a child who, spending the afternoon in a theater of spangled Columbines, returns home to find it has become the dullest place on earth.

She had been disturbed by Viscount Carteret. No man until now had touched her imagination, physically stirred her. She had always laughed and escaped when actors tried to kiss or clutch. This was different. For the first time in her life she imagined not the clouded fantasies of a hero galloping away with her like Byron's Corsair but the embraces of a real man. She thought of herself in his arms, in his bed. She melted against him, hazily imagining what lovemaking with him would be like. Her thoughts tormented her. And it was not only these imaginings which made her miserable. She had been disturbed by every person, every object she had seen in Bagot Park. The great chains of rooms, their ceilings painted with clouds and goddesses, the ladies floating by in rose colors and pearly whites, braceleted gloved hands used for nothing rougher than holding a gold-handled fan. The candelabra burning with a hundred candles, the easy formality of the world of privilege, the servants waiting to carry out the guests' smallest wish. Had Kate asked Isabella what she truly wanted, she would have replied, "Everything." And because the desire was absurd, she sulked.

The play in rehearsal at the North Street theater was, as Thomas printed it on the playbills, "by popular demand." In this case it happened to be true. It was *King Charles's Merrie Days*, and audiences enjoyed any piece on the subject of Charles and Nell Gwynne. Kate had asked if Isabella could play the leading role, but Thomas brusquely refused. Of course Kate must play Nell, who in any case had red hair. Isabella should be Louise, the Duchess of Portsmouth, the Frenchwoman who shared the doubtful joys of the King's bed.

Kate disliked *King Charles's Merrie Days*. She never wished to play any character who was immoral. She was modest and reserved about sex, undressed beneath a wrapper, would never discuss sex even with Isabella. Her sister did not share her prudery, and when the old actors talked of the old wicked days, Isabella always listened openly. The theaters had been filled with soliciting whores. "You should have seen the fights—heard the screams!"

"Horrible," shuddered Isabella delightedly.

But today's tastes were changing; in this new version of *King Charles's Merrie Days* there was not a single scene in a bedchamber.

On the afternoon of the first night, after weeks of bitter cold it began to snow. Isabella, huddled in one of her mother's shawls, sat on the window seat. The snow whirled through the air, seeming to fly up rather than down. When the carriages and carts went by, their wheels spurted up the slush, which spattered the clothes of the passersby.

How pinched everybody looks, she thought, hiding their faces in collars and mufflers. It's time to go to the theater, I suppose. How I hate it! She watched her father picking his way across the street, dodging back as a mail coach clattered by.

She leaned her forehead against the icy windowpane. In her imagination she saw the women in Bagot Park, exquisitely dressed, waited upon, *warm*. Fires burned in great fireplaces, the Viscount—they called him "Carteret," he did not seem to have a Christian name—sat by the fire with his sisters and talked. What did the nobility talk of? Conversation in the Winter family was strictly theatrical and usually about money. Oh, that endless talk of money and the lack of it . . .

"Isabella. We must go."

It was Ellen in the doorway, dressed in her old black cloak with the hood, her hands in her muff. Isabella left the window seat in silence. She glanced at her mother's stony face.

"I'm sorry if I have been disagreeable."

"You certainly have."

"Seeing Bagot Park and everything—I suppose it upset me. I can't *help* feeling like that, Mama!"

Ellen's face altered at once, the cold disapproval vanished as if by magic.

"Of course you can't," she said. "You have Bagot blood in

your veins. You don't have to tell me how you felt, my child. I would have been exactly the same. Your father and sister don't understand things like that."

She fastened Isabella's cloak—Ellen's equivalent of the tenderest kiss—and they went out of the house together. They lifted their skirts as high as modesty allowed and waited for a carriage to go by with its attendant filth and deafening noise of wheels on cobblestones.

Kate and Isabella shared the smallest and pokiest dressing-room in a row of rooms situated under the stage. The callboy was filling the oil lamps in his usual slapdash fashion. Kate gave a shriek.

"Look out for my costume, Jeffrey. Truly, you are so *clumsy*. That's our best lace on the cuffs."

She sat down at the dressing table, lit the candles and began to pin up her long hair, trying to make it resemble Lely's portrait of Nell Gwynn. It was a difficult task and took her a long time.

Watching her, Isabella said, "You should wear a wig."

"I detest to wear a wig."

There was no arguing with Kate when she used that voice. Isabella laced herself into the stock costume of green taffeta, much mended and darned, which was used for court ladies in Shakespeare, Sheridan or any other piece. She had to fasten the dress carefully in case the silk should tear.

"Mama says most of the boxes are empty," she remarked. "It will be a dull performance tonight."

"*I* shall not walk through my part on that account," said Kate disdainfully.

A thump on the door.

"Beginners, please! Beginners—if you perlease!"

The girls stood up, Kate in a white blouse falling from freckled shoulders, a tray of property oranges in her hands. Isabella in the mended taffeta. They went along the narrow passage between the dressing rooms and climbed a ladder toward the stage.

The house was certainly not full but the smallish audience was friendly and settled down to enjoy Nell Gwynne and her antics. Halfway through the first act there was a scene between Nell and the Duchess. Kate had a soliloquy first, ending, "Ah, but I shudder, in spite of my natural courage!"

Isabella entered. Facing Kate haughtily and using her best French accent, she began her speech. Suddenly from nowhere a gust of smoke blew across the stage. It caught both girls by the throat. Trained to continue, as every actor must, Isabella finished her speech, and Kate replied. The smoke belched in again, thicker and yellower. And then there was a terrible sound. A piercing shriek from the audience, the bloodcurdling cry of, "*FIRE!*"

With something between a roar and a groan every man and woman in the audience sprang up and began to rush toward the doors. The smoke grew thicker. There was the noise of crackling and behind Kate a tongue of flame licked up the painted flat showing St. James's Palace.

Kate and Isabella fled to the prompt side, the audience stampeded; voices shouted vainly for calm. Actors rushed by, almost knocking the girls down. In the prompt corner Ellen was dazedly watching the fiercely burning scenery.

"Ma! Come! Come!"

They dragged her, tottering, backstage but she pulled back, screaming, "Your father—Thomas—"

"We'll get him!" Somehow they managed to push Ellen into a passageway and out of the stage door. "Thomas!" shrieked Ellen again. Laurie Spindle, bundling actors and actresses out into the snow-covered street, shouted, "I'll find him. Kate, take your mother and get out before the doorway catches!"

Sobbing and stumbling, the girls and Ellen made their way to the front of the theater. It was chaos. Carriages and stamping horses, shouting people, no sign of the fire engines but only the frightened crowds, tongues of fire flaming at an upper window, the whirling snow.

Suddenly Ellen cried, "Look!"

Down the passageway from the stage door came Laurie Spindle, and beside him, half-dragging, half carrying a basket full of singed costumes, was Thomas.

* * *

By the time the fire engines galloped into North Street and were put into action the theater was burning like a torch.

The fierce flames grew higher as they were fed by stores of materials which ignited at once—rolls of painted back cloths, sized flats made of bone-dry wood, baskets of painted and gilded costumes, dozens of wigs, wooden props, oil lamps, benches, velvet curtains. The heat was so intense that the firemen could not safely get close to the theater. All they could do was prevent the fire from spreading down the street.

The whole of Market Chester, men, women and children, came to watch the fire. It was a spectacle of high drama. The theater drew more crowds on the night it burned down than in all the years it had been a playhouse. The street was packed with tense, silent people staring at the fire, until tiredness and the bitter cold finally drove them indoors.

Thomas, his family, and most of the actors stood at the windows of the house opposite, shocked, white-faced, their faces and clothes smeared and blackened with smoke. Thomas watched the fire in a dreadful silence. It was a holocaust of his life. Scenery, props, costumes, the building that his wife's inheritance had made possible for him to own, his experience, his hopes, all, all consumed in flames which made a horrible roaring noise, like hell itself. The very bricks of the building were burned—later they fell to powder. The smell, acrid and bitter, filled the town afterward for nearly a week.

At last the actors crept away, Ellen put her arm round Thomas and led him up to bed.

Only Kate stayed. She sat crouched on the window seat, looking at the now-smoldering blackened building opposite. Great smuts floated in the air among the snowflakes which settled on a playbill bearing her name.

Chapter Three

SPRING CAME LATE IN NORTHUMBERLAND, eight weeks later than in the south. The wild daffodils in the woods outside the town only budded at the beginning of May, leaves in the cold wind unfurled cautiously. The heather stayed for a long time a brown sea of dry stems. In Sussex, Kate thought, the bluebells would have come and gone in the hazel woods and so would the primroses which grew in the back garden of the house in North Street.

It was over a year since the fire had destroyed the family's livelihood in Market Chester, floating away Thomas's theater and their mother's inheritance in black smuts in the winter air. But Kate still thought of their life there, what it had felt like to have a home, the pleasure and freedom of owning their own theater. What they had done—all they could do—desperately needing work, was to start up the old circuit life of traveling from town to town, taking any circuit in England that would have them.

Jolting painfully in teeth-rattling coaches, the Winters returned to the traveling life. How cold and miserable they often were, racked and battered by day and night. Sometimes the coaches halted interminably at toll gates while someone shouted to the turnpike man, who would *not* wake up. Sometimes the roads were impassable in seas of mud. Sometimes Thomas scarcely had the fares for the journey. Then they arrived at an unfamiliar town, met often unfriendly actors, and unpacked their own few shabby costumes, an essential part of their livelihood.

Thomas had been stunned by the disaster. Had it not been for Ellen, he might have been gravely ill. He was almost bankrupt, and when the actors and some creditors were paid after the fire, the rest of Thomas's debts had to be settled by selling the family's possessions.

Everything had to be sold. The furniture in the North Street house, any costumes and props saved from the fire, a few pieces of scenery, even Ellen's diamond ring and Thomas's gold watch inherited from his father. By the grace of God, the Winters managed to get an engagement on the Manchester circuit. They left Market Chester with luggage consisting of a single box and a bag containing two of Ellen's bonnets.

Thomas might have had a stroke, might have died, but he could not afford it. He obeyed his wife's repeated entreaty: "Tom. Don't be ill, *please!*"

He got through the disaster, took his family to Manchester and began to work again. He was silent, short-tempered and looked older.

Kate was more unhappy than she admitted to anyone, but she was steady and reliable, fixed her mind on her work and tried, in small ways, to comfort her poor father, who scarcely noticed her. The two who came out best during the time of the disaster were Ellen and Isabella. Ellen was positively cheerful: she enjoyed drama. When their furniture was sold, she attended the auction with interest, returned to the stripped house and made a picnic on upturned boxes. When she said good-bye to the actors, she gave them words of encouragement and advice.

She bade Milly good-bye as if parting with a family retainer.

"We must give the servant a farewell gift. She has served us faithfully," said Ellen, tipping her. It was a maxim of Ellen's that while one might be poor, one must never look poor.

Isabella, too, behaved well during the days following the fire, helping to pack the scorched costumes, counting spoons, suggesting her trinkets should be sold, ready with a smile and a cheerful remark day or night.

But such nobility could not last. The drama was over, Market Chester left behind. The life which began again was poor and hard. Thomas called himself "stage manager" but he often did the work of six stage carpenters, setting the stage himself. When there was no money for coach fares, the family walked from one engagement to the next on the open road in pouring rain or icy winds; the weather always seemed unkind. Once, they acted in an old malt house up a long flight of steps—to an audience of three young boys and an old woman.

Thomas's face grew pinched. Sometimes he was morose, sometimes his worry took the form of harassing his daughters. He began insisting every morning that they should say their lines aloud at breakfast time. He would lay down his knife, stare at them with a gray unsmiling face and say, "Well? What comes next? And then? And then?"

Ellen steadily supported him; she called it "bolstering him up" to herself, though not to the girls. With Thomas's lost confidence and fits of gloom, she and Kate had the worst of the family's trouble.

But now they were settled for a season in Newcastle and after their adventures in barns or disused stables in innyards (when they had no circuit engagement they literally became strolling players), the family were part of a company and acting in a good theater again. Things were better.

Kate sat in a lean-to whitewashed attic at the top of the theatrical lodgings where the family were installed. The room was so small that the girls had to sleep together in the narrow bed, top to toe, and when they dressed they edged past each other to fetch a comb or a petticoat. There was only room for one chair, even supposing the landlady would provide another.

Uncomfortable and cramped, Kate felt cheerful. The sun was shining, and as she brushed her bright hair she hummed to herself. Yesterday evening she had been in her dressing room when the door had creaked and a voice chanted in sepulchral tones, "I ha' summat to say, summat at my tongue's end—it must come out. Do you recollect when you sent me away fra' your service? Because I wore given to drink, you turned your back on me, I ha' never been a man since that time."

"Laurie!"

The goblin face had peered round the door and while Kate was still laughing at the words, which came from a melodrama, *Luke The Labourer,* which they had played together, they rushed into each other's arms.

How delightful it was, Kate thought with a sigh of pleasure, to refind one's friends.

"Why did Papa not tell me you were coming?"

"Because I didn't know myself. I was just passing through," said Laurie with all the player's optimism, indifference to the risk of having no work, certainty that his gift would not fail him.

If only Isabella would be a little happier as well, Kate thought, looking at her own face in the glass. Her sister had gone down the alley to the pastrycook's and Kate was guiltily glad of a respite. Isabella was so tiring. Brushing her hair until it crackled, Kate wished for the thousandth time that her sister could care a little about the theater. Since the fire, since life had become harder, Isabella's indifference—no, it was dislike—of her work was more marked. What she talked about was the gentry. She had an almost religious reverence for the "polite world," and her mother's distant relationship to it. When Kate wanted to discuss plays and actors, Isabella talked of Ellen's girlhood, the titled people her mother had or had not met, those now-forgotten Bagots in Sussex, or of some Lord This or Lady That who might have been in the audience the previous evening.

Kate was pleased when well-born people attended the play, but only if they behaved with propriety and raised the tone of the audience. All Kate hoped was that there would be no fighting or shouting.

The attic door opened and Isabella came in, carrying a plate covered with a piece of muslin. She wore her shabby brown frock and her mother's old black bonnet. The dingy colors did not suit her, but her eyes were brighter than usual.

"Kate. Pa has a visitor. He is waiting downstairs. He said would I ask Pa to see him."

Kate looked alarmed.

"Is he someone Papa owes money—"

"Oh, no, I am sure he is an actor."

When their father had gone down to meet the visitor, the girls went into their mother's bedroom, the next-door attic slightly larger than their own.

The lodgings were in a back street fifteen minutes' walk from the theater. The house was Elizabethan, with bulging walls, blackened beams and creaking stairs, and stood in a row of similar houses huddled together like old women gossiping. The alley, none too clean, was so narrow that women strung their washing from one side to the other, like flags.

There was in addition to a pastrycook, a cobbler's and a saddler's, small-windowed cottages smelly and dark, and a dame's school filled during the day with shouting children who poured out in the evening like water through a dam. Ellen Winter did not like the lodgings and liked their owner less, a Mrs. Gunn, who had been an actress. The woman dyed her hair and wore rouge, had eyes like flint and was inquisitive about her lodgers. Mrs. Gunn disliked Ellen in return, particularly when she boasted.

"Your father fetched the tea from the kitchen, since that woman would not bring it up," Ellen said as her daughters came into the room. "Isabella, your back hair is coming down. Kate, why are you wearing a ribbon round your neck?"

"I thought it pretty."

"If you don't own a necklace, it is preferable to wear nothing."

"Some of the actors would enjoy it if she did that!" Isabella giggled.

"Isabella, I do not allow impropriety," said her mother coldly.

But Kate caught her sister's eye and they exchanged a grin, something rare nowadays.

Isabella sprawled on her parents' bed, Kate sat by her mother's side. She took her hand and gave it a kiss, and Ellen, who never showed affection, looked pleased.

"A bun, Isabella?"

Isabella took a large one and was biting into it, her lips covered with sugar, when the door opened.

There was a small commotion as Thomas and a tall young man came into the room. Ellen, who could not bear being taken by surprise, put down the dish. Isabella tried to swallow a mouthful. Only Kate, unself-consciously holding the bun in one hand, bowed pleasantly to the visitor.

"My dear, may I present Buckey Vernon? He is to join our company and has done us the honor of calling—"

"Charmed. Delighted."

Buckey Vernon bowed and smiled, and Ellen, recovering her poise, graciously offered him tea.

"We do prefer our own tea, Mr. Vernon. In lodgings the tea that is served is really a little—"

"I agree, Mrs. Winter. Horrid stuff as black as treacle. Thank you very much, indeed, I would appreciate tea."

Buckley Vernon sat down and began to talk politely and easily.

He was a man who knew how to charm. He was tall but somewhat round-shouldered, his face pale, his brownish hair greasy but plentiful, his nose finely shaped. He had a beautiful thick-lipped mouth which curled upward like a girl's. His manner, noticeably wooing, would have been called ingratiating in a less handsome man. It seemed to say that he knew *he* was fascinating, and if you thought so (but only then), he would be enchanted to admire you in return.

He divided his attention and his smiles very fairly among the Winter family sitting round, larding his conversation to Thomas with "sirs," deferring to Ellen and being subtly gallant to both sisters.

"Your father tells me, Miss Winter," he said to Kate, "that he is planning to revive *King Charles's Merrie Days.* You, of course, will be pretty, witty Nell?"

"Not necessarily. There are other actresses in the company," Kate said. She did not say "good" actresses.

"But the part is suited to you, surely?"

"It is not a case of parts 'suiting' my girls, Mr. Vernon," said Thomas. "In a stock company they have learned the important lesson of being useful. They can play anything— tragedy, burlesque, farce, comedy."

"They are both nice little actresses," put in Ellen.

"There is no question which of us is the better, Mama," said Isabella, not very gracefully. "It's Kate."

Buckley Vernon looked from one girl to the other with an expression of exaggerated languishing and murmured:

> How happy could I be with either
> Were t'other dear charmer away!
> But while ye thus tease me together,
> To neither a word will I say.

The family laughed, and he joined them.

Vernon's arrival in the Newcastle company was greeted with various jealousies. The two leading actresses, Georgiana Coins, a talented hard-faced forty-five, and Margaret Frognal, sickly, pathetic and nearly thirty, paid him too much attention and angrily competed for him. Buckley divided himself between them as neatly as a woman cutting a cake. Some of the young male actors were cold to him. Laurie Spindle would not give an opinion. When Kate asked, he said, "Wait and see, wait and see."

"I wonder why Laurie does not like Mr. Vernon, Mama," said Kate thoughtfully.

"He is put out because Mr. Vernon admires you," said Ellen, who considered Laurie Spindle beneath contempt.

If the ladies, with the possible exception of Isabella, openly admired Buckley, the man who welcomed him was Thomas Winter. The fire in Sussex was history now, and so was Thomas's position as owner of a theater. This engagement at Newcastle was a godsend; but could he make it succeed? He had a horror of debt and sometimes imagined that some creditors—possibly overlooked—would take legal means to have him arrested. Money was short and the Newcastle theater not full. The players in a previous season had not been popular, and Thomas was suffering from the faults of his predecessors.

But Buckley Vernon might be a valuable addition and help in Thomas's choice of plays. There was the old favorite *King Charles's Merrie Days*—it still might have some life in it; Buckley Vernon was to play the King. The play could be pushed into the repertory in a couple of days—no need for more than a few rehearsals. All the circuit actors, including Thomas and his daughters, had fifty or sixty roles at their fingertips. They must be able to act a role at a moment's notice. It was part of the job and demanded by managers just as a newly engaged actor must bring with him some feathered hats, a good cape with a swing to it and a well-handled rapier.

Thomas had also received the news that Davenant, the great Henry Davenant, had consented to visit Newcastle and play with the company for a few weeks. Davenant, a star, as they called famous actors nowadays, would fill the theater every night from pit to gallery. In the meantime, the Merry Monarch and Nell Gwynn must do their best.

Buckey Vernon was as good as Thomas hoped. He had the

right sensuality for King Charles and a pleasing good-
humored stage presence. Once again Kate pinned up her
red hair and carried her tray of property oranges.

One spring evening when *King Charles* ended and Kate
went into the dark little dressing room to change out of her
court dress, there was no sign of Isabella. Kate lit the candles
and hung up Nell's painted shirt and buckram-stiffened petticoats. She buttoned herself into her old green dress. The
theater was quiet. The candle, wavering in a draft, threw
shadows on the brick walls, distorting the shape of a feathered hat hung on a nail into the fat profile of a child, cheeks extended.

Picking up the candle and protecting the flame with her
hand, she went into the passage. Buckley Vernon, wearing a
massive caped coat, was coming toward her.

"Miss Winter, I came looking for you. I asked your father
if I might walk you home."

"Are my family already gone?"

"Your father seems to think I might be trusted," he answered, smiling. He stepped back for her to precede him but
his coat was so bulky that Kate had to squeeze against him,
far closer than she thought proper.

They set off through the streets. The day had been springlike but an east wind was blowing, it seemed to hide round
every corner waiting to spring. She put her hands into her
mother's moth-eaten fur muff.

"The house wasn't full enough," Buckley said.

"Papa says we must wait for Davenant before the theater is
completely full."

"Why can he do it and not us?"

"Because he's a great actor."

Buckley made a dissatisfied sound.

"Perhaps *we* are. He wasn't the idol of the public when he
was young either. Success. Do you want it as much as I do,
Miss Winter?"

"I want to be a good actress," she said solemnly.

He laughed.

"One has to be one of three things, you know. More famous than the others. Or richer. Or bigger."

The gas lamps at the street corners threw yellowish circles of light, but between one lamp and the next the streets were very dark, and Kate was glad to have as a companion someone who was bigger than other people, as he had just indicated. They were walking through mean streets not far from Mrs. Gunn's alleyway when Buckley said, "Look there."

In one tumbledown house every window was glowing with candles. As they drew nearer Kate heard the curious noise, a kind of steady roar, made up of many voices all talking at once. The door of the house was open, and a shabby man stood outlined by the light. Catching sight of Buckley and Kate, both more respectably dressed than was usual in so poor an alleyway, he disappeared indoors, giving the rickety door a violent slam. The men's voices, the slam, the silhouettes showing through torn curtains, made Kate quicken her steps.

Buckley gave her his arm.

"Newcastle is not the peaceful place it used to be. When I was playing here three years ago it was quiet as a church. Now there's a thunderstorm rumbling."

Kate nodded. Everybody kept talking about the price of bread, how hungry people were, and how angry. Sometimes she felt guilty when she sat down to supper with her parents. And her father had said the bad harvest last autumn meant things could only get worse . . .

"Have you seen the crowds in the market every morning, Mr. Vernon? We went through the market on Sunday on our way to church and there was a man making a speech. He had a white face and white hair and was so thin—he looked like a spirit. All the men in the audience, I mean in the crowd, shouted and cheered. I saw one man weeping."

"Did they frighten you?"

"Oh, no," she said, surprised. "They would never harm us. They're poor and hungry, and we have been both. When we were children, Isabella and I were sometimes so hungry

when we went to bed that we made knots in our handkerchiefs and bit on them. Papa was nearly bankrupt, too, you
know," she added unself-consciously, "and in danger of going to prison."

She was silent for a while. He waited, thinking her odd.

"Apart from being sorry for them in the Christian way, of
course, there is something else. I always worry that real life
may interrupt what is in my head. One has to be very strong
as an actor not to be swamped by real life, don't you think?
To use it, not drown in it."

"I am sure it will never drown *you*," he said with a certain
irony.

Isabella sat on the window seat overlooking the roofs and
chimney pots and the cold, bright sky. It was the first week in
May but the room was chilly and the fire, a shovelful of
smoking coal, would soon be out. It would need a battle with
Mrs. Gunn to get the scuttle refilled. Isabella tucked her feet
under her for warmth, balancing on the narrow seat with
difficulty, hands crossed on her breast and hidden under her
arms. In three days it would be her birthday: she would be
eighteen. How old that sounded. Georgiana Coins, now
forty-five, had married at sixteen, even if her husband had
been killed in the duel in *Hamlet* two years later. Margaret
Frognal, who drank too much gin and never laughed, had
been twice married. Isabella's own mother had eloped at
eighteen.· Isabella sat doing the arithmetic of age and ma-
trimony and getting low-spirited about it. Her mother was no
comfort either. One of Ellen's favorite phrases when talking
of any girl planning to marry was "high time—I do dislike
seeing an old bride." When she said that, Kate only laughed.

Kate had taken her own nineteenth birthday, celebrated a
few months before with a party on stage, quite philosophically.

"How does it feel to be nineteen, Kate?"

Kate raised her eyebrows and said Isabella had been
brooding over "the old bride" again.

"I can't help brooding. I wish I was like you."

"Bella, you wouldn't choose to be like me *ever*. What! Worry over acting, get discouraged, spend your time with neckache from bending over a script."

"I suppose not."

"Well, then," said Kate, shrugging.

It was true that Isabella had never envied Kate until now. Perhaps it was a symptom of getting older. Kate was doing what she wanted, she enjoyed things. She even liked playing opposite Buckley Vernon.

Isabella didn't like Buckley Vernon and didn't know why. Her manner to him after the first day or two was noticeably cold, which surprised him, for he rarely failed with women. "The dark one," as he called her to himself, apparently was not interested, and after a few unsuccessful attempts Buckley stopped trying. As she didn't find him attractive, he would persuade himself that she was plain. But it was quite difficult to do that.

Isabella had always discussed her thoughts and feelings with her sister, but she avoided the subject of Buckley. He upset her. Or rather her own feelings when he was near her did. Sometimes even seeing him at a distance, she felt slightly faint. Only stupid women fell in love with actors. She did not want to fall into a trance, spend all her time imagining what it would be like in Buckley's arms, feel her stomach drop when she saw him, hear her voice sound hoarse when she answered him. She kept away.

Her mother's neat head looked round the bedroom door.

"There you are. Kate said you must have gone for a walk."

"I was thinking."

Ellen gave a sharp laugh. "It is no good sitting about with a face like a fiddle. Come into my room and tidy my dressing table drawer."

Ellen liked to give her daughters the tasks of a lady's maid. She sewed all day in the wardrobe but simply could not mend her own gloves or replace her own buttons. She had a pleasure in being waited on and a satisfaction in being obeyed.

Kate was by the window, a script in her hand, when Isabella flounced into the room. Looking at her sister's absorbed figure, Isabella thought Kate's green dress far less shabby than her own old brown. Hers was fuller than Kate's—but she did not own enough petticoats to make it look right and her mother would never allow her to have any more. Where would the money for the cambric come from? Isabella had spent hours with the detested brown dress, unpicking the black braid and sewing on white bobble fringe. It still looked dingy.

"Why can't Kate do your drawer, Ma?"

"Because she is working."

There was no answer to that as far as Ellen was concerned. She had rigid ideas about work. She waited on Thomas tenderly because he was weighed down with work, but she would never lift a finger to help anyone enjoy himself. Work, for instance, did not include reading anything but plays, and when Isabella read history or novels she put paper covers over the books and lettered them "Sheridan" or "Vanbrugh." Work was sewing in the wardrobe but not stitching fringe on one's own dress.

Isabella sat down at the worm-eaten oak dressing table. Like every other piece of Mrs. Gunn's furniture, it was rickety, one leg of the table loose and secured by curl papers wedged into its socket. The looking glass was so spotted that when Isabella looked at her face she might have had the smallpox. The bedcover was clean but scorched, the walls were blackened with candle smoke. Nothing in the room was fresh except the faces of the young girls.

Isabella placed her mother's few possessions in a row on the table. A pot of rouge. A box of rice powder. Some glove stretchers and a shoehorn. A pearl-handled buttonhook, two handkerchiefs embroidered with violets by Kate. In a box was a pair of earrings, circles of seed pearls, not valuable enough to be sold after the fire, Isabella put them through the lobes of her pierced ears and set the circles swinging.

Ellen was watching her.

"They suit you."

"Do you think so?"

"Have them."

"But they're the only ones you've got!"

"Young people look better in jewelry. My face is old."

Kate, still reading, stretched out her hand to her mother.

"Mama, that is just not true."

"You can have the earrings for your birthday," said Ellen. "Which reminds me. Have we decided on your birthday treat?"

Kate closed the play. She knew the part by heart.

"What about a picnic?"

"Papa likes picnics," said Isabella, still making the earrings swing and looking at her own reflection.

"He could go to the market early and buy us some fruit," said Ellen, who enjoyed sending her husband on shopping errands, because however little money they had he was extravagant.

"Did you know there was fighting in the market?" Kate said suddenly. "I meant to tell you. Mr. Vernon saw it. Mr. Vernon said—"

"Oh, Mr. Vernon, Mr. Vernon. Why must you quote him all the time? He isn't God Almighty," interrupted Isabella irritably.

Ellen's expression turned to stone.

"How *dare* you!" she said, fixing Isabella with dark angry eyes. "How dare you swear! It is blasphemous, and what is more it is unladylike. I shall not tell you about it again." Isabella blushed scarlet and Kate began to talk, drawing her mother's attention away from her miserable sister.

"Mr. Vernon was crossing the Buttermarket on his way to Grey Street. He said it was so cheerful with all the carts and the spring vegetables and pigeons in cages, there was even a Punch-and-Judy show. Then suddenly he heard shouting and a scuffle started, and a crowd seemed to come from nowhere, men with cudgels and the stalls were overturned and one man was on the ground. Mr. Vernon got away as quickly as he could."

"Such courage," muttered Isabella, still crushed and refusing to be pleasant.

"But what man of sense would join in a fight he knows nothing about? Besides, how could he play King Charles if some villain had given him a black eye?"

It was agreed in the family that Isabella should have a picnic for her birthday treat, something both girls had been given since they were small children. The weather was good, the skies a clear windswept blue. The picnic would be on the day before her birthday, a Sunday, the only day when there was no performance. They decided to travel to a little fishing village some miles away. Thomas and Ellen had visited the place years ago when they'd been on the Northern circuits, and both girls were eager to see the sea. There was never time to go so far on working days.

The size of the audiences at the theater had improved. *King Charles's Merrie Days* was quite popular, and Thomas also introduced a burletta into the repertory, a romp based on a story from the *Arabian Nights*. The idea had been Laurie Spindle's—he'd played in the piece before.

"The town's unsettled at present," he said to Thomas, looking at him with the confidence of someone very small and very hardy. "People are downright miserable, and as for talking about the price of a loaf! Why not give them a chance to laugh?"

Thomas disliked taking suggestions from other people but agreed. The piece turned out a success. Laurie played a miniature (and grotesque) Lord Chamberlain, Buckley a prince, Kate a lost Arabian princess. On the first night there was loud applause and approving whistles.

When the curtain came down, her painted white cheeks still glowing with excitement Kate came offstage with Isabella and Buckley. They made a strange-looking trio just then. Kate wore purple harem trousers, a vaporous veil, a pearl

circlet round her hair, huge property anklets studded with
paste diamonds. Isabella was in blue, star-patterned, a
wreath of crimson flowers on her head. Buckley wore yellow
satin and a turban sewn with paste diamonds the size of marbles.

"Did you ask your sister about her birthday, Miss Winter?"
asked Buckley. He called other actresses familiarly by their
Christian names.

"Oh, Bella!" exclaimed Kate. "I forgot. Mr. Vernon has
begged he may hire a carriage to take us to the sea. Papa had
said we should go in the public coach, but Mr. Vernon says it
will be so crowded and horrid. And not another coach to
bring us home until ten o'clock at night. So—is it not kind of
him?"

Buckley smiled easily, saying he would be in their debt if
they allowed him to join the party.

Isabella thanked him and escaped as soon as she decently
could, leaving Buckley and Kate to talk absorbedly about the
performance. She heard Kate sigh, "Wasn't it *beautiful?* I
could play it all over again!"

Alone in the dressing room, Isabella lit the candle and sat
down. Why must they have that man at her party tomorrow?
She did not want to be with him for ten minutes, let alone a
whole day.

She nervously clasped her hands. She had the desire,
strong and wild as a nymph in mythology, to run, to flee, to
escape from the only man who could make her tremble.

Chapter Four

THE WINTER FAMILY CAME TROOPING OUT into the sunshine when the carriage arrived. Ellen Winter thought Buckley very smart in his caped coat with the steel clasps and a hat of sporting style. She wished Mrs. Gunn was not standing in the doorway with the air of a woman reckoning to the last half-penny how much the young man had spent hiring the conveyance.

"I am handling the reins myself, Mrs. Winter. I'm a dab hand, you know. Wait until you see me," said Buckley. Ellen gave her upward-running laugh, like a rising scale of notes. For a moment her small brown face had a trace of the girl who had made a romantic runaway marriage.

There was a pleasant bustle as Buckley let down the step and handed Ellen into the carriage. Thomas came out with the picnic baskets, Buckley inquired which of the girls would brave the sea breezes and sit beside him on the box. Before anybody else could reply, Kate said lightly, "Would you think me selfish if I asked to be the one? I know it is Bella's birthday, but last time she sat on a box she felt giddy, did you not, Bella?"

Isabella agreed she had indeed felt very giddy and afterward had a headache. She was relieved as she climbed into the carriage beside her mother; but Kate's intuition made her uneasy. Kate was too clever. What else did she guess about her feelings for Buckley Vernon?

The door was closed, Buckley climbed up on the box beside Kate and away they went, trotting round a corner out of the sight of Mrs. Gunn.

Ellen settled herself comfortably, but her mind was still on her enemy.

"Tom, you will really have to speak to that woman. It is like being dogged by a spy."

"Yes, my dear," said Thomas.

He never would.

The gray stone houses edging hilly streets were left behind, they trotted cheerfully into the country, greener and more springlike than Kate had expected. Buckley pointed out interesting sights with his whip. That ruin yonder had been an abbey. Kate agreed that the arches were lofty and grand but thought it seemed forlorn. Look, said Buckley, we are approaching a bridge over the Tyne. Did Kate know the river was full of salmon? They trotted steadily in the sweet-smelling air on an arrow-straight road which would eventually lead to Scotland.

Isabella, glad to be with her parents and away from Buckley, enjoyed the unaccustomed luxury of traveling in a private carriage not squashed in an omnibus or a public coach. She, too, admired the countryside, wondered at the old abbey, leaned forward to catch a glimpse of the river. The sun grew warmer and the inside of the carriage, smelling of leather, was soon unpleasantly stuffy. But Isabella could not open a window, for her mother was always cold even in summertime. Thomas called Ellen "a chilly mortal."

At last Buckley reined in the horses and drew the carriage to a stop. Thomas had fallen asleep and woke with a start.

"Have we arrived? Good. Let me take the baskets, my dear, don't trouble yourself. Yes, I should fasten that lid, should I not? No, I can manage perfectly—well, if Isabella could manage the small one—"

He collected things and forgot things, generally making the few possessions needed for the picnic seem as numerous as the scenery and costumes of a play.

They took a winding path down the cliffs through high furze bushes which bent in the wind. The air smelled salty and sea birds cried in a melancholy way. Isabella, following Buckley and her sister, thought the sound mournful. Who had told her that gulls were the souls of drowned sailors?

Down on the shore they found a great deserted stretch of rocks and sand damp from the ebb tide.

Ellen took command.

"Where shall we sit? No, no, Mr. Vernon, not where there is a rock pool, one of the girls will be sure to drag her dress in it. Thomas, that place has no shelter. Here among these rocks is just right."

Buckley spread a rug across a flat granite rock, Kate unpacked the food, Thomas uncorked the wine. A gull almost as large as a swan swooped down close to Ellen, folded its wings and stood staring at her with yellow eyes. She stretched out her hand fearlessly and gave it some bread.

The bird opened its curved beak and closed it with a ferocious snap. Isabella gave a little scream.

"Be careful, Mama! It will bite off your fingers."

"Perhaps you shouldn't feed the bird until we are leaving, Mrs. Winter," said Buckley, sitting beside her. "Otherwise we may lose our feast. Once when I was playing at Berwick-on-Tweed some friends and I went for a picnic to Holy Island. Down came a gull during our luncheon, gave a lunge and then flew off. Do you know what it had taken?"

"A bun?" suggested Kate.

"My purse."

Everybody stared and both the girls laughed.

"What happened, my boy?" inquired Thomas, not in the least amused by any story in which money was lost.

"Well, sir, I confess I never saw my purse again. It's my

opinion that bird was heading for Norway. Of course, I was the object of much wonder and sympathy in Berwick afterward. Everybody spoke of the horror of watching my money fly out to sea. It occurred to me to persuade the Berwick Theater to give me a benefit."

"And did they?"

"Papa," murmured Kate, "Mr. Vernon is teasing."

"But how much did you lose?" Thomas asked.

"I don't like to confess it."

"We all feel for you, Mr. Vernon," said Ellen. "Do tell us."

Buckley paused effectively.

"It has always been my secret, but perhaps, as I am with friends, I can reveal it. The bird made off with a considerable sum. Can you guess how much? Precisely sixpence."

Kate hit him with a spoon.

They ate their meal and sat enjoying the sunshine and the sound of the sea. They talked, of course, of the theater.

"Tell me, sir," Buckley said to Thomas, "why should the theater not be a gentlemanly profession? My father is a justice of the peace and was deeply shocked at my choice of calling. But I told him then and I still believe it—I'm determined to prove one can be a gentleman and an actor."

Thomas's face lit up.

"My dear fellow. That is something I've said for years."

After a while Kate stood up and said she would like to walk along the shore. Buckley asked if he might go with her.

"Well . . . I was going to say my lines aloud. I wanted to hear what they sounded like with the waves as an accompaniment."

"An excellent idea. I will cue for you."

"Isabella can go, too," said Ellen, looking at her younger daughter, who was leaning against a rock, her face in the sunshine, her eyes closed.

Isabella answered ungraciously that she would stay where she was.

The two young people walked away across the damp sand. Ellen glanced at Isabella, thinking she was tiresomely moody and best left alone.

When it was time to leave, everybody was lulled by the hours spent in the open air. Kate was again handed up on to the box, Isabella again went inside with her parents. They set off briskly. The fishing village was left behind, the road crossed heather-covered land, then entered a wood of trees in bud. There was a blur of bluebells. Emerging from the deckled woodland light into the sunshine, they saw a high stone wall on the right which seemed to go on for miles. On the other side of the wall were the well-tended lands and great trees of a gentleman's park.

Ellen leaned forward.

"That must be the Fallowfield estate. I thought we passed it on our way out. Yes, there is the house. Handsome, is it not? But too old-fashioned."

On a rise of ground stood a huge old stone house as grim as a fortress. Ellen talked knowledgeably about "the Fallowfields," whom they had married, what were their titles. She always knew about the aristocracy, her memory about their relationships, their property, was extraordinary. She was still talking when the carriage gave a swerve, Buckley tugged at the reins, the horses suddenly checked and Ellen and Isabella were almost thrown from their seats.

"Perhaps we're making way for the public coach," said Ellen, calmly sitting back again.

They were slowing down for another vehicle to pass, but it was not the crowded dusty public coach. A shining yellow and black carriage raced by, drawn by four magnificent chestnut horses. As it dashed past Isabella caught a glimpse of two gentlemen inside and an elaborate coat of arms on the door. A second later the carriage turned through the open gates of the manor.

Isabella had the feeling, as the carriage vanished into the distance, that its brightness had shed a light on her and her surroundings as fierce as that which came nightly from the stage. It shone on her family's genteel poverty. Her cloak was old and shabby, her mother's gloves darned, her father's boots scuffed with polish only on the toes. With a familiar gesture she put her hand to the ribbons of her bonnet.

Those, too, were threadbare from tying and retying. Even the cushions against which she leaned, the cushions of this carriage generously hired by Buckley, smelled of dust.

The great actor Henry Davenant was due in Newcastle that week, and Thomas waited his arrival with nervous trepidation. Thomas had seen Davenant act many times—like most professionals in the theater, Thomas attended the play on any and every occasion, never tired of it, comparing or remembering performances as a wine lover might discuss vintages.

"Kean's Hamlet was at its peak in 1814."

"Kemble's Brutus, to my mind, will never be equaled."

He had favorite theater stories which he liked telling and told well (they bored his daughters). There was the legendary occasion when Nelson had come to see *The Merry Wives of Windsor* at a theater where Thomas was working. When the hero's carriage arrived, the street had rung with the shouts of the crowd, the box office was besieged. At the end of the performance crowds of sailors from Nelson's ship were waiting outside the theater to greet him.

"I never saw such a thing. I shall never forget it."

Thomas always ended the story in the same way.

He was knowledgeable about the theater, acted well but without fire and was a painstaking manager, but Ellen was as worried at the prospect of Henry Davenant's arrival as Thomas was. The man was a great actor, but he was a bully. Stories of Davenant were much repeated and laughed over; his despotism had a kind of largeness which suited his huge reputation. But it was one thing to joke about him in the greenroom, another to cope with him in person. Poor Thomas always "caved in," as Ellen privately called it.

A letter arrived from Davenant.

"Sir. I expect to be at the theater the afternoon of Thursday. I will perform *Lear*, *Othello* and *Hamlet*. *Lear* shall be first. Choose the Cordelia with attention, if you please. She has importance to me. I do not require rehearsals for my plays but wish to see the young lady on the matter of Scene One. Mind she is young. Not above 30. Yours obediently,"

Thomas frowned as he showed the letter to his wife and Kate. He looked fussed.

"I must put up the playbills immediately. It is very soon."

"And no rehearsals at all," said Kate. "Cordelia is difficult. At any rate, I have always found it so."

She looked as anxious as her father.

"Famous actors never rehearse, Kate," said Ellen. "He knows the great parts as you do your own name. We simply have to fit in."

"Is he as fierce as they say?"

"Of course not," snapped Thomas.

Five minutes after Davenant arrived in the town, before he had his boxes taken to his lodgings, he arrived at the theater, marched into Thomas's office without knocking and demanded that the actors be "mustered forthwith."

The company knew about the great man's arrival and were waiting in the greenroom when the message arrived. Raising their eyebrows, making grimaces and jokes, they trooped on to the stage. Kate was excited and curious. She had never worked with a great actor before or even seen one at close quarters.

Davenant was standing onstage, his back to the empty auditorium. He was a stocky man with broad shoulders and brown hair worn brushed upward and curling in the outdated manner of King William. He had heavy whiskers. He was perhaps forty years old, but his face, though lined, could look considerably younger. His cheekbones were high, his nose strong but irregular, his eyes large and a burning blue.

He stood glaring at the actors, who froze into stillness. Georgiana Coins, usually the first to draw attention to herself, looked quite glassy; even Buckley seemed nervous.

"This is the company, Mr. Davenant," said Thomas deferentially, standing beside him with his hands full of papers.

"I can see that, man! Gentlemen, we play *Lear* tonight," said Davenant in a powerful voice with a curious edge to it.

"Who is Kent? Gloucester? Goneril? Oswald?"

He ran through the parts like a father checking the presence of a large ill-behaved family. As each actor stepped forward, he looked him up and down and said nothing. Finally the call came: "Cordelia."

Kate took a pace forward.

"And who may you be?"

"Kate Winter, sir."

"Any relation to the manager fellow?" demanded Davenant as if Thomas were not present, let alone standing at his elbow.

"His daughter."

"Are you, by God?"

Kate said nothing. Davenant looked at her.

"I wish a word with you," he said at last. "The rest of you," glancing along the rows of silent actors, "can go. I do not rehearse my plays. The performance is at seven, but I wish it to start five minutes later to avoid shuffling from the audience. I trust you know your business. That is all."

The actors melted away until, out of earshot, they all began to talk at once.

Kate remained where she was. Her father rustled through his papers, frowning impatiently. Davenant continued to stare at her.

"You are small, miss."

"Not so very, sir."

Her father looked up as if only just noticing his daughter's height. He reminded Kate of a jester standing beside a king, unsurprised at being ignored.

"What do you wish me to do?" inquired Kate respectfully.

Davenant folded his arms.

"Not much. In the rejection scene—'Peace, Kent! Come not between the dragon and his wrath'—you stand with your back to the audience all the while, then you sink very gradually to your knees. While I am cursing you, mind you stay with your eyes fixed on mine. All the speech through."

"Is that all, sir?"

"Yes. You may go, Miss—"

"Winter."

"How could I forget?" he said with wonderful sarcasm.

Everybody at the theater was talking about Davenant. In the dusty greenroom, sitting on benches, thumbing scripts, darning their own costumes, they discussed Davenant's rudeness and expensive clothes, his bullying manners—and his art. Even poor actors traveling the circuits, treated as scarcely better than the "vagabonds" of the past, were awestruck by great talent. The man who had such a thing possessed a talisman. It was as if they were being visited by some kind of ill-behaved angelic presence. It had arrived from above and would return later to paradise. It could never be treated as mortal.

Kate was sent for during the afternoon. Davenant said he would run through the rejection scene with her.

"It's the only scene I rehearse," he said, regarding her again with penetrating blue eyes.

He had shed the greatcoat he'd worn that morning, and was wearing a full-skirted dark blue coat and white trousers. His clothes suited him. But he looked more like a wealthy farmer than an actor. What he could never be taken for was an aristocrat; his body was too stocky, his neck too thick, his whole appearance almost coarse.

They took their places in the center of the stage, and he faced her and began to speak. Everything changed. His face swam, his eyes reflected a kingly anger, when he moved he was old yet infinitely graceful. . .

The theater had never been so full as it was for the first Davenant performance. Thomas was red in the face and excited. He hurried in to see the actor, who was already in his dressing room beginning to make up. Davenant did not turn around when Thomas came respectfully into the room, but continued to draw lines on his face as if on a canvas.

"There's not a seat to be had, sir."

"So I should damned well think."

Kate, too, was excited when the performance began. Rehearsing with Davenant had been extraordinary. Now, when she was actually playing with him in front of an audience, she felt she had never acted before in her life. When the play ended, the audience rose and cheered. Davenant, long white hair round his shoulders, face streaked with paint and real tears, bowed his head. Kate, a halter round her neck, her face gray to simulate her death of a minute before, curtsyed deeply. Davenant kissed her hand. The applause poured over them like golden rain.

The curtains finally bounced together, shutting off the love which had surged over the footlights.

Davenant dropped her hand.

"Winter."

Thomas, who had played Gloucester, hurried forward.

"The lighting is bad. The storm is too loud and she—" pointing at Kate—"speaks too low. One of the walking gentlemen has squeaking boots. Either the boots or the actor must go."

Davenant made Thomas very nervous but the full houses comforted him.

Returning home after being shouted at, Thomas talked to his wife philosophically. Most great actors had some vice or other which had to be borne. They drank. They were bullies. They were sweet as pie to a manager's face and black as pitch behind his back. There was always a flaw, "a vicious mole in nature," that was strong in them; it seemed an inevitable result of fame. Davenant was worse offstage, infinitely better onstage, than others called great whom Thomas had known.

Anxious about so much, Thomas never worried over his daughters. They did him credit. He'd coached them since they were small children, their voices were beautiful, they could hold their own with anybody on a stage. But if Thomas had taught them to act, it was Ellen who had brought them up to be ladies. It had been no easy task in a world where there was much drunkenness, language was Rabelaisian and many of the actors and actresses loose-living.

The Winters had strict rules for their girls. Thomas returned from the theater each night before the evening performance to collect them, while Ellen remained at work in the Wardrobe. The girls were never allowed to walk to the theater alone.

The weather had turned cold, and one evening Kate sat in the attic window on the lookout for her father.

He was usually punctual, and his absence worried her. She leaned for the second time out of the window to look down at the alley.

"I do wish he would come."

"Oh, Kate, don't fuss."

"But he is always on time, Bella."

"Well, he isn't this evening."

How cross she is, thought Kate. She loved her sister dearly, but found her moods hard to bear. She opened the window again, trying not to make a noise, and hung out.

"Goodness. There's Laurie."

"What do you mean?" said Isabella impatiently.

"Laurie Spindle is coming to the house. Do you suppose Papa sent him for us?"

"I trust not. I cannot bear him."

"Bella, he is a dear little man. Yes, I'm sure he has come to collect us," said Kate, snatching up cloak and bonnet and darting down the stairs. Isabella followed slowly, making a face. She disliked Kate's devoted admirer with his stories of being a fiddler, a harlequin, dancing the toe-and-heel, his days of starvation, his brief triumphs. She didn't even think him a good comedian or see why audiences laughed at him.

Laurie Spindle was leaning against the open door much in the way he leaned against the proscenium arch when speaking a soliliquy.

He was hopelessly drunk.

"Guvnor says I'm to 'company you ladies."

"Laurie, dear, you are not very well," said Kate with a gentle sympathy which filled Isabella with scorn.

"P'fctly well. Quick march," said Laurie, clinging to the door. "Gotter see you get t'theater—"

"He's *drunk*," said Isabella in contempt, buttoning her

gloves. "Leave him to fall into the gutter. I will not be seen walking with *him*."

She swept by, and Kate looked at Laurie, sighed and followed her sister. Laurie grinned and began to stagger after them.

"Don't walk so fast, Bella. We will lose the poor man. He is in a dreadful state."

"I hope he breaks his neck."

"You are so hard. He cannot help his weaknesses. He has had an unhappy life."

Isabella gave a snort and walked on. She walked fast, and soon the little unsteady figure was left behind.

It was broad day, but the streets through which they passed were poor and crowded. Kate murmured that their father would not like them to be alone like this, but Isabella tossed her head at such stupidity. She had longer legs than her sister, and Kate had almost to run to keep up.

It seemed to Kate there was a curious atmosphere in the streets this evening. Was it because they'd never walked alone before? Women at open doorways stared at them. There were groups of women—no men seemed to be about—at street corners who looked with hostile faces at the girls. One big woman in a sacking apron suddenly shouted, "Dinna go by Market Street!"

"Bella—we'd better not."

"Oh, for goodness sake!" exclaimed Isabella as they turned a corner. "That's the quickest way."

"But if she said—"

"Don't be such a cake," jeered Isabella. It was their mother's phrase for a coward.

They crossed a deserted courtyard, went down a side street and came into the long cobbled stretch of Market Street. Suddenly they saw something flowing toward them. It was, quite literally, like a great swollen river. A river of men. For one minute the familiar street was almost empty, in the next it was engulfed by a vast moving mass of men walking and talking in grumbling voices, a sound like a long unending growl. The girls were too far down the street to turn back, and before they could run or step aside the river dragged them with it by sheer force of weight and movement.

None of the men took the least notice of the girls. They looked blindly ahead. They were filthy, in reeking clothes and tattered caps, their faces dark from dirt or from exposure. Kate gripped her sister's arm and somehow managed to keep beside her. Her bonnet was knocked off, and hatless, her red hair falling down, she let her slight body be swept along, supported by the crowd and going with them as if she were indeed swimming in a river. When Isabella looked at her she saw with astonishment that her sister was merely excited.

"It's all right," gasped Kate. "Go as they go. Keep calm. We may be able to get out in a little while." She put out a small hand and gripped Isabella's arm. She knew Isabella was terrified out of her wits by crowds. When they had been children their father had taken them to the races, and Isabella had been so frightened by the press of people that Thomas had been forced to carry her on his shoulders.

Desperately clutching at Kate's arm, Isabella was filled with panic. They were being dragged God knows where by this mob of angry men in rags, they were at the crowd's mercy, they were helpless. She clutched at Kate, saw her sister's reassuring face under the cap of red hair; then the crowd surged round a corner and Isabella tottered, scarcely able to keep on her feet. The crowd slowed down and there was a sudden roar. They had halted outside a corn chandler's. Above their heads was the chute used for pushing down the fat corn sacks to wagons waiting below.

"The door, lads! The door!"

Voices yelled, there was a noise of splitting wood, Isabella wrenched round and saw—with terror—that Kate had disappeared. Sobbing and screaming, she tried to fight her way through the bodies to where she'd last seen Kate. She managed to jump up for a moment higher than the crowd and across a sea of caps saw Kate's red head already at a distance and disappearing still further.

The crowd burst into a wild cheer. At the top of the flour chute the figure of a man appeared, then another, clutching bulging sacks of corn, which they pushed into the chute. Down came the sacks, and the crowd broke like a huge wave as men clawed their way toward the corn. The sacks fell to the ground, there was a surge of bodies and just when Isabella thought she could no longer keep on her feet and would be trampled to death there were cries of "No more. All gone! No more!"

"Bakers, t'bakers!" shouted the crowd, beginning to move again, chanting and yelling, "We want bread, and we'll take it, we'll take it."

Half-mad with fear, sometimes nearly fainting, Isabella was swept down the street past houses where shutters were slammed against the mob. In the distance was the solid facade of the coaching inn, its windows full of people, crowds on the entrance steps. If only she could get toward the inn. . . With all her strength she pushed against a great tall man on her left, but he took no more notice of her than if she were a fly. A grayness began at the edges of her eyes, a feeling of nausea and giddyness, then more shouts. Suddenly she was gripped in two arms and lifted sheer out of the struggling mass and borne, as if flying, out of the noise and stink, straight into silence. . .

"Give her air, if you please. Stand back. Look, she is reviving."

The voice was low, and when she managed to open her heavy eyes she faintly saw a man looking down at her and felt her hand clasped. Someone put a cloth on her forehead; it smelled of eau-de-cologne.

The two young men stood looking down at the figure stretched on the sofa. They dismissed the landlord and his wife and ordered that nobody should enter the saloon. A moment before they had snatched this girl from a boiling sea. Now outside in the street a regiment of the militia had arrived and the crowd, so vast and strong, had broken, scattered, vanished down alleyways, leaving smashed windows, corn scattered in the roads, and shattered doors.

The girl on the sofa, her face the color of chalk, had closed her eyes again. Her lashes were black crescents, a jagged mark of dirt ran across her face. One sleeve of her torn dress hung from a bare arm, her hair was a tangled mess on her shoulders. Slowly she opened her eyes again, and the man holding her hand smiled.

"Ah. You have come back to us. Do not try to speak. You are safe now."

She lay looking at him drowsily. At first she did not believe it, then she was sure. It was the young man she had met what seemed a century ago at Bagot Park. It was Viscount Carteret.

Chapter Five

KATE HAD NOT FARED AS BADLY AS HER SISTER in the riot because she managed to use her wits. When the mob pressed
toward the corn chandlers, she saw, for a split second, a gap
between two men rushing at the first sack of corn; she darted
through the gap and stretched out her hand to Isabella too
late. Her sister vanished in the struggling mass, and a moment later Kate was somehow tossed to the edge of the crowd
like a piece of flotsam thrown up by a rough sea on to a
beach.

There was a passageway between the buildings. She
slipped into it, climbed on a ledge and tried to catch a
glimpse of Isabella, but there was no sign of her. When it
looked as if the crowd, too, would come surging in, Kate ran
to the end of the passage, then through a maze of back-
streets, fleeing as if pursued by a devil. Five minutes later,
shaking but not hysterical, she was at the theater getting what
help she could. She insisted on accompanying her father, although it seemed the militia were already on the way. It was
not until a groom from the Bull arrived with a message from
the landlord to say Isabella was safe that Kate burst into
tears.

The riot had risen out of nowhere, terrified the town and vanished as if it had never been. It dissolved into frightened separate men, hiding, skulking, hurrying home to swear they'd never been part of it. In the town it was said men had been arrested and would be hanged. A mounted patrol rode nightly through the streets, bringing a sense not of safety but of fear.

The men who'd marched out, half-starved, to steal bread were afraid of the militia. Other people were afraid of them. In the countryside farmers found their ricks blazing. A speech made two years ago was still lighting fires. "You have only to take a couple of matches and a bundle of straw dipped in pitch, and I will see what the Government and its hundreds of thousands of soldiers will do against this one weapon—if it is used boldly." Now everybody was afraid.

Thomas and Ellen had been horrified at what happened; it had been a miracle neither of the girls had been killed. To Isabella's disgust and Kate's sympathy, poor Laurie Spindle grew even drunker after the riot—he drank from remorse.

Both girls soon recovered their health and spirits with the elasticity of being under twenty years old. Isabella seemed more cheerful than she'd been for weeks. She was not only pleasant to the family, springing up to do little services for her mother and kissing her father when they retired to bed, but hummed tunelessly (she had no ear) when dressing for the performances. Kate sometimes quite longed for the previous gloom, to be spared that little voice always off key.

Kate did not comment to her mother, but she knew Isabella's bright eyes were due to the appearance of Viscount Carteret. He and his cousin Robert Bagot had called at the theater to inquire after Isabella's recovery, and later sent her a magnificent bouquet of roses, deep yellow streaked with pink.

Isabella gave the flowers to her mother. Since the girls had grown up, Ellen was always given any tokens of admiration offered to her daughters; it was a kind of toll. Kate won the heart of an actor, the flowers went to Ellen. An admirer left a pair of fine gloves at the stage door for Isabella, Ellen wore

them to church on Sundays, remarking on the good fortune
that Isabella's hands were as small as her own.

The yellow and pink roses bloomed on Ellen's dressing-
table at their lodgings, to the disgust of Mrs. Gunn. Isabella
pressed one in a book of poetry.

"Tell me about Lord Carteret. I scarcely saw him when he
called at the theater," Kate said. They were in their poky
dressing room before the evening performance; it was two
weeks since the riot. The roses were long since dead.

"I know very little of the Viscount. But he seems to me to
have a very gentle and kind nature," Isabella said, untying
her bonnet. For once she did not scowl at its frayed strings.

"I imagine the nobility must be arrogant. They're always so
in an audience. Quite rude sometimes. They were very hard
to engage at Bagot Park that time, I remember."

"You only think of people as an audience."

"Well, of course. How else would I think of them?"

Kate smiled, and then looked at her sister and gave one of
her sentimental sighs.

"Is it not strange, Bella. That the Viscount should be here
and actually rescue you. I have forgotten the reason he and
that other gentleman—"

"Mr. Robert Bagot. He is Lord Carteret's cousin."

"But why are they here? Mama says something about
property in Northumberland."

"They own half the county," said Isabella carelessly. "They
have shipyards, you know, and so much land—miles and
miles of it. They came to see things are in order."

"You mean because of the riot?"

"No, thank goodness, that was nothing to do with the Bagots," said Isabella, with a happy, know-all air.

"The cousin told me they are determined to see nobody of
theirs wants a livelihood. It worries the Earl that they live so
far from their property and land here."

"They have so much, I suppose."

"They are very rich. You know how it is."

"No, I don't," said Kate. "Shall they be in Newcastle long?"

"I think they have already left," Isabella said indifferently.

"They should have at least come to the play and seen Davenant," said Kate, quite shocked. "And I would have liked your Viscount to see *Lear* because I have a good role in it."

"Egoist. And he isn't *my* Viscount, alas and alack."

Tunelessly humming, Isabella took off her clothes and began to tie on a series of padded petticoats, fasten a wired bodice which pushed her small breasts together and dress in a costume sewn with false ermine.

She was concealing from her family that she'd seen the Viscount and his cousin every day since the riot. It was the first time in her life she was grateful that she knew how to act.

From the moment when she drifted back to consciousness, Isabella knew the two young noblemen were people entirely different from any she'd ever known—except during one lost evening in Sussex. She wouldn't have believed it possible for men to treat her with such delicacy. Had an actor rescued her he would have exaggerated his gallantry, loudly repeated that she owed him her life. The Viscount and his cousin did the reverse. When she was at the Bull they treated her with such exquisite politeness she forgot that her clothes were in tatters and that she was as bedraggled and dirty as a starving wretch in a hovel. They persuaded her to drink a glass of hot negus, sat quietly with her until she regained her self-possession. When she was stronger they drove her to the theater in a private carriage and politely pressed her grubby, gloveless hand.

The following day the gentlemen called at the theater to inquire after the young lady's health. They met both sisters and their parents and asked permission to invite the family to luncheon. But all the family were working except Isabella, so it happened that what she might have dreamed of as a wonderful impossibility came about; with Ellen's permission she had luncheon in the Bagot's private suite alone with the Viscount and his cousin.

Lord Carteret had been faintly interested when, on meeting Thomas Winter, the actor reminded him that once he and his family "had the honor to play at Bagot Park." He remembered then that he had spent some time that evening with the younger of the sisters. He remembered no more than that.

When Isabella arrived for luncheon he scarcely recognized her. Ellen had lent her the only real silk gown in the wardrobe, plain silver-gray, which suited Isabella's dark looks perfectly. Why, she is delightful, he thought, surprised.

During the meal, Isabella was charming, spirited and remarkably pretty, and the gentlemen showed her that they thought so. She interested them. There was an aura of romance about this girl, they thought, it must be that very curious life she leads, full of paint and make-believe.

Sitting between two attractive men who concentrated their attention entirely on herself, Isabella compared them. They were physically rather alike, both dark, both with straight noses and gray eyes. But the Viscount, taller than his cousin and with long well-shaped legs, had a round face, a fascinatingly indolent manner and slow voice. The cousin was a quicker person in every way. He spoke abruptly as if there were so many ideas crowding into his head that he only had time to select a few for the present. He had a restless way of springing up and walking about. He had a longish handsome face and curling, glossy black hair.

It was clear the two Bagots liked each other.

"Are we going to see you perform in a play, Miss Isabella?" inquired Lord Carteret. "My cousin assures me you are not on the playbills this week. Why is that? I shall be deuced disappointed if I do not see you act, you know."

Isabella explained that she was not in every play, although her sister was. The famous Davenant was acting with them at present. They must, of course, have seen him? They assured her they had never done so. Accustomed to theater people, it seemed incredible to Isabella that the Bagot gentlemen had never seen Davenant upon a stage, and clearly they were not going to make the effort to do so. They seemed far more interested in her.

She knew they both admired her, but found it easier to talk to Lord Carteret; it was to him she turned more often. He had such a sweet lazy manner, he looked at her so charmingly, laughed so easily. His gray eyes were full of good nature.

When the Bagot gentlemen drove her back to the theater after luncheon, Lord Carteret said, "May we have the honor of seeing you again?"

The week that followed was full of amusing subterfuges. Isabella explained to the Bagot gentlemen that her family simply must not be told she was meeting them. She knew, she said earnestly, that this was not as it should be, but her father was a taskmaster about her work, and she was supposed to be concentrating on a new role. They accepted what she said; everything connected with the actor's life was mystifying to them. As Robert Bagot said to his cousin after Isabella had told them of the necessity for secrecy, "Possibly her papa disapproves of her having acquaintances outside her own class, you know. There are many different snobberies."

"Is it not absurd to think of that delicious creature *working* for her living?" said Carteret. "But perhaps acting is not really work, d'you think?"

"From what I remember of our theatricals last winter, it's deuced hard work," said Robert, laughing.

It was difficult for Isabella to get to the Bull to meet them, but by fibs and inventions she managed to do so. Lord Carteret never asked to see her alone; his cousin was always present. Nothing could have been more proper than the time she spent in their private saloon, talking to them as if they were friends, old friends. Compared to the pinches and kisses between men and girls backstage, she might have been at Court.

She like both men very much but it was Lord Carteret she preferred. Not because he was the son of an Earl (this thought filled her with awe) but because she knew he considered her beautiful. He called her "the wittiest creature": her smallest joke made him laugh. When he looked at her she felt as if she were standing in sunshine after months spent in the coldest winter.

"The cousin," as she called Robert Bagot to herself, also liked her, but she knew *he* remembered she was an actress.

"I fear it is time you left us, Miss Isabella," Robert Bagot said one evening, looking at his watch. She had been with them an hour.

"Davenant plays King Lear tonight, does he not?" said Lord Carteret. "Do you have a large role? You have told us about your parts, but I forget which is the greatest."

"I do nothing in the play tonight," she said, laughing. "I am just a walking-on lady attendant to Cordelia. That is Kate. Poor Kate quakes in her shoes, you know, but she says Davenant is a genius, so I daresay he is."

"You have great faith in your sister's opinion," said Lord Carteret, looking pleased for some reason.

"About the theater—always. Kate calls us 'children of the arts.' That is what *she* is. For Kate everything must be about the theater or because of it. It is her passion."

"You are very fond of her."

Isabella put her hand under her chin in an unstudied, careless gesture. Carteret thought he had never met a woman so alluring. The well-bred girls in society paled beside her. She was like a fire. A new-lit fire.

"One couldn't be anything but devoted to Kate," she said. "*You* would be, you know. She is so sweet and clever and quick and kind. Except when she's acting, and then she's very strong and rather horrid sometimes! We had happy days when we were children. Mama bundled us into shawls and left us in dressing rooms when she and Papa were working. Kate would invent games. Some went on for weeks, and they always began in the same way. She spoke the words like a spell."

She talked about her sister, exclaiming how much better

an actress, how much kinder a person Kate was than herself. Carteret watched and listened in silence.

Isabella had been let off lightly as far as her acting was concerned; she thought Davenant must have decided not to use her. Certainly any leading part which required a young girl had gone to Kate, to Isabella's intense relief.

Thomas called the company to assemble one morning when the weather outside the theater was beautiful, the freshest and sweetest kind of May. The actors, creatures of the dark, crowded on the stage. Buckley and Kate whispered together, other actors and actresses exchanged glances, raising their eyebrows in questions as to what Davenant wanted, shrugging to indicate that they didn't know.

Davenant was seated on a property throne with a gold crown on its carved back. Thomas, flushed with nervousness and pursing his lips, was consulting the list of players. There was a tense expectancy in the air.

Isabella took her place in the crowd as far back as possible. She had slept badly and woken miserable: she knew the Viscount and his cousin were leaving today or tomorrow. She was uninterested in this gathering, but because she thought Davenant alarming she stood out of the way, hidden by the tallest actors in the company to escape attention. Kate, a bunch of violets pinned under her chin, was in the front row.

"All present, then?" inquired Davenant.

Thomas looked about and nodded.

"I should think so, too. *I* have been here this half hour."

Davenant paused, regarding them.

"I have consented to remain for a few more weeks," he said. "And Thomas Winter earnestly requested me to play *The Welsh Girl*, as you must all know. Deafening my ears to my own good sense, I agreed. But now I have reread the play. It is trash. I shall play *Othello*."

Even Isabella, absorbed in her own selfish thoughts, knew what a blow this was to Kate. *The Welsh Girl* was a part in which Kate had always shone. Looking through the crowd, she saw her sister's face was white.

"*Othello* casting is arranged by Winter," continued Davenant indifferently. "But there is the matter of Desdemona."

As with *Lear*, the only role other than his own which interested him was that of his leading actress.

He *must* give it to Kate! thought Isabella. Georgiana is an old bat and Margaret Frognal is ugly. That beast is too clever not to know what a beautiful actress Kate is.

"Miss Isabella Winter, please."

She stared but didn't move.

The actor beside her gave her a push.

"He wants you."

Isabella stepped forward. Davenant made a gesture as if to say "Closer." She came closer. She looked over at Kate for reassurance: her sister's eyes were fixed on the ground.

"Winter informs me you have played Desdemona."

"I did play it two years ago."

"Speak up. I am not deaf, and neither is the audience. You know the role, then."

"I was not right for it." She was scarlet.

"Not right for it?" he repeated. "What does that mean? Not good enough? Were you not good enough? Winter, I thought you told me the girl could act."

Thomas looked as if he were in the dock facing a hanging judge.

"She is a good actress. Perhaps a little subdued, but when she acted Desdemona the Othello was not strong. The newspaper critic was most encouraging about her. She had grace, he said."

"Is that what you've got?" demanded Davenant.

She met the implacable eyes and knew she had no hope of dissuading him. As well tell the wind not to blow. With as much self-possession as she could manage, she said, "I will do my best, sir."

"Hmm" was the reply. "Winter. See the girl wears a flaxen

wig and white powder. I can't have all that black hair on the stage when the Moor is black."

He made a shooing gesture and the actors began to leave. As Isabella walked away she heard Davenant say, "Winter. I require her for rehearsal with wig at two o'clock, if you please."

Feeling she could bear to speak to nobody, she ran to her dressing room, snatched up her cloak and bonnet and fled to the stage door. It was midday, and the sunshine outside was hot and bright. The cobbled yard was scattered with straw, an old horse was eating from his nosebag, birds pecked round him. There was a cart full of painted scenery, its colors in the sunshine as tawdry as booths at a fair.

"If my family ask for me, I have gone to the milliner. I shall not be long," Isabella said to the stage doorkeeper. He scarcely listened, returning to a mug of beer and a newspaper.

She hurried into the street. Like the sunshine, it had a cheerful air. A man went by on a gray horse. A milk churn had halted, and people crowded round with their basins. Children were laughing.

She walked as fast as she could toward the Bull. At least I'll say good-bye to them if they are there or leave a letter if they are at the shipyard, she thought. She was miserable and angry by turns. How she hated this acting life. She hated her father's humility in front of that bully sprawled on the throne, hated the fact that Davenant had her father in his power and poor Thomas could do nothing. He did not even have the freedom to answer back.

And if she detested from family pride seeing her father in that position, what about herself? Her father of course had lied. She had not even been passable as Desdemona; it was a role she'd always disliked. She was not like Kate, able to melt and merge her personality by imagination into a role, change magically, pearling over the difference, drawing out the likeness between a character and herself. Isabella despised Desdemona. *She* believed in struggling against an unkind fate, not meekly submitting. Imagine a girl knowing she was to be strangled and going to her death like a lamb to the slaughter.

At the thought of playing the role opposite "that beast," she felt sick.

The yard of the Bull was crowded with arrivals for the races. Travelers were climbing from a coach, horses steaming. Servants carried boxes, people greeted one another, the young men in dazzling boots, the old men in heavy coats. Servant girls giggled and eyed the men.

Isabella went into the hallway. The porter, sitting in a hooded leather chair in the corner, stood up and bowed.

"Is his Lordship in just now?" Isabella asked.

The porter had been present when this girl had been dramatically rescued and carried shoulder-high in the arms of the two young gentlemen. A shabby little thing, he thought. Pretty, though.

"The Viscount is in the back parlor, miss. Shall I announce you?"

"Oh, no. I can find my way, thank you."

The parlor was small and dark and two hundred years old, full of moldering books read by nobody. There was a worm-eaten desk which nobody used and on the wall a pair of pistols used by spiders. No sunshine reached the room. It was damply cold.

As she opened the door, it creaked loudly. Lord Carteret was sitting at the desk and at the sound he turned, then sprang up.

"You! I was this moment—"

"Writing to tell me good-bye."

Everything about her just then, her beauty, her poor attire, her slender figure, her desolate face, went to his heart. He felt as if he had been stabbed.

He came to her and took her hand. Something was very unfamiliar: they were alone. They had never been so until now.

"You are leaving, are you not?" she said, and began to cry.

"Ah, don't weep, I cannot bear it if you do!"

He took both her hands and pressed them, then kissed them, closing his eyes. She stood looking down at his bent head, trying to stop her tears. When he opened his eyes he gave her the tenderest look she had ever seen in her life.

"You must know that I love you," he said.

"My Lord . . . "

She began to tremble violently, moved and excited, knowing what he was going to ask. He would ask her to go away with him, perhaps to London, offer her a rich disgraced life as his mistress, his kept woman. Longing to be in his arms, yearning toward him, sure now that he loved her, she was as sure she would refuse. The hard-sounding voice of common sense told her so.

"Please don't ask me," she said in a low voice. "I could never go away with you, my Lord. Never."

"But I want you to be my wife."

"That is impossible!"

"Isabella–"

"No, no, it's impossible, it cannot be!" She was quite distraught now and crying harder, "How *could* you marry me, with your high rank? Don't say such a thing it would never never be allowed. Oh, I am so unhappy!"

"I do say it. I beg you to accept."

She continued to sob.

"Isabella," he said quietly, "I was writing to propose marriage to you. You must know I love you with all my heart. My cousin knows it. You cannot be unaware of it. I beg you to be my wife."

"It's impossible," she said again, rubbing her eyes and looking away, her heart thudding, "How could *you* , a nobleman, marry an actress! The Earl would forbid it."

"Certainly he would," he said calmly. "Which is why we must be married secretly. My dearest, my dearest . . . "

He drew her close and began to kiss her passionately. Her cheeks were wet and the kiss tasted salt.

"Dear, lovely, haunting, irreplaceable girl. I can think of

nothing but you. May I speak to your father—ask him—"

"No, no! He would never allow it!"

She started away from him, and he looked at the shabby woebegone figure in astonishment.

Isabella said, the words tumbling out, "I know I am not your equal and never shall be, but my father doesn't think of that. He would never let me go. I am part of his work. He's afraid of that horrible Davenant, and I must work for him. Oh, but why are we even talking of it? We must say good-bye. Kiss me just once again."

He kissed her, and she clung to him.

"Denys," she said, calling him by his name for the first time. "Oh, Denys. We are both prisoners in different ways."

He smiled at that.

"Of course we are not. We will leave now, and drive to Gretna Green. Robert understands it must be like this. We can be there by nightfall. We will write a word to your parents and send it to the theater, and by the time your father reads it we will be gone."

"But my boxes—my packing—"

He tied the bonnet under her chin by its threadbare green strings.

"I would so much rather you came to me just as you are."

Part Two

Chapter Six

IT WAS LESS THAN A MONTH since Isabella had disappeared, but to Kate the space of time could not be measured in days; it was an epoch. A kind of drastic change, like being a child and growing up overnight. Her sister's elopement had hurt her bitterly. They had grown up unalike, yet so close that there had never been secrets between them. They had shared everything. Now they were separated for the first time in their lives not only by the miles between Newcastle and wherever Isabella had gone but by Isabella's duplicity.

Ellen became pinched and silent when the news first came in a scrawled letter delivered from the Bull. She did not believe Isabella was to be married and from the moment she heard her daughter was gone she scarcely spoke, sat for hours in silence looking out of the window. Kate was alarmed by her mother's state, remembering an actor years ago who had lost his wits. He, too, had sat without speaking for long periods, perfectly quiet and indifferent to his surroundings.

But four days after the disappearance a letter arrived on crested writing paper. It was from both Lord Carteret and Isabella, gave details of the Gretna Green wedding, and enclosed a banker's draft from the Viscount "to buy a memento of a joyful day which alas you could not be with us to share." The banker's draft was for a hundred pounds.

Ellen recovered as if by magic and actually laughed out loud. She became altogether, rather pathetically, happy. She gossiped at the theater, patronized Mrs. Gunn (who was unusually disagreeable) and was more talkative than Kate ever remembered, repeating time and again, "Of course, the Bagots are distant relatives of my own."

Kate had been miserable and Ellen shocked at the time of Isabella's elopement, but Thomas was perfectly furious. He ranted and shouted at Ellen. He was frightened of telling Davenant that the actress chosen for Desdemona had run away.

But Davenant, never predictable, took the news sardonically, pointed at Margaret Frognal and said impolitely, "She'll do." Margaret Frognal was afraid of him, and when she first made her entrance she was shaking so much that she could scarcely hold the famous handkerchief.

With Isabella "safely" married, as Ellen called it, life at the theater continued not without its difficulties. Davenant thought of new demands every day. His name was not large enough on the bills. More lamps were needed in the footlights. The actresses reminded him, one and all, of elephants and must be given lessons by a dancing master in "the art of walking." Thomas arranged for planks to be extended the length of the stage, and Davenant watched while the actresses were made to walk, very slowly at first, then faster and faster until they could walk right along the plank without deviating once from a perfectly straight line. Kate, fired by the challenge, soon became very nimble; Margaret Frognal fell off.

Despite the fact that there were few rehearsals, Kate went to the theater each morning. She spent her time in the greenroom facing a courtyard where the spare scenery was stacked. Here she studied her parts and thought about the plays. Sometimes, looking from the window, she saw a small mass of rats which lived above a stable coming down a rope and gathering round to nibble the paint off the canvases.

Laurie Spindle liked to sit with her.

"Shall I teach you a harlequin trick, Beauty? Can you do a double turn?" Agile as a gnat he would spring up, illustrate a new way of jumping, spinning, almost flying.

Buckley Vernon also came to sit beside her and together they ran through scenes from many different plays. Both wished to have as many parts as possible at their fingertips, and Buckley was always eager to learn a new one. He thought Kate a useful friend.

One morning when she went into the dressing room which she had shared with Isabella and which was now only hers, she found a message on her table. It was scrawled on the back of a handbill and said would Miss Winter do Mr. Davenant the honor of calling at his lodgings. Three o'clock and no later.

Kate was mystified.

She found her father in the wings arguing with one of the stage carpenters, a red-faced man like a sailor, called Pick.

Pick was loudly denying responsibility for an unsteady pillar in *Othello* which the previous night had rocked to and fro and made the audience laugh when Davenant leaned against it.

"You are speaking of *Mister* Davenant. An actor whose name is known the length and breadth of the country. It is outrageous that the scenery should not be correctly secured. It must never happen again."

"Do me best," said Pick, unimpressed. He lounged away.

Thomas, aware his daughter was waiting, said abruptly, "What is it?"

Since Isabella's flight, his manner had been markedly cold to Kate, almost as if it had been her fault. Kate was hurt but refused to be upset about it. Sooner or later her father would have to stop thinking of his daughters as commodities offered for hire with himself and his wife. One actor-manager, one wardrobe mistress, two actresses. She gave him the handbill in silence.

He read it and frowned.

"It is clear enough."

"I wondered, Papa, if you knew what Mr. Davenant wanted?"

"Something to do with your acting, no doubt. You are very uneven. Never the same performance two nights running."

"Did he tell you that?"

"Not in so many words, but I can read his expression. Mind you wear a good frock when you visit him. And remember to give him my compliments."

He hurried away in search of Pick again.

A minor advantage for Kate after Davenant's arrival had been a few shillings extra in her payment. She had saved these and bought herself some muslin for a new dress. It was white with a pattern of copper-colored sprigs of barley with green stalks. Ellen made the dress, sewing every night after she returned from the theater. It had gracefully full skirts, a tiny waist and sleeves full above the elbow. She also retrimmed Kate's bonnet with new flowers and a silk frill at the nape of the neck.

Her mother came into the bedroom while Kate was carefully dressing for the Davenant visit. She watched critically as Kate fastened the belt of the new dress.

"You must use my reticule, child. And my best gloves."

Ellen fetched the reticule and gloves, both treasured and kept wrapped in paper. Kate kissed her.

"You admire Mr. Davenant, do you not?" said Ellen suddenly.

"Of course, Mama. He is a great actor."

"All the more reason, child, to be on your guard."

Kate looked startled and, meeting her mother's ironic brown eyes, blushed.

On her walk to Davenant's lodgings, which were in what Ellen called the "good part" of the town, Kate reflected that she had never for a moment betrayed to her mother that she found Davenant physically alluring. How had her mother guessed her secret thoughts? Acting in *King Lear* with him, she was in one scene closely embraced, and at the end of the play he carried her onstage in his arms. She longed for those scenes. She assured herself it was because of the extraordinary experience of acting close to him. It was not true. She liked him to touch her, and when he did her heart fluttered and her mouth grew dry.

The square of brick-built Georgian houses was stylish. Everything looked clean and cared for, she thought. Nobody shouted from attics or threw stones or strung up washing like flags.

She rang the bell of Number 27, and a neat maid ushered her into a parlor overlooking the back garden. The room was prim, with sprigged wallpaper and watercolor paintings of the countryside.

"The master will be down directly."

Kate sat down in a straight-backed chair and looked about. This was no place to be reprimanded about acting. It was genteel. Theater talk belonged in the dusty stretches of backstage, or actually onstage, where Kate's role as a harlot who painted her face and lay in wait for men in Venetian back streets had a vivid, if temporary life. Not here. She dreaded Davenant scolding her. Suppose that he made her cry?

When he strode in, she wondered if it would be correct for her to stand up. Somehow, she remained seated.

"Good afternoon, miss."

"Good afternoon, sir."

He stood contemplating her, hands behind his back. He did not look unkind, but quizzical, and since her life was spent being looked at she was not embarrassed. She gazed back, thinking his eyes a very extraordinary blue, his face much lined and strangely attractive. There was a sense of power in him. She was sure he had noticed everything about her. Did she please him?

"So your sister galloped off with a lord, is that it?" he said.

"She is a Viscountess now."

"And that impresses you."

"I am sure she finds it very pleasant."

"Sorry you missed the chance?"

"Good gracious, no!"

He gave a roar of laughter, throwing back his head as if he had been looking not at a girl in muslin and ribbons but at a Punch-and-Judy show.

"Miss Winter, I like you. What do you say to that?"

"Naturally, I am honored, sir."

"Now, now," he said, shaking his head. "No sarcasm, if you please. I will not hear a word against myself. I daresay you thought I should have given you Desdemona. Were you mortified because I gave it to Frognal? What a bad actress, eh? A drab. You shall have the role for Saturday. Who says I am not a man with a great heart? But that is not why I asked you to call to see me. There is another matter I wish to speak of."

He had been striding about as he talked, but now he sat down facing her. When he was close to her, not onstage where his art altered his mystifying face, but here, in reality, in life, she thought his burning eyes had a calculating look. She was not sure of him. She was excited and uneasy.

"How would you like to come to London with me?"

A profound silence.

"Did you hear me, miss?"

"I am not sure I understand, sir," said Kate faintly.

"Now, that is odd, for I have always considered you a sharp young lady."

"Do you mean that I could come to London—to act—"

"Exactly so."

He looked pleased as he watched her blush. It was high time the chit showed some appreciation. The blush spread across her freckled face.

"Now we're getting results," he said. "The idea appeals, I see. Then with your permission I will have a word about you with your father."

"*Oh, no!*"

His expression of good humor vanished. He looked at her with his jaw dropping, as if not hearing aright.

"What's that?" he said angrily. "Do I understand you? Are you refusing my offer?"

"Of course not! Of course I want to come!" she cried so far forgetting herself to lean forward and grip his arm. "Mr. Davenant, what I mean is please do *not* speak to my father but allow me to do it. It will be much much better if I may break the news to him. Please!"

At her entreating voice, her face still pink, her beseeching expression, Davenant's manner changed magically back to its former jocularity.

"That is a good daughterly attitude. I like that. Yes, I like that."

During the first days after Isabella's flight, Buckley Vernon had been a great comfort to the Winter family. He had been concerned, understanding, soothing Ellen's fears that her younger daughter was ruined, and assuring her that Isabella was not only virtuous but had a sound head on her shoulders. Buckley had been the only person Ellen was willing to listen to. Later, when news of the marriage arrived it was Buckley who had pointed out to Thomas that a marriage of such eminence could do him nothing but good.

Kate had grown fond of Buckley. She liked to be with him, enjoyed his easy companionship. She looked on him as a friend. He never made tender moves toward her or gave the impression of wanting anything more than a kind of brother-and-sister relationship. This was a relief to Kate, who since her early teens knew how tiresome and importunate some actors could be, clasping her suddenly, kissing her hotly and becoming furious and spiteful when she refused them.

On her return from visiting Davenant the first person she saw at the theater was Buckley. He came toward her along the passageway near her dressing room and stood looking down at her kindly.

"Your father said Davenant sent for you. I trust you are not upset?"

"I am so glad to see you, Mr. Vernon," said Kate. "Could we talk?"

Margaret Frognal, haggard and paler than usual, and the sharp-faced Georgiana Coins went by, looking at Kate with hostility. There were few secrets in theaters.

"Come into my dressing room," he said.

Buckley's dressing room, coveted by other actors because of its nearness to the stage, was in disarray. His costumes, brown holland, painted satin, stiffened with buckram and bulging out with size and weight, lay on chairs or on the floor. Kate nearly tripped over a rapier and a walking stick. Pots of powder and shreds of orange peel were in a china meat dish on the table.

"You cannot imagine what has happened!" exclaimed Kate when he had closed the door. Usually quiet, she spoke in a torrent of excitement, of anxiety about her father, of astonishment and uncertainty about the great offer. Was it too soon for her? What did Mr. Vernon think?

Buckley wouldn't have been human if he hadn't felt a pang of envy at Kate's good fortune. It was true she was gifted, but so was he. She was young and handsome: so was he. She was ambitious, he was more so. To be taken up by Davenant, spirited away from Northumberland to London, was the kind of dream every actor severely dismissed from his mind. Yet here was this slip of a girl, with her red hair and white face, telling him it had actually happened.

"It's wonderful," he said. "Of course you are ready to go. Let me congratulate you. With all admiration."

He bent to kiss her cheek, still in the elder-brother role which suited both of them. She gave him a radiant smile. It was so beautiful and so moving that Buckley stared, wondering why he had never thought of courting this irresistible woman. But the callboy knocked at the doors, the voice cried monotonously, "Curtain up in half an hour! Curtain up in half an hour!"

Kate ran out.

* * *

The news that Davenant had offered Kate an engagement was broken to Thomas Winter when the family returned for supper to their lodgings.

Mrs. Gunn served the usual unappetizing meal. She came into the room, and slammed down half-cold plates of herrings fried in oatmeal, the fish too small and bony to nourish the family, who had worked hard until midnight. She left them to themselves in the stuffy dining room.

Ellen buttered her husband a piece of bread.

"Kate has something to tell you, Tom."

"What is that?" asked Thomas absently. He never paid his daughter any attention.

It took an effort of will for Kate to speak. She drew a deep breath and began. She punctuated her story with "I know you understand, Papa," and "As you have often said, Papa." Her father went first white, then red. Before she could finish speaking he interrupted:

"Do you realize that if I do not meet my commitments I shall be arrested for debt?"

Kate's eyes widened.

"But you said things were so much better since we have been here and—"

"Ingratitude!" exclaimed Thomas in the very tone Davenant used as *King Lear*. "My God! Ingratitude!"

"Please don't be angry with me, Papa," she said, her voice quavering. "I do not think I could bear it if—"

"*You* cannot bear it!" he shouted. "*You* cannot bear it! You have not been ruined, seen the only theater you ever owned go up in flames, lost your wife's inheritance, seen her . . . a woman of birth and breeding, brought down to doing a seamstress' work! You are the fortunate one. Go off with that scoundrel. See where that will get you!"

He had never used such a bitter tone to Kate before in her life, and, bursting into sobs, she ran from the room.

Ellen, showing no emotion, looked at her husband for a moment or two, then poured him a cup of tea.

"Drink it, Tom. It will calm you down."

She left the room, quietly closing the door as if Thomas were ill.

He remained for a long time, looking with unseeing eyes at the smoke-stained walls, the empty fireplace, the dirty plates in front of him. His head ached from his fit of anger; he felt old. He remembered himself at Kate's age, handsome, lively, merry as a cricket, flirting with actresses and ballet dancers. He had thought the theater and its gimcrack finery the most exciting place in the world. He recalled the first time he had met Ellen, a slip of a thing in white wearing long gloves edged with ruffles. He thought of the girl she had been, spritely, mischievous, and as in a dream faintly recalled their violent passion for each other. He remembered the day of their elopement. Their life until now. He and Ellen had given everything to the theater. Every ounce of youth, strength, hope, dedication. What had they got from such devotion? Debts. Disaster. Rudeness from actors like Davenant. One daughter running off to marry some titled fellow they didn't know—he supposed she *was* married—and now Kate leaving, too. And she would get the very thing he and Ellen had worked for, toiled for. The theater owes me something, he thought. For my life. It owes me something. The thought made him more bitter against Kate for being paid when *she* was owed nothing at all.

Ellen found Kate sitting on her bed. The girl had stopped crying and sat knotting and unknotting a torn handkerchief.

She looked up.

"I could tell Mr. Davenant I will not go."

Her mother gave a downward smile.

"You know you don't mean that. You of all people. Your father will get over it. Leave him to me."

"I thought he would be pleased."

"No, you didn't. You knew exactly how he would take it. He has had a hard life. Very hard."

Kate sniffed pathetically and nodded. She turned her face to her mother and Ellen saw in it all the non-comprehension of the young. They paid lip service to the sufferings of the

old, but they couldn't understand them. They were as far
from them as a sparrow hopping beside an old imprisoned
lion. Could the sparrow help being cheerful as it pecked up a
crumb and fluttered off to liberty?

Isabella, Viscountess Cartaret, lay in a four-poster bed, lazily waiting for her husband to finish dressing in the next
room and listening to the murmur of his voice and the discreet replies of his valet.

Every morning Isabella woke wrapped in Denys's arms,
sleepily thought that she must go to the theater and then remembered where she was and who was holding her. How
beautiful it was to make love—and how different from her
imagining. She lay against a heap of lacy pillows, languorous-
ly remembering not only the love of last night but the very
first time.

On her wedding night in Scotland she had been shaking
with nervousness, with the strain of that long and extraordinary journey and the brief—almost brusque—marriage cere-
mony. Then, when supper at the inn was over, she knew the
moment had come, the time when she was to lose her virginity. A man was going to take her, and she was afraid. Reared
in a world of license, she had stayed innocent, protected by
her parents and curiously ignorant of the facts of sex. Her
body was virginal, her knowledge hazy and fearful. She had
never seen a man naked in her life. Denys had treated her
with wonderful delicacy, retiring to a small adjoining dressing room and leaving her in the dark paneled bedroom
alone. She took off her shabby gown, untied the strings of
her petticoats with icy hands. Should she take off her chemise? She stripped it off, blew out all the candles but one and
jumped between the ice-cold sheets, inadequately warmed
five minutes before when a servant had thrust a warm pan
across them.

Isabella waited, her heart thudding so hard that she felt
she could hear it aloud.

The door opened, and Denys came into the dark room lit

by the wavering light of a single candle. He looked very tall, and frighteningly strange, wearing a long brown silk robe tied at the waist. She began to tremble as he came toward her.

She sat hunched in the curtained bed, the covers drawn up to her shoulders like a child feeling the cold. He sat down on the bed beside her. He looked at her caressingly, at her long loose hair, her throat, her pale frightened face. She could not meet his eyes.

"Give me your hand," he said.

She put out her left hand with its heavy gold ring, and he kissed the palm, closing his eyes, pressing the little chilled hand against his face. She had been waiting—she did not know what she had been waiting for—except that she was afraid and clung to the last moments of virginity and its untouched freedoms. She was here to be conquered and invaded. But he did not move closer, or seize or mount her. He merely sat, putting each of her fingers in turn gently between his teeth. The robe had fallen open, and she saw his chest covered with dark wiry hairs; quite suddenly, because he did not move to her, she wanted to touch him. A tremor went through her. She thought of that muscular body soon to be pressed up and into hers, and all fear left her. She bent toward him, took her hand from his lips and put it against his face and then on to his chest. He understood the swimming look in her face and took her strongly in his arms, giving her his first long exploring kiss, his tongue in her mouth . . .

Now they had been married for long, passionate weeks. Denys said once that she was "born for love." Those were the only words he had ever spoken when he was taking her—just that. When he made love he was utterly silent, very strong, never seemed to tire. She had to learn about love, and at first, aware that his body in hers gave her exquisite pleasure and longing, believed *she* would never reach her own climax, and moving her head helplessly, would moan, "I cannot—cannot." He did not reply. He waited, almost unmoving inside her, kissing her eyelids. And at last she did come, for the first

time, and after that it grew easier and more exciting
. . . yes, I was born for love, she thought, leaning back in a
swoon of remembered pleasure.

Wonder and gratefulness came to her when she thought of
all the things she need not do any more. Her old brown dress
need not be darned. Gone was the detested bonnet with its
threadbare green strings. She need not walk to a stupid theater, rehearse a stupid play, eat burned herrings, bear the
rudeness of men like Davenant. She looked back at her
bondage without a shred of loyalty. Her family she loved tenderly—when she remembered to think of them. But the theater was a slavery from which Denys had rescued her.

Thinking of Denys taking her to the jewelers' yesterday in
the Burlington Arcade, she jumped out of bed and ran to
her dressing table. The leather case was open, and the necklace and earrings were even prettier than she remembered.
Seed pearls and gold. The necklace was a string of gold vine
leaves, the pearls made into bunches of grapes. A bunch for
each earring. Three larger bunches on the necklace fell in
the center of her throat. She held the necklace up and put
the pearls between her teeth, scraping them along the unev-
en surface.

Denys is so generous, she thought. Such a princely lover.
Since the long enthralling journey from Scotland, they had
moved into fashionable lodgings in Clarges Street, and her
husband had spent all his time seeing she had everything she
needed. So many clothes. Morning dresses. Walking dresses.
Carriage dresses. Ball dresses. Bonnets. Gloves. Pelisses.
Furs. Fans. Jewelry. Everything, Isabella found, opening her
brown eyes, could be arranged when you were rich.

"Isabella."

Denys had come through the curtained alcove of his dressing room.

"You startled me," she said, laughing. "I was admiring my
necklace. Shall I wear it when we go to Bagot House? Shall
your sisters approve of me?"

She laughed. Since the day they had left for Scotland, he

had told her again and again that his family would forgive the marriage, that they would be reconciled to him and would receive her.

"But so much is due to high rank, and I am an actress!" she always answered, waiting to be contradicted.

He embraced her.

Now, coming into the room, she looked at him with affection. There was a speckless elegance about Denys. It took him hours every morning to look like that—she marveled at how long a gentleman took to dress. But the look stayed with him until he changed for dinner at night when, again after a long, leisurely hour, he emerged as beautifully elegant as in the morning. He wore his clothes carelessly, sprawled rather than sat, leaned rather than stood, yet his silk cravat, dark silver-buttoned coat, exquisite boots, were perfection.

He stood looking at her. The pearls were still in her hands.

"I have received a letter from my father."

"But that is good news!"

"No, it is not, Isabella."

His tone, his face, were blank, and she said uneasily, "May I read the letter?"

He had been holding it in his hand and he folded it decidedly and put it in his pocket.

"I would prefer you did not."

He turned away and walked to the window. His father had hurt him. He had done so many times, and Denys never became accustomed to it. All his youth he had made the best of his father's treatment, sure of affection, telling his cousin, "Robert, you must have noticed how much my father is improved toward me."

Isabella climbed back into bed and pulled the covers.

"Are you not getting up, Isabella?"

She stayed, only her nose and dark eyes showing, hoping to make him laugh. He did not. She pushed back the covers crossly.

"Just because the Earl will not accept us yet," she said, "it isn't the end of the world. Now, I suppose your horrid father has said something unkind about me."

"He has not met you, Isabella, and is in no position to say anything about you."

"Then why are you so cross?"

"It is no use behaving as if this does not matter to us," he said. "It matters a great deal."

She sat up in bed.

"Do you mean we might be poor?"

He laughed angrily. For the first time since their marriage he felt he was looking at the inhabitant of another world. The beautiful girl, lace falling off her bare shoulders, understood nothing. It would be easy to treat her as a child: men often treated women in such a way, and women appeared to enjoy it. But she was no child. She had lived an extraordinary life which he could scarcely imagine, and if she were ignorant of society all he could do was to attempt to explain it. But he was hurt by her lack of intuitive understanding and angry with himself for being so.

He sat down beside the bed and took her hand.

"Dearest one. You must surely see it would not be possible for us to be happy if the family will not accept us. One cannot live like that. Of course we would not be poor, I came into an inheritance when I was twenty-one. The trouble has nothing to do with money. It is with family. You must take your rightful place, I care very much about that. And I love my family and wish always to be close to them. As it should be."

He had never spoken or looked so serious before.

Isabella made a sulky grimace. Using her trick of saying things so that he should contradict her, liking to see him change and melt, she said, "Perhaps the Earl will never accept me."

Denys's face did not change then.

There was a knock at the door.

"Wait, if you please."

He handed her a flimsy shawl to cover her bare shoulders. How modest he is, she thought, draping the shawl round her, it will only be my maid.

But when Denys called and the door quietly opened, it was Mr. Locking. He was the owner of the Clarges Street lodgings, and had been—long ago—butler to the Bagots. Isabella thought her husband rather absurdly devoted to Locking, a steely-haired old man with thin lips and a cold manner. She felt he disapproved of her as the wife of Viscount Carteret, but the old man was far too practiced in the ways of the great world for her to be sure.

"Two ladies have called to see your Lordship. They are downstairs in the parlor."

Denys's grave face suddenly blazed.

"Locking! Is it—"

"I fear not, your Lordship," interrupted Locking, wanting to quench such a painful hope. "The ladies are of her young Ladyship's family, I am given to believe."

Isabella did not see the bitter disappointment of Denys's face or the compassionate look the old man gave him. She burst out laughing.

"Ma and Kate! What in the world are they doing here!"

Chapter Seven

ISABELLA WOULD HAVE RUSHED DOWN AT ONCE in a shawl, but Denys insisted on ringing for her maid and told the girl to help her Ladyship to dress as fast as possible.

He went downstairs to greet the visitors.

Isabella could scarcely wait as her maid, a shy little creature, pinned her hair, fastened her skirts, helped her with her lacy stockings and shoes. "Quick, quick, Rivers, my mama is waiting!"

Rivers thought it very proper that the young lady should be so pleased, but refused to allow Isabella to leave until everything was as it should be. Rivers had been trained by Mr. Locking.

Isabella pelted down the stairs and rushed into the parlor, throwing herself into her mother's arms. Denys, Ellen and Kate had been seated, exchanging somewhat strained compliments when Isabella came flying in, a vision of blue and white striped satin and lace, her face blazing with pleasure. She hugged her mother, kissed Kate, clasped their hands, burst into laughter. Denys watched, smiling. When there was a moment's lull he said, "Your mother has done me the honor to say that she and Miss Winter will stay for luncheon and

101

spend the afternoon with us. I will now leave you, if I may. I have an appointment to see my cousin at Tattersall's." He took graceful leave. When he had gone Isabella exchanged a look with her mother.

"He thinks we would prefer to be alone. He is quite right. Oh! I have so much to tell you both!"

Apart from briefly inquiring why they were in London, and being unsurprised at Kate's news of a London engagement (Isabella already took good fortune for granted), she talked uninterruptedly. She told them the whole story of her elopement, reliving each detail of the adventure, laughing, gesticulating, describing everything in the actor's manner with mimicry, jokes, dramatic effect. She told of the journey to Scotland, the village of Gretna, the blacksmith with ginger whiskers who said to Denys, "It's to my mind that ye'er safely wed at last!"

She took her mother and sister upstairs into her bedroom, showed them wardrobes full of clothes, opened leather cases to display her jewels, held the bunches of pearls to her ears, asking for, getting, their admiration.

"I have a title now, imagine! Does not Viscountess Carteret sound exactly right?"

Kate, listening and marveling, finally glanced at the carriage clock on the chimney piece.

"Surely Lord Carteret will be back soon?"

"I daresay. Then we will have a delicious luncheon. You know the old man who showed you into the house? He is Locking and used to be the Bagot butler. His wife does the cooking, she is *very* good. Wait until you sample her chicken with truffles, Mama. Or a grape sorbet. Not one bit like Mrs. Gunn's herrings!"

"Bella," Kate said thoughtfully. "You haven't spoken about Lord Carteret's family."

"You will have to start calling him Denys."

"Have you not met them?" asked Kate, ignoring that.

Isabella fiddled with a tourquoise bracelet on her wrist.

"Denys says they will come round eventually."

Her mother started. All the morning she had sat by her

younger daughter, bemused at seeing the girl so beautiful, rich and happy.

"The Earl of Bagot refuses to see you?"

"For the present, but—"

"He must have been furiously angry when the Viscount married an actress," said Kate. "Of all people. Society still thinks we players inferior creatures. Slaves of the public." She smiled.

Isabella didn't smile back. She did not want her triumph spoiled, her family's admiration lost. A story, *her* story, must have a happy end.

"They will come round," she said sharply, "Denys says so."

Her sister and mother knew that mulish look.

The three women made a curious contrast, Isabella gleaming in satin, Ellen and Kate poorly and neatly dressed in old dresses and darned cloaks.

Ellen thoughtfully rubbed her chin.

"You know, it's possible they never will accept you," she said, examining the thought. "It happens more often than not with a misalliance in a family as high as the Bagots. They are not only proud, they're adamant. I came merely from small gentry, but you both know my parents never forgave me for marrying your father. When my own father lay dying I was not permitted to return home."

"Oh, Mama!" exclaimed Isabella, stung by the often told story. "That was twenty years ago. Things are changing, they're different now. I *know* the Bagots will accept us. Denys has told me so and I believe him."

She glared at her mother, her chin set.

Kate went over to the window and gazed down. The street, the shops, were bright and prosperous, pavements swept, windows shining and full of costly objects. Passersby were rich-looking. Carriages and horses, too. As she watched, she saw Lord Carteret in the distance, walking slowly down the street toward the house. He looked tall and very elegant and for a moment she merely admired him. Then a lady and gentleman passed. Lord Carteret bowed gracefully, raising his hat. The gentleman hesitated, as if about to reply with a bow, but the lady, dressed in black and elderly, swept by as if Lord Carteret did not exist.

Kate, saying nothing, went back and sat beside her mother. Ellen was still thoughtful.

"How much, exactly, have you told the Viscount about us?"

Isabella had become nervous. She started up, went over to a vase of yellow roses and began crossly pushing the flowers about.

"Very little, of course."

"'I have often seen a gentleman soldier and a gentleman sailor, and other sorts of gentlemen, but I have never yet seen a gentleman player,'" quoted Kate. "The less said about us the better."

Ellen raised her eyebrows.

"I mean, Isabella, did you mention to the Viscount that I am related to him?"

"Oh, Mama, of course not! He is the son of the Earl of Bagot, his family are one of the proudest in England, they had titles four hundred years ago. What would he care for cousins ten times removed? Please don't mention such a thing. He would think it pathetic. I know we're proud of being gentry. Somebody like Denys never thinks of such a thing."

Her mother gave Isabella a look very different from her previous glances of spellbound admiration.

Denys arrived after that and Locking announced luncheon.

During the meal Isabella recovered her spirits. Ellen sat on Lord Carteret's right, and he paid a great deal of attention to her. In a way she was a shy person, and when treated so warmly she blossomed. Lord Carteret also asked Kate about her London engagement, and talked more about her career than her sister had done.

But when the meal was over and the family had returned to the Carterets' private drawing room Ellen gave Isabella a chill of dismay.

"Lord Carteret. My daughter tells me your family refuses to receive you both."

He was taken aback by the directness of the question and by a subject of such embarrassment. Far too polite to show this, he murmured he was sure the reconcilement was a matter of time. Kate, watching, was convinced Lord Carteret was now looking for some gentlemanly excuse to leave, so that further conversation on the matter could be avoided.

Before he could speak again Ellen said matter-of-factly, "My daughter also tells me you are unaware that my family and yours are distantly related."

He looked astounded. How stupid and naive of Mama, thought Isabella angrily, now she has made us look perfect fools. She was about to try to make it into a joke when Denys said, "My dear Mrs. Winter. In what way are we related? It is very strange Isabella has never mentioned this."

"Through your third cousins, my Lord," said Ellen settling down to a favorite conversation. "The Marchmonts of Ware."

"The Marchmonts? They were with us at Bagot Park last autumn. How very interesting. Wait a moment, Mrs. Winter, I beg—"

He went to a desk in the corner of the room where he kept his papers. Rummaging through some documents, he took out a large folded paper, which he spread on the table, anchoring it with a heavy, silver inkwell. Isabella had never seen the paper before; it was a family tree going back to 1450, a long, complicated, spidery-written pattern of dates and names. He and Ellen pored over it.

"There are the Marchmonts," said Ellen, pointing with a small brown hand wearing a small diamond, often pawned, often retrieved. "That Marchmont, Anthony Delaval, was my mother's second cousin. My mother's maiden name was Capell. I believe they were Italian, they came over in the seventeenth century, Mama used to tell me. . ."

The talk turned to technicalities.

Isabella looked at the absorbed faces of her husband and

her mother and then glanced automatically in Kate's direction. It was what she'd always done as a child, looking for a friendly confirmation that adults were ridiculous. Kate looked up at the same time. Across the table, the sisters gave slight, mystified shrugs. Their mother and the Viscount were mad.

"Really extraordinary," Denys said when he and Ellen stopped studying the family tree. "So I must greet you as a cousin, ma'am."

To Isabella's amazement he bent forward and kissed her mother's cheek. Ellen, shy as a girl, laughed in the way she did when she was very pleased, a laugh running up the scale like a little ascending trill of music.

"I am very proud of the connection, my Lord."

"And Isabella knew this all the time," said Denys, taking his wife's hand. "What a noodle you are, my dearest, for not telling me."

"About what? Being a cousin ten times removed?"

Ellen shook her head. "I thought I had taught you the importance of birth, my child. Do not show your ignorance."

"You are pleased Mama is a kind of relative, then, Lord Carteret?" put in Kate, seeing her sister, who detested to be put down by her mother, had blushed an angry pink.

"More than pleased, Miss Winter, relieved. I am not sure, but it is possible the Earl may accept our marriage when this is known to him. I will write to him at once. Ladies, if you will excuse me?"

Locking was sitting in his own back parlor cleaning the house silver, something which took him five hours once a week, and twice a week when there was a London fog. Candlesticks, trays, coffeepots, ring holders, candle snuffers, were ranged on the table in front of him. Locking, wearing cotton gloves, was using a curved brush on a tiresomely curved candlestick. He was thinking about the Viscount and the arrival of the two ladies.

He thought a good deal about the Viscount, whom he remembered as a dreamy little boy in Sussex, who had learned to ride a pony from the age of three and used to come into Locking's domain, the Servant's Hall, and sit on the table and ask questions. Reserved, cold-seeming, tight-buttoned as his black coat, Locking was deeply touched that Lord Carteret had now come to stay in his house. It was almost like the old days to see him about, talk to him, serve him. But as for that runaway marriage, Locking disapproved as strongly as the old Earl himself.

The young Viscountess was very pretty, and she had manners, which surprised Locking, who considered actresses no better than harlots. But to think of the future heirs being mothered by a woman who had appeared in the theater with a painted face, lived a possibly immoral life! Locking's manner to the young Ladyship could not be faulted. But it was as cold as iron.

There was a tap on the parlor door, and Lord Carteret came into the room. He smiled at the old man, showing beautiful even teeth.

"Locking, forgive me for disturbing you. Is there someone who might go round to Berkeley Square for me? It is to deliver a letter to the Earl. I would very much like him to receive it this evening."

"I will take it myself, my Lord."

Lord Carteret looked pleased.

"If it is not too inconvenient, Locking, that would do me a great service. I confess I much prefer you to be the bearer of the letter."

"I will go at once, my Lord."

The old man took off his cotton gloves. They looked at each other. Old friends, separated by birth and riches and nothing else.

"I think this letter may bring good news," Lord Carteret said. "I have just learned from the lady who is visiting us, her Ladyship's mother, that—well—the fact is the family are some sort of cousins of ours. Mrs. Winter traced it for me on the genealogy. Her mother was a Capell. Related to the Marchmonts."

Locking's impassive face gleamed with a sudden interest.

"The Marchmonts of Ware, my Lord?"

"Exactly so."

"I will be at Bagot House in exactly twelve minutes, my Lord," said Locking.

Lord Carteret laughed and Locking allowed himself a smile. He did indeed know the precise time that it took him to walk to Bagot House; he walked there once a week to spend a pleasant hour or two with the present Bagot butler. Family news was always known to Locking well in advance of the Bagots themselves. As now.

Carteret was more affected by what Ellen had told him than good manners allowed him to show. Even the smallest hope of healing the breach with his family was something he most desperately longed for. His father's treatment since his marriage had wounded him to the heart.

He had written to the Earl from Scotland, telling him of his marriage and begging forgiveness. It had been an impulsive letter, very simple and direct, an appeal to a father's affectionate heart. It had been certain to fail. But Carteret had made himself believe the contrary. He never despaired of winning his father's understanding, continued to hope for the impossible. The girl he had married was totally unacceptable yet he believed the Earl would relent. The old man was hard as a rock, yet Carteret thought he might soften. He loved his father and went on hoping without reason to be loved in return. He was both reserved and passionate. He was like his father in that.

Carteret was nervous during the evening after the letter had been taken to Berkeley Square, but Isabella didn't notice and chattered happily about her own affairs. Her pretty voice, her way of laughing, seemed pathetic to him just then.

The Earl's reply was brought by Locking the next morning. It was written in the third person and consisted of three lines. The Earl of Bagot presents his compliments to Viscount Carteret and will receive him and the Viscountess at five o'clock.

Denys gave a sigh of pure happiness.

He put his arms tenderly round Isabella and kissed her,

saying how wonderful it was that her mother should have brought them such a blessing yesterday; he could scarce believe it.

Bagot House, a great mansion consisting of a central house and two large wings, stood back from the road near Berkeley Square in a wide courtyard into which the carriages could comfortably drive. It had been built in the late seventeenth century, four stories high of brick somberly faced with stone, its windows tall, its roof as square as a Florentine palace, each corner decorated with a kind of stone cannon ball on a plinth. The Bagot arms were on either side of the heavy gates, which stood open permanently during the London season.

For many months of the year Bagot House was empty. The family lived in their favorite house in Sussex, where the Earl, although he was sixty, hunted regularly and where his lands were looked after and his tenants cared for. The Bagots had strong country roots and came to London during the season for rather shorter periods than most society families.

When the family left London at the end of the summer Bagot House was silent. The chandeliers hung in huge cotton bags as if containing swarms of bees. The furniture was ghostly under sheeting, carpets rolled, doors barred. For months the house, smelling damp and bitterly cold, was inhabited only by mice. The mice, more and more daring, would execute merry dances in the ballroom, run like water along the windowsills, make nests in the most chewable volumes in the Book Room.

But at last the hunting season would end, the London plane trees begin to bud, spring arrive and Bagot House come alive again.

Feet hurried in, windows opened to the light and air. Down the long passages came pails of soapy water, mops, brushes, the sound of voices exclaiming over cobwebs. The sunshine, locked out for months, jumped in and invaded the house. Hooves and heels echoed on the courtyard stones, coaches opened their doors and the Earl and his daughters and their personal servants rustled into the new-burnished house for the season. The mice retired to their holes in the paneling and wainscots and bided their time.

It was already late in the season, the family would soon be gone, when Denys and Isabella traveled to Berkeley Square in the elegant carriage he had hired for their London stay. Isabella wore a new gown of creamy silk, patterned with pink daisies, and there were daisies bunched inside her bonnet brim. She looked pretty and composed. Denys seemed to prefer her not to talk about the theater, so she didn't tell him she felt as if she were about to go on in a difficult role in a brand new play. She had the same taut nerves, dry feeling in the roof of her mouth, the same longing for the opening scene to begin. The Earl, in her mind, had become a sort of Davenant.

The carriage galloped through the open gates and drew up at Bagot House. The family butler was waiting to receive them. Isabella distinctly remembered him, and Kate's long-ago triumph over him. Swayne was elderly, high-shouldered, with great dignity and an ironic face under yellowing-white hair. He bowed low, saying, "My Lord and Lady!"

It was the first time except for that far-off occasion when the Winters had visited Bagot Park that Isabella had seen Denys in his own home. Everybody greeted him, everybody was glad to see him. There were dozens of servants in the marble-floored hall and in the long corridors. They bowed or bobbed curtsies. As Denys and Isabella walked down a white and gold passageway lined with mirrors, he said in a low voice:

"You know who *they* have been looking out for."

"Do you mean me?"

"You must have been the only topic of conversation since Gretna."

A liveried footman went by, politely lowered his eyes, then raised them to snatch a quick observant look.

They arrived at two enormous doors and Denys took her gloved hand.

"Now, my dearest. Stand your straightest and be your bravest."

The Earl, sitting in a carved chair, stood up as they came into the room. He was a big broad-shouldered handsome man of sixty with a misshapen back due to a hunting accident. Seated, he looked younger. Standing and bent sideways, he looked old. Something about him reminded Isabella of a bird she had seen sitting on a post on the Sussex downs; her father had told her it was called a Montagu's Harrier. Hunched, its powerful dark wings folded, it had a fiercely curved beak and hooded eyes. The old Earl's nose was beaked, his clothes dark, his eyes thick-lidded and very sharp.

"Father, may I present Isabella? My wife."

Deny's voice sounded forced.

"How do you do, Lord Bagot."

Isabella sank into the curtsy she had learned for *The Merrie Days of Nell Gwynne.*

The old man put out a hand as well-shaped as his son's, the Bagot seal ring showing up the thin fingers, and lifted her up.

"So you're the hussy who ran away with my son."

"No, sir, it was I who did the wooing," said Denys, with a laugh as strained as his voice.

"Let the girl speak for herself."

Isabella noticed the Earl's eyebrows, tufted and whiter than his hair, met in the middle when he scowled.

"Surely the Bagots always do the wooing," she murmured. The old man looked at her sardonically.

"Hmm. Well, I suppose I must drag you round the rest of them. Come along. Put the girls out of their misery. Their eyes are out on stalks."

He marched her round the room. He presented her to two young women and then to Robert Bagot, whose familiar face and pleasant grin were a distinct relief.

The first lady to whom she was presented was Denys's elder sister, Lady Frances, a slim young person with a prim manner, dressed in unbecoming pink. Lady Frances had a face which reminded Isabella of engravings in Shakespeare's *Henry VIII*—she looked like a Tudor princess. Her face was oval, her eyes narrow, the Tudor impression strengthened by her stiff manner. She looked not exactly unfriendly but guarded. She faintly pressed Isabella's hand.

Sitting by the window, wearing apple green and white silk, was the youngest of the Bagot children, Lady Clare. Isabella faintly remembered her from the night of the play, saw she was beautiful and felt a pang of jealousy.

"This is the baby of the family," the Earl said. "She likes to keep us all in order, don't you, miss?"

Lady Clare gave her father the smile of a girl who knows her power and held out her hand to Isabella, giving the impression that she wished to do no such thing. When Isabella took the hand she received no answering pressure, it was like shaking hands with a wax image. She was glad to let it go. Lady Clare was lovely, yet it was difficult to know why this was so, for her nose was too large and her mouth too wide, her cheeks too thin, her fair hair almost colorless. In a way, she was like a sulky-looking boy. But there was something feline as well as female about her.

Robert Bagot gave Isabella the first real smile she had received since she entered the room.

"Here's my nephew Robert. I gather you have already made his acquaintance. I've told him I hold him entirely responsible for this marriage of yours. He is supposed to see Carteret behaves himself."

Robert laughed. Apart from the old bird of prey, Robert was the most self-possessed person in the room, for Lady Frances looked uneasy and Lady Clare like a stone.

Denys had spoken a great deal about his cousin to Isabella since their marriage, and she knew how much Denys loved and admired him. Meeting him now, she felt he was an ally. Yet in Newcastle he had seemed the contrary. She envied his easy assurance with the Earl, the way he laughed at the old man's brusque jokes, while poor Denys stood by looking at a loss.

Tea was brought on a silver tray; the silver teapot with a silver acorn on the lid was so huge that Isabella wondered how Lady Frances managed to lift it up. Conversation was commanded by the Earl, consisting of anecdotes which he told rather well, and at which he expected his family to laugh. As an actress, Isabella knew he'd told those stories before; he spoke them too skillfully for them to be new. All three of his children and his nephew laughed dutifully. After that he became silent, now and again shooting looks at Isabella from under heavy-lidded eyes. There was no way of knowing what he was thinking.

When tea was over he put his tea cup down with a clatter.

"Got to be off," he said to everybody present. "Robert, that damned fool Wreford will be here directly with a parcel of questions a child of seven wouldn't ask. You had best come, for if I'm left alone with the fellow I shall most certainly shoot him."

Standing up with his curious sideways stoop, he gave Isabella and his son a frowning glance.

"Swayne will send round for your boxes. Fanny will arrange your rooms. Fanny?"

"Of course, Papa."

"In this house we dine at seven," he added, glaring at Isabella.

She gave him an almost roguish smile. It did not appear to surprise him. He continued to look at her appraisingly, then, calling Robert to heel as if whistling a hunting dog, he went out.

Chapter Eight

WHEN ELLEN AND KATE LEFT CLARGES STREET they walked through the crowded streets on their way to the lodgings which were to be Kate's future home. They had spent the previous night at a coaching inn in Holborn.

The name of the owners and the address of the lodgings had been given to Ellen by Mrs. Gunn. It had "ground into Ellen's soul," as she confessed to Kate, to ask her old enemy for help, but neither Ellen nor Thomas had stayed in London longer than a night and, even to resolute Ellen, finding lodgings in the metropolis was an alarming prospect.

"Mrs. Hastings keeps a house in which many of my actors have stayed," said Mrs. Gunn. "I played with her in *Henry Four*. She was a passable Mistress Quickly. She tells everybody she was once Lady Macbeth opposite Kean but I have my doubts about *that*."

Ellen had her doubts about lodgings recommended by Mrs. Gunn and about lodgings kept by any retired actress. She also had doubts about leaving Kate in London. For the first time since the days when her children as babies had been muffled in shawls and left in dressing rooms, she was anxious about the girl walking sedately beside her.

There was much to ponder over. She was satisfied with Isabella's "great" marriage, thought the young Viscount a pleasant, tender-hearted man and congratulated herself on the
stroke of informing him of Isabella's gentle birth. It was satis-
fying to think that her own ancestry might be instrumental in
Isabella taking her place in society.

"Every act reacts," she thought. It was a favorite maxim,
used by Ellen to mean only that things repeated themselves.

Kate was quiet, and when her mother glanced at her, the
girl was staring at the pavement lost in thought. Farley
Street, not far from Oxford Street, was reached at last. It was
not encouraging. The houses were shabby, the railings peel-
ing, there was an air of neglect and dirt. Number 33 was a tall
house, five stories and built sixty or more years ago. It had
seen better days, its windowsills were dusty, the area steps
had a broken handrail. The maid who opened the door was a
haggard child of fourteen with a none-too-clean apron.

"Mrs. Hastings says to take you in 'ere."

She took them into a stuffy room of the kind Ellen and
Kate knew only too well. The walls were hung with flyblown
engravings of famous actors of the past—the Kembles, the
Keans. The carpet was threadbare, the heavy curtains looked
as if when pulled they regularly dropped showers of dust. A
canary in a cage hopped monotonously from one perch to
another like a prisoner.

"Dicky, dicky, dicky," said Ellen who loved all creatures.
She put her brown face close to the cage and chirruped. The
bird immediately began to sing.

"A bird fancier!" cried a powerful voice, and framed in the
doorway was a tall figure in black. The lady could have been
in mourning except that in place of jet she wore coral earrings and a coral-colored ribbon in a white cap too youthful
for her. The sleeves of the dress, early 1830's style, billowed
like wings; since she herself was both tall and large, the effect
was of a giantess.

"I am Mrs. Hastings," she said. "And this must be Miss
Winter, about whom my dear friend Hester Gunn has written."

Kate curtsied politely. She did not like the look of Mrs. Hastings and wished the windows of this oppressive room were open. Mrs. Hastings rang for tea. A tray was brought in by the haggard child, who carried it awkwardly and put it down with a clatter. She had forgotten the muffins.

"Sybil, you have a head on your shoulders, have you not? Use it, use it," cried Mrs. Hastings in a voice for filling theaters. When the girl had slopped out she sighed.

"Mrs. Winter, ma'am, I'm sure you agree that servants are not what they were. Supposing I ring this bell for her to hurry, do you suppose she will do so? But I shall continue to press it. I have always been a bell ringer."

During tea Mrs. Hastings talked of "the profession." Had Mrs. Winter seen this? Had she enjoyed that? News of theater in the provinces and in London was at her fingertips, and she enjoyed discussing it, opening her painted eyes, laughing in her big low-toned voice, full of vitality. After tea she showed them up a creaking staircase to a bedroom at the back of the house. It was as small as the lean-to attic in Newcastle, and the view was similar except that the London sky was dark with smoke. My life, thought Kate, seems spent looking at chimney pots.

"Everything for your comfort," said Mrs. Hastings, gesturing at the rickety washstand. "And remember, Miss Winter, if you need anything, Sybil is here to serve."

She left them.

Kate silently began to unknot the cord on her box. Ellen waited until the footsteps had receded, then said in a low voice, "If you don't like it, child, you must not stay."

"It is perfectly adequate, Mama."

"Not very clean, I'm afraid."

"We are used to that, Mama."

"Yes," Ellen said and sighed. "I suppose we are. Do you promise if you are not happy you will ask someone to help you to move? Mr. Davenant, I feel sure . . . "

"I promise," Kate said calmly.

Her mother helped her to unpack, and they left the house

together so that Ellen should be in good time to catch the
night coach.

Ellen was flustered by the size of London and anxious at
the thought of leaving Kate. Isabella's glory slipped from her
mind.

When Kate arrived at the theater next morning after a
long walk through both shabby and fashionable streets
crowded with horses, carriages, and jostling crowds, she was
awed at the theater facade. It had the air of a great mansion
or a temple, Shakespeare's statue was on the roof over the
portico, other statues, Garrick among them, stood in niches
on either side of the entrance. Imposing, dazzlingly white, it
was far removed from the theaters Kate was used to, most of
which looked like warehouses. But when she went down a
narrow passage to the stage door she felt at home. The stage
door, situated in a dull alleyway at the back of the theater,
was exactly like every stage door she had known, ill-lit, dark
and confined, and the doorkeeper was like all the other
doorkeepers. He was small and brusque with mottled cheeks
and a peremptory manner. Kate knew that one of his duties
was to keep out the duns, as her father called them. The
duns—creditors, bailiffs—haunted every stage door in England. If the doorkeepers were rude, they were also the actors'
friends. They were their shields against the outside world,
their allies. They alone knew the poor actors' secrets, defend-
ed them and told lies for them.

"Morning, miss. Name's Jack."

"Good morning, Jack. Kate Winter."

"Good egg," said Jack surprisingly. He returned to his sen-
try box behind a screen of glass.

Kate found her way, using her instinct, through the pass
door into the auditorium. The place was lit and seemed
enormous, a positive landscape of plush seats, draped boxes,
a heaven full of chandeliers, a long crimson hoop of circle
above which fat gold cherubs held bunches of gas globes.

She stood and stared for a while, then slipped back

through the pass door and went on to the stage to join the actors already assembled there. There were far more actors than she was accustomed to. But everything today was on a huge scale . . . the streets, the theater, even the chandeliers.

A stumpy little woman with a knob of dyed black hair and a timid manner came up to her.

"Miss Winter? I'm Gwynyth. Your dresser."

"I'm glad to meet you, Gwynyth," Kate said. "Everything is very strange to me at present, I'm afraid. The only person I know is Mr. Davenant."

"He is the only one you need to know, miss. Mr. Davenant is a great man. I've known him since he was young, you know. Think of the splendor of his name now!" murmured Gwynyth, her old face wearing an expression of worship.

On cue, Davenant strode on to the stage and Kate heard Gwynyth give a sigh of pleasure.

He looked, Kate had to admit, very magnificent. His handsome figure was enhanced by a dark green coat with engraved silver buttons and perfectly fitting trousers of dove color.

He walked to the footlights and turned to face the actors. Kate remembered his trick of studying them as if, his eyes ranging up and down, he was picking out what he disliked about each of them. The crowd became very still.

"The list, Bryson, if you please."

Davenant put out a hand without looking at the man at his side who reverently placed a paper into the hand, rather like an acolyte attending a priest on an altar.

Kate guessed that the man addressed as "Bryson" must be the manager whom Mrs. Hastings had spoken of the previous evening, claiming a friendship with him "from years back, my dear." Bryson was tall, over six feet, and towered over Davenant, but stooped as if apologizing for his height. He was foppishly elegant in lavender-colored clothes with velvet cuffs and much black frogging, his hair dressed in a fashion too young for him. But Kate thought he looked fussed: just like her poor father.

"Well, friends, I am here to talk about the program," said Davenant, in a voice which could have been heard in the furthest seats of the stalls. "Bryson wished me to do one of those French fal-lals which he says are all the rage. They are not the rage with *me*. Today we start rehearsing *The Iron Chest*."

Kate drew a breath. She knew the play, which both Kemble and Kean had made famous. It was a curious mixture of domestic comedy and melodrama, it had songs and glees and humorous "catches," as they were called. What made Kate's heart begin to beat faster was that there were two main roles for young girls—Barbara, the child of a poor family in the New Forest, and Helen, who lives in the house of Sir Edward Mortimer (the Kemble/Kean role).

Perhaps—oh, perhaps—Davenant had asked her to come to London to play one of those.

Davenant called out the names of the characters in the play as he had done in Newcastle with *King Lear*. At each name, an actor or actress stood in front of him.

"Barbara?" called Davenant.

A blonde actress, considerably older than Kate, with a pert face and a tilted nose, came to the center of the stage.

"See you behave yourself this time, Violet."

"Get on with you," said Violet. Davenant laughed.

More roles were called. Then: "Madam Helen?"

This *must* be it, thought Kate, blushing with expectancy.

A tall young woman with copper hair, not Kate's flaming red but of a darker tone, stepped out of the line of actors to face Davenant. She had an expressionless pale face.

"Well, Jessie?"

"Well, Mr. Davenant?"

"I hope you're going to work hard and show your paces."

"Oh, yes," said the girl with a condescending smile. Davenant nodded.

The rest of the roles were called. Then the list of "New Forest countryfolk." Kate was one of these.

When Davenant dismissed the company Kate walked off the stage in a state of such nervous disappointment that for a moment she did not hear somebody speaking to her. It was old Gwynyth.

"Would you like me to take you up to your dressing room, dear?"

Kate thanked her and followed her up a steep flight of stone steps. Gwynyth explained that the "big dressing rooms," in which four or five of the young actresses dressed together, were all full, and Kate was very lucky for a new arrival—she had a dressing room on her own.

In silence, Kate followed Gwynyth along what seemed to be miles of chilly corridors. They went through rooms hung with costumes stiffened, fantastic, seeming to be inhabited. At the end of a passage longer and narrower than the rest, Gwynyth stopped at last and opened a door. She took Kate into a stone-floored room the size of a large cupboard.

"This is to be yours, Miss Winter. Nice, isn't it?"

She gave the dusty table a dab with her handkerchief.

"I hope you don't find it a little small?"

"It is very nice. Thank you."

Kate was too miserable even to smile, either at the hideous little room or the kind old woman.

"Just you settle in, then," said Gwynyth, looking round as if expecting to see a costume hanging there. "Then Mr. Davenant wishes to see you."

"Oh."

"Yes. He spoke to me this morning," said Gwynyth, with her look of adoration again.

She took Kate on another long journey, and while they descended stairs and made their way through a honeycomb of passages, Kate's spirits rose. Davenant must have news for her. He was going to explain that although she must be bitterly disappointed by what had happened this morning, there was another play, another role he had in mind for her.

Gwynyth left her when they reached a pair of lofty doors.

Kate had thought today was on a large scale, but she had never seen anything like the suite which Gwynyth had called Davenant's "dressing room." She went into two high-ceilinged rooms divided by a door which was thrown open to make a chamber large enough for a banquet. The rooms were carpeted in white garlanded with roses. The curtains were royal blue velvet, the furniture large and heavy, polished to so high a sheen that it glittered. Between her stone-floored boxroom and this place was the distance of a prison to a palace.

Davenant was sitting in a large high-backed chair with an air of weariness, his head on his hand, while Augustus Bryson sat beside him, talking in a complaining voice as if he would never stop.

When Kate came into the room Bryson gave a polite smile and continued to talk. Davenant gestured her to sit down.

"The problem, sir," said Bryson earnestly, "is that the public requires novelty. Novelty is what they want."

"You have told me that four times."

"Novelty," repeated Bryson, as if not hearing. "It is my duty to point out to you, sir, how many times *The Iron Chest* has been seen. What is more, over so many years."

"Kemble. Kean. That is the whole point," said Davenant, sighing. "It worked then and it will work again. *I* am playing in it."

"But the public likes spectacle, sir, In my experience—"

"*Your* experience! If you are referring to what was allowed on this stage a few months ago, Bryson, all I can say is I pity you. Two boa constrictors and an elephant. Serpents writhing to Hindoo music. Do you wish me to share my theater with *them?* Go away, Bryson, and stop bothering me with your serpents."

He waved Bryson, who looked offended, from the room.

Kate was sitting quietly, her hands folded. She wished her dress, though freshly laundered, was not so faded, her green slippers not so scuffed. Davenant had a hawk's eye. And then . . . close to him again she had that feeling she had known in Newcastle. A restless kind of unease. She was aware of the toughness of the man. But he stirred her.

He paid no attention to her for a while, sitting at his desk in thought. She ventured to speak.

"*The Iron Chest* is a wonderful play. I have acted in it many times."

He was not interested.

"I daresay," he said indifferently. Then he did look at her.

"Do you remember an actor who played Romeo in Newcastle? Fellow with a lot of hair and a good conceit of himself?"

"Do you mean Buckley Vernon?"

"That's the name. Good." He scribbled on a piece of paper, then nodded to her in the way he had dismissed Bryson. She waited, her hands not folded now but gripped. Surely he would tell her!

"Well," he said. "What are you waiting for?"

Suddenly, she could not do it. Could not open her mouth and ask him what her parts were going to be. Perhaps it was the trepidation of coming to a vast, unfamiliar theater, having no friends, missing the confidence of knowing her parents were there to help her. There was something challenging in Davenant's face. She quailed before those sardonic blue eyes. She must trust him, she thought painfully. At least she was here, in his theater, close to him. She *would* trust him.

"I wanted to thank you for engaging me," was all she managed.

He raised an eyebrow but said nothing.

When she was gone he scratched his nose. She was a little on his conscience at present. Not much, but slightly. Was the chit being sarcastic just now? Difficult to tell with a face like that.

The theater was Kate's life and passion, but she never deceived herself about it. She knew it was all work and study and practice and many, many disappointments, whether playing in a converted malt house, or in Drury Lane. But Isabella had invented a fantasy about the aristocracy. She thought that their ordered and ceremonious life must, could not help but, be happy. She thought living in a sumptuous mansion, waited upon, meeting the rank and fashion, spending the season with a round of balls and soirées, must be a state of bliss.

Lord Carteret and his bride moved from the comfortable Clarges Street lodgings and the care of Locking into a suite in Bagot House for the last weeks of the season.

The rooms given to the Viscount and his wife were very fine. Tall windows overlooked the garden, where a bronze state of a Roman emperor, not unlike a more youthful version of the Earl, but in breastplate and sandals, stood on a lawn surrounded by lilac trees. The Carterets had a beautiful lofty-ceilinged bedroom with a huge ancient four-poster hung with embroidered curtains. There were dressing rooms for the Viscount and his lady, a private drawing room also with a garden view. Lord Carteret's valet, a tall Scot called Robertson, quiet and neat-handed, returned to his master's service. Denys treated him as he treated Locking, as a friend.

But Isabella lost the kindly little Rivers, the girl who had maided her at Clarges Street, and was given as her maid the Bagot's retired family nurse, Hopton.

Isabella disliked Hopton on sight. She was a big slow-moving old woman with a white face and a pinched mouth and expressionless hazel eyes. She had the powerful look of a peasant. Hopton did everything well; she ironed beautifully, did Isabella's hair to perfection (but hurt her when she washed it; her fingers were like steel). She scarcely replied if Isabella made a pleasant remark, bringing with her an atmosphere of silent disapproval, almost of dislike. You may be "my Lady," but you are not so to me, she seemed to say. It was useless for Isabella to complain to her husband. He'd known Hopton since he was born. He had this trait of being devotedly fond of the servants. They served *him* with smiles and kindness. It was vexing, but Isabella had to put up with it.

There were other things to put up with. The strict formality of the manners. The meals at the Earl's table, at which he talked solely of his own affairs. The many things Isabella was supposed to know (such as that no lady could go shopping in Bond Street in the afternoon, it was not proper).

Lady Frances, "Fanny," as they called her, soon became a friend. Lady Fanny loved clothes, and she and Isabella discovered this interest in common, spent hours consulting over dresses and went shopping together in the Bagot carriage.

"Lady Quenington was telling me the Queen is going to change the way she does her hair." Isabella was an entranced audience to remarks like that.

Paradoxically, the most considerable member of the Bagot family—its head—was the one with whom Isabella was a complete success. Denys was surprised and impressed by Isabella's way with the Earl. He himself was afraid of his father or it was more true to say he was afraid his father would hurt him by the brusque impatience of an unloving heart. Isabella saw the Earl as a man—and therefore to be managed.

Of course he was difficult, but she had been expecting that. He did not know the meaning of making himself pleasant, and looked at anybody who spoke to him from under hooded eyelids as if about to pounce. He was usually rude.

"There's a dam' fool thing to talk about!" he exclaimed, when Lady Fanny spoke to Isabella about a new gown.

The worst of Isabella's troubles at Bagot House came from Lady Clare. And since Denys was fond of his young sister, as he was devoted to his family, to the servants, to everybody in the world, it seemed to Isabella, she had to wage this new domestic war alone.

It had never occurred to her, naive, spirited, hopeful and eighteen years old, that when she stepped through the rich doors of Bagot House and made her curtsy to the Earl she was also about to meet an enemy. Lady Clare proved to be exactly that.

Lady Clare was the traditionally spoiled child, and the fact that her mother had died when she was born made her all the more precious and petted. She had inherited her strange blonde looks from a Scottish great grandmother, daughter of a Duke, whose name had been Melisant. Melisant had also been a lady of strong will, imperious, difficult, who had made a brilliant marriage. Melisant was talked of when Lady Clare was at her worst. Isabella never saw Lady Clare at anything but her worst, since Lady Clare either ignored her or made disagreeable remarks aimed at her in a drawling voice and with a cold smile.

"Why do you all allow Clare to be so absurd?" asked Isabella when she and Denys were dressing for a ball, "When we went out in the carriage this afternoon she wrapped her skirts round her so that they would not touch mine. I longed to ask her if she thought her sister-in-law had the smallpox."

"Clare is only a child, my dearest," said Denys, rearranging his white silk cravat and brushing his hair.

Isabella rustled over in her petticoat and wound her arms round his waist.

"She is not a child, she is seventeen years old. When I was her age—"

"Ah, yes. We know all about that."

"You mean I must hold my tongue."

He merely smiled, turning to press a kiss on her lips. Drawing back and looking at his face, so sweet, so reserved, she wished he did not imply—he was too tender to do more—that he preferred her not to talk of her past life. How could that be anything but uncomfortable?

"Anyway, you must defend me against your younger sister. She is very ill-natured."

"I will talk to her. Clare is a dear girl *au fond*. All my friends want to marry her, you know. She's clever, too."

There was no answer to that.

The news that Bagot and his son were reconciled and the new bride installed at Bagot House soon spread. Streams of visitors drove up, sometimes three carriages together, and

Lady Fanny did the honors when her father was absent. Invitation cards arrived, far more than could be accepted for any single day. Isabella was greeted (not without looks of great curiosity) by London society. Being launched into the great world turned out to be as hard work, she thought, as being an actress. It was like playing a matinee and an evening performance every day of the week. She was surrounded by new acquaintances and on show from morning until night.

Denys was always beside her except when he "rode out," as he called it, each morning in the Park, or sometimes when he and Robert went to their Club, Brooks's, in St. James's.

It was generally agreed in society that although Carteret had made a mesalliance the girl was beautiful and seemed to have a head on her shoulders. The Earl had put it firmly about that Isabella was related to the Bagots, and this interesting fact began to grow. From being a distant relative of the Marchmonts of Ware, Isabella soon became closely related to a ducal family in Northumberland, a romantic figure whose father had fallen on hard times so that she, daughter of a noble house, had been forced for a short while to earn her bread as an actress. The days before the season's end went by in luncheons, garden parties, dinner parties and splendid balls.

"You are bidden to a Drawing Room next week, my dearest," Denys said one morning as he came in from riding in the Row, fresh-faced and handsome in black and white.

"To make my curtsy?" exclaimed Isabella. She knew something of the Queen's drawing rooms from Lady Fanny, but had never asked when she herself was to be presented.

"To be kissed by Her Majesty," said Denys, sitting beside her and stretching out his long indolent legs.

"I thought the ladies kissed the Queen's hand."

"Not the daughters of Dukes, Marquises or Earls." Denys always knew things like that. "Her Majesty will kiss your forehead or your cheek."

Looking at her sparkling face he added, "Now you can enjoy planning your presentation frock."

"I do think of other things besides attire," said Isabella shortly.

He looked at her genuinely surprised.

"But why should a lady not think of attire?"

That afternoon the Earl said, "Glad to be making your bob to Her Majesty?" He had condescended to come into the long drawing room to take tea with the family. Everybody was expected to be there as a consequence, including Lady Clare.

"It was good of you, my Lord, to arrange such an honor," said Isabella in the right tone.

"Melbourne gave your name to the Lord Chamberlain," he said. "Told me he liked the look of you. 'She doesn't fidget,' he said, 'I detest a fidgety woman.' Always liked Melbourne. He makes me laugh." He gave her a glance. "My mother will present you by the by." He relapsed into silence.

"I suppose you should have a lesson, Isabella," murmured Lady Fanny, from behind the giant silver teapot. "Making your curtsy to the Queen is not the usual obeisance, you know."

"Will this do?"

Isabella stood up, faced her father-in-law and gracefully fell into the lowest curtsy, bending her head in deepest respect. Then magically rose again without effort in a movement of exquisite slowness. It was the curtsy she and Kate had perfected when playing ladies-in-waiting to Ann Boleyn.

Lady Fanny looked amazed, Lady Clare furious.

"Hmm," said the Earl. "I daresay it will serve."

There were strict rules for Royal Drawing Rooms. Isabella must wear white, her headdress of three white plumes must be set off with a lace veil (only unmarried girls wore tulle). Her train, jeweled and embroidered, must be at least three and a half yards long. When nearing the Presence, Isabella must drop her train, which would then be spread out by the Court officer.

"Drawing Rooms are in the early afternoon. You will have to begin dressing after breakfast," Lady Fanny said.

The dressmaker and two assistants were summoned to Bagot House with bookfuls of pictures of the newest styles from Paris. Isabella was entranced.

"Do you like this one, Fanny?"

Her sister-in-law had recently requested her to drop the "Lady."

"Oh, no, Isabella. It is much too—well, it is too much."

"And this one?"

"No. That is quite impossible," said Lady Fanny, looking at the design Isabella admired, an elaborate affair of flounces, with far too low a neckline. The style was finally approved, and Isabella had to stand for hours while yards and yards of white Spitalfields silk were pinned and tacked round her. It reminded her of the days when her mother had made her costume for *The Smuggler's Bride.*

Three days before the Drawing Room presentation, she was sent for by the Earl. A footman took her to the study which Isabella had never visited before; it was on the other side of the house.

The room was full of sunlight and smelled of leather, from books, from furniture. Isabella walked in, conscious that she looked her best. She wore a silk dress of black with a pattern of brilliant crimson flowers. It was a new fashion, a dramatic change from the old white and pale pink muslins of the past. She had changed her hair in imitation of the young Queen; it was plaited and looped in a manner to leave her ears bare. A thick chignon was knotted in the center of her head at the back.

Robert Bagot and the Earl stood up as Isabella sat down, arranging her skirts in a bright circle.

The Earl looked at her. She never knew what he was thinking. Faces like his, she thought, have no discernible expression, they are just handsome and wicked. But Robert gave her an admiring glance and a grin as if for encouragement.

The Earl gestured for her to wait a moment while he settled something in his mind. Isabella sat, upright, unself-conscious, in respectful silence. Robert sorted through a heap of letters.

Before Isabella had come in, his uncle had been talking about the embarrassing matter of the Bagot diamonds. By rights, at a Drawing Room at which she made her curtsy to the Queen, Isabella should wear the diamonds. She was the wife of the Viscount, the Bagot heir. It was true the tiara and necklace were very old-fashioned and heavy and she might not like them much, but she had every right to wear them. However, there was the little matter of Clare. "She'll not stand it," said the Earl, in a voice of mixed amusement and relish. "If she sees the girl wearing the things, Clare will raise the roof."

"Like Melisant?"

"As you say, my boy."

"Is there any possible solution, sir?" inquired Robert. He had thought of one, and he guessed that his uncle had done the same.

"I believe so."

Now the Earl roused himself from his thoughts and told his nephew to be off (he pronounced it "orf").

"I am taking my daughter-in-law to buy her a few diamonds."

"When, sir?" said Isabella. Perhaps a shade too quickly.

"Now, of course. Off and get your bonnet."

Returning briskly through the corridors and up the staircase to her own rooms, Isabella grinned to herself. Like Kate, she was afraid of very few people and knew how to deal with men. It was an art taught to both girls by Ellen, who had always considered that the male sex should be managed. Managing meant coaxing, deferring, treating men as superiors. And enslaving them.

Denys's feelings about his father irritated Isabella. Nobody must hold sway over Denys but herself; she did not like to see her elegant, lazy, sweet-natured lover unmanned when he was with that ill-tempered old man. Why was Denys afraid of him? What was there to fear?

Sitting next to the Earl in the carriage, Isabella was enchanted at the thought of their destination. The man beside her did not bother to speak, and when she glanced at him from under her eyelashes he reminded her more than ever of that bird, the Montagu's Harrier, with curved beak and hooded eyes. This bird of prey was taking her to buy her something very expensive indeed. Surely that must mean she had tamed it?

The carriage halted at a small early eighteenth-century house in South Audley Street which did not look like a shop at all.

"The Frenchman who owns this place has taste," said the Earl. "T'any rate, I think so."

The footman coming to the carriage door seemed to recognize the Earl, and when Isabella and he were ushered into the house, a well-dressed haggard man, short, dark and with a crooked nose, greeted the Earl with respect and a kind of gleam which Isabella did not miss.

"Gautry, this is Viscountess Carteret," said the Earl, seating his bulky crooked frame on a small cane chair. "She needs diamonds."

"A necklace, my Lord?"

"Necklace, parure, tiara, bracelets, the whole shooting match."

Gautry disappeared, returning with his hands full of morocco leather cases.

Isabella was requested to remove her bonnet and closefitting jacket. She sat at a table with a looking glass in front of her, and Monsieur Gautry placed a diamond tiara on her glossy hair. Earrings larger than pear-drops followed. There were necklaces which cunningly took to pieces, bracelets made like chains of flowers.

The Earl talked weights and carats with Gautry, using phrases Isabella found as mystifying as Chinese. He held pieces to the light, narrowing his eyes. Some of the jewels he pushed aside as "vulgar," other as "unimportant." He appeared to know a great deal about diamonds, picking them up in his beautiful hands, swinging them between his fingers, muttering, "Try these," and looking at Isabella with his harrier eyes, his grizzled head on one side.

Finally, without asking which she preferred, he chose a magnificent tiara with a rose of diamonds in its center; the rose, set on wire, slightly trembled when the tiara was worn. There was a matching necklace, earrings and bracelets all with the rose design. There was also the parure, a smaller necklace, to be worn with a brooch and earrings.

"Bring them round tomorrow."

Gauntry bowed deeply. And so he should, thought Isabella, wondering at the fortune the Earl had just spent on her.

During the journey homeward she looked over at her father-in-law slumped in the corner of the carriage, deep in his own thoughts.

She leaned forward and lightly touched his sleeve.

"How do I say thank you, my Lord?"

"How would you like to?" he said sardonically.

"Like this."

She faintly kissed his wrinkled cheek.

"You women think that pays the piper, don't you?"

There were many answers to that. She could have replied teasingly or with affectionate propriety. She could, actresslike, have been as ladylike as Fanny, as farouche as Clare.

She said, "If I am the most beautiful woman at the drawing room, it will be thanks to you."

"Certainly it will," he said, very drily indeed.

Chapter Nine

FOR ALL HER HOPE AND AMBITION, Kate had been afraid of living in London. She had been happy with her parents, even if "home" had been lodgings in dreary towns and playing in half-filled theaters, except during the glorious year in Sussex when they had owned the North Street theater. As an artist, she had been free from responsibility when she lived with her parents. All she had to do was act. Everyday things were left to Ellen, who gladly exclaimed if Kate were overtired and needed caring for. Mothering her (though never admiring her in words) made Ellen happy. Thomas, too, took the responsibility for giving Kate roles which would stretch her talent. She had interest and love and encouragement, and the company of beloved parents. Why had she been mad enough to leave?

Davenant had offered her what every actress burned for, a chance to conquer London. Or so she had thought, leaving her parents and the old circuit life behind. Now a year had gone by since he had asked her to join the Royalty. A long, dragging, exhausting year of risen and fallen hopes. Davenant had given her nothing but parts of a few meager lines.

Violet was given every comedy part. She was good enough, but Kate knew that she herself was better. More hurtful still was his treatment of Jessie Ramsey—he cast her in every coveted and important dramatic role. But why? Jessie Ramsey was supercilious, only passably good looking with her expressionless pale face and copper hair. She was conceited and of questionable talent. Onstage she was nobody. Offstage she gave herself airs, queened it in a ludicrous fashion. Gwynyth told Kate that Jessie Ramsey was wealthy. Kate had seen her leaving the theater in a very smart phaeton.

Perhaps, thought Kate, Jessie Ramsey was more than merely an actress to Davenant.

She was jealous of her because of her roles, but scarcely less jealous of her as a woman. Kate was slightly—more than slightly—in love with the actor who treated her so ill. She despised herself for that. Was Jessie Ramsey his mistress? That would be nothing new in the theater. Peg Woffington had been Garrick's lover—and the lover of many other men. But *she* had acted like an angel; London was wild about her. Woffington's name, glimmering from the past like a burned-down candle, meant art as well as sexual love. Jessie Ramsey had nothing but conceit and copper-colored hair.

Prim in her speech but not in her thoughts, Kate spoke of Jessie and Davenant to Gwynyth.

"Perhaps they are more to each other?"

"Gracious, no, Kate!" exclaimed Gwynyth. "Why, Mr. Davenant and Jessie's father are intimate friends. Jessie is Mr. Davenant's *goddaughter!*" The reply was innocent. Perhaps it was true.

Kate knew that she should have faced Davenant long ago about her career and made the kind of scene that actresses deliberately provoked when they were dissatisfied with their roles. She should have angrily demanded why he had brought her to London, when all he had given her were the despised roles of "walking ladies." But a miserable lethargy had come over her. Perhaps he believed she had no talent. *She* knew she had, but was too crushed to think how to prove this. And although she thought of him bitterly, his physical fascination had not left her. This, too, weakened her resolution.

She was lonely, unhappy over her work, and she was poor. It was difficult even to pay for her laundry. And now, in the early summer, she received a letter saying that her parents were taking ship for Ireland. They were going on a tour of eight cities. They planned to take ten actors with them, many of whom were old friends; most of the plays they were to perform Kate knew very well—even the dear old *Welsh Girl.*

Reading her mother's letter posted from Liverpool, Kate felt homesick and guilty, too. She was not there to share her parents' discomforts, support her mother in small affectionate plots to save Thomas from worrying, or coax him from one of his fits of despondency. Ellen wrote that "your father is very pleased about the Irish engagement. He has collected such a satisfactory company. They are very cheerful and gifted and your father is more sanguine."

Kate didn't believe a word of it.

The letter brought strongly back the familiar, higgledy-piggledy, anxious, bedraggled, on-the-edge-of-debt life she and Isabella had known since they were born. Why did I long to come to London? she thought miserably. Why did Davenant bring me here, why did he bother? He had tempted her with false promises, implying (though never saying) that he would give her good parts. She thought of him now, saw him now, with the greatest bitterness.

She took her mother's letter downstairs to Mrs. Hastings, not because she was fond of her landlady but because Mrs. Hastings would be offended if she did not.

The landlady was in the parlor, a dingy room overlooking the backs of a row of houses. She spent most of her time here, drinking tea (which she kept locked away and allowed nobody to brew but herself), doing her accounts, quarreling with her husband and grumbling at the servant Sybil. In between times she read plays. She never read books or newspapers.

It was a rainy chilly London day of the kind that comes in summer, making townspeople believe they will never see the sun again. Mrs. Hastings put down a dog-eared prompt copy of *Hamlet*.

"Good afternoon, child."

"I have had a letter from my Mama, Mrs. Hastings," said Kate. Sybil had brought up the letter, but Kate knew Mrs. Hastings always looked through the post and studied every postmark.

"I wondered if you might like to see it."

"Thank you, dear. I would be most interested," said the landlady, putting out a large hand genteelly buttoned into a black lace mitten.

Kate was not offered tea.

"Irish touring is very tiresome," remarked Mrs. Hastings, returning the letter and fixing eyes of surprising brilliance on the girl. "I was in a fire at Dublin and a riot in Londonderry. They threw turnips," she added, her voice at its deepest.

"My father was hit by a tomato once. And in Sussex when we played *Nell Gwynne* a man threw a firecracker on the stage."

"Of course, of course," said Mrs. Hastings with the disinterest of one actress in another's career. "Did Mr. Hastings remember to tell you we cannot provide supper on Sunday? It is his birthday, and we are giving a collation for a few friends. I should ask Sybil to buy you a pie if I were you. Imagine, dear," she added, lowering her voice, although they were alone and the door closed. "Mr. Hastings is *fifty*."

"Indeed, Mrs. Hastings."

"Fifty," echoed Mrs. Hastings in wonder. She gave Kate the look of one young girl to another. "I'm told one has to expect, when a man reaches that age, that there is a decline in his powers of enjoyment. I remember my poor Papa . . ."

When she was leaving for the theater, Kate met Mr. Hastings coming up the front steps, under a large umbrella. He was a small neat man with a girlishly thin figure, and although his clothes were very worn they had once been stylish. He was far more energetic and quicker-moving than his spouse. His face reminded Kate of a turnip lantern, with holes for eyes and mouth, very circular and white. One had no idea what he thought of his life, his wife or the actors who clattered in and out of his house. His turnip face never looked pleased. He shook his umbrella carefully, gave her a cold smile and disappeared indoors.

Kate walked to the theater, picking her way through the cobbled streets, which were covered in mud. She went down a street full of shawl and fan shops, along Drury Lane with its windows full of ballet shoes and to the back of Covent Garden, where the inns and lodging houses were dark-windowed. Horses steamed in the chill air. Windows were gaslit although it was June. The road widened as she approached the white palace of the theater.

A slight figure in a gray cloak, she slipped through the stage door. Two or three members of the orchestra went by, carrying clarinet and violin cases, their coats spangled with rain.

As Kate glanced through the doorkeeper's glass window she saw a figure she thought she recognized. Surely it could not be—yes, it was! Buckley Vernon.

"You'd best take the filly, sir," Jack was saying in his grating voice with its unidentified country accent imitated by scores of actors. "A pretty little goer she is and no mistake. You choose Delicate Lass."

"Put me down for a guinea. And here's another delicate lass," exclaimed Buckley, striding out to greet Kate.

"Isn't this the best moment of the week?" he said, almost kissing her.

"I am glad to see you after all this time, Mr. Vernon."

He burst out laughing.

"Don't sound so formal, Miss Winter! You can't be surprised at seeing me, since I have you to thank for my engagement."

"Me?"

"You told Davenant where to find me."

"That was months and months ago."

"Yes, it was, and he offered me something but it wasn't big or interesting enough."

"Did you refuse him?" she said in a small voice.

"Of course. I waited for a better offer," he said with the look which waited for applause. He little knew the pang his boast gave her just then. *She* hadn't had such courage.

They met again during the first act interval in the greenroom. Buckley was spirited and cheerful; he already knew a number of the actors in the company and Kate, sitting in a corner by herself, was grateful when he came across the room to join her.

"We can't have you sitting there like a mouse," he said, giving her his flattering boyish smile. "Is this the girl who set them all by the ears in Newcastle? Tell me how you are. Tell me about yourself. Are you a little triste, or do I imagine it?"

"Perhaps a little," she said. "I had a letter from my parents today. They have left for Ireland."

"So?"

"How hardhearted you are," she said, laughing in spite of herself. "I miss them very much. As they must miss Bella and me. They lost both their daughters."

"Do you seriously expect me to be sorry for them when one daughter is a full-blown coroneted Countess or whatever she is and the other daughter is at a London theater?"

"Since I have been here I have only been a walking lady."

It was difficult to confess it, and when he scoffed she was pleased.

"Don't be a ninny. What does it matter if you have no speaking part yet? You are *here*. That pretty little foot is in the door. Great things will follow."

"Do you truly think so?"

"I truly do," he said, with the inward-looking expression he always wore when talking about work. "For us both."

"I suppose you must know that Mr. Davenant is reviving *The Iron Chest* again," she said. "He did it when I first came to London and wants to do it again. I think it is a stupid play.

But Gwynyth, who's my dresser and who knows everything, says Mr. Davenant loves it."

"Anything Kemble and Kean succeeded in," said Buckley, grinning at her.

"Mr. Vernon!" exclaimed Kate scornfully. "It is almost sixty years since Kemble played in it. Goodness, that was in 1780! Even when Kean was in the play I was *eight* years old!"

He laughed at her impassioned voice.

"I have to confess I find the play interesting."

"Then you must have a leading role in it."

"It is not quite settled," he said, with the actor's caution and superstition. "The piece has a great deal to offer, you know. Comedy and drama."

"I call it melodrama."

"Perhaps so. But Davenant is always extraordinary. And there is music and songs. What more can one ask for?"

"I would ask for Shakespeare."

"*Macbeth?*" he said. "Our audiences want to enjoy themselves. It is very natural. Don't look sad," he added in a tone of a man to whom good fortune is so close that he can afford kindness to spare.

The bells rang for the next act, and Kate stood up. She did so automatically but with no feeling of excitement. She wished tonight's performance held, as it used to do when she played real parts, a sense of danger. All she did now was to be a "walking lady," sing a song with the other girls, stand about. She thought of her mother's old phrase, "it grinds into my soul."

To have worked all her life with dedication and to achieve *nothing*. She had made the wrong decision in accepting Davenant's offer, she could not forgive herself or him. She was poor and disappointed, living in the teeming capital, and despite Buckley Vernon's kind company, alone. It was true she was too busy to notice loneliness much of the time, but there were hours when she passionately wished to be with her parents on their way to Ireland in the old rattletrap life she understood.

Another thing which saddened her was that she had lost Isabella. Her sister had left London for months, going to Bagot Park with the family after her husband had been reconciled to them. Since Isabella's return for the season, weeks ago, Kate had received one short letter from her. "I'm at Bagot House again. Come and take tea tomorrow. Do!"

But there had been a rehearsal on that day and after Kate had written saying she could not come, she had not received another word.

Unhappy over her work, anxious at the frightening lack of money, disillusioned in Davenant, she remembered her sister's companionship painfully. The separation was widening and soon would be something neither of them could cross. Years ago Kate had seen two people skating. There had been a very thin crack across the ice and quite suddenly, with a strange sound, it began to widen so that the couple, a man and a girl, were left on separate stretches of ice. They had managed to scramble to safety but it had been very terrifying to see them one moment happily close, the next separated by a great path of dangerous black water. . .

She was not called for the first rehearsal of *The Iron Chest*; she had a part of a mere four lines at the end of the play. The rain had stopped, it was warm and dull, and she made up her mind suddenly to walk to Bagot House and leave a message for her sister. Isabella might even be at home. How absurd, how hurtful, to live so close at present, scarcely a mile from each other, and never meet.

She had never visited Bagot House and asked the way of a bored-looking footman standing on the steps of a house in Conduit Street. Two minutes later she had walked through the gates of Isabella's home. It was very magnificent. She could see tall vases of flowers through the lofty windows, and the front door up a flight of steps reminded her of the studded doors of a patrician mansion in *Julius Caesar*.

A footman in livery said non-commitally, "Yes, ma'am?"

"If Lady Carteret is at home would you inform her, please, that her sister is here. I am Miss Winter."

"I will ascertain," said the footman, ushering her into the hallway.

It was a great spacious place, the floor patterned in black and white like a chessboard. Marble statues stood in alcoves, and more statues on either side of a noble staircase. I was right about *Julius Caesar*, thought Kate. He and Cassius should make their entrance from the opposite side.

The house was perfectly silent. Kate sat on a stiff-backed chair and looked at her worn slippers. How different it is here, she thought, to the rustle and life of a theater, the snatches of song as actors go to their dressing rooms, the sound of hammering, slam of doors, strains of music as the orchestra rehearses, bursts of laughter. . .

"Lady Carteret is taking tea with Lady Frances. Would you be good enough to join them," said the footman, coming quietly back.

Kate followed him up the staircase, along corridors hung with paintings and carpeted with crimson, to a pair of double doors. The footman announced as if at a Lord Mayor's reception, "Miss Winter, my Lady."

Isabella started up, hands outstretched.

"Kate, how delightful to see you!"

She kissed her fondly, took her hand. "Lady Frances, may I present my sister. Lady Clare, my sister, Kate."

Kate curtsied politely and was answered by a kindly pressure of the hand from one lady and a stiff bow from the other.

Isabella, to her sister's eyes, had changed again and looked quite different from the girl she had seen almost a year ago in Clarges Street.

She wore a silky silvery dress of myriads of little tucks with a deep lace collar and sleeves with lilac-colored bows at the elbows. Her hair, marvelously plaited at the back, was dressed to show her ears. She wore amethysts. Her air was poised, she was quite at her ease.

Kate, watching the Earl's two daughters, thought Lady Frances very missish with a pursed little mouth and an air of stately decorum that would suit a lady twenty years older, but she seemed kindly. Lady Clare was another matter. Here was that recognizable character, the jealous foe. Every actress sooner or later met one in her career, and Kate knew this lady was Isabella's enemy. When Kate curtsied, Lady Clare had raised her eyebrows as if to say, "What, pray, are *you* doing in *this* house?" Actresslike, jackdawlike, Kate noted the expression. She might use it sometime in a play.

Isabella made Kate sit beside her, and they drank tea. Lady Frances, having poured a cup out for Kate, waited for the footman to carry it across the six feet of carpet which separated them.

"My sister tells me," Lady Frances said (she meant Isabella), "that you are performing at the Royalty Theater."

"Yes, Lady Frances."

"I think my grandfather saw Kemble once," said Lady Frances, looking for a subject to interest her guest. She reflected.

"I don't exactly recall what he thought of him. Wooden, would it be?"

Both the Winter sisters burst out laughing. There was a pause of astonishment from the Bagot ladies. Kate did not dare look to see if Lady Clare's eyebrows had gone up again.

Conversation was stilted, and although Lady Frances made an effort, talked in her tinkling voice about going to the play and listened courteously when Kate answered, it was a relief to them all when tea ended and Isabella extricated Kate from the drawing room.

"I will take my sister to show her our apartments, Fanny. You shall not mind?" said Isabella, whisking Kate out of the room.

When they were in the corridor Isabella whispered.

"Thank goodness, that's over. We had to stay to tea or it would have been talked about. Is not Clare a *gorgon*?"

She bustled Kate across a landing which overlooked the black and white entrance hall, up more stairs and into a different wing of the house.

"The relief to go through this door!" said Isabella. "This is all Denys's and mine. For the moment, anyway. We can make as much noise as we like." She gave the door a slam.

The sisters spent an hour in Isabella's drawing room overlooking the garden. It seemed Denys was gone to Richmond to visit his grandmother, who had asked that he should come alone.

"The old lady doesn't like me very much. She's the image of Clare, so Denys will have a horrid time," said Isabella, laughing. "Oh! it is lovely to see you! But you do look a little thin."

"*You* look beautiful."

"The dress is pretty, is it not?" was the careless reply. "But wait until I show you what the Earl bought me last season when I was presented. Diamonds, Kate. My own diamonds. A sackful! He is a frightening man, you know, everybody is afraid of him. Even Clare, who is his pet. Cousin Robert understands him but treats him with kid gloves."

"Does he frighten you?"

"Not one bit," said Isabella, smiling to herself. "He does not like anybody. I mean he does not love them. He is not that sort of man. He is cold and clever and strong. He makes my dear Denys so unhappy. Do you know why? Because it is so evident that he despises him."

"How could anybody despise Lord Carteret?" exclaimed Kate, shocked.

"He doesn't stand up to his father. How I wish he would. But Denys is too kind. I tell him that so often. And then, you know, Kate, if your mama had died when you were a child perhaps you would *wish* to love your father much more. Oh, don't let us talk about the Earl and Denys, it only makes me cross. What do you think of Fanny?"

"The tinkling one in pink?"

"She is my favorite. She takes me shopping."

There was a picture of Lord Carteret over the chimney piece, a pencil drawing which exactly caught a look of indolence and kindness in his face. Something in its expression gave Kate a stab of the heart.

"How is your husband?"

"Oh, Denys is a dear dear man, and I shall love him forever. Shall we ring and get the diamonds? They have to be kept in a safe. Imagine. Don't take any notice of my maid Hopton. One just has to put up with her. Ah, Hopton," as the door opened and a tall, stout old woman in a dark gray dress came into the room, "this is Miss Winter, my sister. She wishes to see the diamonds Lord Bagot bought for me. Could you ask Mr. Robert if they may be removed from the safe, please?"

When the woman had gone Isabella made a fearful grimace.

"Can you imagine her as the witch in *Hansel and Gretel?* Oh, Kate, the things one must endure. What with Lady Clare looking as if she would willingly kill me and sweeping in and out as if she is on her way to mix me cold poison. Why? I don't do the creature any harm. We never speak. And as if Lady Clare were not enough, there is Hopton who brought her up and is now *my* maid. She and Lady Clare hobnob together like an old witch and a young one. And then—" continued Isabella, with a gesture—"there is not being allowed to do things."

"What sort of things?" Kate asked curiously.

Isabella giggled.

"The other evening I began to fold up a card table, and Fanny nearly swooned. 'The footman does that' she gasped. Then last week when I was talking to Robert I pulled one of the chairs slightly closer to him. Lady Clare looked at me as if I were the crossing sweeper. 'What do you imagine servants are for?'"

With the actress's gift of mimicry, she caught the drawl and the stare.

She shrugged, looking helplessly at Kate.

"One has to remember not to do anything. Not to undress oneself. Not to fasten a belt or button a glove. I must hold out my hands—so. I must not do my own hair. Nor pass a cup and saucer. Nor open a carriage door. It is like being a doll. Or too ill to move. Yet there is a sort of fascination about just standing and watching people spring forward to wait on you."

"Don't you feel guilty?"

"Oh, Kate, don't be so holy! If I did things for myself, the servants would be offended, they would be much much more shocked than horrid Lady Clare. One just has to get used to *not* doing anything."

"It is a very odd world you've strayed into," said Kate drily.

Robert Bagot had a natural authority he had been born with, as he had been born with dark springy hair. He was a cousin of the Bagots, his parents had died and the old Earl had taken him into his house when the boy was a handsome twelve-year-old. From that time Robert had shown himself to be what old Locking used to call "a born leader."

Carteret was the heir and three years older than his cousin, but it was Robert who led and Carteret who followed. Robert's pranks were more daring, he studied harder, he made the decisions, he was the one Carteret turned to. Carteret, it was true, excelled in physical things; he rode better, was a more accurate shot, could box and fence and win at any kind of game, which he picked up without effort.

When the boys grew up, the Viscount went into the Army for a while. The Earl considered a year or two in the Army would be good for the heir; it was an alternative to University where Robert went to study and did well.

Robert grew up to be the Earl's right hand. He managed the complex matters of the great estate, the shipyards, coalfields, thousands of acres, tenant farmers. Everybody in the Bagot household consulted Robert. He had scarcely any property or income of his own, his father had gambled it away. But to possess wealth genuinely did not interest him. He enjoyed the problems, the challenges, the responsibilities, the weight itself. When Carteret left the Army, Robert

constantly suggested he should be consulted and involved in
the matter of managing the estates. But it was clear to the
Earl, to Robert and to Carteret himself, that such things
bored the Viscount and that he did them badly.

The affection between the two young men had no trace of
jealousy. Carteret admired his cousin's quickness and sure-
ness, his thoughtful intelligence, tact, authority. Carteret
went too far in his admiration and "Robert's a wonderful fellow" was always the answer. Robert must be turned to and
consulted about everything but Carteret's own provinces . . .
horses, guns, clothes, sport . . . and the matter of choosing
a wife.

The old Earl had been very bitter against Robert after the
runaway marriage. Carteret was a fool and his cousin knew
it; why had he not stopped such a disaster? Robert stood up
to the Earl with a coolness Lord Bagot found it impossible to
crack.

"I know, sir. It could not please you. But Deno—" Robert's
nickname for his cousin since childhood—"Deno would not
listen. Might as well tell the north wind not to blow as stop a
Bagot when he's made his mind up."

"Marry an *actress.*"

"I had a faint idea, perhaps I have it wrong, that the fourth
Earl . . ."

Robert knew and so did his uncle and the rest of the family
that the fourth earl had wedded an actress in James I's time,
that the lady had been much respected and that one of their
sons had become an ambassador.

The storm had been over now for months as far as the Earl
was concerned. Robert saw Carteret's wife managing his uncle and approved. But she hadn't won over Clare and probably never would, Robert thought. He sighed over a character as tough-fibered as his own.

Returning from seeing his grandmother, Carteret sought
out Robert in the study adjoining the Book Room, where
Robert worked for some part of each day.

The room was kept in severe order. The old-fashioned

desk, a Sheraton, held papers tied with colored tape, the heavy silver inkwell was refilled every morning, there were comfortable leather chairs and, for reading matter, any books from the Earl's collection which Robert considered useful. Law books, peerages of England and the Continent, agricultural books, English history, Bagot history.

Robert glanced up as his cousin came into the room.

"How was the old lady?"

"Not very agreeable. She was very sharp about Isabella."

"Did you get a little angry?"

"How could I? Her back is painful."

"Sometimes I find myself wondering about the Dowager's painful back," said Robert, grinning. But when he looked at Denys, his cousin did not smile.

Denys's round sweet-natured face no longer had the lazy contentment of the past and Robert was sorry to see that but not surprised. He had been moved by Denys's fierce romantic gesture at marrying Isabella. He envied its rashness but knew what it entailed.

"Why are you looking anxious, Deno? Surely not after drinking tea with one arrogant old lady on Richmond Green."

"My grandmother is part of it. A strong part, I suppose, because Clare listens to her. Even Fanny does sometimes. Family troubles are upsetting, Robert. I do not seem to have the knack of settling them."

"Or ignoring them?"

Carteret sighed.

"How can they not like Isabella? After a year of knowing her, too. She's handsome and getting handsomer every day. As for manners, she can give points to Clare any day of the week. Besides, she is related to us, ain't she?"

"What did your grandmother say?"

"What else but that she is making another will, that I was a grief to her in her old age. At one time she cried," Carteret added, in a low voice. He had not liked to see the old woman, who looked so like his sister, with her eyes full of tears.

"Poor Deno. Is there anything I can do, dear fellow?"

Carteret had been contemplating the toes of his brightly shining boots. He looked up.

"Could you perhaps speak to Clare? I tried, but she was hurtful. Most hurtful. See if you can persuade her to be more pleasant to Isabella. Clare is so stubborn. She gets it from my father. But she listens to you."

"When it suits her."

"You could think of a way of making her believe it did suit her."

"I can try. What does Isabella feel about Clare?"

"She is an extraordinary girl. One moment she is offended and angry, the next minute she bursts out laughing. I don't understand her. I never have understood women. But I am sure you do."

Before the gong warned that it was time to dress for dinner Robert went in search of Clare, and by luck found her alone in the upstairs drawing room, reading with the impatient air of somebody who despises the book. She wore white, which did not suit her pale hair and skin. She looked up and frowned as he came into the room.

Robert rather admired his cousin Clare, but then so did every man. There was something teasing and sulky about her, something which demanded a challenge. She was like a young lioness whose coloring she resembled; one felt compelled to stroke, rather hoping the animal would snap and scratch.

"Deno and I are riding out tomorrow morning. Shall you come with us, Clare?"

"I don't expect so."

"Why not? You like to ride. And we like you with us."

"*She* will be there."

"Isabella, you mean?"

No reply.

"Isabella never rides out, as you know."

"I don't expect she can ride, except perhaps a donkey."

He laughed and sat down near her. Clare looked out of the

window. He found her very attractive; her farouche manner and coldness added to it.

"Why don't you give it up?"

No reply again.

"Clare. I spoke to you."

She turned, then, full-face toward him, her large long eyes, almond shaped, glittering.

"Carteret sent you as peacemaker, I suppose. How like him. Why can't he fight his own battles? Does he think I'd eat her? No, Robert, I will not accept that *woman* as one of us. She painted her face and strutted about for show—everybody knows actresses are harlots. My father took her into the family because of some trumped-up story about being related to us. To the Bagots. That creature is no more related to me than I am to a scullery maid. Do you know what happened yesterday? Her sister had the impertinence to come here. Another actress, and sitting here with Fanny, bold as brass. Don't you expect me to change my tune, Robert Bagot, because I shall not. I shall do everything in my power to persuade my father to come round to my way of thinking."

"You're very hard, Clare."

She half-closed her eyes in contempt at that.

"And very pretty," he added, and laughed.

Chapter Ten

DENYS'S AFFECTIONATE HEART told him he ought not to spoil his wife so absurdly, but he simply couldn't help it. As their marriage progressed, he was more in her spell than before, treated her more tenderly, indulged and protected her.

Isabella had developed a dazzling self-assurance and seemed to grow more beautiful. She was certainly not more sweet-tempered. But if she was sometimes jaded, Denys perfectly understood it. When the season ended she would welcome, as they all did, the refreshment of the country.

Isabella now belonged in this close-knit world walled with privilege, where she was expected to be always at her beautiful best. Wearing a bonnet heaped with roses, she ate strawberries at a duchess's garden party, walked in the gardens with admiring friends; she returned home to change into a satin ball dress, put round her hair a wreath of cornstalks made of gold which Denys had made for her and leave again for a soirée or a ball. Across a lofty room full of people wearing diamonds, orders, Garter ribbons, she sometimes saw the little plump figure of the young Queen on the arm of her handsome Consort.

Isabella danced more lightly, answered more wittily, than almost any other lady. Men were captivated by her. A visiting foreign Prince inquired, "Who is the enchantress in white?"

It was very late, very quiet, when the Carterets' carriage trotted home through squares still lit by the wavering light of flambeaux. Most of the nobility in May Fair resisted gaslighting, and preferred the torches their ancestors had known.

Sweeping in to Bagot House, tired and satisfied, Isabella knew that the next day would be as busy, as demanding. Her best would be expected of her and she would give it. She was a success.

She slept late in the hot summer mornings, and when she drowsily opened her eyes she heard the noise of the fountain in the garden. But one morning when her old maid (and enemy) Hopton came into the bedroom to pull the curtains, Isabella heard Denys's voice. He was talking to Hopton, who answered in a gruff friendly way and laughed. Hopton never used a tone like that with Isabella.

The curtains were looped back and the sun pounced fiercely into the room, blazing on Isabella's face.

"Gracious, what time is it? Dawn?"

Isabella burrowed under a pillow.

"It is eight-thirty, my Lady," said Hopton, glancing at her master and not at the figure hiding in the bed. She left the room and Denys sat down, gently pulling Isabella out into the sunlight. He had the fresh look of a man who has been out of doors for hours. His coat smelled of green leaves.

"I want to go back to sleep."

"But I have something to tell you, my dearest."

"It can wait," said Isabella, beginning a long yawn.

"I fear not. I have been in the Row with Robert, and we have had a long talk. It has been decided that we will be traveling to Northumberland. Today."

Isabella, who had begun another yawn, shut her mouth with a snap like a dog catching a fly.

"To *Northumberland?* Are you out of your wits? Do you suppose I am strong enough to travel—"

"Isabella, don't be foolish. Of course you will not go. My cousin even suggested that as it meant leaving you he would make the journey alone but I won't hear of that. There is a lot to be done and he needs my help. We must visit the estates, and there's some matters about mining rights. There are the shipyards. Robert received a letter from the agent this morning. I won't trouble you about it, but it is more urgent than we thought. We must go at once."

She gave a furious frown. Such an expression, which her sister and mother used to know only too well, was rare nowadays. The Carterets never quarreled, since she always had her own way.

"Robert can go alone," she said sulkily. "He works for your father, doesn't he?"

She knew she had hurt him.

"You must not say things like that, Isabella. It's the greatest good fortune Robert is in the family. He's the best and kindest of men. And he's such a clever fellow. He does all the things I should do."

"Why don't you do them, then?"

He did not reply. Meeting his eloquent look, her eyes brimmed with angry tears.

"Oh, you're *stupid!* You've spoiled everything. Had you forgotten I want to go to the Royalty to see Kate playing? It's months and months since I saw her, and I thought it would be so amusing to give her a surprise. I *told* you. Fanny and I both have new gowns. Now it's all spoiled, and I shan't go."

He leaned forward and took her in his arms, kissing her, saying of course she must go to the play and see her sister and should he invite someone to escort her? What about James Fane? Isabella always said how much she liked him. He didn't scold her for ill-temper or say that he would be traveling hundreds of miles on the family's business. He had been taught, and deeply believed, that women were despots—in a way. They had the right to be bowed to and in return for the embraces of this beautiful girl he must always pay with love, indulgence, gentleness and generosity.

Isabella crossly refused the company of James Fane. She did not wish to be with "strangers," as she called the attractive man with whom she often mildly flirted.

"If you are going away, I shall not go to the play at all."

"But my father has taken a box, Isabella."

"Then I shall go as a member of the family," conceded Isabella, "but nobody will notice my gown."

It was a final arrow to wound her kind husband's heart.

Lord Carteret and his cousin left that afternoon for the long northward journey. It would take days to reach Northumberland, but the young men liked to be together, and although he would never admit it to himself, Lord Carteret often missed the careless pleasures of masculine company. He took a remarkable number of boxes, guns and fishing tackle with him. It was a regret he could not take his own horses, but Robert was certain some of the Northumberland cousins would "find something ridable."

Isabella came into the courtyard to see them off and allowed her husband to give her a tender embrace. She had not exactly forgiven him for going away so tiresomely. But Lady Clare's eye was on her. She wasn't giving her the satisfaction of looking vexed.

Having Buckley Vernon in the Royalty company was a comfort to Kate. He was a lively companion, and the year or more since they had met had oddly strengthened their friendship. Part of her affection was their shared remembrance of the past. He was like a member of her family, she thought gratefully.

When they talked together in the greenroom or Buckley gallantly walked home with her to her lodgings sometimes (always politely leaving her at the front door) he was encouraging about her future.

"Davenant would never have put himself out to engage you merely as a walking lady," he said.

"But Jessie Ramsey gets every part, Mr. Vernon. And truly, she is *not* a good actress."

Jessie Ramsey was a thorn, and a festering one, in Kate's thoughts. Why, why, why did Davenant give that particular actress the best parts? She had a face which reminded Kate of a bun, a muffled voice, little stage presence. The newspaper critics did not like her. It was true they did not dislike her either. They simply dismissed her as "pretty little Miss Ramsey gave a pleasant reading."

"Actors have these blind spots about casting. Davenant will get tired of Ramsey in the end, and then you will have your chance," Buckley comforted her.

He himself was doing well. In the much-discussed *Iron Chest* which Davenant had revived during the summer, Buckley was given the important role of the hero, Wilford, the young man who "offers to be killed if it will do Sir Edward any service." He had many dramatic scenes with Davenant and acquitted himself gracefully.

Davenant was at present rehearsing a new play, *A Game of Chance*, in which once again Kate was given nothing but a few lines and Buckley an important role. Buckley had to work hard but always took any chance to be with Kate and be kind to her. At eight one sultry evening when the rehearsals had broken—the Royalty had been dark for a week—Buckley found her in the greenroom bent over an old volume of Shakespeare.

"There you are. I thought you might have gone home. The rest of the rehearsals are between Davenant and myself."

"I don't seem to want to go home," Kate said.

Buckley put out his large hand and covered hers.

"Are you unhappy?"

"Disheartened."

"Don't be. Think of other artists who had to be patient. What about Sarah Siddons? She was a failure and forced to leave the stage and become a lady's maid. What about Kean and all his trials and tribulations?"

Kate grimaced. Her father used to speak of the chance of late-arriving success in just the same way. Was that what happened to some people, including herself? Born full of hope and working so hard and trying so passionately, and in the end repeating for comfort the worn-out tale of Sarah Siddons becoming a maid.

"I have decided, Mr. Vernon, that if nothing alters, nothing gets better, I mean, I shall return to my parents."

"That will never happen!" He smiled at her, full of vitality and confidence. He radiated his belief in her and said impulsively, "I will speak to Davenant about you."

"No. Please do not do that."

He didn't argue but made a gesture as if to say, "I will do as you wish. I am your friend." Privately he was relieved. He had kindly impulses, sometimes generous ones, but he knew he had just impulsively offered to do something unwise. His own acting career was at a vital point just now. Better to concentrate on that.

Before the opening night, Kate was taken aback to receive a card from Isabella, heavily coroneted.

"I thought I would surprise you, Kate, by coming to the Royalty first night. You are always so mysterious about your work, and this time I simply can't keep away. It will be delightful to see you play again, dear Kate. The family have taken Box D, so don't forget to look up! Denys has gone North, which is very vexing. I will come round to see you afterward. I don't expect the others will!"

Kate tore the card up. She wished she'd had the courage to see Isabella more and to confess that her career was going badly. But when they did meet, rarely, Isabella was so full of her own affairs, and Kate so glad not to talk about hers. Like every actor, she detested failure and had the superstitious belief that if she did not speak of it, it would stop.

Since her marriage, Isabella had not once visited the theater. The Bagot family had never been playgoers, although they went to the opera on Royal occasions. Isabella sometimes thought their marked disinterest in playgoing might be a mutual, silent, agreement between the family to keep away from a world where Isabella might recognize some undesirable friend. Who could say? The Bagots never talked of such things.

When the Bagot family arrived at the Royalty and were shown into their box, Isabella was quite excited. She and Fanny took their places at the front, the old Earl and Lady Fanny's rather dull escort, a fair young man in the Guards, sat in the armchairs behind them. The Earl ordered his chair to be pushed well into the shadow of the box curtains and Isabella, who knew him, guessed it was because he would go to sleep.

Lady Fanny sat, glancing round interestedly. She looked, Isabella thought, quite pretty tonight in her yellow and white embroidered net gown, with a wreath of yellow rosebuds in her hair. Lady Fanny smiled and bowed, raising her gloved hand to acknowledge the bows and salutes of friends.

Isabella stared round. How elaborate this theater was. The gaslights, covered in soft rainbow shades, the front of the boxes festooned with crimson silk, chandeliers held by gilded cupids. On the ceiling goddesses floated on fat white clouds. It was all strange, rich, yet curiously familiar. The audience making that curious noise, like bees, the feeling of expectancy, the rustle, the movement of figures making their way to their seats, the elaborately decorated theater, the dazzling crystal chandeliers. Isabella, absorbed, quite forgot to look at her program. When the vast curtains flew up, she didn't know which role Kate was playing.

The play began. Scene after scene went by, marvelously played by Davenant. But there wasn't a sign of Kate. After the first act she began to suspect that her sister had no part worth playing; Isabella was shocked. Poor Kate, how disgusting of that beast Davenant! It just showed that her opinion of him so long ago had been right.

But why give her sister nothing when Kate was so clever? For the first time since her marriage, Isabella mentally traveled back, sat in greenrooms, joined in arguments over who should play which role. She watched, disliked, the actress playing the lead, a pudding-faced girl with an inferior voice.

And when Kate finally appeared, so pretty and remarkable with her white face and red hair, Isabella had quite a pang of love and indignation. She scarcely heard the snort which came from the Earl, now deeply asleep.

Then a man came on to the stage. A strong broad-shouldered man, whose figure reminded her of the figure of a soldier, whose voice had a caress in it. It was Buckley Vernon. She'd known he was in the Royalty company, Kate had told her so, but seeing him gave her a shock.

She had not thought of Buckley Vernon and his effect on her since the day Denys had taken her from Newcastle. Buckley Vernon had vanished from her life like a ghost. He belonged to a time when everything had been miserable, when money was short and lodgings were cold, parents worried and food was sparse and nothing was beautiful or luxurious.

Seated in the box, a posy of heavily scented gardenias in her lap, she thought of Buckley. The curtains flew up for the second act and her spirits flew with them. I shall go round and see Kate and speak to him, she thought. I am a Viscountess now.

The play was long and the old Earl slept again. This time Lady Fanny heard him snore, turned to look at him and, catching Isabella's eye, pursed her lips. But the climax of the piece, which was dramatic, woke him with a series of revolver shots, and he enjoyed the final half hour and applauded vigorously when the curtain fell.

The applause and cheers rose almost to a roar. Aware he had them in the palm of his hand, Davenant bowed, indicating with the very angle of his body that he was their servant.

Old humbug, thought Isabella, discovering as she clapped that gloved hands do not make a satisfactory sound.

"We ought to come to the play more often, Isabella," said Lady Fanny, standing up and arranging her vaporous skirts. Her little face was quite vivacious with enjoyment.

"Did you enjoy it as much as I did, Mr. Coterill?"

"Indeed, yes, Lady Fanny. Magnificent. Just the thing," murmured her escort obediently.

As they were leaving the box, Isabella said, "Would you like to come round, Fan?"

Her sister-in-law looked as if Isabella had spoken in a foreign tongue.

"Come round backstage. To see my sister and congratulate her," translated Isabella impatiently.

Lady Fanny, intrigued, wondered if it would be allowed. She spoke to her father, who was fastening the buckle of his cloak.

"Isabella wishes to congratulate Miss Winter. May we go if it is only for a minute or two, Papa?"

"If Coterill goes with you," grunted the Earl. "Where's the fellow got to?"

"He is in the next box," said Isabella who had no idea where Fanny's young man had gone and didn't care.

The Earl took out a gold hunter and consulted it by narrowing his eyes. He detested wearing spectacles.

"You can have five minutes and no more. By rights I should come with you, but I am not going to and Coterill will have to serve. Off you go. I suppose," he added, glancing at Isabella, "you know the way to get down behind the scenery?"

"I think I can manage, my Lord."

"Tell Coterill to keep you both close, then."

Isabella and Lady Fanny sped down the staircase. Lady Fanny looked round in a harassed way for her escort but he was not to be seen.

"Oh, come on, Fanny, or we won't be able to get into the stage door at all. Mr. Coterill will find us. Stop fussing," Isabella said, taking her sister-in-law's arm. Leaving the crowds in the foyer, the girls walked down the side of the theater. Scores of carriages were waiting and footmen on the lookout for their masters. Isabella took Lady Fanny through the stage door. She made her practiced way past crowds of admirers, actors, writers, men of fashion, women of dubious reputation, dancers, footmen, a motley collection pouring down the corridors toward the dressing rooms.

Lady Fanny looked dazed as Isabella walked indifferently through the mass of people and arrived at two open doors.

She guessed they belonged to the star dressing room and was sure that Buckley Vernon would be there (but not Kate). Buckley, she faintly remembered, was the kind of man who would always try to be where the important people were.

"Where is your sister? Can you see her?" asked Lady Fanny, pink with excitement and shyness as she looked at the actors and actresses, talking and loudly laughing with Davenant. These were people she had never seen before, unfamiliar as rare animals. Their faces were haggard and full of life, they seemed to have something dangerous about them, something laid bare, not hidden, not controlled. They frightened her.

"Kate must be somewhere here," said Isabella coolly looking about. She had seen Buckley.

He had also seen her and gave a very deliberate smile and began to walk toward her. It fascinated him to see this woman, her bare shoulders rising from an exquisite evening dress, diamond stars in her hair, and remember the girl he'd driven to the seaside.

He gave the ladies a low bow.

"Mr. Vernon," said Isabella, using a manner borrowed from Lady Clare. "I am glad to see you. Lady Frances, may I present Mr. Buckley Vernon, whom you saw in the play just now."

"I trust we pleased you, ma'am."

Lady Fanny smiled and murmured something. She wore a look of delight at actually talking to a live actor. But he embarrassed her.

Buckley, self-conscious and determined to look the reverse, said to Isabella, "I scarcely recognized you."

He did not use her title.

"Indeed, Mr. Vernon? I recognized you at once!"

They both laughed. Buckley because he liked to be with young women as dazzling as these two. Isabella because at that moment she thought she would faint with pleasure.

On the morning following the first night, Lady Fanny sent a message saying she would be paying calls and would be glad if Isabella could accompany her. The carriage was ordered for eleven.

"Her Ladyship wishes to know your reply, my Lady," said Hopton, standing four-square in the bedroom while Isabella languidly drank her coffee in bed.

Isabella looked at the maid and remained silent to annoy her. How the woman disliked her, and how easy it was to show dislike while yet staying perfectly correct! Hopton did everything well. She was a fine needlewoman, could iron the minutest frills to perfection, dressed her skillfully, never forgot a pin or a button. It was she who chose Isabella's bonnets, gloves, boots, slippers, fans, parasols to go with whatever dress Isabella's whim decided upon. Hopton was a treasure. And a foe. She had a great broad body and muscular hands and steady narrow eyes. Isabella had seen that peasant's face melt with Denys and with his sisters.

"Tell Lady Frances I will be glad to go," she said coldly. "And hurry back, since it seems I have to be ready shortly."

She leaned back on her pillows, incapable of dressing without help.

The calls took most of the morning. Lady Fanny enjoyed them, and enjoyed gossiping with Isabella. She talked of their friends, examined the details of news. Did Isabella know Lady Quenington had the migraine for a whole day? Imagine, the Nicholls heir has lost heavily at cards again and his papa refused to pay his debts. People said Lady Sarah was in love with cousin Robert but he only danced with her once, had Isabella noticed?

Isabella answered automatically, nodding and smiling and scarcely hearing a word. The carriage trotted from Park Lane to Belgrave Square, the girls descended, were received, smiled, paid and received compliments, rustled back into the carriage and were trotted off to another great house. Lady Fanny, precise in matters of social give and take, sat beside Isabella after the fourth call looking satisfied at the morning's achievements from under the shadow of her violet parasol.

"Now we have only two calls to do tomorrow. By the way, have you sent your sister some flowers, since we did not manage to find her at the theater last night?"

"I thought I might go to the Royalty this afternoon."

"Would Carteret not mind?" asked Lady Fanny, shocked at the idea of Isabella driving to a theater, not to see a performance, but to go behind the scenes. It had been a place she was sure she did not approve, alluring though it was.

"Denys encourages me to see my family," Isabella said. She did not say that Denys had always been quiet, almost stern, on the matter of her own connection with the theater.

After luncheon, Bagot House sank into its afternoon trance. Isabella rang for Hopton to dress her. The old maidservant, disagreeable but neat-fingered, dressed Isabella in a frilled russet and white silk dress. The carriage set off through sleepy streets emptied of carriages and riders. Nobody was allowed to trade or sell things in the quiet acres of May Fair, except the women who sold lavender and the men who sold muffins, whose parents and grandparents had done the same. No omnibuses came into the beautiful, leisurely squares. The tall plane trees shed a grateful shade, but nobody played or sprawled under them.

Isabella's heart was thudding as the carriage left the quiet part of London where she lived and began to enter shabbier streets. It drew up at the front of the theater.

"No, Edwards, tell the coachman to take me to the stage door where he took Lady Frances and myself last night," Isabella said. The footman looked just slightly surprised.

Isabella sat straight. She wore the air, believed for the moment in the role, of a lady of quality visiting a sister who was a poor player.

Edwards opened the door again and respectfully asked if he should leave Her Ladyship's card?

"No, I will speak to the doorkeeper."

She picked her way, a mass of silken frills, across a pavement littered with straw. Jack was sitting with his feet on the table, but he jumped up at once. He knew a lady when he saw one.

Isabella graciously inquired if Mr. Vernon were perhaps in the theater? She took a card from her reticule.

"As it happens, madam, he's just this minute stepped out on a matter of business," said Jack. He had seen Buckley go into the Cross Keys with two elderly actors half an hour ago. "Don't know as he'll be back for a bit."

Isabella was so disappointed she felt slightly sick. This ridiculous gamble of hers had failed. Still remaining cool, standing there in her graceful rich clothes, she inquired for her sister. It seemed prudent to do that.

"Miss Winter won't be in until six for the evening performance, madam. Sorry," said Jack sympathetically.

A tall man in an elaborate double-breasted coat with heavy velvet cuffs had swung into the stage door. Seeing her, he bowed with affable formality.

"Surely it is Viscountess Carteret? Did I not see you in Mr. Davenant's dressing room last night? Buckley Vernon mentioned that it was you who had done us the honor of calling. I gather you are related to a member of our company, my Lady?"

Isabella was gracious, Bryson was bland. They talked a little. Something in Bryson's way of speaking about Kate penetrated Isabella's disappointed self-absorption. This man with the foxy face and vulgar clothes was patronizing Kate.

"I always say," drawled Bryson, "the young' lady has a pleasing little talent."

There was a slight pause.

"Mr. Bryson," Isabella said slowly, "I am glad of this opportunity of speaking to you. My family, the Bagots, as you must know, have always been patrons of your theater." It was pure invention, but Bryson did not know it, and of course the name worked.

"I was deeply shocked to see how my sister has been overlooked," continued Isabella. "Surely you could speak to Mr. Davenant about her? Use your influence in some way. I do assure you it is a grave waste of high talent."

"Yes, yes, I understand. Just so," said Bryson, very taken aback by the request.

"Ask Mr. Davenant to reconsider. I'm sure you could insist that my sister is given her chance," said Isabella. "Promise me you will do this for me."

She gave him her coolest smile.

He gravely promised to do so. There was no sign of Buckley in the street outside, and Isabella had no further excuse for lingering. Bryson, who had not the slightest influence over Davenant, repeated he would speak to the actor and was certain something would be done for Kate at once.

Isabella allowed him to take her hand.

The carriage returned to Bagot House.

She felt extraordinarily tired. The thought of the coming adventure had buoyed her up through the day from the first moment when she woke this morning. All during those interminable calls, during the long luncheon when the Earl was at his most abrupt and rude, on her journey to the theater, she had been trembling with anticipation—for what? Just to see Buckley again.

"Anyway, I did Kate some good," she thought. "That overdressed fool won't dare not to help her now."

She wandered into the upstairs drawing room. The tall front windows were open on to the courtyard, and the side windows on to the street. The clip-clop of a single rider went by. Then a carriage. Then silence. She sat down in the old Earl's chair with carved arms ending in a lion's claws.

She put her hands on the polished claws and pressed hard. She thought of Denys with a yearning melancholy. Not of Denys himself but of her own feelings about him until Buckley had walked on to the stage last night. Her affection for

her husband had always been as unquestioning as when she
had admired him in Newcastle. To be made love to by Denys
was as happy as she'd imagined it would be. He was an experienced, ardent, tender lover. He never spoke about love
making. He was passionate, and silent when the loving was
over. She could not bear to think about Denys now. It was
Buckley who haunted her, Buckley whose figure, face, voice,
self-conscious smile filled her mind.

There was a knock at the door, and one of the footmen, a
tall man with hollow cheeks, came into the room.

"A letter for you, my Lady."

"Thank you."

"A person is awaiting a reply, my Lady."

"A person, Kingsley?" said Isabella, raising her eyebrows.

"A porter from the theater, my Lady."

"It must be from Miss Winter. I will ring when I have written my answer."

He left the room.

She knew the handwriting was not Kate's, and when she
tore open the envelope she was trembling.

"How did I miss you? Let us meet. Why not at the theater
for some champagne. Tell *the nobs* you are visiting Kate.

                                                    B."

She turned the letter over, scribbled, "Yes. At five," and
sealed it in a fresh envelope, using the Bagot wax and crest.

When the letter had gone she went back to the chair with
the lion's claws and sat down. She leaned back and shut her
eyes. It was as if that moment she was at the top of a steep
hill, almost a precipice, and could choose whether to descend
or stay. It was as if, sitting on a kind of sledge guaranteeing
no safety, she hesitated for a second at the slope's top, looking downward. Then deliberately pushed with both her feet.
Down, down went the sledge faster and faster, ripping round
corners, hurtling down polished slopes, every moment the

speed quickening, while she gripped its sides, felt its speed, was unconscious what waited for her at the end of that journey to God knew where. . .

Robert and Denys had been away a fortnight, and Robert in his reliable manner wrote regularly to the Earl with news of the shipyards, the mountain property, the various problems and successes of the visit.

"We have seen a mort of people and there are more to be visited," wrote Robert to his uncle. "But we have also been out sailing, the sea was calm as a millpond and Deno is a dab hand in a boat. We have been riding a great deal and Deno has a good horse but mine is a bad-tempered old woman who almost bit me last night when we arrived back at the inn. We hope to be back with you shortly but things must be tidied up first, particularly with Carrisbrooke and Browne's, there has been some difficulties over the men's Sunday. . . . " And so on.

The Earl missed Robert, his "right hand," as he called him. It was when Robert was absent that he noticed, couldn't miss, the inadequacy of his London agent, a young man who seemed to the Earl positively to enjoy pointing out the difficulties both of his job and of the Earl's great responsibilities. The Earl grew very short-tempered. Apart from needing his nephew, he disliked a house which was a nestful of women and lacked his male relatives. He liked women about him, of course, but in their place. Silly women he despised. He had despised his wife, Cecilia, who died when Clare was born. Cecilia had been of high rank, better than himself, a duke's daughter. She'd been as pretty as a rose when she was a girl. One of those women in whom frivolity and beauty make an irresistible combination, being helpless, confiding, light-hearted, full of ribbons and nonsense, vulnerable, innocent, merry. She would probably have been stupid and dull when she was old but she died too soon for him to know that. Poor thing.

He was not at present inclined to seek out Clare's company

(Fanny bored him) because, although he admired Clare's spirit and she reminded him of himself, he recognized that she was going through a tiresome period of growing up. "Some man," the Earl said to himself, would settle all that soon enough. He must find a man who could cope with Clare and then she'd behave herself.

Robert-less, the Earl looked round for entertainment while he was at home—courtesy demanded he should be home at least part of every day—and his hooded old eyes landed on his spritely daughter-in-law. He liked the girl. He knew Clare considered Denys had made a mesalliance; he himself was satisfied with Isabella's slender pretensions to gentility, a third cousin once removed or some such. It would serve. She was a lass of mettle with eyes that looked at him sometimes with a certain acuteness. She might be clever, for all he knew. She was certainly a beauty and getting more so. He had enjoyed, in his cynical way, buying her those diamonds. It must be slow for her just now. That minx Clare did not like her, but Clare was a Bagot, and a touch of arrogance never came amiss. Carteret's wife was very thick with Fanny, but that could not be very amusing for the girl. Fanny bored him, as his wife had sometimes done. They were women who never took the trouble—perhaps did not know it was necessary—to interest a man in their talk. They discussed fripperies every time they opened their mouths. At least Clare rode well, read a book or two, and sometimes came out with intelligent if unkind observations about their friends. Fanny chattered about clothes, servants and other women. . .

His thoughts returned to his daughter-in-law. She must be missing Carteret. That would explain the absent look in her eye, her lack of appetite. Isabella sat at his right hand when they dined, and he had noticed recently that she had not the appetite of a wren. Was she ailing? She looked perfectly well, indeed, she seemed to grow more handsome as the days went by.

He found his son's youthful and seductive wife rather disturbing. She was the kind of spirited creature he himself had chosen for his bed in the past. He liked women with style, but they must be lusty, too. This one was just to his taste. She reminded him very much of a girl he had had when he was young, Katharine Harvey. He had called her Kat, a delicious little courtesan who had conquered and kept him with her for almost a year. His father had finally insisted on the affair ending, and he had married. Much Kat had cared when he said good bye. It had been he who ached for those practiced embraces. His daughter-in-law had Kat's look, a heaviness above the eyelids, an inviting lower lip, breasts which teasingly moved under her silk clothes. His own daughters were flatchested. Carteret's wife had a way of walking, too, which stirred a man. One way or another, he rather wished Carteret had chosen some whey-faced high-born Miss with no breasts. But Carteret, though a fool, was his own son. His once-lusty blood ran in the boy's veins.

He went in search of Isabella one afternoon and found her, in white with blue ribbons and lace flounces, sitting at her desk in her own drawing room, head bent, writing a letter.

Walking in his half-crippled way, shoulder sloping as if he might fall, the Earl sidled into the room. Isabella gave a violent start. It was the time when Bagot House was at its quietest. The Earl had never entered this part of the house since Denys and she had come to live here.

"Startled you, did I?"

He gave an abrupt, unkind laugh. "Shouldn't leave your door open if you want to keep people out."

He stood looking down at her with his harrier's face.

"Thought I'd pay you a call."

She showed him to the best chair, welcomed him, asked if she should ring to have the blinds lowered as the sun was bright. She had no idea why he had come; she had been writing to Buckley and felt so nervous that her heart pounded. The color in her cheeks only made her prettier.

"Don't put yourself out, the sun does not bother me,

brought up in the country, used to daylight. Wish some ladies we visit didn't see fit to keep us all in the half-dark.
Well," he said, falling, more than sitting, into an armchair.
He immediately looked younger because he no longer bent
sideways. "Missing the Viscount, are you?"

Isabella said of course.

"Writing to tell him so?"

"Denys is a dreadful letter writer. I count myself lucky if I
receive half a page from him," said Isabella, closing the blot-
ter and picking up a letter she had received from Northumberland two days ago.

"You don't have to show my son's epistles to me. He never
could write a letter. Told him so when he was at Eton. Sent
one of his letters back, 'do better,' I wrote on it. Not like his
cousin Robert—there's a boy who knows how to put a letter
together. Or anything else, come to think of it."

"Denys never claims to be clever."

"He'd better not," said the Earl with another laugh. Isabella slowly rearranged a fold of her dress. She thought for a
moment of defending Denys, but what notice would his iron-
willed old father take of that? When she glanced up, his
hooded eyes were looking at her ruminatively. He's a handsome old devil when sitting down, she thought. I wish he
would go.

"You don't like living here, do you?"

Taken aback, she blushed a second time, then began a con-
ventionally polite reply. He interrupted with a "tt-tt" and an
impatient wave of the hand. He hadn't come all the way from
the other side of the house to hear her talk such missish stuff.

"Yes, yes, it was very *kind* of me to have you and Carteret
to live here," he said, finishing her sentence satirically. "But
who wants to live in a mausoleum?"

"Don't you like this house, sir?"

"Can't stick it. I used to come here when my grandfather
was alive, that was 1800 and London was a sight livelier than
it is today, but I didn't like the place then. T'anyrate, it is too
small."

She was happy this afternoon, excited, full of trembling expectation; she gave an enchanting smile. He was delighted.

"What I came to say," he said, "was that it comes into my mind you and Carteret need a house of your own. Not a few rooms in a corner," he said, contemptuously gesturing, "but a piece of property. Something worth having. Would you like to look at a house or two with me?"

Isabella accepted with more smiles. The Earl, still pleased with her, said he would waste no more of her time (by which he meant his own) and would be ready to take her out tomorrow morning to look at houses. Did that suit her? So it should.

When he was gone she finished her letter to Buckley and then calmly began a letter to Denys. "Imagine, dearest Denys! Your papa has decided to buy us a house! Does that not astonish you? I am to go out with him tomorrow to look at some. I hope, dearest Denys, you will not mind I shall look without you. You always say you approve my taste and now it will be the Earl's, too. Perhaps by the time you return we will already be the owners of a *house* where we can do as we please and enjoy ourselves and invite all your friends to dine and—for my part—escape your sister Clare!!"

The letter was affectionate and so was her expression as she wrote it in her sprawling girlish writing. She ended the letter with her love, sealed it, glad to think how surprised and pleased he would be to know the news. Thinking of her husband, she did not have a single pang of conscience. Exactly twenty-four hours before she had been in Buckley's lodgings, lying in his arms.

Chapter Eleven

THE DAYS OF LONGING FOR BUCKLEY had been a kind of nightmare. Sometimes it felt as if she were going mad. All she could think of was Buckley, Buckley. When she drove out in the carriage every male figure riding or walking looked like him. It seemed in her feverish state as if the whole of London, every street, park, great reception rooms, gardens, ballrooms, were haunted by Buckley. She saw his swaying walk, the shape of his head, his strong figure . . .

She did not think of him as companion, admirer, friend from the past, but as the only creature who could stop, by his body, the constant fever, thirst, ache, which possessed her. She woke at night, she could not sleep, she had no appetite for food, she often felt faint. She had hallucinatory imaginings which she repeated in her mind, over and over again. Somehow she and Buckley had managed to meet, and had driven to a cottage in the country. Yes, she could see the house. In her mind she walked up the path with him, and the leaves of overgrown shrubs brushed against her, catching at her skirts so that she had to pull them away with a tearing sound. Buckley opened the cottage door, and she was so full of desire that she was sweating. She sweated in her imagination. He put up his hand and ripped her silk dress from shoulder to knee so that half of her was naked. Why, in the dream, did he treat her so? Then he took her, forcing his body into hers, hurting her, outraging her, at last releasing her . . .

During those feverish days, in real life and not in her fantasy, it was she who did the pursuing. Buckley had written one single letter, but after that, after their brief first meeting, it was never he who suggested they should see each other again. Yes, he desired her, she knew that. But he did nothing to possess her. For some reason of his own, vanity or sheer perversity, *she* must beg. And he knew, saying nothing but staring at her, how desperate she was. She almost believed he knew the dream, the cottage with its overgrown branches, the moment he had forced himself into her . . .

Yet she was the one who risked everything if they were discovered. Perhaps that was why. Isabella knew instinctively that here was a man of no strong character despite her violent desire for him. He was ambitious and selfish and that was all. Perhaps he would not take the responsibility of making Denys a cuckold. If *she* were mad enough to do it, he would enjoy her. But he was going to make no decision.

The feeling that he would not lift a finger to get her made her craving all the stronger. If only he would fall in love with her as Denys had done, give her the feeling that she had power over him. But it was always Isabella who, after some brief and contrived meeting, said, "When shall I see you again?"

After half a dozen such meetings she could bear it no longer. Sometimes when he merely brushed accidentally against her she felt she would scream and beg for him. Her body was an agony for her. They were walking one afternoon toward the theater, having spent a mere quarter of an hour together—she had not dared stay longer—when she suddenly said in a low voice, "Cannot we be alone?"

He turned and looked at her.

"Come to my lodgings," he said. "If you dare."

Ignoring the insane risk she was taking, her mind clouded, she nodded. Her face was ashen. Buckley hailed a hackney carriage, and they drove to a street of shabby lodging houses behind Oxford Street. It was a London Isabella had never seen, crowded, dirty and foul-smelling. Buckley paid the driver and led her through a battered front door into a hallway dark with dirt.

"Not your style, is it? I mean to move one of these days. But it suits me, and it is cheap."

He opened the door of a bedroom like a hundred rooms she had seen when her parents were at their poorest, but which her mother had never allowed them to lodge in. The curtains were ragged, the bed unmade, the two chairs had broken backs. Buckley's clothes, a frilled shirt, stockings and a silk cravat, lay anyhow. There had never been a fire in the dust-filled grate, and in winter the room must be as bitterly cold as now it was airless and stuffy.

"No locks in this place. They broke long since," he said, and pushed a chair under the door handle.

He tugged off his cravat, threw his coat aside, preparing to make love like a fighter stripping for battle. She shut her eyes. Now the moment had come she was filled with shame.

He gave a low laugh.

"Take off your clothes. This is what you have been thinking about all the time, isn't it?"

He stood beside her, naked, his skin like ivory, his body risen and ready. She could not move and he fumbled with her skirts, putting his hand up them and forcing it between her legs as she resisted him.

"Take off your clothes or I shall tear them off," he said, as in the dream.

She began to undress, leaving her clothes in heaps upon the dirty floor. He stood watching, half-smiling. When she was naked she was still ashamed, tried to cover herself with her hands, and when he took her in his arms she struggled. Her resistance excited him, and he forced her lips open, pressing his hard body against but not into her, then pulled her roughly on to the disordered bed and took her savagely and at once. He whispered in her ear as he thrust into her.

"You are a whore. I found you in a whorehouse where they have a school to teach women like you how to please. If you don't do as I want I shall beat you."

He smacked her across the face, thrusting himself more quickly into her with the blow. She gasped in pain, and they reached the climax together. It was scarcely ten minutes since they had entered the room . . .

When she thought afterward about his lovemaking, she did not care how short it had been, the blow on her face was nothing, he had satisfied her, released her, given her himself, coarse and hard and strong. It had been utterly different from lovemaking with Denys. Denys was loving, expert, silent, oddly chaste. Being loved by the two men was like eating a dishful of both their lives, Buckley's disreputable and dirty and almost savage, Denys's good and wholesome, as things should be.

Other women, the world over, had lovers when they were married. Why not she? I'm nicer, happier, because of Buckley, she thought. She jumped up and ran to a looking glass over the chimney piece and looked at her reflection. "And I'm more beautiful."

The open carriage stood in the courtyard. Sun sparkled on the chestnut coats of the horses, the brass fittings, the yellow and black doors painted with the Bagot arms. Two unicorns, upright, held shields on which were castles shaped like those in a game of chess. To the left, a small poignard.

When Isabella came down the staircase, doing up the pearl button of her gloves, the Earl was in the hall. His valet, a little whitehaired spider of a man, years older than himself, was brushing the Earl's crooked shoulders and fussing over him as if he were a baby. The Earl's bent figure, wearing his customary full-skirted black, gave Isabella a faint frisson.

"There you are," he said as she came toward him. She

wore pale green and white flounces, a bonnet curled with
tiny feathers which lifted as she moved. He looked her up
and down critically.

"I've told William to drive us to Regent's Park again," said
the Earl. "Wreford is to meet us there."

She smiled delightedly.

The house in Regent's Park which she and the Earl had
seen on the previous day was the one she preferred. But he
had said that it was too expensive.

Trotting through the streets, they talked of the house. Or,
rather, Isabella talked, because that was what he required.
Without stirring himself to interest or amuse her, he made it
plain that he wished to be both interested and amused. The
only compliment he paid her was that of listening attentively,
and occasionally giving his abrupt laugh.

When she was with him, Isabella had the sensation of being close to some aging but still ferocious animal whom she
must charm with a spell. While she used the spell, looking at
him with melting eyes, tossing her head, fluttering her
gloved hands, he would not menace her . . .

The old Earl, indeed, was momentarily tamed by being
with her. She looked at him with her languorous eyes, so like
Kat Harvey's, and turned her head in just the same way. In
his memory he saw Kat stretched naked on a curtained bed,
legs apart, waiting for him. Well . . . those days were done.

The sun blazed down, and Isabella opened a white lace
parasol to shade her face. They trotted into Regent's Park.
Swans floated on the lake, and children ran about with
hoops. Beyond a crescent built when the Regent was alive
was a house standing in its own garden, with a curved car-
riageway and wrought-iron gates. Isabella had liked it immediately. It was spacious but not overlarge, the dark polished staircase was handsome, a long landing opened on to
bedrooms with views of the lake.

"*If* I buy it for you," the Earl said—he liked to tease her—
"if I do, it will be my gift to you. Not to Carteret. Your own
house. Your property."

As the carriage neared the house, she gave a murmur of pleasure, a kind of sigh. He looked at her from under his heavy eyelids. There was something about her these days. Something sensuous, at times lazy, at times excited. "Mettlesome," thought the Earl.

The carriage drew up, the front door stood open, and the Earl's agent, Tom Wreford, was waiting for them. He was a gloomy pale-faced young man with rings under his eyes from working late for a despotic master.

"Wreford," said the Earl, "I take it you told Sherington he's asking too much for this place?"

"I have been with Mr. Herriot, my Lord."

"Who the devil's he?"

"Lord Sherington's steward, my Lord."

"Steward? What do I want with him? The house is Sherington's, ain't it? Tell him I won't pay a penny more than the price I offered. Look at the condition of the place. It's falling down," said the Earl, pointing contemptuously at a carved pearwood fireplace. "My daughter-in-law will cost me a small fortune putting it all to rights. You tell Sherington himself, none of your stewards. Tell him plainly that my offer stands and my daughter-in-law will be moving in as soon as the place is habitable. Are you pleased, young woman? You're costing me a mint of money."

"Denys will be enchanted."

"I am not buying it for Carteret. It is for you. What the French call a *bonne-bouche*. And if you wish to thank me," he added, seeing she was about to make him a graceful and therefore tedious speech, "take Wreford off my hands."

He looked over at Wreford, who was despondently examining a loose banister. The Earl glowered.

"Gloomy beggar. What are a few repairs? The place merely needs a nail knocked in here and there. You tell him what's to be done. I shall go to my club for luncheon, you have worn me out enough for today. Do not ask for another house, if you please. I can't afford daughters-in-law like you."

* * *

It was weeks since Denys and Robert had left London, and to Isabella it seemed a year. The days were crammed with lies and subterfuges so that she could get to Buckley, be with him, in his arms again. She had thought before she had Buckley as her lover that once his body had been in hers, just once, the fever would stop. The reverse was true. Now that he mounted her, half-savaged her with his body, she ached for more. In her mind she became the whore in a school for love. He satisfied her—for that day. Sometimes he took her twice, always fiercely and quickly, but never more. Most of the times when they met he only took her once. And in a few hours she was longing again, shamefully, for his weight, the scent of his sweat, his body thrusting into her.

To have him was so difficult that she was often frantic. Social laws made her a prisoner, and even using her sister as an excuse was insufficient. Lady Fanny disapproved of Isabella going out alone from the start.

"I am going to see Kate," Isabella said, light as air as she came down the great staircase dressed to go out.

"You must take Hopton."

"My dear Fanny—"

"Ladies are always accompanied by their maids," Lady Fanny said, lowering her voice so the servants should not hear her. "Send for Hopton, Isabella. She will be glad to wait for you at the theater."

Isabella's face became set, her brown eyes like stones. Murmuring she would talk the matter over with her sister-in-law later, she had swept from the house, leaving Lady Fanny much distressed.

It was only by persuasion and ill-temper in a judicious mixture, at which Isabella became more skillful as she became more desperate, that she managed to escape from Bagot House on her pretended visits to Kate.

Then something totally unexpected happened. Isabella received a letter from Kate. It was so angry and so rude that she could scarcely believe her gentle sister had written it.

Kate had discovered from Bryson that Isabella had visited the Royalty and interceded for her.

"How *dare* you patronize me! Do you think because you are now married into the nobility you can drive round to the theater and order them to give me roles as if they—and I— were so many servants? Do you suppose I cannot look after myself, do not know what I am doing? If Mama knew. . . ."

And so on for three pages written when Kate was so furious that had Isabella been present, she would have slapped her face.

The letter upset Isabella, who was out of the habit of quarrels, though she and Kate had had many spirited, vindictive but always short-lived rows in the past. She refused to admit she had been interfering or unimaginative, and she thought Kate stupid and touchy. She was convinced Kate would cool down and saw no reason to apologize, at present, anyway. What worried her far more than her sister's feelings was that Isabella saw a danger to her passionate, desperate, complicated plans. She did not dare use Kate as an excuse now Kate was angry with her. Suppose Kate suddenly took it into her head—it would be just like her—to march round to Bagot House and talk the matter out? One sentence in front of Lady Fanny—"I have not seen my sister for weeks"—and Isabella was lost.

But just when Isabella was wildly thinking how she could resolve this, the Earl bought her Finstock Lodge. Here was a new excuse to be alone. She went shopping, carelessly adding that she would "probably call to see Kate as well." Taking the carriage, she alighted at Regent Street, five minutes from Buckley's lodgings, and told the footman she would be some time choosing silks or visiting this warehouse or that. She wished to be collected in an hour, perhaps two. She even had time on occasion to collect snippets of silk or news of furniture which she used in conversations with Lady Fanny.

These half hours—they were never more—spent in Buckley's arms gave the days a rising excitement until the time she stripped naked and he took her.

She had arranged to see him one afternoon in the "usual" way, as it had become, after she had visited an India silk warehouse. A short letter was brought to her, just as she was leaving Bagot House.

"My dearest. At last we are returning home."

Isabella went white.

The door of Buckley's lodgings was ajar, and she ran up the dark staircase and entered his bedroom. He lay, as usual, sprawled on the bed, studying a script.

He gave her a slow smile.

"I have had a key put in the lock. Now you can feel safe."

She ran to him. He kissed her, then untied her bodice and pulled out her breasts, fondling them, pinching them. She gasped.

"You hurt me."

"I mean to. I do as I like with you."

When she was naked he made her sit astride him, thrusting upward into her and watching her face. Then he withdrew from her, and when she had shamefully begged, returned to finish her in his customary way, violently and fast, whispering in her ear of the whore's school and what she must learn there. They were sweating when he reached his climax and pushed her roughly aside.

She lay silent, still breathless, sated with lovemaking for *now*. But would it be her last time? Till when?

After he had finished with her he never lay in her arms and slept. He always left her, washed in the basin in the corner and put on his shirt and trousers while she, naked, watched him. This afternoon he dressed in silence, then went to the fly-spotted mirror on the wall and began to comb his hair. Looking at his own face, he wore a curious half-smile.

"You think you are very handsome, don't you?" she said defiantly. She was always slightly afraid to say such things in case he hurt her. But since, striking her, he had been excited, she herself was roused by her own courage.

Now he merely grinned and arranged his thick hair.

"So you are," she said in a low voice.

"You are quite handsome, too."

His voice had no meaning. The moment he had withdrawn himself from her, leaving her sprawled and shaking, he scarcely saw her. He became, at once, absorbed in his own thoughts. She had noticed it many times, and it made her suffer. Made her feel horribly ashamed of her own cravings. But then he desired her again, and then she forgot it. Every time he was in her she forgot, and then when he was finished with her she remembered that complete indifference.

"Buck. Sit by me."

He pulled up a broken chair and sat beside her where she lay, legs still apart, like a conquered Sabine. He did not notice a scarlet weal across her breasts which *he* had made. He did not notice her at all.

"I have something to tell you," she said in a low voice.

"Now what is it?" he said, in the tone he might use to a tiresome child.

Isabella reached for her chemise and covered herself. When she was naked and he did not want her, she felt degraded.

"Denys has written me. He and his cousin will be in London by tomorrow."

She waited for his face to change.

"So?"

"Don't you understand? How can we meet when Denys is returned?"

He gave his empty, absent-minded smile.

"You will think of a way, I suppose. You can be an ingenious creature."

Humiliated, desperate, feeling already the returning craving for him, she turned away, with her back to him.

He gave her a slap on her naked buttocks.

"For heaven's sake, get dressed and don't be stupid. You scarcely have time to get back to that warehouse if you stay longer. Hurry up."

He slapped her again, harder.

Longing to burst into a storm of sobs, she dressed in a hurried silence, putting on her white embroidered stockings and rosetted shoes, tying the tapes of her petticoats. She waited while he buttoned the back of her dress, and then she borrowed his dirty, broken comb. She put on her bonnet with its rosebuds and feathers, and arranged her India shawl. Dressed, she was again the Viscountess.

"Now, don't sulk," he said, laughing and showing his teeth. "I will have to be patient until I hear from you. You are the one who must think how we can manage to meet. You will think how, I am sure. You *need* to, don't you?"

"But do you *want* to?"

She despised herself for saying that.

When he met her eyes she thought her heart would crack. He looked so perfectly cheerful and indifferent, opening the script in his hand and marking the place.

"Buck, for God's sake—"

"Isabella, what a child you are. Do you suppose after the last hour I don't want to see you?"

With this, and only this, she had to be content. They walked down the musty-smelling stairs and out into the street. Buckley always ordered a hackney carriage which waited at the door to take her as far as Regent Street. But that afternoon when they came out of the house there was no sign of the carriage. Buckley stared up and down the street.

"What a damned thing. It hasn't come."

"I cannot wait," she said, in a voice suddenly taut with anxiety. "I must go at once."

"Then I'll walk you to Regent Street."

"But that's impossible! I can't be seen with you. I daren't."

He laughed.

"Would you rather go through these stinking alleys on your own, then?"

With a shaking hand, she pulled the lace veil on her bonnet down to cover her face and began to hurry beside him. Buckley strode along cheerfully while Isabella bent her head, almost fainting with nerves. She began to imagine she could hear footsteps—she did not dare look back.

"Is there someone behind us, Buckley?"

"About half a hundred," he said, as they passed a filthy doorway crowded with ragged people and made their way through hawkers and rough-looking men who could be ostlers. Guessing from her tone and bent head that she was frightened, he took her arm. She shook him off. There was that step again! This time she could not help glancing over her shoulder. She was convinced she caught sight of a broad, dark-clad figure which vanished into a doorway.

"Look. There's a hackney," Buckley said suddenly. He waved and the driver reined in his horse.

"What a fuss over a little walk," Buckley said, helping her into the carriage. "Off you go. We'll meet soon."

He raised his hat and strode away.

Safe in Regent's Street, Isabella paid the driver and walked into a warehouse. She was immediately greeted, bowed to, surrounded by a reverent attention. But as she sat talking to the warehouse manager and examining some new silks, her heart was thudding. *Had* that been Hopton following her just now?

When she returned to Bagot House she went to her room, her head splitting, lay down and tried to sleep. An hour went by. But when the gong for dressing was rung, she was no calmer.

Hopton came quietly into the room, went over to the long wardrobe and took out one of Isabella's dinner gowns. Isabella watched as the old servant unbuttoned the dress, smoothed its white silk folds and came slowly toward Isabella, then raised her eyes and looked at her. Hopton's expression was as inscrutable as ever. Did Isabella imagine that there was something new in that stern old face? It's my imagination, she thought, as Hopton began to unpin her hair. I feel guilty because I was in the street with him. So I begin to imagine things . . .

Lady Fanny took the burden and responsibility of being the eldest in the family seriously; and she liked both her sister and Isabella to take tea in the upper drawing room every afternoon, sometimes with guests, sometimes alone. Lady Fanny was firm on the matter. Even Lady Clare submitted to her sister's ruling, though she never made the meeting anything but uncomfortable if the ladies happened to be alone.

The relationship between Isabella and the youngest of the Bagots was rather worse than better.

Robert had failed to mend it. Denys did not know how to do so. Lady Fanny, half afraid of her sister, pretended things were as they should be. Lady Clare had established at the very first meeting that she deeply resented Isabella marrying into the family; her manner—sometimes laughably rude— had not changed since then.

The news that "the boys," as she called them, were on their way home made Lady Fanny particularly happy, and during tea, with Lady Clare seated as far as possible from Isabella and nobody else present, Lady Fanny kept repeating, "Surely *that* is the carriage?"

"No, Fan, it is not."

"But Clare, dear, do look from the window. The boys might see you and . . ."

Lady Clare shrugged, repeated there was no carriage yet, sent a footman to the window, who confirmed there was no sign of it.

Lady Clare began to talk about a ball the Montacutes were giving.

"Violet Montacute hoped the Queen might come but it seems she and Prince Albert are to be at Windsor. Violet says the Prince enjoys Windsor very much. She and the family went to a ball there. The Queen was in white but very décolléte and a wreath of white roses. I think it odd we are not lately invited," said Lady Clare, staring at her sister. "Why would you suppose we have not had a card?"

Lady Fanny lifted the monstrously heavy teapot topped with the silver acorn. Isabella rearranged a ruffle at her wrist. The footman took the teacup on his salver and walked across the room to give it to Lady Clare. Everybody in the room, including the footman, knew that what Lady Clare actually

meant was, "Now there is an actress in the Bagot family, the
Palace has decided we are not to be invited." The young
Queen, it was said, was strict about such things.

Lady Fanny had already discussed this difficult subject
with the Earl, who had told her to stop behaving like an old
hen. Melbourne, he said, had distinctly told him the Queen
was cutting down her guests because she was with child and
became easily tired. Lady Fanny did not consider this a proper subject to discuss at the tea table. Once again she fancied
she heard carriage wheels.

This time even Lady Clare couldn't deny the clatter in the
courtyard and darted to the window, then turned and said,
her face lit with a rare, brilliant smile, "It's *them!*"

All three ladies, Lady Clare the quickest, then Lady Fanny
and Isabella more sedately, left the drawing room and went
to the head of the staircase.

Below in the hall the great double doors were open and
servants were bustling in and out with boxes and hampers,
commanded by Swayne, who arrived like a general on the
battlefield. There was an air of excitement, as if the old
house had woken from its sleep with a start.

And there, carrying large bunches of flowers which made
them look charming and absurd, were Denys and Robert.
Before the two young men could take another step Lady
Clare had flown down the staircase, jumping the last two in
her haste, and rushed to embrace them. She looked so happy
that Isabella had a pang of the sharpest envy.

While Lady Clare was laughing, exclaiming, taking their
hands, Isabella too had hurried down to Denys who put out
both arms. He pressed her to him, then drew away and bent
to kiss her hands.

"How I've missed you!" he said, looking at her as if his eyes
were hungry. "Robert and I thought we would never get
home!" He still held her hands, his eyes tracing her face, her
glossy hair, every detail about her.

"Are you well, my dearest? Of course you are. More beautiful than ever."

He himself looked tired, pale, transformed with happiness.

Everyone talked at once. Lady Fanny exclaimed over the quantity of luggage which seemed to have grown from the boxes "the boys" had taken away. How lovely the roses were. But where had they come from?

"They are very fresh from their travels all the way from the North," said Robert, laughing. "We bought them for you in the Burlington Arcade."

Swayne and Mrs. Judge, the housekeeper, greeted both young men. Lady Fanny explained that the Earl was at Richmond with his mother.

"And did you bring us presents, cousin?" asked Lady Clare hanging on Robert's arm.

"By thunder, you're just the one who slipped our minds," said Robert.

As they walked up the stairs, Lady Clare burst out laughing. It was a sound Isabella did not remember having ever heard before.

They went into the drawing room, where fresh tea was ordered; Robert and Denys told them the news of their weeks away, of the shipbuilding yards and their problems, the estates, farms, the inns they had stayed in, the week spent with Lord Lennox, the girls Robert had flirted with, the sailing, the shooting, the weather. There was a great deal of teasing and nonsense, and everybody laughed. What a difference, Isabella thought, between now and the weeks gone by. Between a family which included two young men and a parcel of women on their own with one elderly male despot, usually out of sight.

She was glad of the noise and talk, glad to sit and listen and smile, and so nervous that at times she shook. Denys, long legs stretched out beside her, caught her eye at every moment, giving his sweet, lazy smile. Her heart hurt when he smiled like that. Suddenly and for the first time, she wished she had never met Buckley. Never succumbed to that dreadful hunger, that coiled tension begging for release, that madness. It had been madness. What did she mean, "it had been"? It still was. Sitting here full of meaningless alarm just because Denys was near her, she could still remember Buckley physically; the sensation made her feel she was falling from a height. She could remember his body thrusting into hers, his voice whispering. She longed for him between her thighs. And in a way she hated him because Denys looked so blissful, indolent, handsome and her own.

He will make love to me tonight, she thought. *He* will be where Buckley was. Will he know then?

Chapter Twelve

"A visitor to see you, Miss Winter," said Mrs. Hastings, panting to indicate the exhaustion of ascending her own staircase.

Kate, standing by the attic window looking at the chimney pots and a flock of dusty quarreling sparrows, was surprised.

"I am expecting no one, Mrs. Hastings."

"Personally I never had dealings with the circus, Miss Winter. Your visitor has the appearance of a *juggler,* to my way of thinking," said Mrs. Hastings, sweeping out.

Not having been invited into the house and philosophically leaning his small frame against the front door was the dwarf-like figure of Laurie Spindle. Kate rushed toward him.

"Oh, Laurie! Laurie! Where have you come from? Why are you in London? How did you find me?"

The beautiful girl and the little man clung together. Mrs. Hastings, raising her eyes heavenward, made off to the back parlor.

Laurie and Kate talked at the same time, stopped, laughed, continued to talk. Laurie had, it seemed, been engaged by Davenant. Wasn't that a stroke of good fortune? He

had called at the theater and met an old friend of his, no less
a crony than Gwynyth, and she had told him Kate's address.

They set off together to walk through the streets. Laurie,
not at first mentioning Kate's slight air of melancholy when
the first joy at seeing him was over, told her of his adventures
since the Newcastle days.

"And what about you, Beauty?" he said, finishing a saga of
the circuits.

The smile in her face died.

"Nothing at all. Parts of walking ladies. One role of four
lines."

He was deeply shocked.

"After his promises! You've complained and made him a
scene, of course."

"I couldn't."

"But that is ridiculous!" exclaimed Laurie, stopping to
turn and shake her fiercely by the arm. "Actors have to speak
out for themselves, otherwise who'll help them? Your trouble
is you were looked after too long by your father. You must
beard Davenant in his den. You're not afraid of him, are
you? What worse can he possibly give you than to be a walking lady? Comfort yourself with that."

It was very different advice from Buckley Vernon, who
had counseled a waiting game, assured her everything would
be well in time.

"How do you know what the beast is up to until you've
faced him with it?" demanded Laurie.

By the end of the walk to the theater, which took nearly an
hour, she was convinced. She had absorbed a little of the
small man's attitudes. If Laurie could confront fate, why, so
could she.

"You must hang about near his dressing room. It is the
oldest trick in the profession," Laurie said. "Then, as he
hoves into view, pounce!"

Kate took his advice. She quaked at the thought of ad-
dressing Davenant, afraid that he would reply sarcastically
and hurt her easily wounded feelings. After what seemed an

hour, she saw the actor swinging toward his dressing room, wearing one of his stylish dark blue coats with silver buttons.

"May I speak to you, sir?"

He stopped. She thought he had a wary look on that mobile face as he regarded her.

"I daresay."

She followed him meekly into the magnificent suite of rooms. He threw some play scripts on a table, then turned to her, folding his arms.

"Well?"

"It is about my work."

"What about it? I am not complaining."

She met his eyes, and at her expression he frowned.

"That was a jolly little part I gave you in *The Iron Chest*. Plenty of points to it."

"It was four lines, sir."

"I used to make my mark with *two*."

Kate had a feeling of painful dismay. She knew, now, that what she had refused to believe was true. She did have a genuine complaint against him. He had brought her here to London with promises, and for some reason decided to break them. He felt guilty about her. And it showed.

But Davenant had a fine technique for putting any actor asking for advancement into the wrong. Everybody came to Davenant. Everybody wanted favors. If they didn't like what he gave them, they could leave, could they not?

She looked earnestly, almost longingly, at him. He seemed to her, just then, so unobtainable as well as unkind that it was extraordinary to think he had carried her on a stage in his arms, and they had mingled their tears.

"To do such work, sir," she said timidly, "is very dull."

"Dull? How can that be? Do you know all the parts in *The Iron Chest* ?"

"I am not an understudy in the play."

"I never said you were, miss. Take your profession seriously, then time won't hang heavy on your hands. Learn the three I's. Imagination, intelligence and industry. Put your mind to *industry.* And that is valuable advice," he added, using a fall of the voice to show that the interview was over.

She was walking miserably down the passage when Augustus Bryson stopped her.

"Ah, Miss Winter. I have been thinking about the Viscountess and her visit. So gracious of her. And the word she had about you. She clearly feels that with my influence . . . of course, it will not be easy." He looked meaningfully at the door of Davenant's suite.

Sore at Davenant's treatment, heartsick, humiliated, Kate was so angry she could have screamed.

Her voice shook as she said, "Please do not trouble yourself."

"No trouble, I do assure you."

"I do not wish any kind of preference. Please refrain from speaking to Mr. Davenant. Or to anybody else."

Meeting her eyes, which were unusually bright and glittering, he bowed. It was clear the girl resented his help, and when it came down to it he didn't want to give it to her. That was a relief.

During the afternoon, Kate was not called for a rehearsal at which both Buckley and Laurie Spindle were needed. She went into the greenroom, sat down in a corner and tried to take Davenant's advice. She would learn all the female parts in that favorite play of his, *The Iron Chest.* But the words blurred, her mind would not work. Her career was coming to nothing. Davenant would never help her. And then there was Isabella. She'd tried to forget how angry her sister had made her, but Bryson had brought it back with renewed and violent bitterness. Did Isabella remember *nothing* of their lives together? Did she now look on Kate as a housemaid dependent on my Lady's recommendation to get employment?

Too miserable and angry to work and with four hours stretching between now and the time of the evening performance, she decided to go home. Home. That was a stupid word. Back to her lodgings, where she would stare at the chimney pots. Walking down the dusty streets, sometimes

jostled and pushed into the gutter, she thought of Isabella at
Bagot House, of long cool rooms, marble-floored, smelling
of roses . . .

When she let herself into the lodgings she heard Mrs.
Hastings' voice arguing and now and then a low reply, apparently from Mr. Hastings. Then the woman's voice again,
declaiming, complaining.

Kate toiled up the staircase. The arguing voices oppressed
her, and the smell of stale food and the dust which a long
sunbeam showed on windowsills and dirty windowpanes. She
opened her bedroom door.

Sib, the maid of all work, was standing at Kate's dressing
table, rifling through the drawers. When she saw Kate, she
gave a violent start and recoiled as if she expected a blow.

Kate came into the room slowly and shut the door.

"What have you taken, Sib?"

"Nothing."

"Please give it back."

The girl looked away, frightened and furious. How thin
she is, Kate thought, her bones stick out. Her face looks
dirty, but is it dirt? I've seen actors look like that from exhaustion. But Sib is dirty, too, her dress is torn and that
apron is disgusting . . .

Kate sat down on the bed. Sib stood facing her, terrified
and fierce as a wild animal.

"What have you taken of mine?"

"Look for yerself. Nothing. Didn't 'ave time," was the vicious answer. "How was I ter know you'd come 'ome this time
o' day. Yer never does."

"That's true. And there isn't much to take, is there? My
bracelet. The ring my mother gave me. My clothes, I suppose."

Sib took hold of the handle of a drawer and began to open
it and slam it. Open, slam, open, slam.

"Are you in trouble?"

"Whatyermean?"

The voice was so violent that Kate understood.

"I didn't mean a baby. I mean other trouble. Money or your family. Why did you have to steal?"

Not a word.

Kate sighed.

"Yer'll be off an' tell Missus and she'll throw me into the street, the old bitch, so off and tell her."

Kate saw with pity and horror that the girl's eyes, large, dark, the color of Isabella's, were full of tears.

"Of course I do not mean to tell Mrs. Hastings. What has it to do with her? Just don't do it again, or someone else will catch you and then you'll go to prison. Use your common sense. I know you won't tell me what the trouble is," Kate said, looking at the mute, stubborn face. "So get on with your work and we'll forget it ever happened."

Before Kate had finished speaking, the girl went past like a bird released from a net and rushed down the stairs.

Late that night after the performance when Kate returned home she discovered that Sib must have found the purse under Ellen's letters. It contained every penny she had in the world.

She simply did not know what to do. The money, saved in pence from her meager wages, was to pay Mrs. Hastings the next month's rent, which the landlady insisted on having in advance. It was also money for Kate's slender meals, bought in cook houses, eaten in the greenroom. It was for her laundry. For her very existence, living thinly from one week's pay to the next. It was impossible to hope she would get a farthing back from Sib. For all Kate knew Sib had stolen the money for a family nearly starving, a drunken father, a lover, who could say? Kate could not sleep and rose with the dawn. She set off to walk to the theater.

It was very early, and in Covent Garden the crowds of carts, horses, men, baskets, was so great that she could scarcely make her way. Great toppling masses of flowers and fruit were everywhere. The pavement was thick with petals, crushed oranges, cabbage leaves, the air smelled like the inside of a fruit barrel. She felt bruised and stupid when she finally escaped the shouting carters and shying horses and turned into the alleyway and made her way to the stage door.

Jack, his nose in the morning newspaper, looked up at her.

"Early bird, Miss Winter."

"You once told me that Mr. Davenant is always early, Jack."

"Guvnor come in half an hour since."

Kate walked down the corridor for the second time in two days. It was horrible to be forced to return.

The door of his suite was open as it always was unless Davenant was closeted with an actor, and when she tapped on it his voice, full-toned, with the edge that gave it its beauty, called, "Come!"

Davenent, sitting at a desk under the high window, was busy with a pile of letters, and he turned round to look at her.

"Good grief, you again? What do you want at this ungodly hour, pray? Come to scold me about your career again. Have you no shame?"

"It is nothing to do with my career, sir."

He gestured to her to sit down, but she remained standing. She made a sober little figure in her shabby cotton dress of gray and white and that unbecoming bonnet. Governessy. Why doesn't she dress like an actress, he thought.

"Someone came to my lodgings during the performance last night and stole all my money. I wonder if you could help me."

"Help you catch the thief, you mean?"

"Oh, no."

"Why not? Thieves must be brought to justice. You've informed your lodging house keeper, I take it?"

"No."

"I don't make much of that," he said. "You don't wish the thief caught. You don't tell your landlady of the crime. What *do* you want?"

"A little money."

"Indeed. For what?"

She had lived too long in the company of poverty to be ashamed of it, and although this man was powerful and famous she had never been afraid of him. It seemed to her that he was duty-bound to help her.

"Mr. Davenant, I cannot pay my rent, which is due today. Neither can I eat or pay for my laundry. I had saved enough to live for a month. Now I must manage until I receive my wages again."

"Yes, yes, all very sad," he said impatiently. "What is more interesting is why you don't wish thieves apprehended and landladies informed."

"Because I know who did it and the person is in distress."

He looked at her in deliberately feigned amazement.

"Beware, Miss Winter. You are turning into one of those milksop heroines you played so constantly in Newcastle."

"At least I had something to play in Newcastle," she snapped.

He raised his eyebrows.

"Dissatisfied here, are you?"

No answer.

"Well, well, I suppose we can't let poor Nelly starve," he said. "Here are two sovereigns." He took the coins out of his pocket and, coming over to her, pressed them into her hand. The coins were still warm.

"That is too much, Mr. Davenant. One sovereign would be quite—"

"Stuff."

Taking the hand which was not holding the money, he lifted her slowly to her feet. His grip tightened, so that it was difficult not to cry out. She felt as if her finger bones would be broken. He was looking at her, not coolly as he usually did, but appraisingly, running his eyes up and down her figure. It was as if he could see through her garments. She instinctively shrank back, trying to withdraw her hand, but he gripped it more strongly.

"Well, miss. And how do you intend to repay me for my munificence?"

Before she could answer—before she realized what he was going to do—he pulled her into his arms, kissed her violently and pressed his body against hers. Holding her in arms like steel, he put his hand down her bodice. She struggled frantically, but she was little and light and helpless as he continued to press his open mouth to her closed lips, to push his hand down in search of her nipple, which he fondled between two fingers. When he finally let her go she was so angry she was weeping.

"How *dare* you! How dare you touch me—do you think I am a—a—" She could not use the word. "One of those women! Take your horrible money, to think you can b-buy me, you treat me like a—" The word again refused to be spoken in her disgust and rage, and with a gesture of fury she threw the sovereigns so violently across the room that they hit the further wall.

"Now there's a stupid thing!" he exclaimed. "I show my generosity, help in your hour of need, and you throw my money about as if it were so much muck. Tut tut. That will not do, miss, it will not do."

He walked across the room, knelt down and peered along the floor until he found the sovereigns, which had rolled under a table. He returned to Kate.

She could not meet his eyes but looked away, knowing a button was ripped from her bodice and too ashamed to drag the open dress together with her hand.

"So it is still the virtuous virgin, is it?" he said in a harsh, mocking voice. The struggle with her had left him, it seemed, perfectly cool. But his blue eyes looked dangerous. "You intend to cling to that, do you? Curious. I imagined—was I wrong—that you found my *person* not to be exactly despised."

He came closer, and she blushed. It was not just a mild blush but a flood of scarlet, which made her feel her face had been scalded. She blushed from rage at being treated like a whore—she could still feel his fingers catching at her nipple—and from shame because he had rightly guessed her strong attraction for him.

"I came to ask your help," she said, her voice hoarse and unnaturally loud. "And you treat me disgustingly. I cannot stay at this theater—cannot—"

"Calm yourself, for the sake of heaven, woman," he interrupted impatiently, "What a to-do about a mere kiss. I shall not demand the payment you are so afraid of. Violating virgins has never been to my taste. A woman, for me, must be willing if she is to satisfy me. So forget your pious indignation, miss. It is damned dull. As for leaving my theater, you may please yourself. *I* shall not require you to leave over such a trifle. Here, then."

He put the sovereigns into her hand.

"Take the money, and see you don't waste it. It is hard-earned and should be respected. Not pitched into the faces of one's friends."

She hesitated, then said coldly, "Thank you. I will pay it back."

"So I should think. Now leave me, please."

Even that. Even his arrogant way of dismissing her after what had happened made her angry and humiliated all over again.

When she was alone she thought of him with fury and shame, and however much she tried to push away the remembrance of his kisses, his exploring hand down her bodice, she could not. Only when her thoughts had finally exhausted her did she begin to see the matter in proportion. Davenant was famous and powerful, she could see now that he had any woman he wished for. He had thought she was willing to be his kept woman, the next in line. It confirmed her jealous suspicions about Jessie Ramsey, who was given the roles that she herself wanted so desperately. Davenant only gave to a woman if she gave in return. Her body. Herself. As for the money, the two sovereigns, Kate decided it was perfectly proper to accept them. Davenant was responsible for her being in London—indeed, he was responsible for her poverty. She was glad she had not been forced to ask Laurie or Buckley for money. When she had better roles— and it *must* come that she would, even if it was never to be at the Royalty—she would pay Davenant back the despised sovereigns. She would do that with pleasure and with spite.

She was insulted at his low opinion of her and despised him for his loose morals. Her own were rigid. The old bad days in the theater were changing, and she was glad of it. She remembered audiences when she was in her early teens, their filthy language and behavior, the way they looked on actresses as harlots. It was not like that today, and Kate thanked heaven for it. As for Davenant, he had been in his twenties when George IV was on the throne, and everybody knew what morals were like *then*. The way he embraced me, what he took for granted are not only wrong, they're out of date, she thought, with twenty-year-old disdain.

She paid Mrs. Hastings the rent. Her landlady counted the money carefully and locked it in a sewing box.

"If one could only have *guests* and not be forced to take emoluments," said Mrs. Hastings, sighing. "But I regard you, Kate, as a friend. Almost as a daughter. Will you take a cup of tea?"

Kate also went in search of Sib, whom she found on her hands and knees scrubbing the stone-floored basement kitchen. Sib looked up from under sweaty black hair.

"Whatyerwant?"

"Don't look at me like that, Sybil, I am not going to eat you. Mrs. Hastings has dropped off to sleep, and Mr. Hastings is out. I came to give you this."

Kate held out her hand with sixpence in it.

Sib regarded the hand as if it were a serpent.

"Keep yer money. I don't want it."

"Don't be a donkey. You've already had my money so don't bother to deny it. I can spare sixpence. Why not," said Kate, without much hope, "at least buy a new apron?"

Sib pocketed the money in silence.

Kate thought it likely that the sixpence had made her an enemy, but to her amusement Sib did buy a new apron, and occasionally brushed her hair and washed her face. Meeting Kate on the stairs, she actually gave a wink.

But if things at her lodgings were slightly better, Kate had made matters infinitely worse by refusing Davenant's embrace. He began to single her out. For ridicule. He picked her up on the smallest point, declaring there was never such a laughably bad performance as she gave in the two sentences grudgingly allotted to her.

Kate found his persecution hard to bear. When he lashed her with his sarcasms she felt as if he were physically beating her. Her friends were shocked at his treatment, declaring that it was inexcusable to be so cruel to an actress who was a professional and was given scarcely a word to say. Gwynyth made her tea. Laurie Spindle sat on an upturned skip and talked shop to comfort her. Kindest of all was Buckley. It was comforting to have this handsome man as her friend; *he* made her feel of consequence. He sought her out, flattered her with his look, sometimes gallantly pressed her hand to his lips.

It was painful to be ill-treated by Davenant, yet in a way she understood it. He was having his male revenge because she had refused him. Some of the most hostile actresses began to hope Davenant would get rid of her; particularly as she was pretty.

The leaves of the plane trees had begun, very slightly, to yellow, and the last dinners and balls were being given before the great houses were closed. Society would soon be gone to what most of them infinitely preferred—the country life. Since his return Denys had been so glad to be reunited with Isabella that he was at her side constantly. He approved of everything—the new house still being prepared for the furniture, her choice of silks and colors, her new gowns, the hot bright weather, the interminable dinners, the drives in the

park by his lovely wife's side where he sat lazily, saluting
friends galloping past. Except for his morning rides, Denys
was never away from her. It was weeks since she had set eyes
on Buckley.

Until one morning during the last week of the season
when Denys and Robert decided they must go to Sussex
ahead of the family to buy some new carriage horses. Denys
was full of apologies to his "dearest," but he and Robert did
not trust the agent at Bagot Park to buy the horses because,
"poor fellow, he does not have the eye."

Isabella assured him he must not feel guilty for a moment,
and was tenderly kissed for her goodness. When Denys and
Robert had driven away she ordered the smaller Bagot carriage to take her to Regent's Park. On her way she would call
in, she told the coachman, to leave a word for her sister at the
theater.

It was a letter to Buckley.

"Imperative I see you at once. My new house Finstock
Lodge, Regent's Park, any hour between now and four. Do
not fail me for God's sake. I."

It was sultry and airless and Isabella alighted from the carriage and handed the footman the key for the house. He
opened the door and stood back.

"Don't keep the carriage waiting for me, Edwards. Lady
Fanny needs it, and I am meeting Mr. Wreford. We may be
some time. He will bring me home."

The footman bowed, the horses were whipped up and
trotted away. As the sound of hooves and wheels slowly faded, Isabella went into the house, leaving the door open. Lad-
ders leaned against walls. Furniture was pushed in corners
and shrouded in sheets. There were wallpapers, paints, carpets, paintings stitched into cotton coverings. It was like a
play before the scene was set.

She looked back into the park where the grass was dying
after the long summer and the trees were turning brown. In

the distance the lake gleamed. Despite the thinness of her muslin dress, she felt suffocatingly hot. She pulled off her long gloves; her hands were sweating.

For half an hour she wandered through the empty and unfinished house like a ghost. Then she heard a sound and rushed into the hall. Buckley came through the open door.

He stood, with the panorama of the deserted park behind him, smiling at her, dressed in dark green, his tall hat in his hand. There was something untidy and rough about him after Denys's immaculate elegance.

"Bella. I am sorry I could not come sooner. Rehearsals. How is it with you, hmm?"

When she saw him she had the falling sensation in the pit of her stomach.

"Buck."

Answering the note in her voice, he strode across and took her into his arms, pressed his open mouth to hers, enjoying forcing her lips open—it had been something they often did, she resisting, he taking pleasure in making her yield. She felt giddy when he released her.

"I suppose there is a bed somewhere in this house?" he said, putting one hand against her mouth.

"No. There is nothing."

"And you are too much the aristocrat to lie on the ground."

He laced his arms round her waist, pressed his hardened body against her so that she could feel him, fondled her breasts through the thin dress, rocked her to and fro. She dragged herself from him, her senses reeling, taut with desire.

"Don't touch me like that or I will never be able to talk."

"Why should you talk? Don't talk. Mmm."

But she still kept at a distance from him and, seeing his expression, no longer excited by her resistance but growing cold, she burst out, "Don't be angry! I have so longed for you—I do now! I thought I would be sick with want. All these weeks. But there is something you must know. I am with child."

Over and over again Isabella had imagined speaking these words. Her thoughts never went further than that. She did not know how he would take them, what he would do. Rush to her? Love her?

He said, drawling affectedly, "An heir for the Viscount. That will make you popular with the nobs."

She put her hands, unconsciously, to her heart.

"Don't joke. I cannot bear it."

With a strained, worldly smile he said, "What do you want me to say, my love?"

"It is your child. Yours and mine."

"Now, why should that be? You're a married woman, Bella, and in cases like this—"

"Buckley," she interrupted, convulsively gripping his arm, "I am more than two months gone and Denys has been with me but two weeks."

There was a pause.

He stared.

"What do you want me to do?"

Isabella sighed. Now he accepted it, now he shared it, she was no longer afraid. A little color came back into her cheeks, and she loosened her tight grasp and took his hand. He pressed it kindly, and a rush of suffocating tenderness came over her. She loved him so intensely that anything, everything was possible. What happiness just to stand here with him knowing that in a while they would make love, that there was a whole hour together. Even bearing his child made her happy.

"Oh, Buck, what shall we do?" she said, with a timid smile. "Do you think we might go away together? Would it not be wonderful? I shall not be peniless, there was money settled on me when I was married, and Denys is so generous. Why cannot we share our life, have our child? It is what we want, isn't it? Isn't it?"

She threw her arms round his neck. As he embraced her and she knew he wanted her, she thought they would lie down on the floor and make love. She strained against him. But he said no, not here, not with the child, wasn't it sometimes dangerous? "I could never be gentle with you. Never," he said.

Her body demanded the pressure and thrust of his, she ached for it, but she knew instinctively that he was not going to take her now and accepted it, holding his hand almost meekly. They went out of the house, and she locked the doors. Along the road under the trees Buckley saw a hackney carriage and hailed it for her. He stood by while Isabella settled herself, arranging her lacy skirts, putting out a gloved hand, which he pressed.

"You will hear from me."

"Do you promise?"

"I swear," he said, making a kissing movement with his lips. She looked at him with heavy eyes, still taut, unreleased. The hackney carriage trotted away through the park gates.

Buckley stood for a while staring at the house, its windows shuttered, its door locked. Then, at the park, where the grass was dying and nobody seemed about in this dozing afternoon. Whistling absently, he made his way out of the park along the dusty streets. What a mess, he thought, what an unlucky mess. Isabella was as pretty a piece of flesh as he'd known for years, but did the stupid fool really imagine he'd run off with her? She was mad. Why, his career was only just beginning to work. God knows it wasn't every actor who had the chance of working with Davenant. Go back to the provinces and live on twopence with a pregnant woman! And she'd be penniless if he knew anything about the nobility and the way they behaved with women who played them false. What would life be with a squawking brat and a woman who'd learned to live rich? There was another thing, too. The little matter of seducing a Viscount's wife. Duelling was supposed to be a thing of the past, it would soon be against the law, but it was accepted among the nobility. Someone told him a man had been killed in Battersea Fields only last week. "A matter of honor" had been settled with revolvers. Buckley despised such claptrap; but Isabella's husband, that Viscount, might think very differently. He might consider it an excellent thing to kill the man who had broken his marriage and impregnated his wife.

He would kill me, too, thought Buckley. Men like that are prime shots. I've never handled a revolver in my life except a stage prop. God, what a coil. Why didn't I keep my hands off her? But it had been Isabella, not he, who had done the pursuing. He'd never been able to say no to a beautiful woman who, by her insistent desire, proved how irresistible he was.

He was hot and disagreeable when he arrived at the theater. The stone-walled building was gratefully cool backstage, and he heard the familiar sound of actors arriving for the evening performance, laughter, slamming doors. He went into his dressing room, wrenched his satin stock loose and threw himself into a chair.

There was a tap at the door.

"Go away."

A freckled face, a tress of red hair, peered in.

"I only called for a moment," said Kate, "but if you are working of course I won't stay."

"Come in," he said, brightening. He scarcely remembered that this shabby little thing with hair the color of new money was the sister of Isabella. This girl was an actress and a professional; he respected her.

"My parents have returned from Ireland," she said. "They will be in London tonight lodging at Holborn Bars. Would you take supper with us, Mr. Vernon? They'd be so glad to see you."

"I would like to very much."

Kate looked pleased.

"Laurie has accepted, too."

She gave him such a pretty look that he was unable to resist answering in a flirtatious tone.

"Why do you call Laurie by his first name? You never do that with me."

"Because he is old, I suppose. Like an uncle."

"I could be a cousin, couldn't I?"

"I'm not sure."

"Of course I could. Try it. It's not so difficult. Say 'Buckley.'"

She looked at him, laughed and said, "Buckley."

"That's better. Very nice, in fact. I am glad Davenant has stopped harassing you lately. Poor girl. You had a most unhappy time."

"I knew why he was like that—" Kate began and blushed.

Always sex-conscious, he understood at once what she meant.

"Did he make advances toward you? Now I understand his behavior. What a swine!"

He was full of chivalrous indignation.

Kate sat down, crouching as she did sometimes, arms folded. She looked very young.

"It is sometimes a nuisance, you know, being twenty and unattached and an actress. It was different on the circuits, you see, because Papa was there. I know he never seemed to pay us much attention, but his presence mattered. The men, any men, respected Bella and me because we were daughters with parents. Now it's as if I am fair game. That's what they think. I do hate it so."

"You have Laurie Spindle. And you have me."

"Oh, yes." She looked at him in a way which, despite her commonsensical nature, was very innocent.

"I am grateful."

He liked her very much just then. Then something occurred to him which by its very simplicity seemed an inspired way out.

"Kate. May I say something to you? As a newly accepted cousin of yours?"

"I am not sure." She had heard something change in his voice.

He went to her and took her hand. An hour ago he had held Isabella's hand, hot and damp, heavy with emeralds and diamonds. Kate's hand was cool, small, ringless and firm.

"It would do me the greatest honor," he said, "if you would, one day soon, consider that we might be married."

* * *

The snow lay crisping on the fields for weeks. It was icy cold. Sometimes a half-thaw began but then the slush froze and it began to snow again. A freezing wind blew across the fields from the sea.

The family had returned to Bagot Park at the end of the summer and had been in residence for months. The green leather visitors' book with the Bagot coronet on the cover, which always lay open on a table in the entrance hall, was filled with signatures. Carriages and riders came and went at all times and in all weathers, there were never less than a dozen visitors, sometimes the number rose to thirty or more. At night the windows shone and music was heard faintly across the icy fields.

The house was far more lively than the old "mausoleum" in London disliked by the Earl. The Earl, his son and nephew all preferred the country, they liked to live among their tenantry, liked the business of the estates, the hard riding and daily hunting, the cold rooms and blazing fires, the crowds of visitors, the bustle of a great house full of people. Lady Clare was much in demand in the country and often away staying with friends for days at a time, returning with more admirers to dangle after her. She grew prettier but never more pleasant to Isabella. Lady Fanny was busy with guests from morning until night.

Isabella took little part in the dinners, games, music and winter fun. Once when she was in the drawing room and the guests were dancing, she fainted. After that Denys refused to allow her to tire herself with people, and she kept much in her own rooms, occasionally coming downstairs for a while to see visitors.

She looked very haggard during the final months of her pregnancy. She slept badly. Often on winter nights, uncomfortable with her growing bulk, she rose in the middle of the night and sat wrapped in a shawl, looking through a gap in the curtains at the fields under the snow. But she never woke, never rose without Denys waking at once, as if she had shaken him by the arm.

"How are you, my dearest? Let me ring for Hopton. You need a hot drink. Your feet are cold. Let me wrap this round you."

Tired after a day in the cold air, deeply asleep, he was always instantly awake and beside her, sharing everything with his gentle, tender company.

The Earl considered such solicitude absurd, and scoffed to Robert, "What a fuss the boy makes. He's like an old hen."

"Deno has a kind heart, sir, and Isabella is not well."

"Pooh. When Denys was born I was out hunting. Remember the day distinctly. We found a fox in Queen's Spinney, but the beggar got clean away across the river."

From the very first, Isabella's health was not good. She felt continually sick, and sometimes so unwell it was as if she'd been poisoned. She had no energy, and was languid and exhausted. But she behaved very well, and Denys thought her courage a marvelous thing. That, at least, made her smile. She did not say, because he wouldn't let her talk of the past, that *she'd* been reared in a world where nobody complained when they were ill. What was the use, when there was a performance to be got through? As a sick child she had been bundled into a shawl and left in her parents' dressing room or in bed in their lodgings, longing for her mother to come home. Now, if she gave the slightest grimace of pain, Denys was at her side. She accepted such proof of love. He had always been like that.

She forgot for days that the child leaping inside her, growing so heavy, was not his. The first weeks when she had known she was pregnant, when she'd had the lunatic hope of running away with Buckley, seemed so long ago she could scarcely remember them. Much, much longer ago than when she had been an actress and come to Bagot Park and first set eyes on Denys.

Sometimes fate, or God, did spare you from ordeals, she once thought. Her mother and Kate had called at Bagot House to tell her the news of Kate's coming marriage. By chance Isabella was prostrate with a migraine, something she

had had on rare occasions since a child; it had been Denys
who was told the news, who had kissed them kindly and congratulated them, explaining that his Isabella was too sick to
see them.

"She will be so disappointed not to see you and so glad for
you all."

So Isabella was spared from being told of Buckley's perfidy
by Kate. Denys sent a magnificent wedding present of silver.
Isabella wrote her congratulations. The Bagots left London
for Sussex the day following her family's visit and she had
not seen Kate, Buckley or her parents since then, although
her mother and Kate both wrote regularly.

Her passion for Buckley, the feverish desire, the ecstatic
pleasure of being in his arms, had utterly vanished. She remembered those feelings rarely and with a sort of wonder.
She was now simply the Viscount's lady about to give birth—
possibly to a son. She lay in a four-poster bed and watched
the fire twinkling and the snow whirling outside the windows. Denys strode in, bringing an auriole of winter air, a
sweet smell of the country clinging to his clothes.

Isabella's son was born in March, earlier than expected,
with a long painful labor which she bore with great fortitude.
The child was a small, perfect boy with a thatch of dark hair
and a nose like a miniature beak. He was, declared the entranced Lady Fanny, the image of his grandfather. It was decided by the family and not by his mother that he should be
christened Frederick, which was the Earl's first name.

Denys was scarcely interested in the baby for the first day,
he was so relieved, so full of joy that Isabella was safe. He
had been more frightened than she, had sat with her until
the doctor and the monthly nurse drove him from the room,
then waited in the outside dressing room in an agony of
mind as sharp as Isabella's birth pains.

Now it was a time of the greatest joy. Everywhere in the
house people heard the sound of Carteret's laugh.

Robert was greatly interested by the new baby. He took to
calling into the nursery next door to Isabella's bedroom and

then coming to see her with reports of the baby's progress.

"Young Freddy knows me already. When I stood by his cot just now he distinctly winked," said Robert, coming briskly into Isabella's room. "I see I have an ally there."

Isabella, finishing her luncheon which she ate with little appetite, smiled.

Denys, for the first time since the baby's birth, had been persuaded by his father and a score of the Bagot visitors to go hunting. Isabella's tall windows were slightly ajar and she had heard the hunt leave, the sound of the horns, the bay of hounds. The weather was misty and the snow had long ago melted. Spring was nearly here.

She lay against a pile of pillows, wearing a tiny cap of stiffened lace which Robert amusedly thought looked like a halo. Everything about her was soft and lacy. Her dresses always reminded him of Herrick's poem *Julia's Clothes*: "the liquefaction of her clothes." Now the child was born the haggard look which had made her olive-skinned face so plain was gone. She was like a tea rose.

"Stay and talk to me, Robert. It is wearisome in bed. I do so long to get up."

"When shall you do that, Bella?"

He was the only Bagot who called her that. "Not a foot on the ground until Sunday, Nurse says. You would think nobody in the world had ever had a baby before."

"Ah, but this isn't any old baby, is it?"

He laughed, looking at her with eyes as dark as her own. Robert is very good-looking, she thought idly. She liked his narrow bony face, springy dark hair. He had an air of quickness, impatience, of being in command of life, taking it over. He was as strong as the old Earl in a way.

"What a devoted father Deno is, to be sure," he said, burying his nose in a huge bowl of white narcissi which Denys had brought her. The flowers were beside her bed, and the air smelled of their heavy scent. There were other presents from Denys. A round silver box with a cherub on it, a bracelet of pearls on a gold chain, a piece of porcelain of a child crowned with daisies, an India shawl.

"He is glad Frederick is a boy," she said languidly.

"The Bagot heir."

"But you were the heir until Frederick arrived."

He burst out laughing.

"Has it been weighing on your mind, cousin? Certainly I used to come second after Deno. But you and he will have a quiverful. And with every boy, Bella, I shall get pushed a little further down the ladder. Think of that. Think how I shall shake in my shoes when the monthly nurse arrives again."

"You don't take anything seriously."

"It looks as if I'll have to take the christening seriously," he said briskly. "My uncle has asked me to help Fanny with it, and I fear Fanny makes work rather than simplifies it. Freddy will, of course, be done at St. Mary the Virgin like all the other Bagots who kneel about in marble glaring at us every Sunday. Have you ever noticed the third Earl and his wife under that huge canopy? I wonder what annoyed them in 1572? The vicar's sermons, I daresay.

"The reception will be here and we think there'll be about two hundred and fifty. Bagots enjoy christenings."

"Do we have luncheon or will it be dinner afterward?" asked Isabella.

She had always followed her mother's advice after she married Denys, remembering "never to show her ignorance," picking up from Lady Fanny or the Earl anything she did not know, rarely asking questions even of Denys. It was usually easy, and she was very quick. But with Robert she never minded in the least showing there were society matters of which she was still perfectly ignorant.

"Luncheon first. Then the carriages to the church. Then champagne in the blue drawing room, and the cake and Freddy to be shown to the admiring ladies—you know he has to be shown to the staff next morning, too, Bella, and they have their own cake quite as big but with a different recipe,

Mrs. Judge informed me this morning. Forty or so are staying at present, so we thought we might dance. What do you
say?"

She smiled and stretched.

"Lovely to dance again. It all sounds delicious. So important. And all for baby Frederick."

"Yes, Freddy is important," was the matter-of-fact reply.

When he left her Isabella lay back for a while listening to
the sounds of the busy house in the distance, to voices on the
terrace, to a horse trotting by, a dog barking, to the birds.
Spring was on its way, her baby was born, everything was safe
and beautiful. She would write to her mother with the news.
Kate, too. She faintly smiled at the thought of Buckley learning in such a way that he had a son. For a moment she
thought of the little creature in his elaborate cot next door,
with the Bagot crest in silver holding the transparent curtains embroidered with flowers, the nurse seated beside him.
Would little "important" Frederick look like Buckley? In her
sanguine forgetting-yesterday way she was certain he would
not. She was filled with dreamy, idle, pleasing, selfish
thoughts. It was spring, and she was twenty years old.

Part Three

Chapter Thirteen

KATE STOOD AT THE WINDOW of her Kensington house, slowly brushing her hair. She was thinking about the theater. It was 1844, and in the last four years it seemed to her that her life had been swallowed, completely absorbed, by child-bearing. The theater, her passion, her great love, had been pushed to one side. She had married Buckley, born him a daughter and a son, and learned the art needed for living with a difficult man. But now she was beginning to feel she might, perhaps, think about herself again.

It was a dull spring morning, and she could hear the children romping downstairs. There were bursts of laughter, scuffling, slamming doors. She frowned. How loudly Matilda shouts, she thought, and how I dislike the noise of raised voices in the house. Buckley had already left for the theater, and Kate decided to spend a quiet morning, walking, reading and thinking, while the nursemaid took the children into Kensington Gardens to use up some of those high spirits in the open air.

The London season was beginning again, the social columns of the newspapers announced the return of the Duke of This and the Marchioness of That to town. There were elegant riders in the Row now, and the great Piccadilly houses behind their high walls had begun to open their shutters like eyes.

Kate, too, felt she was waking up. She knew she'd changed. The births of her children had given her new energy and a new glow. The men friends whom Buckley brought home to dine were more gallant than they used to be. If only, she thought, I could use my attraction to draw audiences instead of merely friends!

She envied Buckley the progress he had made: Davenant now gave him leading roles, Buckley's good looks and ease on the stage were "useful"—Davenant's word. Audiences liked Buckley, but Kate knew they did not fall in love with him. They still did with Davenant. When he was on a stage they looked at nobody else. Perhaps Buckley's lack of magic is why Davenant keeps him in the company, she thought. It is odd that a great actor can be jealous. But it's just as curious that Buckley is actually jealous of a talent as huge as Davenant's. As if Buckley could ever measure up to *him.*

Happily married, the mother of two young children, she was infinitely further removed from Davenant now. It was strange to remember that in those forgotten circuit days she had played Cordelia, and he had carried her onstage in those muscular actor's arms. She had never lost her fascinated feelings for him, and when she saw him backstage she always had a restless, almost angry sensation, as if something was irretrievably lost that once might have been hers. What could that be?

Kate was fond of her husband and treated his feelings tenderly. She never regretted her marriage and in her way she loved him. Buckley was selfish, but what man was not? He was generous with money, liked to laugh, was easy to please except when sunk in his moods of self-dissatisfaction. These came over him when he felt that success was not arriving fast enough. He would become gloomy and silent, asking himself why fame was not beginning to pour down on him like a river of golden sovereigns. Kate never comforted him at these times, and did not approve of his self-indulgence and vanity. She kept herself and the children out of his way when he was in his dark mood.

Buckley visited the Garrick Club a good deal: he liked to be seen with well-known actors and authors. When a gloomy fit was on him he would go to the Garrick, drink too much and arrive home intoxicated and vulgar. Kate, with a calm face, was silently angry. But it would all blow over and life became pleasant again.

The Vernons lived in a not-large house in the village of Kensington, which was less than an hour by carriage from the theater. But it was a country place, with farms and stretching fields, and the children thrived. Matilda, now three and a half, and William, a sturdy two, went for country walks every day, liked to visit the farmyard down the road, watched the cows being milked. They were handsome children, Matilda much resembled Buckley with curling hair and gray eyes; William had Kate's red hair, straight nose and freckles.

There was a knock on her bedroom door as Kate was tying on her bonnet.

The nursemaid, a pretty blonde girl called Mary Anne, poked her head round the door. She was too pretty, Kate thought, but what could one do when staff were hard to find?

"Letter for you, ma'am. And a brougham at the door waiting. I do wonder why!"

"That will do, Mary Anne," said Kate, in much the repressive voice her mother still used. Mary Anne bounced out of the room again and began shouting at the children. Kate was about to spring up and scold her when she turned the letter over and recognized the thick, scrawling writing. It was from Davenant.

From surprise, from a kind of intuition, she blushed. She tore open the envelope.

Scrawled across a card with the Royalty Theater coat of arms at the top were a few words:

"Come to the theater this morning if you please. Brougham will bring you. Trust not incommoded. H.D."

She stared at the card for a moment or two. It was the first
time since she had left Newcastle as a raw girl that Davenant
had shown interest in her as an actress. It must mean something. But what?

She put the letter in her silk muff, bent to look at herself in
the glass, rearranged a loop of red hair against her cheek
and went down the staircase.

There was a flick of Mary Anne's white apron, a giggle of
children's voices from behind the dining room door.

"Mary Anne."

"Yes, ma'am?" said the girl, coming out of the room as
guiltily as if she were one of the children.

"Please take Miss Matilda and Master Billy out for their
morning walk at once. You know I do not wish them to play
about the house. Tell Cook Mr. Vernon and I will not be in
for luncheon, we will both be at the theater. And see Miss
Matilda eats properly. No getting down from the table."

Mary Anne said meek yesses to all the instructions and
waited until Kate left the house. When the front door was
closed Matilda put a round red-cheeked face round the dining room door and made a hideous grimace at her. Mary
Anne gave her a slap. Matilda, since her mother was out of
the way, did not bother to cry.

Kate settled herself in the brougham and the journey to
London began. The winding road under tall old elm trees
was deserted except when the mail coach went galloping
noisily by. She saw farm carts behind great patient drays, and
a man cutting the first crop of early hay. She took the card
from her muff and looked at it again. Davenant. The man
who mystifyingly had brought her away from her parents,
then given her no acting parts worth having, treated her almost contemptuously. How unhappy he had made her, and
how she'd longed to understand why.

But then her life had dramatically changed. She had married her dear Buckley. It had been, Kate thought sentimen-
tally, a whirlwind courtship.

Davenant had not been either pleased or kind when she broke the news to him. He'd had the gall to tell her that if she married Buckley she would be "wasting her talent." Kate had answered, very sharply, that on the contrary it had been Davenant who had wasted her talent. He hadn't liked it when she said that. For a moment she had thought he was going to explain something to her. But all he'd done was stare at her oddly and then say nothing. Kate had the idea, perhaps it was vain and stupid but she somehow believed it, that her marriage hurt Davenant. She felt pleased at that.

She had of course continued to act at the Royalty, and her roles were never any larger or more important. But child-bearing meant a great deal of absence from the company; as time went by she knew Davenant had no interest in her at all. *She* wasn't useful.

Until now?

She was so lost in thought that when the horses were reined in, she saw with surprise that she was already at the stage door. Jack, the stage doorkeeper, greeted her as a friend.

"Coming back to us then, Miss Winter? Guvnor sent word he's expecting you."

Walking along the passages on the ground floor, the first person Kate saw was Gwynyth.

"Kate!"

The two women kissed fondly, looking—Kate in lilac silk, Gwynyth in rusty black—like figures of Youth and Age.

The door of Davenant's suite was open. Kate tapped lightly and went into the room. He was at his desk, his back to the door, and without turning round said, "Sit down, my girl. I will be with you shortly."

Davenant went on writing. The quill made a loud scratching sound and suddenly caught the paper and spurted. He swore under his breath. He continued to write.

Kate studied the back of his head. His plentiful hair was graying and broke into curls on the nape of a neck as thick as a column. That thick neck might be the reason for his extraordinary voice. His shoulders were heavy, he was not as tall as Buckley. Kate, accustomed to Buckley's grace, thought Davenant's shape, though powerful, very middle-aged. There was nothing pliant about it.

He finished the letter, sealed it, addressed it, then swung round.

He looked at the young woman, in her discreet, stylish dress of lavender silk with braided epaulettes and flounced skirts. She met his eye with interest.

"When is your next lying-in?" he demanded.

She was excited by being alone with him, and couldn't help laughing.

"Does it matter to you, sir?"

The answer seemed to annoy him.

"That's a damned stupid question, Kate."

"I was only teasing you."

"Then don't waste my time."

He was making it clear that if in the long distant past he had made advances to her he had no such intention now. She felt he looked at her as a sculptor might at a lump of clay.

"You've never played Shakespeare, have you?"

Before she could answer he held up his hand.

"Don't tell me you played every role while you were on the circuits at the ripe old age of sixteen. The point is are you up to *my* Shakespeare?"

Another actress might have exclaimed at once that she was waiting like a greyhound in the slips for any—every— Shakespeare role. Kate said nothing.

"Know how to make 'em laugh?" said Davenant sharply.

"Oh, yes."

"Indeed?"

"Yes," was the firm reply.

He picked up the quill and turned it this way and that in his hand.

"I'll tell you something curious, Kate. The Shakespeare comedies are coming back. That's odd, eh? When I was a young nobody, managers wouldn't have dared try *Twelfth Night*. People thought it was stuff. What they wanted was *Lear* and *Othello*. Shakespeare's comedies collected dust on top shelves. Forgotten. Now it is all different. Do you know what audiences want? Romance. Romance!"

"Do you dislike romance?"

"Me? I am the most romantic man alive," he said savagely. "So what is on the bill of fare today? *As You Like It.*"

She was silent again. She had an eloquent way of being so.

"You think I treated you badly in the past, don't you?" he suddenly said.

"Not after I was married."

"And before that?"

"Very."

Meeting her eyes steadily fixed on him he appeared—for Davenant—very slightly uncomfortable.

"You are not still holding it against me that I gave you a kiss donkey's years ago? I apologized at the time for succumbing to your beauty. Always thought you a taking little thing."

"Neither of us is referring to that."

He looked at her slyly as if making up his mind about something.

"Oh, very well. I know I promised I would do something for you when you came to London. Now, do not interrupt, hear me out. The fact is, I ran into difficulties. The Royalty was a damned sight more costly than I'd reckoned."

"I don't understand."

"Kate, use your wits. Jessie Ramsey is the daughter of an old friend. In plain English, Ramsey lent me a considerable sum of money toward the lease. If it were not for Ramsey, you and I would never have been at the Royalty at all. I pay my debts."

There was a pause.

"And what does that look mean, pray?" he said, gazing at her.

Almost involuntarily Kate said, "Jessie Ramsey was more to you than the daughter of a man who lent you money."

The moment she had spoken she could have bitten out her tongue.

"*Was* she, now?" he said mockingly. "And what has such an

indelicate subject to do with you? However, I will have mercy on you and not expect you to answer that question. Besides. Jessie Ramsey has decided to retire. The long and the short of it is that the lass is to be married."

Years ago, in another life, Kate remembered the exit of a marble Venus, one broken hand accusingly pointing. But it was she who had had the Venus removed. I was stronger then, she thought.

"So," said Davenant, who had been watching her thoughtfully. "*Du courage.*"

"Oh, I don't need that."

He raised his eyebrows.

"I can see that you don't. Here's the matter in hand, then. I thought I would offer you Rosalind in *As You Like It.* How does that strike you?"

He stood up and grasped her hands. Her eyes widened, her face swam.

"Aha," he said, tightening his hold of her hands as if on a possession, "*Now* that face of yours has a different look on it!"

The news that "Miss Winter" was back in the company, not in small parts with judicious vanishings toward child-bed, but in the role of Rosalind in Davenant's new production of *As You Like It*, was greeted by the company of actors at Drury Lane in various guessable ways. The men without exception were momentarily pleased, since Kate's attractions, that glow and ripeness, shone upon all. The elder women actresses enjoyed foretelling "disaster, my love" to one another. The younger actresses were angry and jealous but too practiced to show it, although when Kate was discussed they never joined the conversation.

Buckley was offended. He considered Davenant should have spoken to him before approaching Kate. Kate was his wife: he would say whether she could accept the offer or no. Besides, he wished to be treated as an important member of the company, one with whom Davenant discussed such things. However, he was offered Orlando and decided to be magnanimous.

"You're clever, Kate," he said, his mouth full of oyster pie, when they were dining at home that evening.

Kate could scarcely eat. She'd been white in the face all day.

"I hope I can do it, Buckley."

"So do I," he said, with a loud laugh.

She knew what he was thinking, recognized the self-absorbed, glassy look on his face. If she failed, *his* career could be damaged.

It had been a joke in the Winter family when she was a child that Isabella must have happy endings at all costs. Kate had said that if someone told her sister about a man losing his leg, Isabella would be sure he "walked quite well on his wooden one afterward." Isabella forgot things which made her uneasy, pearled over anything unhappy.

Her life on the circuits, her passion for Buckley, had disappeared from her mind; the Honorable Frederick Bagot was simply her son and Denys's, doted upon by the family, even by Lady Clare. The old Earl bought him anything he fancied, from a pony to a greyhound. Denys taught him to ride when he was so small he could scarcely balance on a horse; Robert picked him up and swung him round every time he saw the little boy. Freddy was spoiled. He was a clever child, and the small face which at birth had the look of a beaky newborn bird grew handsome. He had large dreamy brown eyes, a proud air. "How like his grandfather he is!" was Lady Fanny's constant exclamation.

Two years after Freddy's birth Isabella was brought to bed of a daughter, a pretty little creature with Denys's smile and grace. She was christened Elizabeth Lucy Effingham Bagot and known only as Betsy. From the moment Betsy could crawl she made straight toward her brother. She followed him on all fours, then in tottering steps, then with dancing feet, his admirer, his loving slave. If Denys asked, "Will you

come for a walk, Betsy?" the answer was always the same.
"*And* Freddy." Frederick treated his sister with a kindly contempt. He would rather spend his time being petted by the
grown-ups.

Isabella's life had settled into the life of people of rank,
with the liberties of wealth and the restrictions of manners.
She took for granted the pattern of the year, as ordered as
the seasons: the short time in London full of social things,
the return to Bagot Park for long months of country life.
The Bagots ruled their district like benevolent patriarchs,
hunted with farmers, knew every farmer and laborer on
their Sussex estates. Isabella learned to be interested in the
building of cottages, in family dinners at Christmas or harvest time given for "the neighborhood"—five hundred people sat down to dinners in the gardens or the house. She
went to village cricket matches, sat under the oak trees, her
flounced parasol a circle of pink over her head, and watched
Denys loping across the green or hitting a six. At sports Denys was always best of all.

Her parents had not long continued the hard work of the
circuits. On their return from Ireland, Denys insisted on settling some money upon them. Thomas accepted this with an
effusive gratitude when he met the Viscount and private resentment afterward. But practical Ellen bought a cottage in
Richmond and soothed Thomas's ruffled self-respect.

Isabella found Denys's kindness to her parents obscurely
annoying, particularly since Denys never spoke of her own
life in the theater and it was mutually understood that she
must not do so, either.

"Truly, Denys, you don't *have* to give my parents money.
Papa is quite proud, you know, and has never lacked work."

"Don't be a goose, Isabella. Your father cannot refuse a
small gift if it comes from his own child."

"But I did not give it."

"I said it was from you."

Oh, Denys, Denys, she thought sometimes. There was

something disturbing in living with anybody so good and so kind. At times his goodness was stifling. Robert, for all his manners, had moments of being rather heartless, and shocking Denys very much. Isabella enjoyed listening to Robert advancing some theory not based on virtue but on common sense and selfishness as well.

After six years of marriage, she knew her husband like the back of her hand. There was something immovable in him. He always had a certainty of what should or should not be done. He always knew without hesitating the choice between right and wrong. It was this adamant quality in his son, together with his lack of intellect, which the old Earl despised. *He* did not see life as black and white, nor did anybody with brains or a pair of eyes. It wasn't possible to continue to be such a simpleton, yet Carteret managed it. The Earl had grown up in the disreputable days of the Prince Regent. He had spent a raffish youth and thoroughly enjoyed it. He knew on which side his bread should be buttered and was damned well going to see that's how it was. His son never seemed to be conscious of such a thing. "I'll swear he wouldn't stretch out his hand if the butter was in front of him," said the Earl to Robert. Carteret never went to the House, showed no interest in the violent arguments of the day. He was curiously free of the arrogance one would expect from a Bagot with immense properties and power to match.

It was true Carteret was rather a lazy man. He was also unselfish, affectionate, too straightforward for his father's taste. The old Earl turned as always to his worldly nephew.

Carteret's attitude toward Isabella's family was kindly but distant, and Isabella had seen to it that neither she nor Carteret ever met Buckley. It was not difficult. She herself sometimes visited Kåte and her children when Buckley was playing and Denys was with Robert. But the sisters did not meet very much. Kate accepted that. Bella was lost to her, and she and Ellen sometimes talked of it, both with philosophy.

"It's the way of the great world," Ellen said.

"The fact is your sister is too good for her own family," said Thomas.

The women refused to admit that.

Kate wrote to Isabella with the wonderful news about her role as Rosalind, and Isabella showed the letter to Denys, who looked pleased. He rarely saw Kate, but he respected her. He sensed in the little redheaded actress with correct manners an attitude toward life rather similar to his own.

"We must arrange to take a box to see your sister," Denys said, sprawling by the open window waiting for Isabella to finish dressing. They were going to drive in the park.

Isabella waited while Rivers, the little maid from Clarges Street now promoted to be Isabella's personal maid, opened a glove box and took out Isabella's long gray suede gloves.

"No, Rivers. I prefer the dove color."

She held out her arm and Rivers pushed on the gloves and buttoned them.

"What day does the play open at the Royalty Theater?" Denys asked, idly regarding his exquisite boots. He could hear pigeons cooing in the garden trees. He had been up for hours, had ridden out in the park with both the children and a groom. He was handsome, slightly fatter, as specklessly elegant as of old.

"Next week or the week after that. I am not sure."

Denys looked surprised, but waited until Rivers had left the room.

"My dearest, surely you know the date of your sister's play?"

"No, I do not. I haven't seen Kate for weeks, and her letter says nothing about dates," said Isabella crossly.

Her relationship with Kate was something she felt uncomfortable about with Denys. She needed, was given always, her husband's intense love and admiration. The least hint of criticism or reproach in his voice made her angry.

"We will find out," he said comfortably.

He always says "we," she thought, when he means I am in the wrong.

Denys idly glanced out of the high windows at a lime tree, its leaves opening, shiny, yellowish. The sky was full of golden-white clouds against pure blue, the air soft, smelling of growing things. How well Freddy rode, how red Betsy's cheeks were when they were in the park, he thought. And my father loves them and is proud of them. He smiled to himself.

Isabella, with one of her sudden impulses, darted across to him and threw her arms round his neck.

Even Isabella, young and strong and ready for enjoyment, found the London season tiring and grew pale after so many late nights and days full of social engagements. Three miles away across London her sister was weary for a different reason.

Kate had played no big role since she'd acted with her parents in the provinces, and now she had begun to work in *As You Like It* she found it an intense strain. Everything was strange. She must be at the theater from morning until night; she scarcely saw her children. By nine every morning the carriage was at the door in Kensington ready to take her and Buckley to the Royalty.

The journeys were not cheerful, for Buckley, who had recently been criticized somewhat harshly at a rehearsal by Davenant, was irritable and silent.

Huddled in the carriage each morning, Kate left Buckley to his thoughts and tried to concentrate on her own role. It seemed almost impossible. Perhaps my talent is lost, she thought. Perhaps Davenant was right when he only gave me parts of four lines. I *could* act once. But that was when I was young and didn't know the dangers. It is the same as dreaming one can fly. I used to do that too . . . climb to the top of cliffs and spires and spread my arms and swim through the air. I never do that now.

During the rehearsals she worked with a tense concentrated attention, listened to every word Davenant said, her pale face absorbed. Watching him rehearse—he was playing Jaques—she tried to discover his mystifying secret. How did he manage such power, such subtlety?

When she arrived one morning in the dark boxroom which was still her dressing room, Gwynyth was waiting.

"First dress rehearsal, dear. You'll enjoy that." Kate said nothing as Gwynyth tenderly took the muslin shawl from her shoulders.

"Mr. Davenant sent you a message. When you are in costume, you're to go and see him."

"Oh, *Gwynyth.*"

Gwynyth dressed her in her Rosalind's first act costume, an elaborate court dress of white patterned with gold. She unpinned Kate's bright hair and threaded it with pearls. The sickly daylight coming through a high window small as that in a dungeon shone down on Kate's costume, making it tawdry, turning her painted face into a mask.

Davenant was not in costume but standing in his salon with his hands in the pockets of his elegant trousers when Kate rustled into the room.

"I wanted a word with you."

She said nothing.

He looked at her and frowned.

"You're not to be anxious. You're in the right way of it."

Taking his hands from his pockets, he gestured as if catching things which floated in the air.

"Grace. Ease. Delicacy. True feeling."

They stood looking at the invisible.

"All there to grasp. Off with you. And give it beans."

The playbills were freshly posted, the necklace of gaslamps hung like yellow bubbles. The night was chilly. Crowds gathered before the performance was due to begin, to stare as the long lines of carriages began to draw up. The horses and turnouts were the finest in the world, they murmured, and as for the crests on the carriage doors—why, half Burke's Peerage was coming to the Royalty tonight!

Red carpets were laid across the pavement, stretching up the steps into the Royalty Theater foyer, so that the ladies would not soil the hems of their skirts. Up this red path came gentlemen in black cloaks, ladies in the colors of a fading rainbow, their heads crowned with diamonds or flowers. The butterfly creatures moved slowly up the curved stair, carrying fans or knots of flowers, bowing and smiling to each other.

Isabella, on Denys's arm, walked up the staircase among their friends. She looked beautiful in white satin embroidered with loops of pale blue velvet. The gown showed her thin graceful shoulders and the Earl's diamonds, which she liked to wear a good deal. She'd noticed how her diamonds still angered Lady Clare.

The Bagots had taken a box on the right, well placed for Lady Fanny to enjoy a good view of the audience. As the family trooped into the box the Earl sidled over to the largest chair in a corner, into which he fell rather than sat. His stooping figure seemed, to his son's saddened eyes, to grow more crooked as time went by.

Isabella, for all the worldly air which in the past she had aped and which was now real to her, was excited at the coming performance. She looked round the theater filled with expectant, exquisitely dressed people. She looked at the red velvet curtains, a wall between Kate's world and her own. Behind the curtains Kate must be shaking with fright. She was filled with sympathy and a forgotten sisterly pride.

Down the ill-lit passage in her boxroom Kate was being dressed by Gwynyth. The old woman had brought extra candles and the room for once was bright with light. Gwynyth blessedly said nothing as she tied the laces at the back of Kate's costume, low-cut white, displaying more bosom than Kate approved. Kate gave the neck of the dress an unsuccessful tug to hide the division between her breasts.

In the distance they heard the callboy's voice: "Overture

and beginners. Overture and beginners, IF you please."
There was a sharp rap at her door. Kate felt slightly faint.
"Miss Winter. Your call, please!"

She put out both hands, and Gwynyth pressed them.
Then, not looking back, Kate left the dressing room with a
firm step. As she walked down the passage her heart beat so
violently that she felt stifled, her breath was short and quick,
there was a dazzle in her eyes.

It was the turning point of her life.

Kate woke next morning full of painful uncertainty. The
audience had cheered and after the performance everybody,
even Davenant, had congratulated her. But only the morning papers could tell her if she had succeeded.

Buckley was silent during breakfast—she did not like to
talk about the performance when he was in this mood. He
left in a brougham immediately after the meal, saying he had
"work to do." She supposed he would go to the Garrick, talk
and drink with his friends and get over his disappointment at
the cool applause for his Orlando. Poor Buckley. What stupid creatures we actors are, she thought, egotists, children.

She herself could not settle, wandered into the nursery,
tried to read, changed her dress twice and finally—telling
Mary Anne to keep the children quiet and take them out into
Kensington Gardens at once, please—left for the Royalty.

When the brougham drew up at the theater and she saw
her name in large letters on the playbills her heart fluttered.
It was an emotion she hadn't felt since she was a girl and her
name had been posted on the walls. On the circuits she used
to cross to the other side of the street to avoid passing a playbill with "KATE WINTER" on it. Going through the stage
door, she averted her eyes.

Davenant's doors stood open, and when she tapped his familiar voice called, "I wondered how long it would be before
you came."

He was sitting comfortably in a tapestry chair, a silver

coffeepot in front of him. Would she take a cup? No? Various newspapers, the *Morning Post,* the *Times* and the *Athenaeum* were spread on the table.

"Of course you have read the morning press," he said indifferently.

She shook her head in silence.

"And after your Rosalind last night, you slept like a log."

"Very badly, sir."

"Must be the artistic temperament."

How waggish theater people are, she thought, inwardly sighing. They'll make jokes on Judgment Day.

"You were worried about me, Kate, confess it. You were in a state of painful uncertainty about my great performance. Do they realize he *continues* to be great, you thought, lying on your sleepless couch."

"You were superb."

"Of course I was, dammit. You may now read the public journals, madam, and judge for yourself if I succeeded. There are also one or two words about you. No more than that, I fear."

She picked up the journals and began to read. All he could see was a little foreshortened nose and chin, the red curls escaping from her straw bonnet. She looked demure. It amused him to think of her last night, face passionate, voice trembling with emotion. She was a mixture of innocence and the keenest apprehension, of soft sensibility and hardness. She intrigued him. Kate was reading what the critics had thought of her.

"Radiantly   beautiful . . . emotion,   grace,   spirit . . . signs of youthful genius," she read. "Exquisitely managed and melodious voice," "high comedy which left nothing to be desired. . . ."

She swallowed.

"You have gone very pale," remarked Davenant with interest.

There was a knock on the door, and Augustus Bryson

came into the room. He wore an exaggeratedly waisted dark purple coat and a stock of elaborate frilled satin. The scent of eau-de-cologne came in strongly with him.

He bowed with assiduous politeness to Davenant and then gave Kate a nicely judged nod.

"Might I have a word with you, sir?"

"Sit down first," was the barked reply.

When Bryson sat he was on the same eye level as the actor. He should have known after years with Davenant that this was essential. Davenant would never speak, when seated, to a person standing over him.

"You mentioned last night the matter of Miss Winter's dressing room," said Bryson. "I have been endeavoring to ascertain how the position of her room may be altered."

"So she's closer to me and the stage, of course," said Davenant.

"Yes, yes, precisely so," said Bryson, his long face frowning with concentration; he reminded Kate slightly of her father. He produced a plan of the dressing rooms, much folded and tattered, and spread it on the table on top of the notices. Davenant nodded indifferently.

"Ask Miss Winter. You have to start worrying now whether *she* is pleased or not."

Kate was privately amused. So that little dark box room was a thing of the past, was it?

"I thought perhaps here," said Bryson, indicating a room.

"Oh. But that is Mrs. Courtenay's dressing room," said Kate.

"Mrs. Courtenay informs me she wishes to be on another corridor where she can keep an eye on her daughter."

"The redoubtable Kitty," remarked Davenant.

Kate detested Kitty Courtenay, who was eight years old, clever and a perfect beast.

She looked at the plan, then up at Bryson and gave him a slow radiant smile.

"It is a lovely room, and so close to the stage. Thank you, Mr. Bryson."

"Don't thank him. My idea. You can go, Bryson, when you've told me the state of the box office. Good? I'm glad to hear it. Later I mean to talk to you about the size of my name on the playbills."

Bryson left the room, frowning and looking self-important. Davenant watched him go sardonically, then leaned back in his chair.

"So you are to be the new one who delights London. They're going to flock to see you. All the men will fall in love with you; that's certain."

She smiled again.

"How shall you like that, hmm?"

"I suppose I'll be a little sorry for them."

"Hypocrite."

Chapter Fourteen

EARLY DURING THE SUMMER OF 1844 Lady Fanny was married. Her husband, the eldest son of a friend of the old Earl, was suitable in every way. Lord John Ransome was thin, tall, quiet, pleasantly humorous, with one of those skull-like faces which the Earl had noticed went with the constitution of an ox. He was probably not in love with Lady Fanny, but he paid her the right gallantries, danced with her at every ball, spent every hour of the day riding or walking with her, sitting at Bagot House with her and generally behaving as a devoted suitor should.

"You certain he's what you want, Fan?" demanded her father, after the offer had been made.

"Oh, yes, Papa."

"Strong enough to manage him? He's no fool."

"John will manage *me*," was the inevitable reply.

The Earl had to be content with that. He had never understood his eldest child, but she seemed happy, and there was nothing wrong with young Ransome or his fortune. He even had the expectation of a future fortune, which was to the good. Daughters must marry judiciously and maintain the interest and honor of the family.

Lady Fanny was married with pomp and richness at St.
Margaret's, Westminster, and left for a Scottish honeymoon.

The family was oddly diminished with Lady Fanny gone.
There was no prim-faced correct little person to pour tea in
the drawing room, wearing her air of head of the household.
Even Lady Clare missed her. There were many responsibilities in the running of a great house which, despite skillful
and devoted upper servants, ought to be taken on by the mistress. Lady Fanny had enjoyed them. Lady Clare had no intention of doing one of them. *She* would rule when the
household was her own. In short, when she married.

Throughout her twenty-three years Lady Clare had been
ludicrously spoiled. Her beloved old Hopton had begun it,
her governess had followed suit, the Bagot servants admired
and served her, her family indulged her. From a little child
she had been called "the pretty one," as Carteret was "the
heir" and her sister "the eldest." Isabella had taken away
Lady Clare's claim to be sole Bagot beauty. It wasn't only for
her low birth that Lady Clare disliked her sister-in-law.

Society looked on Lady Clare as one of the richest prizes in
the marriage market. Lady Fanny had a fortune as large, but
there was no excitement in seeing Lady Fanny courted and
wed—she resembled everybody else. Lady Clare was known
to be difficult, and men thought it would be challenging to
win such a rich beautiful shrew. Young men arrived, one after the other, to pay court to her.

Lady Clare wasted no time in her refusals. She told her
family about them, dismissing her suitors with one sentence
for each gentleman.

"Papa, the man is a booby."

" Carteret, can you mean I should marry a man who wears
scent?"

"Cousin, you have never seen my new suitor on a horse."

It was the Bagots' fault that she behaved so badly, that her
opinion of herself was so high, that as the months went by
she became more and more difficult to please. She had lost
the awkwardnesses of her teens, and her poise and beauty
grew. Despite the large Bagot nose and occasional air of an

angry boy, she could look enchantingly pretty. But her character, like that of a vicious horse, grew worse as she grew older.

The family, with the exception of Isabella, who was not a blood relation, were amused. Clare's dismissal of suitors was a kind of proof of breeding.

"She's taking her time, and I'm damned glad of it," said her father to Robert.

The Earl sent for her one morning when she was about to go riding in the Row. She came into his study in her dark habit, carrying her trailing skirt over her arm. Her fair hair was netted behind her ears and without its softness on either side of her cheeks her nose stood out, uncompromising and large.

"Sit down, girl," said the Earl, scowling over a pile of papers on his desk which he considered Robert should have "finished off" the previous evening.

Lady Clare took a high-backed chair by the window.

"The horses are waiting, Papa."

"I daresay. Let 'em."

There was a pause.

"How's Hopton?" he said abruptly.

Clare looked at him.

"Not better."

"What does the doctor say now?"

"That it's a matter of time."

He said nothing. He had an idea she was suffering.

"And don't say," said Lady Clare in a grating voice, "that we all have to die sometime."

He knew the old woman had been ill for weeks; Robert and he had consulted with the doctor, but nothing much could be done. Hopton, devotedly nursed, was in the servants' quarters, visited daily by Clare. The girl had always loved her the most.

"Your cousin tells me Beauchamp's son has offered for you," said the Earl, changing the subject.

"So he says."

"To whom? To you?"

"I would not think much of a man who went to you before speaking to me of such a thing."

The Earl looked at her in a ruminative way. He let her impertinence and the incorrect manner of the marriage offer go for the moment.

"Are you interested in Beauchamp's son? What's his name?"

"Lord Paul. He is a clever fellow. No, I shall not marry him."

"You can't spend the next ten years, y'know, refusing every eligible man in London."

"I am two years younger than Fanny," was the sharp reply.

"Not getting any younger, though. All these refusals. It comes to my mind it is getting a silly habit with you."

"I fail to see why this matter is so pressing," she said, quite furious at the unaccustomed criticism. "The last hasty marriage in our family was disastrous enough."

"Carteret's marriage is now accepted, miss. We will hear no more about that old story."

She stood up, fastening a button of her tight black glove and turned to her father with the light full on her face.

"Papa, I will marry when I am ready to do so. You need not trouble yourself about my choice. *I*, at any rate, will not bring disgrace on the family."

She swept out of the room.

Robert was waiting outside, already mounted, looking handsome in his bright yellow riding coat and mounted on a magnificent gray. Clare's own horse, fretting and bored, was being led up and down the courtyard by the groom. Robert grinned and nodded and the two set off toward the park, Clare riding lightly and effortlessly, followed by two grooms who were as much her slaves as every other young man in London.

It was one of those crisp mornings when people's breath, horses' breath, made a smoke in the air, and Robert and Clare were glad to feel the chill air making their faces tingle;

the Row was crowded . . . horses and riders, ladies and
their tall-hatted escorts galloped to and fro, throwing up the
tan in spurts round the horses' feet; rows of young men
leaned on the railings watching the equestrians and judging
the horseflesh. In the center of the Row people walked, daw-
dled and talked, wrapped in cloaks and heavy coats against
the chill, moving in a mass of vivid colors.

Robert and Clare stopped at the far end of the Row. Clare
dismounted and tossed the reins to her groom.

"We will walk for a while."

She didn't suggest Robert should accompany her, taking
his presence for granted as she did the waiting groom, the
horse at her door. Robert offered her his arm but she refused. She walked, skirt looped over her wrist, in silence.
Looking at her severe profile he said, "How is Hopton today?"

"Don't you ask me that, too."

"Did my uncle inquire?"

"He could go and see her if he wanted."

"Clare, you know quite well if the Earl suddenly appeared
in poor old Hopton's bedroom he'd frighten her out of her
wits. Then she *would* think she was going to die."

"She's very ill, I don't want to talk about it."

Like Carteret, with whom she shared few family traits,
Clare's feeling for the family servants was passionate. She
seemed to love them far more than she did her father, sister,
brother. It was to them that she gave her sudden, wonderful
smiles. Hopton had been her nurse since Clare was born.

"Have you anything on your mind, Clare?" Robert suddenly said, glancing at her again.

"I don't know what you mean."

"My dear coz, I am not one of your dancing partners.
There's something, apart from feeling sad over poor old
Hopton, that is worrying you."

She walked beside him in silence. Robert waited.

"Suppose," she said, after a while. "Suppose you came into

possession of a damaging fact against a man. What would you do with it?"

"It would depend on who might be damaged. And why."

"Suppose he deserved to be so."

"It doesn't necessarily mean one would do it."

"You're so chicken-hearted."

He said drily, "I will not admit to that. Come, cousin. Tell me something interesting. Generalities are tedious."

She looked at him for the first time.

"You wouldn't find this tedious. It is to do with Carteret's wife."

Robert stopped walking. He put his hand across his mouth in an unconscious gesture. The eyes looking at her about the hand were as sharp as her own.

"What have you been up to?"

"*I?*"

"Have you been asking questions about Isabella's past? Discovering what her life was like when she was an actress. How very unbecoming to you."

She bit her lip at his cold, changed voice. Her face was thunderous. Some people went by and bowed, and she replied with a stiff nod of the head. When they were alone again she said abruptly, "Who mentioned her life before she was married? I did not."

Suddenly he took her by the arm, gripped her and forced her to stop walking.

"What do you know against Isabella?"

"I am not sure yet."

She's like a vixen, he thought. They have sharp teeth.

"If you are not sure, why are you telling me this?"

"I have not told you anything yet."

"Stop behaving like a spiteful child. What do you know against her that you're using like a threat?"

"Hopton says," said Clare, with the strangest expression on her face, "that Frederick is not Carteret's child."

* * *

When they returned to Bagot House Robert made her solemnly swear she would hold her tongue, tell nobody. She agreed. After she had spoken, her manner changed. She began to make excuses for listening to Hopton. She even apologized.

"Just keep your word," he said and left her.

Lady Clare went up to her room, threw herself on the bed and began to cry.

Robert went to his study, told the footman he was not to be disturbed, locked the door and sat down to think.

He had remained cool when he'd been with Clare because the less he showed how he felt the better. But what she said had filled him with horror.

Was it true? He could scarcely bear to ask himself that. Merely knowing the existence of such a rumor could be tragic.

His thoughts were not on Isabella or the little boy, whom he dearly loved, but on his cousin. On Denys.

He'd known Denys since the death of his own parents when he'd come to live with the Bagots as a boy scarce twelve years old. He knew Denys with such an intuitive love that he seemed to know always what Denys would do, how Denys would feel.

That day when they'd been in Newcastle and struggled together to rescue a young girl trapped in the mob . . . she'd fainted when they carried her back to the hotel and placed her on a sofa. Then she had opened her eyes as Denys bent over her. At that moment Robert had known his cousin would love her.

What of now?

The tragedy growing in Robert's thoughts was not the fact, true or false, of the child's parentage but of his cousin's nature. The thing in Denys he revered, his loving nature, a deep sense of the old-fashioned quality of honor. If only his cousin were like the Earl, a realist, a cynic. How did one grapple with something as strong, as immovable, as plain virtue?

Robert saw no solution should Clare's story prove true. Even if it were not, what terrible wound would it inflict on Denys's trust in his wife? It might be physically true that Frederick *was* Denys's child. There was still the matter of whether Isabella had betrayed her husband. Hopton's accusation must have some basis—surely?

Poor Isabella. She had grace and spirit and was in the full tide of social success. She had taken the near-impossible step into a closed and jealous world. If this rumor were true, she was either a fool or had remarkable courage. Either way she was to be pitied.

Then he forgot Isabella and thought with growing desperation of how to help his cousin. He didn't see a single ray of hope.

The old Earl was out at his club or the Lords, both places he enjoyed for company exclusively masculine. Robert stayed alone until the short spring evening fell and it was time to change for dinner.

At last the footman knocked on the door and Robert unlocked it, the lamps were lit and the heavy curtains pulled, and Robert heard his uncle's deep voice and footstep. The Earl came in with sidling gait and looked at Robert in surprise.

"Not changed yet? I'm late. Londonerry caught me about some scheme he's putting up for the railways. Waiting for me, were you?"

"Yes, sir. May I have a moment with you?"

"Not more than one. All right, Swayne," to the butler. "Off you go. Stop fussing. You're like an old woman."

He shooed the butler out of the room and waited until the door was shut.

Then, collapsing into his chair, "Well?"

"Trouble, sir."

"I can see that."

"It is something I'm afraid I cannot manage alone."

The Earl waited.

"Clare has got hold of some kind of servants' scandal."

"*Clare* has?"

"I know. It isn't like her, and I told her so. But—"

Robert hesitated, looking for a way of making the fact sound less horrible There wasn't one.

"You know how much time she's been spending with Hopton since she was taken ill. She and Hopton have always been close. Hopton worships her. You remember Hopton was maid to Isabella when Carteret and she lived here after their marriage."

"What trash is this you are talking?"

The Earl's face was hard as stone.

There was nothing else for it.

"Hopton has told Clare that Frederick is not my cousin's child."

There was a profound silence.

The old man, deeply thoughtful, stared beyond Robert at the fact. He did not bother to say furiously that the story must be a lie. He was silent. His thoughts apparently gave him as little comfort as Robert's had done. Finally he stirred.

"Carteret will not stand for it."

"I know, sir."

The Earl scratched his chin.

"Times have changed, that's the devil of it. When I was young . . . I could name you two fellows in society now who are bastards, one of them Royal at that. But Freddy—"

His parchment-colored face twisted for a moment.

"It may not be true, sir. Clare and Hopton—"

"Stirring up a witches' cauldron. Nothing you can tell me about young Clare. She can be the devil. How's she behaving?"

"Frightened."

"By God, I should say so."

"I've told her to hold her tongue."

"She wouldn't dare do anything else," said the Earl. He sighed, took out a fob watch no bigger than a penny and looked at it shortsightedly, narrowing his eyes.

"We must change. I'll see Carteret's wife." Robert noticed

the lack of her Christian name. "The sooner the better. Does Carteret ride out in the morning?"

"Always, sir. Mostly with me."

"Good. I'll call in the morning."

The two men left the room together. As they reached the staircase the Earl said suddenly, "I feel old."

Isabella was surprised when she was told the Earl was waiting for her in the small drawing room. She was in the nursery with the children and their nurse and had been playing with a wooden horse on wheels, pushing it across the floor, making Freddy go quite crimson with laughter. When she heard that the Earl was waiting, Isabella thought what a mercy she was wearing her gray and yellow silk, and why was her father-in-law abroad so early? He never called at Finstock House except in the late afternoon for tea.

The front drawing room was full of sunlight, but when she entered the room he stood with his back to the window. He wore his customary black, and a black satin stock, making a sombre figure in this room of soft blues and little gilt sofas.

"My Lord, how good of you to come," she said, all grace and welcome.

He scarcely touched her hand. They sat down. Like the actress she had been, she sensed something was changed. She was inexplicably frightened, as she gave a charming smile.

"Are you a liar, my girl?" he said suddenly.

"I do not understand you, my Lord. Are you making a joke—"

"You are in trouble. Grave trouble. Are you going to lie yourself out of it?"

His harshest voice was very harsh indeed, a cruel tone she had never heard before. He no longer looked at her as the seductive woman, the latter-day Kat Harvey for whom he had an old man's stir of lust. He was like iron. He noticed grimly that she did not go red, as people usually did when they were threatened. Her expressive face went very pale. She sat still.

"Are you going to ask me what I am talking about?"

"That is not necessary, my Lord, since it is why you are here."

A cool customer. All the better.

"Carteret knows nothing of this," he said, "which is why I called while he is out of the house. Word has come to me of a grave scandal attached to your name."

She remained with her eyes fixed on him.

"It's being said the boy is not my son's child."

Isabella flashed round at him, her eyes full of anger.

"Who dares say such a thing?"

He folded his hands over the top of his silver-handled stick and leaned his chin on it. He had the look of a bird of prey facing some soft thing. A mouse. A mole.

"So you deny it, eh?"

"Deny it? That Freddy is not my husband's son! What a gross, disgusting thing to be said. By whom? To whom?"

Her face was white but brilliant with indignation. The fact that a second earlier she'd been with Freddy and seen him laughing and playing with his sister made her anger real. In the role of insulted great lady, she threw back her head.

"If it's a pack of lies it will soon be proved," he said. "And nobody will be more glad than I. But I came to warn you that it may not be possible to keep it quiet. Robert says it may have gone too far."

"Robert!"

"Oh, yes, he knows. I think," said the Earl, standing up and giving her a look in which there was no trace of affection or even humanity, "you'd best tell Carteret."

"Tell him what? That people have been spreading lies!"

"Yes. Tell him that."

He gave a brief inclination of the head and went out.

As his carriage left the house he saw the children, Frederick and Betsy; romping under the trees with their nurse.

Isabella's courage, like that of the actress who must step onstage despite fainting nerves, deserted her the moment the Earl was gone. She felt deathly sick. She went upstairs to her boudoir, scarcely knowing how she managed to climb the stair, and sat down on the window seat. Like a creature in pain, she could not keep still and sat rocking to and fro, clasping and unclasping her hands. How had this started, who had begun it? Who knew? What did they know? It could not be Buckley, with every reason to forget what had happened between them. Nobody *could* know but Buckley and herself. And yet . . . rolling and unrolling a lace handkerchief, she tore it to shreds. She sat thinking of the secret and who could have betrayed it. The monthly nurse at the time of Freddy's birth? The woman must have known the baby was not premature, but it was not a matter of interest to such a woman, all kinds of mistakes were made in the calculations of when a child was due. Isabella during her pregnancy had taken considerable trouble to tell the doctor and the nurse of her own absent-mindedness. Neither had known of Denys's absence that time . . . why should they?

Hugging her shoulders in an unconscious position of fear and defense, she thought who might have watched her during those lunatic weeks with Buckley. A servant at Bagot House? Surely impossible.

"Nobody can really *know*," she thought feverishly. "Only Buckley and me. I shall just deny it and deny it. Oh, God."

She shut her eyes, tearless, desolate, wondering how she could have done that fatal thing. The fever for Buckley, the sleeplessness, the desire and its desperately exciting reward, were gone. She could remember nothing. Only fear and pain. And a feeling, worst of all, that she had lost Denys.

Chapter Fifteen

She had never lacked courage. Denys came in from riding, wandered lazily into her room and kissed her. She spoke at once.

She was indignant, angry but steady.

"You can imagine. I am completely horrified," she finished.

He listened in silence. He had been sitting by the window in the seat he always used, long legs stretched in front of him and when she stopped speaking she waited, almost in agony, for him to look up. But he did not. Staring at the ground, he asked her a question. Who had started the story? What had the Earl said, what had been done to stop it? She could not tell him.

"Oh Denys—" she instinctively stretched out her hands as she had done in even the smallest trouble, for him to grasp them.

He stood up, excused himself courteously and left the room.

It seemed to Isabella from that moment as if there was no

water or sunshine any more. She had been happy. It was gone. From the moment the Earl had come to the house everything was changed. Her life altered, slowly at first and then with a terrible swiftness.

In the days that followed she scarcely saw her husband. Politely he explained it would be necessary for him to stay for a while at Bagot House.

"There are matters to be talked over with the Earl."

"But Denys—"

"We will meet at the Lennoxes' dinner tonight, and I will, of course, bring you home before I return to Bagot House."

For the first time in their lives together Isabella did not dare to argue. She had no power over him, and nothing she said could touch him. He was like a cold stranger. It was worse than that because he was so polite.

At Bagot House it was Denys, not the Earl or Robert, who closeted himself for a long time with Clare. He would not speak to Hopton, who was more ill than ever, and he knew he would upset the old woman. But he forced his sister to ask Hopton questions. The old Earl was moved by his son as he'd never been before, admired and grieved over him.

What Denys discovered was not proof. Hopton had seen Isabella leave the silk merchants', returning an hour later. She had actually followed Isabella and a gentleman, a fact which she was ashamed of. Hopton had intercepted a letter, which Denys read. No proof. But suspicions . . . disturbing, uncertain, degrading.

Scandals, thought the Earl, were curious things. By merely existing in a few people's thoughts they seemed to come alive like mosquitoes, to sting and multiply. Within a week there were rumors in society.

One wet afternoon when he and Robert were in the study Carteret came into the room.

"You're drenched," exclaimed his father. "Swayne must fetch you a dry coat."

He rang for the butler. Carteret gave the coat to Swayne

and stood in his embroidered waistcoat, mopping the rain from his face. His usually perfect boots were splashed with mud.

"The rain came on while I was riding," he said indifferently. "I hope I do not disturb you both."

His appearance shocked them.

"Gentle heavens, boy, have you been swimming in the Thames? Here's Swayne with a dry coat. Swayne, have the fire lit, the room's cold as charity, and a glass of Madeira for the Viscount."

"Nothing, I thank you, Swayne."

Swayne looked at Carteret much as his father had done, then bent to put a match to the fire. When he had gone, the Earl and Robert waited for Carteret so speak. They both suffered for him just then. The Earl looked at his son's haggard face. God, he thought, when you marry an actress you take a mad risk. Bagots had done such things in the past, and a dance it led them. A dance of death on more than one occasion when dueling was the thing. Damn Clare. And damn the boy for looking as if he'd been shot in the breast.

Robert thought his cousin's appearance ghastly. He looked as if he had not slept for days. To see him gave Robert a physical pain as if somebody had bruised his own heart.

"I have come from the Temple. I saw Lord Whitfield," Carteret said.

"What in Hades did you do that for?" growled his father.

Denys made a slight movement with his hand. "We cannot leave it as it is. How long is it since Clare told you, Robert? Two weeks? It is beginning to be known in London. Isabella will not go out of the house."

"What did Lord Whitfield say?" Robert asked.

"That it should be kept out of the hands of the lawyers."

"I agree," said the Earl. Neither he nor Robert looked at each other—both had a sense of overwhelming relief.

Carteret said nothing for a while. He held out his hands to the fire.

"She has to be cleared," he said at last.

"From what? A parcel of lies?"

"Father. I don't know."

"Vicious falsehoods about the boy. Babblings of an old woman out of her wits."

He used, deliberately, a tone of contemptuous dismissal. But when his father spoke of the child, Carteret shut his eyes.

"There's no proof he is mine."

"Of course Frederick is yours!" burst out the Earl angrily. "The boy's a Bagot. Any fool can see it. Are you telling me you'll ignore Whitfield and bring in the lawyers like a pack of jackals to destroy us? Submit the family to such a thing? By God, I won't stand for it!"

The veins stood out on either side of his forehead. His usually parchment-colored face was crimson.

"No, I won't do that, sir."

"Then what shall you do?"

"I don't know."

Denys stared into the fire, and his father and his cousin stared at him. He looked up and said in the exhausted voice now natural to him, "I have told Isabella I think the children should go to Bagot Park for the present. I am sure my grandmother would go with them. Do you agree?"

"Certainly."

"Thank you."

"I saw your grandmother yesterday," said the Earl. "She doesn't know anything yet, so the sooner they leave the better. Give her something to do, fussing over the children. Better for them, too. Get some country air."

"So you agree, sir. With Lord Whitfield."

"I agree with anything that's best for the family, Carteret. Do you wish me to see Whitfield and have a further talk?"

It was curious to hear the Earl ask him such a question, to hear the Earl ask his son anything.

"If you would, I would be very grateful."

Thanking them, he went quickly out of the room.

* * *

When the children left London, Isabella was so crushed in spirit that she didn't know how to get through the days.

Denys had returned from his stay at Bagot House, but no longer shared her bedroom. Would she forgive him if he moved out for a little? He was sleeping badly and might disturb her.

He also said that perhaps she should not go about much in society "for the present."

He only once mentioned the scandal, when he came into the drawing room where Isabella was trying to read and asked if she would be good enough to see Lord Whitfield at the Temple sometime.

"Lord Whitfield is a friend of my father's and a distinguished advocate. He only concerns himself with advice," Denys said. "My cousin will accompany you." He paused and added in a colorless voice, "Lord Whitfield may wish to see that other person but he will make those arrangements."

That was all.

Isabella had sworn the morning she'd told him what Hopton and what Clare had said about her that she was innocent. Denys never spoke of it again, never asked her a single question. Now he was going through a kind of farce which she supposed was done to protect her. She knew he had been aware from the first that the accusation was true.

His heart and his senses told him so. He did not necessarily believe Frederick was not his son, but he did know Buckley had been her lover that summer when he had been away for weeks in Newcastle.

What was terrible was that Denys no longer loved her. From the moment she'd spoken of the scandal his love had withered and died. Or perhaps he *did* still love her, which was why he looked so haunted. But would never take her in his arms again, never make love to her, never be her real husband, never be happy, never laugh, never be Denys again. The thought filled her with terror. Surely to change like that was impossible? Would he not recover, forgive and accept her—though still pretending she was innocent—as a fallible but not despicable woman worth loving and living with.

For the first time since she had unthinkingly married a high-born stranger Isabella was faced with the substance of his nature. He was a patrician, a man of honor, a man to whom betrayal was like treason against one's country, a mortal sin. He might forgive her. He would never take her back.

She was waited upon and maided, dressed in beautiful clothes, and Denys took her out in the carriage. They drove to places where there were the least of the season's crowds. Certainly they were bowed to. One or two of Denys's men friends came to dine and were gallant to her. No ladies were invited.

The great world, it seemed, had given her up. She was a parvenu and had never been genuinely part of them.

Lonely and frightened, at times filled with hate for Clare and her old, sick enemy Hopton, at other times miserably condemning herself because she had been found out, Isabella dared not see Kate. How much did Kate know? Society and the theater were widely apart, yet now and again the circles intersected. Actresses, particularly successful ones as Kate had recently become, were invited into society now and then. Men of rank always enjoyed entering the world of the theater, in the hope that it was as immoral as its reputation.

Isabella wrote to Ellen at the Winters' cottage in Richmond, saying she would like to spend the day with them. She ordered the carriage early while Denys was out riding. It was a relief to leave the house, which was horribly quiet since the children were gone.

The rain of the last few days had ended, the sun was out. The road to Richmond was lined with budding trees, the fields were fresh green. She saw some new season's lambs. It was a long time since she had visited her mother; in her mood of despondency she thought how little she had made the effort to see her parents during the last years. It had been Denys whose generosity had released them from the bondage of the circuits: he had bought them their house. It had been Denys who arranged for the children to be driven down to see her parents and spend the day with them. Denys. Always Denys. Isabella had visited Richmond very rarely; she always meant to do so and Denys used to scold her lovingly for her broken promises . . .

The cottage, with a walled garden, was built at the edge of the park and reached by a secluded path beside a small stream. At the front of the cottage a flowering currant bush was covered with sweet-smelling pink flowers; there was a mass of daffodils in the grass under a cherry tree. Isabella told the groom not to come back for her until late. "I will dine with Mrs. Winter," she said.

The groom, a sturdy young man whose family had been with the Bagots for years, said politely, "His Lordship dines at home tonight, my Lady."

"I know, Longstaffe, but his Lordship does not expect me."

As the carriage drove away, Ellen opened the door and Isabella threw her arms round her mother's neck.

Ellen, embarrassed and pleased, laughed as she led Isabella into the house.

"What a change, my child, to see you here. I'm afraid your father will not be home for some time; he has gone to the theater at Richmond. He cannot keep away from the old life. I think he finds it too quiet, leading the life of a gentleman, you know. He tells me there is talk of the manager giving him an engagement for the summer. Poor Thomas!"

She laughed in her unsympathetic little voice. She looked older, smaller, She was slightly tanned from the spring sunshine, her pale blue dress with gold and blue buttons down the front suited her aging brown face and still-dark hair tidily coiled. She was so dear and familiar, so far from the rich world in which Isabella had despaired for what seemed eternity that she almost began to cry.

The cottage drawing room was homely and neat, with chintz covers, a piano, a canary in a cage. Isabella, for the first time in years, sank down on the floor. Her mother patted her hair. Not as a caress but to tuck a stray curl in place.

"I am in trouble, Mama."

"So I see."

Ellen looked at her with dark unblinking eyes.

"Don't say anything until you've heard, Ma. I want to tell you exactly what happened."

Isabella sat by her mother's side, picking at the braid on her pale dress and poured out the official, untrue story. Lady Clare hated her and so did the old nurse. Together they had invented lies about herself and Buckley Vernon. What was worse they said that Freddy . . .

The words tumbled out. She was to be taken, it seemed, to Lord Whitfield. "He is a Law Lord, whatever that means. Everything is frightening, Ma. They have taken the children away. To Sussex."

When Isabella stopped speaking Ellen said, looking at her, "You have not mentioned your husband."

"He is very upset."

Her own hollow words shocked her.

"No, no, it's worse than that. It is as if he were ill. He is quite changed."

"You mean he believes it."

"He would never say so."

"That makes it worse," Ellen said.

She did not ask whether it was true. Isabella, who all the way to Richmond had not been able to decide whether to confess or not, realized that her mother had no intention of asking the question. Maybe Isabella had deceived her husband. Maybe the little boy, her grandson, was not a Bagot at all. Ellen's attitude was steady: she accepted on its face value that Isabella needed family love and support. Ellen would give her both, together with sometimes penetrating counsel.

They sat without talking while Isabella picked at the braid of her beautiful yellow dress, and the canary sang so loudly that its body trembled.

"Do the family stand for or against you?"

"Robert is the only one who speaks to me. He has come to Finstock Lodge to dine."

"Why must you go to this Law Lord?"

"Robert told me it is only for advice."

"Who gains, suppose they decide you guilty?"

"But they can't! I told you—"

"I said *suppose*. Would Freddy be disinherited?"

"I don't know. Yes. I suppose so."

"Who is next in succession after Viscount Carteret?"

"Freddy, of course. Oh, after that it is Robert, the cousin, who would inherit."

"Perhaps cousin Robert began the scandal. He has much to gain."

Isabella gave a shocked choking laugh.

"You don't know him. That is literally impossible."

"Nothing is 'literally' impossible, Isabella" said her mother, as cynically as the old Earl.

Ellen, telling her daughter to undo her bonnet or she would get a headache, left the room to speak to the cook about luncheon. Isabella was alone. Looking drearily round, she noticed that the room was full of objects from her childhood. There was a watercolor of a mountain she herself had painted when she was twelve years old. There was a china box with sailors on the lid used by her father for his cigars. Two blue vases decorated with white flowers which her mother had bought in the market at Newcastle. A patchwork cushion made by Kate. Kate! She had not spoken to her mother about Kate.

Ellen returned, saying the meal would soon be ready and that Isabella must eat.

"You are too thin."

"Am I? I hadn't noticed."

"Your neck is scrawny. You should wear a necklace to cover those saltcellars." She pointed to the hollows at the base of Isabella's throat. "Being scraggy doesn't suit you."

"Ma—" burst out Isabella, not listening, "do you think Kate knows?"

"I wondered when we would come to your sister."

"Oh, I'm sorry! Everything is so horrible and I've got so selfish."

The moment Isabella said that, her mother's hard expression changed.

"I am sure Kate and Buckley have heard nothing. They were here with the children yesterday, cheerful as crickets. I will have to tell them. Or perhaps your father should do it."

"Oh, no! I must do it!"

"Are you sure you're strong enough?" Ellen said. "You'll have to be tactful. You're in no state to use your brains just now."

"I shall tell Buckley at once," Isabella said. "He must know before he hears it from somebody else. I certainly could not—*should* not—tell Kate. Buck must do that."

By the way she spoke, the look, the determined way she folded her lips, even the manner of speaking Buckley's name, Ellen knew he'd been her lover. Isabella's no actress, she thought grimly. She never was.

The next day, during which Denys seemed to be out almost all the time, Isabella drove to the theater an hour before the performance. It was *As You Like It*, and the bills had "KATE WINTER" in letters three inches high. Isabella ordered the carriage to wait, ignoring the martyred expression of the coachman, who disliked keeping his horses in a crowded street. At the stage door she asked for Mr. Vernon.

She had deliberately chosen dark clothes, a mole-colored velvet cloak with a hood over her hair, and when Buckley swung down the passage he did not recognize her. He came up with his swaying walk, wearing a questioning, merry expression. She had not seen him for months, and his male beauty struck her with a feeling of forgotten familiarity.

"Isabella! I scarcely knew you—how very pleasant. Let me give you a glass of madeira in my dressing room. Star dressing room now, you know. Coming up in the world. Have you come to see Kate?"

He laughed and pressed her hand. They walked down a long stone corridor echoing with the noise of actors getting ready for the performance, with the smell of size and lamp oil strong.

Buckley's dressing room was large and spacious with a skylight. Gilded, stiffened costumes hung like puppets or lay on chairs like men collapsed when drunk. Dishes of colored powders lay in front of the looking glass. The smell of them, sweetish, dusty, came to her as if she could literally smell the past. She sat down and the hood fell away from her hair.

"I've come with bad news. People know. About us, I mean."

He was so shocked by her words that he looked ridiculous. His mouth fell open.

"What the hell are you talking about?"

Oh, I've played this scene before, Isabella thought.

She repeated everything she had told her mother but with a difference. He and she knew the slander was true.

Buckley remained aghast.

"What do they know? Who do you mean? What proof?"

"A letter, I think. I have not seen it."

"The only notes I had from you I burned the moment I'd read them. Most of them, at any rate."

What practice, she thought indifferently.

"I suppose Hopton stole it. She could easily have followed me into the shops, even to your lodgings. It is not impossible. They have told me nothing of what they *do* know. It's as if they won't put me on trial. Or are afraid to."

"What does your husband think of all this?" demanded Buckley. She saw he was frightened, and she despised him for it. How stupid he looked. She was wrong to think him handsome just now. Did I sacrifice Denys, she thought, and my happiness and my name and my life for *this?*"

"He has not said."

"Has he left you?"

She gave a cold smile.

"People like Denys are different from you and me. No. He is standing by me."

"But he believes you innocent. You've sworn."

"Oh, yes. I have sworn."

He looked at her, still with the thunderstruck expression on his face.

"Kate mustn't find out. My God! What would happen if she knew?"

Isabella stood up, pulling the cloak round her. She felt tired, and the room, with its scented smell, oppressed her.

"Buckley, I came to say that you must tell her at once. The story has got about, I don't know how, but people are talking. You must tell her before she hears it from someone else."

"Tell her! Tell her what, for God's sake? Go to her and say I'm sorry, dear, but I slept with your sister, and the child she calls Lord Frederick Bagot is my bastard! Kate adores me. She'd never forgive you."

"You mean she would not forgive *you*," she exclaimed, blushing at his brutal manner. Nobody had spoken to her in such a way since she was married. She had forgotten men could behave like that to women.

She held up both hands to stop him from speaking again.

"I don't want to hear another word. I came to warn you because we're in dreadful trouble. I shall continue to deny it and you must, too. But I tell you, if you don't speak to Kate in time, she is *certain* to hear of it. Now good-bye."

She ran from the room, leaving the theater muffled like a mourner at a funeral.

The streets were crowded with coaches and riders, so the journey back to Regent's Park took longer than usual. When she went into the house the butler told her a visitor was waiting for her. For a moment she thought it was the Earl, and a pang of fright went through her. But the butler said it was Mr. Robert.

She went into the drawing room; Robert, who had been looking out the window, came over to her quickly and kissed her hands. It gave her a curious feeling of pain to see his dark head bent over her hands.

"I'm glad to see you, cousin," she said.

"I'm afraid you will not be. I have bad news."

"The children!"

He made a sudden movement full of concern and kindness.

"No, no, they are well. Very happy and spending time with their grandmother in the gardens. I saw them two days ago, and they are quite settled. It is something else. I have just come from Brooks's where I was with Deno. Lord Gough is a friend of my uncle's—they were in the same regiment years ago. Deno applied to serve under him and has just received his papers. His regiment is going abroad. To India."

She stared at him with horror. Half an hour ago she had shocked and frightened Buckley and despised him for the way he had taken her news. As if heaven were revenged on her hard heart, she was now the one to receive a blow.

"Oh, no, I cannot bear it."

"I asked if I might be the one to tell you," he said, and took her hands again. A feeling of such grief came over her. Tears rolled slowly down her cheeks. They were the first tears she had shed since that horrible day weeks ago when the Earl had stood in this room. So she had been wrong when she said Denys would stand by her. He was leaving after all. He had given her up in his heart, and now had quietly found the best way to cut himself free. She saw his face, his tall lazy figure, heard his voice, felt his arms strongly round her. She began to cry bitterly.

Robert took her gently by the shoulders and stroked her hair.

"Poor girl. Don't cry, Bella, you will break my heart. It is not forever, you know, only for a while. It really is best just now. The man has been so grieved, so broken up, desperately unhappy. I am sure it is for the best. The Army life, work, comrades . . . and he is not leaving you unprotected; he asks me to do everything for you, look after you, care for you. My poor girl. Don't cry. Ah, don't cry."

When he left her, she went up to her room, asked Rivers to pull the curtains because her head ached and lay down.

The slow spring evening began to wane.

Isabella lay with her eyes closed. All her spirit, her energetic meeting-life-halfway, her optimism, common sense were gone. She couldn't remember what it felt like to be happy. She imagined, though it was not true, that she'd known all the time that Denys would go. First the children. Now Denys. Then she would be quite alone. She had lost everything, and for what? For lying on Buckley's disordered bed and possessing his muscular white body for a short time—how long, twenty minutes? Half an hour? They had never loved for long, and "loved" was not the word since Buckley had lusted after her and nothing else. Why, when the pleasure was over he'd picked up the script of a play! For that she had lost the deep love of a husband she had never understood or treasured, the safeness of his home, the company of her children, her name, her honor.

Before she had been discovered she often forgot the past for months at a time. Now it hung over her like a grimacing face, stronger and more hideous when she was alone in the dark.

I suppose that is being found out, she thought. I'm selfish, and I'm a liar, I wanted Buckley and that time when I had him I never even thought of doing wrong or hurting anybody, just of pleasing myself. Now I don't even like him. It is Denys I love.

She did love him more than she had ever done before and in a different way. Leaving her, he was tearing her life in half.

When she went downstairs, changed into a dark silk evening gown, her hair freshly coiled, she walked into the dining room as the butler was lighting the candles. It was growing dark. Denys, tall and thin in his black evening coat, was standing with his arm along the chimney piece in the indolent way he often stood. The heavy Bagot ring shone on his hand.

He murmured good evening.

During the meal, which neither of them could eat, they managed a kind of conversation for the benefit of the footmen. Isabella told him she had been to Richmond. He inquired about her parents. The farce of this talk told on Isabella's nerves. She was trembling when the butler finally brought in the tray of coffee, extinguished most of the candles, leaving only two burning (something Isabella in the past had thought romantic). He left them alone, closing the double doors.

They sat at each end of a table too long for only two people, separated by an expanse of shining mahogany covered
with silver objects so burnished that the silver was almost
blue. She poured his coffee and handed it to him. The cup
shook in the saucer.

"Robert told me."

She looked beseechingly across the table toward him. He
did not respond. He never smiled now and had been a man
who smiled more easily than anybody. His round face was
like the face of a sick child. With an effort he said, "Robert
asked if he might tell you, he seemed to think you would
prefer it. I would have told you myself but be insisted."

"It was better I heard it from him. Denys. Oh, Denys.
Please, please don't go!"

She hadn't meant to beg or weep and did both. She hid her
face in her hands. He did not move. He, the kindest of men,
who would have ridden through a storm to save her the
slightest headache or disappointment. Without comfort or
word she stopped crying. His silence frightened her.

"I am sorry if you are grieved, Isabella. But it is for the
best. I do assure you of that. It has often troubled me that I
gave up my regiment—"

"You never said so!"

"And Lord Gough is allowing me to be on his personal
staff. He is a brave old man, much loved," he went on, as if he
hadn't heard her. "The children are well cared for with their
grandmother, and Robert says he will take you to visit them.
He is very good. I have arranged with the bankers—"

"Denys, for pity's sake—"

He stood up then and did come toward her, and for a moment, her face piteous in the wavering candlelight, she
thought he was going to touch her. She looked up, mournful
and lost, but he only gazed at her intently and gave a kind of
bow and went out of the room.

Chapter Sixteen

KATE HAD BEEN REHEARSING ALL DAY, and when she returned to Kensington she was tired. Davenant had decided
to revive an old melodrama, *The Orphan of Geneva,* and she
was to play the virginal (and mawkish, she thought) heroine
pursued by a villain played by Davenant. The play, Davenant
informed the actors, was to be "spectacular. Storms, castles,
ghosts, lightning and suchlike. Make the audience's eyes
pop."

She came into the house feeling nervous and irritable. Acting with Davenant always did that to her. She wished she
were immune to the feelings he gave her. Sometimes when,
in the play, he had to touch her, her nerves were so taut that
she almost started back. She had developed a stupid habit of
slightly trembling when she was close to him. She tensed like
a coiled spring. Yet when they played together she knew she
acted at her peak—he made her do so.

The children were in bed, the house was quiet. She found
Buckley sprawled on a sofa, staring into the garden. He did
not get up but turned and looked at her.

"Are you well, Buckley?"

"Perfectly well," he said, so rudely that she thinned her lips, picked up her script and sat down in silence.

"Kate, we're in the hell of a mess."

As she looked up, her beauty and poise stung him. He was afraid of her, and said loudly, "It's your sister. All lies and rubbish, but she thinks you have to know."

Kate's eyes grew wide. But she said nothing.

"Isabella came to see me at the theater this afternoon. She says there's some servants' tittle-tattle that she and I—in short that we had a love affair years ago before you and I married. A lot of lies. Makes you sick."

He didn't know what he expected of his wife. Experienced with women, he was used to tears and vows of love, all the promises forced from him (and forgotten immediately afterward) which came at the end of a liaison. He'd had two or three since his marriage. Girls in the theater were easy game and usually moved off to some other fellow after he'd given them the push.

He admired and resented Kate. Her silence. The erect way she sat. Her dress was too young for her, he thought, those ridiculous flounces. . .

"You're a cool customer, I must say," he said spitefully. "Anyway, there's more. They're saying your sister's boy is—well—is my child."

"*Lord Frederick!*"

"More lies. Your sister's told them till she's blue in the face. But society people eat and drink scandal. Isabella said I was to tell you. Warn you."

"Warn *me?*" Kate said, looking at him fixedly. "What has it to do with me?"

She stood up and went to the window, standing with her back to him and staring out at the garden. She felt very sick. But she knew that if she stood calmly and breathed deeply the sensation would soon go. She had had it many times in the theater, only then it was that old-fashioned thing of strung nerves and fear which was called stage fright.

What was curious was that after the first moment of intense shock she was not surprised. She remembered a dozen things about Buckley and Isabella from the past, things she had been too self-absorbed to notice very closely. Her sister's manner with Buckley, long ago in the North, had been strangely uneasy. . . Isabella's excited white face once, when was it—at the theater before she and Buckley were married. Buckley's own manner sometimes when she talked of Isabella. . . it was oddly forced. She thought of the little boy she had only rarely seen, a spoiled, titled, handsome little person, her own children's half-brother, her own husband's bastard.

Buckley came to her, put out his hands and turned her round to face him. He looked stupid and at a loss. She'd never seen him look quite like that before. He liked to arrange life so that he shone. She had a pang of regret because she was stronger than he. He put his hand quite tenderly and cupped her chin, looking at her with lustrous, nervous eyes.

"I shall write and tell Isabella that I can't see her. I really would rather not," Kate said. "Please don't talk about this to me any more."

She moved away from him, returned to the sofa, picked up the script and began to read.

Denys's regiment, the Fourth Cavalry, had been mustering in Gravesend for the last couple of days. As soldiers did at the end of leave, the men arrived in the town haphazardly, bringing their families with them. Lodging houses were crammed and the streets full of soldiers in scarlet and wives in tartan shawls. Many of the young women carried babies in their arms or led little children by the hands. The soldiers had brought their parents, too, gray-haired men who had known other campaigns, thin-faced women with worn faces.

The *Durham* would be sailing before dawn, when the high tide was just on the ebb. The old slow East Indiamen of the past would have taken weeks, even months, to reach the Indian Ocean, but the *Durham* was fast. The redcoated soldiers would soon be in India. So far away! The atmosphere in the little riverside town was hectic, tense and sad.

On the evening the *Durham* was due to sail, Denys and Robert arrived at Gravesend in the Bagot coach. The Earl had wanted to accompany them, but somehow Robert had dissuaded him, and father and son had said good-bye at Bagot House. Robert knew Denys was too wretched to bear a long-drawn-out parting from his father.

When the cousins arrived at the Nelson Arms on the quayside they found the old-fashioned inn as crowded as the town. Boxes were heaped in every corner, candles brightly shone, laughter was loud, waiters rushed by carrying trays loaded with food and wine. Robert and Denys were taken up a crooked staircase to a room which had been reserved for them. Like the inn, it was old, beamed, panelled, askew, the floor at an angle, the windows so low that the young men had to stoop to look out of them. It was a bedroom, but Denys would leave it long before dawn.

Robert ordered supper and then joined Denys at the window.

"There she is."

The *Durham*, tall twin masts topped with single lamps, was high in the water, the ship as bright with light as the inn. The stretch of water between ship and shore was bobbing with small boats. They plied to and fro, packed with people, and Robert could see the crowd swarming up the ship's side on to the deck.

Denys stood leaning on the windowsill, watching in silence. His scarlet uniform altered him; he was no longer the indolent companion who rode every day in the Row with Robert or went to Tattersalls, joked or talked of horses. Robert could feel what Denys was feeling. Everything happening just now, in the inn, in the boats, on the quayside, in the ship, the tears and good-byes, the feeling of love heightened by coming separation, the families clasping each other close, made Denys's own state worse. He stood, serious and sad and longing to be gone.

Robert always breakfasted with the Earl in the mornings. It had been something insisted on when he and Denys were boys, punctiliously continued by Denys when they were older although the Earl was morose at breakfast time, almost daring either young man to utter a word.

On the morning following Denys's departure, Robert went to the breakfast room where the Earl, grizzled, silent, was reading a newspaper. There was the usual sideboard of hot dishes but Robert ate little.

"Have some salmon," said his uncle suddenly.

"I don't think so, thank you, sir."

"Stewed kidneys. You like those. Swayne. Give Mr. Robert a dish of kidneys."

After Robert had again refused the Earl returned to his newspaper.

The old man was offering him a kind of challenge, as if to demand proof that Robert was in good spirits, that nothing was upsetting him. It's hard for him, Robert thought. He loves Deno and never showed it, knows he hurt him and is suffering in consequence. There is nothing to be done.

In the afternoon Robert rode from Berkeley Square to Finstock Lodge. It was sunny, misty, hot. His thoughts, as he turned his horse into Regent's Park were on Denys. The sea would be calm for the beginning of that long journey.

Finstock Lodge lay in the sunshine, looking rich and well cared for. It was a pleasant house with its velvety lawns and tall windows, a pretty aspen tree in a corner and a bronze statue of a nereid that Denys had brought from Sussex when he and Isabella first moved into the house. The statue, Denys said, reminded him of her; Robert, glancing at it now, thought that in the nymph's short nose and high cheekbones there was a slight look of Isabella. . .

He was shown into the drawing room, which overlooked

the park. He found Isabella, in a rose pink dress, sitting on the window seat with her hands in her lap. It was an effort for her to smile when she greeted him.

"When did he sail?"

"On the ebb. From Gravesend."

"And you saw him off?"

"Yes. The *Durham* was packed to the gunwales with troops. You never saw such crowds. It was pandemonium when the ship was about to move off—"

He realized what he had unwittingly told her.

"Many women came to say good-bye to their men," Isabella said. "I wish I had been there. I do wish I had been there."

He was about to answer, but she said, "Don't say it is for the best. Denys kept saying that, and we all know, Robert, that it is *for the worst*. Don't let's talk about it."

"I'm afraid we must for a little," he said matter-of-factly. "We have an appointment this afternoon with Lord Whitfield. Don't start like that, Bella. He won't eat you. You'll like him. He's one of those bluff down-to-earth people, everybody likes him. Best get the visit over, don't you think? Unless you have other plans for this afternoon?"

"I am doing nothing."

"Then that's settled," said Robert briskly. "Now. About you. Lady Quenington told me she had invited you to dine with her but you refused. The old Countess of Bovill was also inquiring."

"They are very kind."

He gave a slight grin.

"I doubt that, Bella. Well, old Bovill is rather a duck; Lady Q. is another matter. You know about scandal, you've heard enough of it in past seasons. It can turn into a hurricane and pull its victim up by the roots. Or it can just die away. We may be able to weather the storm."

"*We?*"

"Of course. You and I. My uncle. Deno—at a distance. Even Clare, who incidentally has left London and gone to Bagot Park. Poor old Hopton died last week."

"I am so sorry."

The conventional reply was a shock, spoken in that empty voice. He would have preferred her to say something almost wicked—that she was glad Hopton was dead, for instance. It was like being with a sleepwalker.

"Shall we go, then?" he said. "Go and put on your prettiest bonnet to charm Lord Whitfield. He has an eye for a handsome woman, my uncle tells me."

During the journey to the Temple, Robert talked and Isabella listened, sometimes faintly smiling when he made one of his disjointed Robertish jokes. The carriage took them through the crowded streets, passing four-horse omnibuses full of people, phaetons, riders, carriages lined up at the bonnet shops and lace warehouses in Regent Street. Riding down Regent's Circus, helmets flashing, plumes waving, was a cavalcade of scarlet-coated Household cavalry. The scene was cheerful, noisy, and Isabella had a curious thought she half believed: that every single human being she saw walking or riding in the busy streets was happy. Save herself.

The carriage drew up in the hush of the Temple gardens. Telling the coachman to wait, Robert escorted her across a courtyard into an ancient house in Kings Bench Walk.

A clerk bowed them into a large dark room with low latticed windows.

A man at a table stood up.

"Lady Carteret, Mr. Bagot. My service to you."

He greeted them pleasantly, and Isabella was given a chair facing the lawyer.

Lord Whitfield was a ruddy-faced man in his sixties, with curling white whiskers and curling white hair. There was something sporting rather than legal about him. He wore a white cravat fastened with a gold horseshoe pin, a white rose in his buttonhole. His manner was as brisk as Robert's but without Robert's grace. He reminded Isabella of a country doctor.

"Best come to the point right away, Lady Carteret, don't you think?" he said, having dismissed the clerk. "Robert here, and Carteret himself, have laid the whole of this thing on my desk. I've been spending quite some time on it. I have seen the party in question—"

Isabella wondered who that was. Buckley? Clare?

Lord Whitfield looked at her, and she met his eyes without looking away.

He picked up a sheaf of closely written papers.

"The old nurse's evidence. Well, you can't call it evidence, it is the tittle-tattle she repeated to Clare, poor old thing. I gather she died last week, Robert?"

"Yes, sir. Clare was very upset."

Lord Whitfield raised an eyebrow.

"I saw Clare, too," he said. "She doesn't know what to make of what she's done. Wishes she'd never begun the thing one minute, and insists it was Hopton's dying wish to confess the next. Clare," said Lord Whitfield reflectively, "is no more responsible for her actions than a boy of ten with a hand grenade. There's no strong case here."

"My cousin never intended there should be a case at all," Robert said.

"I know that, my boy. He wanted the thing silenced. Cleared up. If there was anything actually to clear, if you take my meaning."

He put on some small round spectacles and looked over the top of them at Isabella.

Now and again he'd had cases, curious and interesting they were, that involved dealing with women of quality; he was accustomed to the inevitable bursts of feminine denials. Tears, too. The woman sitting opposite him did not behave in the expected way. If it were not for a letter lying on the desk this moment, Lord Whitfield could have believed her innocent. He admired her pluck.

"Of course," he said, "I haven't consulted my colleague yet, he's the great expert in these things. If he advises it I'm in duty bound to inform the Viscount that the child should not—*could* not by law—be the Bagot inheritor."

"Yes, yes, Lord Whitfield, we know, my cousin and my uncle are perfectly aware of that," said Robert, in a voice as practical as if discussing the decision to transfer an estate, not Freddy's future life. "But I take it that, from your remark just now, there *is* no real case."

"I couldn't say that," said Lord Whitfield, with a lawyer's perversity. He paused.

"Now, this letter, Lady Carteret."

He picked it up and looked at it. She could see, upside down, her own writing of five years ago. "Foolish," he said, reading it, then laying it down. "Very foolish."

"Buckley Vernon was a friend of Lady Carteret's long before she married. They were in the theater together," said Robert. It was curious to hear him mention such a thing. Isabella thought from his voice that he had also read the letter. What had she said in it? Why—when—had she written it?

"Oh, Buck, of course, at twelve, even before," Lord Whitfield read aloud. He passed the letter to her.

"I daresay you don't remember a word of it, do you?"

The letter had the look of paper, even paper as thick as this was, which has been much handled. It was creased. The ink had faded. It could have been a hundred years old.

"Oh, Buck, of course, at twelve, even before. I am going to the Quadrant, then to Jay for silks. *How* I long! Bella."

"According to a colleague, and I agree, that letter can be read in six different ways," Lord Whitfield remarked. "It has taken a deal of our time. A deal of it. I said just now that the matter is not exactly closed, but I don't want to sound despondent. We'll see what can be done to mend things. One point worth mentioning, Lady Carteret. Your sister-in-law. I've known the child since she was in short petticoats, but, not to mince words, Clare can be a vixen. You have an enemy there."

"I know."

"Well, well, it happens in the best families. That's all I have to say for the present. I wanted to make your acquaintance, Lady Carteret. It's always necessary in matters like this. Feel assured of my best services."

He stood up and grasped her hand firmly, almost fiercely.

Isabella was silent when she and Robert left King's Bench Walk, and the carriage began its journey back to Regent's Park.

If she had surprised Lord Whitfield by her self-command, her silence now surprised Robert even more. She didn't say, as would have been human, thank God it looked as if things were settled. She didn't exclaim that everything could now return to normal. He saw Isabella accepted that things could never be the same. Who believed her innocent? Poor Deno never had. The old Earl, he himself, Lord Whitfield, all suspected she'd been that actor's lover. Between the Bagots and this beautiful woman lay only her rather admirable lie.

The carriage turned in at the park gates and trotted under the shady trees. When it halted at Finstock Lodge he saw Isabella give a slight shudder.

Chapter Seventeen

BY THE TIME KATE'S SECOND important season at the Royalty was begun, she was what they called in greenrooms a star. The town adored her. She now had scores of ardent friends, while in her days of obscurity she had scarcely had two. She played Viola in *Twelfth Night,* Beatrice in *Much Ado About Nothing.* Boldly ignoring the difference in their ages, Davenant played Benedick. They were the most fascinating pair of actors in London. Kate was so famous that crowds collected every night at the stage door to see her arrive and leave the theater, flowers thrown on to the stage at the end of the performances lay at her feet as if at a Roman triumph, letters arrived in heaps every day begging her to meet foreign marquises and English baronets. When she stepped on the stage every night, the audience roared as if welcoming a lover.

Davenant seemed pleased by the adoration. He had discovered and trained her, taught her all she knew. If Kate was the toast of London, it was he they were actually toasting. The roars for him, in any case, never lessened. Why should they?

Kate was not hardened by the stream of light and money

which poured down on her. She became rather softer now
she was the acknowledged queen of the London theater. But
her life altered. She and Buckley moved to a larger house in
Kensington. There was a walled garden and an orchard, a
fountain in a courtyard outside the drawing room, a covered
entrance from the road to the front door. The Vernons had
their own carriage now, which took them daily on the country drive to the theater and waited for them at night after the
performance. Matilda and Billy had a nurserymaid as well as
the fairhaired Mary Anne, who had been promoted to Nurse
in a smart navy-blue starched frock. Kate's clothes were now
created by a fashionable dressmaker.

With success, Kate's looks flowered. Her russet hair was
worn, like that of the society women, in imitation of the
young Queen, parted in the center and plaited over her ears.
Her pale skin had a glow, her luminous eyes were bright. She
entertained, went out a good deal. More than fame and
accompanying wealth, what made her happy was playing opposite Davenant. Her life was filled from morning to night
with work, with Davenant and work, one inseparable from
the other. He taught her to "plaster her voice" as he called it
"on to the back wall of the gallery." He taught her that if a
costume was to cling, it must first be wet, then knotted and
left to dry so that it became clinging and wrinkled. He taught
her—while acting—how to laugh. He never needed to teach
her how to cry, for her eyes brimmed when her speeches
were sad, and her moving voice made audiences weep with
her.

Two things darkened the brightness round Kate; and
whenever she was not actually working they continued to
hurt her. She had refused for more than a year to see her sister. And Buckley had begun to drink too much.

Kate had lived in the theater since she was born, and knew
every sign of a man who is taking to drink. She had inherited
from both parents almost a revulsion against drink. In her
short life she had seen talent ruined and men die of it. The
one exception for her was Laurie Spindle, but when *he* drank

he became stupid and sleepy. When Buckley drank he was frightening.

She had told nobody that he was sometimes violent to her. Once he had pushed her across the room so hard she had hit her head against the edge of a cupboard and fainted. On two or three occasions he had returned home drunk and taken her crudely, against her will. She knew a wife must submit, and she did love him. But to be siezed by a drunken man, forced down onto the floor and nearly raped, in a coupling which lasted less than a few minutes, left her outraged and disgusted, her body and mind both violated and bruised. He used her as if she were a whore; she felt soiled.

But she was fiercely independent and kept such things a secret. Nobody was to feel sorry for her. Besides, she knew why Buckley drank. It was from furious disappointment. She was sure, too, that as well as taking her so crudely, he had other women. She shut her mind to that. Both the drink and the sex were anodynes, because Davenant did not give him leading roles anymore, while she herself had become as famous as Buckley had always believed he would be. It hurt her conscience to see Buckley drinking. Gloomy and spiteful, his handsome face blurred, he filled her with concern and even with remorse. It was as if there were a spell over them which, if it enhanced her, must damage him. . .

Her feelings about her sister were very different. She still loved Buckley, or at least was fond of him and felt guilty and sad about him. But Isabella shocked her. Isabella, a married woman and a lady of nobility, going to bed with Buckley. She knew the affair had been before her own marriage, Buckley had admitted it and when she thought of it she was sure that it was true. She also suspected that Buckley's sudden proposal of marriage—which had so delighted and flattered her— must have been at the time his affair with her sister was at an end. Knowing Buckley so well, she perfectly understood that. She did not resent it.

But what had been the result of Isabella's wickedness? Ellen had told Kate that poor Lord Carteret had left England,

and that pretty little Lord Frederick might lose his title. It was very strange to think he could be Buckley's child, her own children's half-brother. What a tragic mess.

Playing the great passions upon the stage, she had never felt them in reality. At best, Buckley's lovemaking stirred her, but it dissatisfied her, too. Prudish and reserved about sex, she had talked of it to nobody and was oddly ignorant of its details. She must, she thought, be one of those women who could never have a climax in love. She put it out of her thoughts.

She was dressing for the theater one afternoon, waited on by her maid, when Buckley came into the bedroom. Looking quickly at him, Kate said, "Thank you, Janet. That will be all."

The maid left the room, and Kate calmly tied the enormous green silk ribbons of her bonnet under her chin.

Buckley leaned against the wall, staring at her. His face had the blurred look she had begun to hate. Never tidy or cared for in his person, his expensive dark green coat was marked with dust, as if he'd been lying on the ground.

"Buckley, don't you think you should rest?"

He gave her a jeering smile.

"Go on," he said. "Hurry off to the theater and give the mob a treat. Mustn't keep them waiting, they'll be hanging round the stage door by now, won't they? Do you know something? Your acting makes me sick. You're Davenant's puppet, that's all you are."

"You are drunk."

Her collected manner infuriated him. She was small, neatly and fashionably dressed, calm, everything about her invulnerable. Did she think she acted better than he did? Did she conspire with Davenant to rob him of importance?

"Yes, I'm drunk, and I'll get more drunk," he said, coming toward her. "And don't look at me like that, you stupid vain little—"

Using a filthy word, he struck her hard across the face.

Kate tottered and almost fell, then with a kind of gasp ran out of the room and rushed down the stairs.

She had no veil to her bonnet and huddled in the corner of the carriage, her hand up against her face. The bruise throbbed, and when she dabbed her cheek there was a little blood. She was too angry to feel any pain, and when she had hurried with bowed head through the stage door and up to her dressing room the first thing she did was to rush to the pier glass to look at her face. A great black bruise was forming on her cheek round the thin gash of dried blood. She began to cry, not from pain but from helpless anxiety. How could she play now? She bent close to the glass, examining the bruise and cut when there was a loud knock at the door.

"Don't come in!"

"Why not?"

It was Davenant. Coming into the room, he saw her standing by the long glass and at once came over to her. He took her chin in his hands.

"That's some black eye you are going to get there. Don't waste time explaining. We will talk later. I came in to ask you to have supper with me after the performance. No, no, don't speak—"

Still holding her chin, he continued to study the bruise.

"Sit down," he said. "We'll see what we can do in the way of repairs."

On a clean linen cloth on Kate's dressing table were the small pans and dishes of moistened watercolor which she used for her makeup. Gwynyth prepared them freshly for every performance. A large dish held the flesh tint, which Kate put on with a sponge, and when that was dry she painted with a brush the lines to stress bone structure, the white for highlights.

"Now," he said, skillfully beginning to make up her face, using the base tint more thickly than she usually did. "I had a black eye myself once when I was playing Hamlet. Had a few words with a fellow actor, a nincompoop acting the Ghost.

The man hit me. It would have been a fine thing to appear in customary suits of solemn black with an eye to match. I did it like this. . ."

He went on working at her upturned face.

"There."

When she looked in the glass, there was not a mark on her face.

"We can show them a trick or two," he said. "I don't know what they'd make of Benedick if he'd been knocking the lady about before the play started. Don't forget. A little supper in my dressing room after the performance. Just a few friends. . ."

When the play ended, Gwynyth helped her to dress in an evening gown. Kate's dressing room on the first floor was scarcely less grand than Davenant's, and she and Gwynyth often laughed over the end-of-the-passage box room. In the cupboard running the full length of the room, Kate kept a number of gowns into which she changed when she was going to suppers or receptions after the play.

Gwynyth knew nothing about the blow, and Kate was not going to tell her. She couldn't bear to discuss it. She merely told Gwynyth she had "decided to keep on her stage make-up." Gwynyth accepted this unusual decision without comment. Anything Kate did was right.

"Did you see the lilies?" she said. "Aren't they magnificent? Can't make out the writing, it looks foreign to me. There's red roses again. And all the little violets, and that big basket of camellias in the corner."

"Lovely, dear," said Kate, so accustomed to living in a roomful of flowers, fresh every day and sent by people to show that they adored her, that she scarcely noticed them. "Do you know who is to be at Mr. Davenant's party tonight?"

"Haven't heard a word," said Gwynyth, "Funny, I usually always do."

The two women kissed each other an affectionate good night, and Kate went down the corridor slowly arranging her silk gauze scarf on her arms. She had taken a long time to

dress—she preferred to—and the theater was settling down
to its midnight silences. She was tired. Now the performance
with all its sparkling color was over, she felt shaken and
shocked again.

In Davenant's suite two waiters were laying a table and
Davenant was supervising, examining plates and cutlery.

"This fork has a crooked prong. No, the flowers and candles go there, if you please."

He had changed into evening dress. The dandyish style of
his clothes showed off his stocky, powerful figure. His hair,
parted at the side and curled, was grayer than when Kate
had first met him. His face was more lined. But his eyes were
as blue, his voice more alluring than ever.

"Here you are, madam. Not before time. You are the most
unpunctual of my actresses. That will do," to the waiters, "I
will ring when I need you. No, no, I prefer to pour the champagne myself. Off with you both, but remember to ice the
Chablis correctly and no bits floating in the turtle soup. The
lady dislikes them."

He shooed out the waiters.

"I had thought of ordering my favorite supper of kippers
and champagne," he said. "But somehow I decided it might
not suit."

"Where are the other guests?" asked Kate.

"Did I say there would be any?"

"A few friends, you said."

"A good description. Sit down and try this champagne. It
is not bad. The Comte de Chambrunier brought it for me
from France."

She took the glass in silence.

"Are you feeling better?" he said, looking at her.

"Thanks to you, yes."

"I fear you will need to paint thick for a week or two.
Bruises take a time to go. Do you want to tell me about it?"

"I would prefer not to. A private matter."

"Very right and proper," agreed Davenant, filling his
glass.

Kate enjoyed the meal because nobody in the world could resist Davenant if he had made up his mind to amuse and fascinate. He had no intention of allowing her to think about anybody at present but him. He had an extraordinary, irresistible way with him, and her outraged thoughts about Buckley faded from her mind. But as she listened, and watched Davenant, and laughed, she sensed something altered in his manner to her. She felt uneasy. She had not acted with this man, lived beside him onstage and played his lover or wife, his daughter or mistress, without having strong intuitions about him.

When the meal was over he pushed back his chair and poured himself some brandy. Putting down the glass with deliberation, he said, "Did I ever tell you that I was married, Kate?"

She answered coolly enough, "Everybody says that you are."

"Why do you suppose they have never met this invisible wife of mine?"

"There are various rumors."

"There certainly are, and I can tell you every one of them. That she left me for a foreigner. That she is mad, God forgive them, and I had her locked up. One kind friend suggested that, like the Earl of Leicester with poor Amy Robsart, I had made away with her. But that was after we had been playing *The Pit of Hell* to packed houses."

"Why are you speaking to me of your wife?"

"Why not? We are friends. I like your company. And there is something sympathetic about you."

She smiled faintly, still uneasy. She had a curious sensation of danger. He *was* dangerous, for all he seemed so mild this evening. The bruise, too, worried her. Now that she was no longer concentrated and uplifted by acting, it ached painfully. I am sure my face is swollen, she thought. I must look a fright.

"Yes, I did marry years ago," Davenant said, "A pretty little thing who fell sick within a year and nearly lost her life giving birth to a stillborn son. She has been in Wales on a mountain top ever since, living with an old aunt of hers. I go—I went—to see her as often as I could. Sometimes I had to travel all through the night to reach her, and return the next day for a performance. Poor child, it was pitiful to see her fading. She lingered on for years. She scarcely knew me, and there was never much hope, for all I consulted so many doctors. Last month she died."

"I am so sorry," Kate said in a low voice.

He shook his head.

"No need. It was best. Terrible, to be so ill and weak, bedridden, in a kind of swoon most of the time. I gave her the best I could. But I have wished, God knows, that I never met her. It was bearing my child that ruined her health. Because of me she is dead, if truth be told."

He stopped speaking, staring into the brandy glass, not picking it up. He was deep in thought.

What he had told her moved Kate almost to tears. She had not known the poor dead creature, and her sympathy and sadness were all for him in this hidden part of his life. She waited a little, sharing his sadness. He did not stir. The sense of danger was gone, and, feeling she could say nothing which did not intrude on his private thoughts, she stood up hesitatingly. He roused himself, got to his feet, came round the table and with a kind of push made her sit down again.

"Don't you make me a missish speech and then say goodnight, Kate, because I decided to tell you Eliza is dead. I am not a block of wood. Of course I am grieved. But the poor thing was never a wife, and during her years-long illness she was like a sick stranger. What is reality is my work, my life in the theater, the friends who understand me. You are not proposing to go, are you?"

"But I thought—"

"What?" he said, gazing at her with his brilliant eyes. "What did you think? That I made an improper suggestion to you, once upon a time?"

"I have forgotten it."

"What a Miss Prim," he said satirically. "You remember the occasion perfectly. I can see it in your eyes. Will you have some more strawberries?"

She shook her head.

"I see I have taken your appetite away. Now we come to the matter on hand. I am, as I have told you, Kate, now a widower. Why not marry me?"

Her usually pale face blushed scarlet. Even her nose and ears went red.

"What on earth can you mean!"

"What I say, of course."

"But I am married!"

"Not much of a husband, is he?" he said, deliberately touching his own cheek at the spot where Buckley had hit her on the cheekbone.

"He's unhappy, he didn't mean it, sometimes he drinks— oh, how *could* you say such a thing?" she cried hysterically, sprang to her feet and a glass of wine tipped up, spilling in a crimson stain across the skirt of her white satin dress. She burst into tears.

He put out his arms and clasped her, putting his hand on her hair, pressing her head against his chest.

"Cry away. Cry away."

"I don't want to cry," she sobbed angrily. "Let me go. Leave me alone."

"No, I will not. You don't love that self-indulgent selfish man you married. I know you have two pretty children, and why shouldn't you keep them? But Vernon doesn't suit you. Didn't I hear talk of him and that titled sister of yours? He's a woman-chaser. He drinks, too. In my experience it is drink in men that makes them brutal to women. What is more," he said, finally releasing her, "he is not the actor he was."

"He would improve if you gave him a chance."

"*If* he improves, I will."

She mopped helplessly at her stained skirt with a small lace handkerchief, still half-crying.

"Poor Buckley," she said. "He needs me."

Davenant looked at her pityingly. "Kate, Kate, Buckley is an egotist. He would find another woman tomorrow. If I am any judge of men, there is one who never thinks of a single human creature but himself. Are you simpleminded enough to think he needs *you?* He bitterly resents you. Now, now, turn off the tap, for heaven's sake. You are not crying because you are shocked at my suggestion. Or because I have offended those delicate feelings you are so proud of. This is why you are weeping."

Suddenly, he caught her in his arms. It was the danger she had feared yet waited for. She was pressed close against him, kissed, not violently, but with a long, exploring, lingering promise. When he drew away her head had begun to swim, she was more frightened than before.

"You are crying because you want *me*. As I want you," he said, looking down at her.

They were alone in the great empty silent theater which a few hours ago had teemed with life. There was not a sound except—to Kate—her thudding, fearful heart. He kissed her again, pressing so close that she could feel his body against her.

"Don't—oh, please don't—I must not—"

"But you *must*," he said, and, picking her up effortlessly, carried her across to the divan and laid her down. He went to the double doors and locked them. Struggling against her senses as if she had fallen into a river in flood, she shook her head as he moved toward her, saying helplessly, "No—no—no—"

She was tense and trembling as he knelt beside her and began slowly to undress her. He stopped when he had unfastened her bodice and kissed her breasts in turn, putting the raised pink nipples into his mouth so that she gasped. He pulled off her silk petticoats and underclothes, and at last she lay in front of him naked, her skin tinged with gold in the candlelight, the triangle of curling hair between her thighs a dark coppery red. He had been kneeling beside her, but now he stood up, looking at her naked body with appraising eyes.

Kate, lying at his mercy, could not stop trembling and pulled a fallen petticoat across herself to hide from his eyes. He smiled and began to undress. Then the petticoat was ripped away, his heavy weight pressed down on her, her legs were roughly forced apart. He felt her resist him, tensed against him, as he went into her. Pressing his face against her thick red hair he whispered, "Come to me, come *with* me, this is what you need, this—and this—and this—"

She still resisted, stiffened against his invading body, and he kissed her mouth slowly, matching the kisses with the thrusting drives of his hard body inside hers. She could fight her senses no longer, felt herself melting, helpless, fainting with pleasure as he brought her to her climax quickly, then again and again, until she was exhausted, sore and bruised with lovemaking.

At last he finished with her, wrapped her in his arms like a child, and they slept.

When she opened her eyes a gray dawn light was filtering through the heavy velvet curtains. The candles were burned out. She lay awake, not able to move, for Davenant was still lying covering her, as if keeping his possession. Her whole body ached deliciously as it had never done before in her life. Buckley's lovemaking had been so short, had never once satisfied her, and she always thought she was a woman who would never know a climax in love. Lying under Davenant's weight, remembering how he had brought her to that over and over again, she felt ecstatic, worn out, lost. He had taken her at first against her will, forcing himself into her, knowing how it would be between them. She moved slightly, to look at his sleeping face. He had not stirred, still pinning her to the divan, but when she looked at him he was awake.

"So you love me," he said. "Is that what I am to think?"

She put her arms round his naked back and clung.

"Are you tired, Kate?" His voice mocked her. "Too tired to show me all over again?"

*   *   *

Buckley was astounded when his prudish wife, on the day following their quarrel, calmly informed him she was considering a divorce.

"What do you mean! You have no evidence."

It seemed she had just found out about a recent affair Buckley had had with a dancer in the Royalty ballet. It was clear Kate knew all about it. The girl, Kate said, had "confessed."

"A woman can't divorce a man for that," exclaimed Buckley angrily. "You'd need to cite cruelty!"

He was so flabbergasted that he had completely forgotten.

"That, too," said Kate. She left the room.

For the first few days after this conversation he simply could not believe that his wife, with her rigid moral code, would go to the lengths of divorcing him. It was out of the question. He comforted himself with this thought and behaved, on the whole, rather well. He apologized for striking her and said he would stop drinking to excess. She merely listened. He did not mention Floss Buxton, who had vanished from the ballet without trace—he supposed Kate had put the fear of God into the poor kid. What was a mere dancer if the star actress wished the girl removed?

After a few days of guarded peace he was astounded when Kate said at breakfast (she had been advised to do so by Davenant the previous evening), "I am afraid, Buckley, you cannot live here any longer. Not in the circumstances. You will have to leave as soon as it is convenient for you to do so."

"You actually mean you want a divorce!"

"I think so. I am considering it. But you will have to leave in any case. You can see the children, of course, whenever you like."

"That's kind," he said, so bitterly that she sighed.

"I'm sorry. You did bring this on yourself, though. If you want any extra money . . ."

That really stung. He'd never loved her, although he had liked and respected her. He'd married her because he had been afraid of the very scandal which had now broken over Isabella, damned near drowning her. Kate had been dutiful rather than passionate. She was a brilliant actress and could be a good friend. But she was sentimental and played the part of wife and mother rather than feeling either very deeply. As for his taking her money—how dare she!

"Listen to me," he said viciously, "I wouldn't touch a sovereign of yours if I was starving in a ditch. I've put up with a lot from you. Only a lunatic marries an ambitious woman. That's your sin. You don't like hearing that, do you? Your duty was to *me*. You should have helped and supported me, your husband. All you did was push yourself into the front of the stage. What's more, I act better than that old played-out Davenant and I'm twenty years younger. Keep your money for him when his hair and teeth fall out. I don't want to hear another word."

He slammed out of the room.

He left that afternoon, when the servants were out and the children in Kensington Gardens. The carriage was heaped with his luggage, boxes of clothes, guns, fishing tackle, a set of rapiers with chased steel handles. His own portrait. Neither Kate nor Buckley himself had ever stopped him having any possible thing he wanted.

He opened the drawing room door, did not come into the room, but said loudly, "Good-bye."

She started up and ran toward him, for a moment very troubled.

He did not give her time to speak but was gone.

Something like remorse kept coming over her for the rest of the day, every time she thought of Buckley and remembered he was gone from the house. When she arrived at the theater she talked to Gwynyth earnestly about the matter, but Gwynyth was full of approval and loving, prejudiced encouragement. Kate, dressed in her costume as Beatrice, made up her face and went down to the wings. She liked to hear the noise on the other side of the curtains, the rustle, the murmur, as the great theater began to fill. The music of the overture began.

She stood in her vaporous green dress threaded with pearls, her hair loosed and falling in a golden-red mass round her shoulders, quietly listening. A strong hand gripped her waist, and a muscular body pressed against her back. Davenant whispered, "Don't think *they* have come to see *you*."

She pressed back against him, trembling, and he put his other hand caressingly against her buttocks.

"I shall make love to you tonight until you cry out for me to stop," he said, then let her go suddenly, leaving her breathless.

Chapter Eighteen

ISABELLA DID NOT CLOSE FINSTOCK LODGE in the autumn, when the rest of society left town. She stayed. London emptied, and in a way she welcomed it. She lived a lonely life. During the winter her children were sometimes brought from Sussex to stay with her, but she knew herself to be a dull companion, and was well aware that they preferred the merry country life of a great house.

Robert visited her occasionally when he came to London in the winter, and what he saw of her disturbed him.

Finally, when the Bagot family returned to London at the beginning of the season in the following spring, he decided to go to Regent's Park, determined to help her in some way. But how?

The park looked fresh and green, children shouted and ran about. Finstock Lodge itself was crisply white as he rode up to the door. He was anxious to see Isabella, and when he was shown into the drawing room, he saw her sitting in the window seat. She turned toward him, but did not stir.

Robert took her hand and kissed it, looking at her searchingly. She moved him. She was so delicate, so pale, in a cling-

ing dress of olive green which did not suit her. He held her
hand a moment longer.

"How is it with you, Cousin?"

She said she was well enough.

He sat down beside her, and talked of family matters. To
make things feel natural, he spoke of Denys. Had Isabella received a letter, as the old Earl had, telling of the terrible
storms and of how the Regiment was being cut off by floods?

"A serpent in his riding boot!" Robert said, laughing. "The
horror of it. His news is so dramatic. Ours must be very tame
to him."

There was the kind of silence which was better broken.

"Well, Isabella, what are your plans?" he asked in his energetic way. "Do you intend to stay here at Finstock?"

She looked round the room just then and he thought he
saw her give a slight shudder. She'd done that once before.
Marriage is the devil, he thought. Why didn't I see that this
room is full of Deno? There was a pencil portrait of him on
the wall, a silver box for his cigars on the table beside them.
There was the Bagot crest on every damned piece of silver
one looked at. There was even Denys's much-thumbed book
of form in its old place, where he could pick it up and flip
through it, commenting on horses and owners.

"Why not pack up and leave here?" he said suddenly.

"Where could I go?"

He thought the question, from this beautiful woman in her
unbecoming dress, very pathetic.

"I don't know, Bella—what about Brighton? It's cheerful
there, I'm told, and full of life. There are all kinds of enter-
taining things to do. Sea-bathing if you are brave enough!
You might persuade your Mama to go with you. Let me arrange things. Yes?"

Ellen agreed to go with her daughter to stay at Brighton—
Robert suggested the fashionable Bedford Hotel. Ellen had
hesitated at leaving Thomas, but he insisted. The post he had
obtained at the Richmond theater interested him; (now that
Viscount Carteret had settled some money on the Winters,

Thomas was stronger and less fussed about his work). He would be well looked after by Ellen's small staff of servants at the cottage. Of course she must be with their daughter.

"The girl's made an unholy mess of everything and the more she sees of you, my dear, the better for her."

Ellen was inclined to agree.

When they arrived in Brighton, Ellen liked the town at once. The sun shone after weeks of cold weather, the climate was kind, the sea breezes refreshing. In squares of pillared houses were beautiful flowers—Ellen saw a magnolia covered with white and purple blossoms. She enjoyed the fashionable crowds, the carriages and riders going by on the road by the sea, the ships, the feeling of being somewhere lively, modish. The hotel was comfortable and well furnished; princes and princesses sometimes stayed there.

"What more can we want?" Ellen said with her upward trill of a laugh. From the windows of Isabella's suite, there was a magnificent view of the sea.

But in the months that followed, although Ellen was a practical and not weakeningly sympathetic companion, although her father came to visit them and everything was done for her well-being, Isabella remained listless.

A misty autumn look began to come to the sunny mornings. Soon, Ellen thought, she must return home. Sitting by the window, looking at the calm sea, she wondered if the Michaelmas daisies were out in her Richmond garden yet. Thomas had written to her yesterday—but he never told her things like that.

It was too early for the morning parade of carriages or horsemen, and when Ellen heard the clatter of a carriage arriving at the front of the hotel she looked down curiously; then stared, her face sharp with interest.

Isabella had come through the archway leading from her bedroom.

"Are you expecting a visitor, Isabella? Because *I* think the Bagot carriage has just drawn up."

Isabella sat down very suddenly.

A few moments later Robert was announced. He came in

with his quick way of walking, greeted Isabella with affection and Ellen with graceful respect. She had never met him before and was charmed. She might have stayed talking for quite a time but it was noticeable that her daughter never said a word. Regretfully, Ellen curtsied and left them.

Robert looked sharply at Isabella when they were alone. The strong light from the sky shone full on her. He had not seen her for weeks, and she had grown even thinner. There were rings under her eyes and her skin was no longer olive but yellowish, as if she suffered from malaria. Her gray embroidered dress hung round her, emphasizing her wasted figure.

"I was not expecting you, Robert. It was good of you to come. How are the children? Are they still at Bagot Park?"

"Yes, and thriving. But they would so much like to see you. May I take you there? It is only two hours from Brighton, and in this fine weather—"

"I don't feel quite strong enough at present."

He leaned forward.

"Cousin, are you ill? May I send you a doctor? Tell me what I may do for you. You know I am always at your service."

"I am perfectly well, Robert. A little thin, I suppose." She grimaced and bunched the loose waist of her dress. "Mama scolds me, and Rivers wants to alter the dress, but I don't wish it."

There was a trace of the old, willful, difficult girl in her insistence on wearing a dress which emphasized how she was changed.

He still looked at her concernedly, and she said, "Have you heard from Lord Whitfield? I do wonder if the Earl has decided poor little Freddy must be sent packing."

"Bella!"

"Why not? If they decide he is not a *lord* any more. Why should they give him house room?"

"You're very bitter," he said, at a loss—something rare for him. "I don't like to hear you talk like this. Do you hate us now, Bella?"

She twisted a heavy emerald ring Denys had given her years ago. It, too, was overlarge and the stone slipped from the front to the back of her finger.

"I don't hate anyone. Not even Clare. I've thought about what happened with Clare. I've thought of little else. Hopton adored her so. I suppose she knew Clare was in love with you and thought her *secret* would straighten the path of true love."

"You are talking nonsense."

She gave a smile of such irony that he was shocked at the change in her.

"You're not being honest with me, Robert. You and I both know how much Clare was attached to you, probably still is. Denys told me so. I suppose she was glad when Hopton told her those things. With poor Freddy out of the way—Denys, too—you would inherit. And maybe Clare with you."

Although what Isabella said might be true—he'd never faced Clare with it and never would—the accusation was a disgusting one. It imputed horrible motives to Clare and by inference to himself. A plot, whether Isabella were guilty or not, to become the Bagot heir by ruining Denys's life. But Isabella's words couldn't hurt him because, for himself, the idea was ludicrous. He'd never for a single moment in his life desired to be the heir. A strong man, he never wanted to rule except by a vicarious authority. A kind of energetic indifference stood between him and ambition. And he loved Denys.

He stood up, because Robert never sat still, walked about, opened the window wider, bent to sniff some roses in a bowl, came back and stood beside her. He looked down at her thoughtfully. She met his look as if he exhausted her.

"Forget all this nonsense, Bella. You've suffered very much, and you mustn't sit about getting so thin and sad-looking and spend your time on sick fancies. I'm glad I came. My clever idea about the healthy Brighton air is a great failure, I see. Why not go home?"

"To Finstock Lodge. Please don't ask me to."

"Do you still dislike it so much? Then let me sell it for you."

She shook her head, saying merely, "Oh, Robert."

"Where would you like to live?" he said, ignoring that. "I went to dine at Twickenham last season. It's an enchanting place, do you know it? Pope used to live there, they tell me. And Lady Mary Wortley Montagu and all kinds of last-century grandees. Why don't we go to Twickenham and look together?"

Isabella was about to refuse. She was too indifferent, too worn out with misery, to make any kind of decision. But Robert took both her hands and raised her to her feet. Clasping her hands, he seemed to force some of his own energy through his fingers into her own. She had a feeling of his strength and affection.

"That's settled, then."

It was early winter when Isabella moved into the new Twickenham house, only a twenty minute ride from her parents' cottage in Richmond. Lockton House had been built in the early 1700's. A gnarled wisteria grew against its handsome brick front, and it was a rambling old place full of irregular-shaped oddly attractive rooms. The garden was spacious, sloping lawns ran down to the river's edge. It had been built for one of George II's ladies-in-waiting.

Robert spent all his time with Isabella, helped her to choose the house (just as the old Earl had done, Isabella thought wryly), and waited on her with unselfish kindness. No detail was too small to interest him.

She dreaded returning to Finstock Lodge, but Robert made the ordeal less painful. He pointed out, in a practical way, how foolish it would be not to return, and that he would help her to decide which furniture was to be saved or sold. Because he was interested, amusing and energetic, she revived. His companionship was lively, and she felt in it a kind of unspoken championship. As if he were saying, without words, "I am here. Lean on me."

At first she was glad to see him because he reminded her of Denys and the days when she had been happy. But then she began to look forward to Robert's visits, and would run to the window to see if the carriage had come, looking for his elegant figure and clever, dark face. Sometimes she quite longed for him, and when at last he arrived and clasped her hands strongly she blushed with pleasure. She enjoyed the days of shopping with him, enjoyed being teased and cared for. She admired him. Sometimes, catching his thoughtful glance, she felt that perhaps he shared her feelings. But that was impossible. . .

When she was at last settled in the new house, he broke the news that he must return to Sussex.

"My uncle is getting crotchety. He keeps saying in his letters that he is not getting any younger. What he means is that I am behind with my work on the estate."

Isabella sighed. They were sitting in the dining room of her new home, having luncheon. Looking across at her, he felt moved, and oddly satisfied, almost as if he were an artist who had completed a picture. She wore a creamy velvet day dress with a scalloped skirt and a beautiful rose-patterned shawl. She was *almost* the girl who had been Deno's wife. If Deno had seen the poor thing looking so ill, Robert thought, he must have relented.

"Fanny and her husband are at Bagot at present," he said, "and Lord knows who Fan has invited, the place is bursting with visitors. I shall miss you and this nice house and the fun we've had."

"I shall miss you, too."

Robert disappeared from Isabella's life as suddenly as he appeared. For weeks he had been her companion, coaxing her back to life. Then he was gone. He arranged for the children to return to her. They were taller, noisier, more beautiful than Isabella remembered. Freddy was autocratic, Betsy plump and loving, with a rosy face. They seemed delighted with their new home, soon forgot to mention Bagot Park. They brought their nurse with them, a fat country girl all smiles. But although Isabella hugged them and went for riverside walks with them, she did not feel close to them. It was to their nurse they ran, crying, when they fell over.

She began to receive a few cautious invitations from people in society and once or twice nerved herself to accept

(Robert had told her that she must). But at a small dinner at Lady Quenington's the talk was of the Queen and Prince Albert and a ball of the previous week at the Palace. One deaf old lady from the country said loudly, "Why weren't you there, my dear?"

Isabella went scarlet.

She was more conscious of her curious situation now that society half-received her again. She was at the mercy of people's generous thoughts and disliked that very much.

The children had been with her at Lockton House for a few weeks when she received a letter from Robert suggesting they should come back to Bagot Park for Christmas "if she could spare them." When she told Freddy he fixed his large dark eyes on her and said, "Mama, I think we *need* to go. Our ponies miss us."

"And I'll be with Freddy," chimed Betsy. Inevitably.

In the way of children, they gave her desperate hugs and kisses and danced off into the Bagot carriage as if on their way to a party.

It was late November and had begun to be very cold. On the day the children left Isabella went for a walk by the river, returning before it was dark. A fire was lit in the drawing room and she sat staring into the flames and thinking of Denys. She had received another letter, covered with strange stamps, creased, travel-stained. It had been written on a journey to the North of India. It was brief and dutiful and meaningless, ending, "Affectionately yours, D." All his letters ended like that.

She picked up the letter and read it again. Tears stood in her eyes. He'd been away now for much more than a year. She had thought when he closed his heart against her that she passionately loved him, but perhaps that had not been so. Perhaps what she ached for had been *his* love, which had so surrounded her that when he took it away she felt ill. That same feeling, that she'd possessed something infinitely previous and had lost it forever, came back whenever she received a letter. Even his slanting handwriting made her cry.

There was a knock, and the butler came into the room. He

was a thin quiet man, white-haired and gentle, who had been chosen by Robert. "I am sure he will suit, Bella. His name is right. People are affected by their names, you know."

The butler's name was True.

"A visitor for you, my lady."

The card was engraved in letters much too large and looked more like a playbill than a visiting card.

"Buckley Vernon."

Isabella had a moment of genuine shock. She hesitated, then said, "You may show him in, True."

"Bella!" exclaimed a resonant voice. Buckley strode in, hands outstretched. "I only heard this morning that you were here. I felt I must pay you a call. I arrived for a new engagement at the Richmond theater, and who was the first person I set eyes on? Your father!"

From the moment she saw him, the nervous flutter of her heart stopped. Surprisingly, pleasantly, his presence did not upset her.

They sat by the fire in the way that old friends do, comfortably. Buckley talked and Isabella listened in her charming, attentive way, her dark eyes on his face. She only half-heard the story of his arrival at Richmond. He was not, she thought, as handsome as of old. His face, his thick girlish mouth, were coarser: there was a dissolute look about him. But she liked his panache. It wasn't easy to speak of leaving the brilliance of the Royalty and taking a role at a little theater in Richmond Green, but he managed to make it sound a clever thing to have done. His bravado touched her as much as his boyish smile.

"I am to play the lead in a burletta. Did you know I sing beautifully!"

He laughed, showing his white teeth.

The past was not mentioned. He briefly touched on his family, spoke of Kate, changed the conversation back to himself at once. Isabella was genuinely glad he had come. She'd forgotten that captivating manner, the way he laughed, his childish habit of boasting and waiting for praise, then if it was given returning it extravagantly, a kind of reward made of gold.

When he said good-bye she put out her hand.

"Come again, Buck. It is good to see you."

"And you, Bella. You are looking very beautiful."

Buckley soon knew every stick and stone of the road from Richmond to Twickenham by heart. He called to see her almost daily, at any time when he was not rehearsing at Richmond. She began to look forward to his visits. When he strode into the room she brightened.

But it was odd that the relationship seemed to have reversed. During that summer years ago, when she had been frantically in love with him she had been the pursuer. It was strange to remember that. She had begged to know when they would meet again, she had counted the hours. Now she would never think of suggesting a meeting. She simply did not wish to. He must do the asking or there would be no meeting at all.

Deserted by her husband, scarcely accepted by society for all her beauty and wealth, Isabella knew that sooner or later she would go to bed with Buckley again. They'd once been lovers, there was no natural barrier, no reason why they should not. But to put off the moment of discovering whether he could still give her such pleasure (which she doubted), to dally, did her good. She did not tell her parents she was seeing him, and he agreed not to mention it to Thomas at the theater. It added a flavor to this renewed friendship.

One afternoon they went for a walk along the towpath; the day was wild with a strong wind blowing fiercely through trees now bare of leaves. Buckley had bought Isabella a spaniel pup and the little dog lolloped in front of them, running for sticks, then returning hopefully with them in her mouth.

"Will Chloe like Ireland, do you suppose?" Buckley said, throwing another stick. The wind had blown some color into his usually pale face. He winked at her.

"Why should my poor little dog be banished to Ireland?"

"To be with her mistress, naturally."

"Buck. What nonsense are you talking?"

"Not nonsense at all. I've been offered a good engagement in Ireland for six months. Maybe longer. Come with me."

She actually laughed and told him not to be absurd. But she had slightly blushed.

"It isn't absurd, Bella. I shall be free soon, you know. Your sister has decided to divorce me."

She stared and said nothing.

He took her hand casually for a moment, saying wryly, in a manner she very much liked, "I know, I behaved badly. I often do. I'm a fool. But not about you, never about you. Come and be happy with me. Come with me, beautiful one."

He took her in his arms and kissed her. The kiss, the first they had exchanged, turned her bones to water.

"It's impossible—I can't—"

"It's impossible for us *not* to be together," he said, embracing her again.

It was hours before she could sleep that night. She had not allowed him to make love to her, but when she refused he'd merely smiled, accepting the refusal for what it was worth— her waiting game. Alone in her room long after midnight, the candles still burning, she walked up and down barefoot, wrapped in a long lacy shawl, her hair round her shoulders. She looked at the drawing of Denys on the wall by the dressing table. He returned her look with lazy smiling eyes. When you last looked at me you were turned to stone, she thought. She compared her memory of that sad stony face with Buckley's this evening, when he'd pressed his cheek against hers.

It snowed in the night, and when Isabella woke the world outside was changed. There was a strange glare, a kind of light from below. Garden, trees, pathway, lawns, were under a counterpane of blazing white.

The house was bitterly cold, and she ordered fires to be lit in every room, including those she did not use. Isabella's sudden fits of extravagance were much approved of by her servants, many of whom had worked for rich people who counted every penny. Footmen and maids bustled to and fro with logs. There was the sweet smell of wood smoke, the air was faintly warmer, fires crackled.

Isabella came downstairs wearing a dark red braided dress with many petticoats, and a great white fringed shawl Denys had given her. She picked up the puppy and went to sit on the window seat. I always seem to sit on window seats at fatal moments of my life, she thought. When I was a girl and saw the Bagot carriage. And in Newcastle. And now. She had made up her mind to go with Buckley.

When she remembered Denys she found she no longer suffered in the same way. The pain was dying, fading. Buckley wanted her—Denys did not. Even her little children were Bagots. Paradoxically Freddy was more a member of that proud family than Denys's own daughter. She didn't blame the children for being happier away from her—their life was in Sussex, they were part of it now. And Freddy was safe, it seemed. The Bagots wanted him.

So I can go a-roving, Isabella thought. Her senses swam. She gave a langourous sigh.

It had begun to snow again, and the house and the garden and the whole world seemed hushed. But then she thought she heard the muffled sound of horses on the snow. A moment later round the corner, turning into her gates, she knew a familiar carriage. Yellow and black, with two footmen on the box. Robert! The last person she wanted to see now.

He came into the room with his quick, confident walk, so much less studied than Buckley's. He kissed her hand. She smiled at him, but he did not return the smile. Did she imagine an air of haste and sadness?

"How pleasant to see you, Cousin."

He looked as if he hadn't heard her.

"Isabella. Deno is on his way home."

Her eyes widened. She swallowed and said nothing.

"He is on the *Lancashire,* the fastest of the steamers from the East. He will be in England within the fortnight."

"But I didn't know the Regiment has been ordered home—in the newspapers—"

"It isn't that. He is invalided out. He is ill."

She gave a start, leaned forward and touched his hand.

"Oh, Robert, I'm so very sorry." She might have been speaking of a friend of years ago.

"It's a kind of fever. It's been with him for weeks. The doctors don't understand it. He is very ill."

She pressed his hand but still said nothing.

Robert looked at her steadily and said, "I have come from the Earl. He begs you to return."

"But that's impossible!"

"Isabella, listen to me—"

"The *Earl* asks me!" she interrupted. "How could the Earl ask me? He cannot stand to see me, nor can any of the family. I am deeply sorry poor Denys is ill, but he is young, and he will be nursed back to health. All the family know the last person he would want near him is me! You know how it is with us, Robert. His father knows it. How could you come here and ask me such a thing?"

"You are wrong."

"Robert, it isn't to be discussed."

"Yes, it is. Because Deno loves you."

She made a kind of involuntary recoil, as if he'd burned her.

"Don't say things like that. Don't upset me."

"Why not? Why should I not upset you, as you call it?" he said harshly. "Deno needs you. He always has done, and how much more now that he's gravely ill, might even die. Were you blind enough to think he stopped loving you when all that happened? Isabella, I beg you. Be at the house when they bring him home."

She shook her head. She was mute.

"Is it pride? Do you think the family would not be good to you? If I promise—"

"I'm leaving England," she said flatly. "Very soon. In a few days."

He looked horrified.

"Leaving? With whom?"

"Why should it be 'with' anybody?" she said, stung. "I'm free to do as I wish. You've told me so often enough."

He walked over to the window and stood looking out at the snow, now steadily falling and making the sky very dark. Then he turned and said, "Tell me the truth."

A few minutes ago she had felt so happy. She wanted to feel like that still. But more than that, she wanted to keep the affection of this man looking at her in such a cold, unfamiliar way.

"I'm going away with Buckley Vernon. My sister has decided to divorce him. Buckley has an engagement in Ireland, and has asked me to go with him."

"I see."

"Robert," she said pleadingly. "I am lonely. Please understand."

"I understand this, Isabella. You've been hurt, and your marriage is broken. Whether it was through your own fault or not, whether I believe you innocent or not, is up to me. But isn't it time you began thinking of somebody else for a change?"

"You think me selfish?"

"Very."

"I am fond of Buckley. And he is of me."

"Fond?" he repeated, with such disdain that she blushed crimson. "Fond? What is that? Deno loves you. It was *because* he loved you that you cut him to the heart. Isabella, try. For once in your life try to think of someone except yourself."

"You can't ask me to give up being happy now," she said. Her eyes were full of tears.

There was a pause. She heard the clock ticking on the chimney piece, a door closing somewhere in the depth of the house.

"Can't I?"

Chapter Nineteen

THE WINDOWS OF THE OLD HOUSE GLOWED, but all round in the park and gardens and fields and woods lay a waste of whiteness. Isabella had made the long journey alone, leaving Robert to wait for the arrival of the ship at Gravesend.

Tired and gray-faced, she was shown into the long drawing room, which seemed to her dazzled eyes too brightly lit with dozens of candles.

The old Earl and Lady Clare were by the fire. The Earl sidled over to take her hand.

"You're half-frozen."

"Yes, the journey was cold. The carriage was stuck in the snow for a while."

"By the marsh? It's done that before. Did they manage the horses? Come to the fire, girl, you look perished. Clare, are you going to greet your sister?"

Lady Clare came over and pressed a thin cheek against Isabella's. It was the first time she'd done such a thing. She murmured something and then returned to her chair.

Sitting in the elaborate room filled with the treasures and trophies of the past, the most composed person was Isabella.

Her face had lost its reviving brightness but she was poised and calm. She had made a decision to do something selfless and after that everything had become curiously simple. Always self-indulgent and childish, the feeling was new to her. She had no resentment or dislike left for the Earl or Lady Clare. Lady Clare had wronged her. *She* had wronged Denys.

They were suffering more than she. Denys had lived in their thoughts all the time he had been away because he still loved them. But in Isabella's spirit he had dwindled, not because she wanted that, but because he had rejected her.

The Earl sat down in the old way, as if falling. Lady Clare began to sew.

"Robert says the ship is expected in Gravesend in a week or so," Isabella said, holding her hands to the fire.

"Might be sooner," said the Earl. "If they have a following wind."

"I always forget the wind."

"Sailors don't," said the Earl.

A second later he had fallen suddenly asleep. He began to snore.

Lady Clare put the small embroidery frame down on her knee and looked across at Isabella.

"He often does that. He is getting old."

"He looks quite well," said Isabella involuntarily, with the old trick of needing a happy ending.

"I do not think so. If Carteret dies, it will kill him."

"Don't say that, Clare!"

It was the first time Isabella had called her by her name or that she and Clare had talked normally.

"He's been so sad since my brother went to India," Clare said, beginning to sew again. "He blames himself, you know, because he was not good to Carteret. He never appreciated him. He treated him like a fool. Now he's very unhappy, poor old man. One can do nothing to help him. The thing that upsets him most is that it was he who spoke to Lord Gough and persuaded him to get Carteret back into the Regiment . . . "

Isabella listened and Clare talked of Denys and his father. The old Earl with his beaked, fierce face, lay deeply asleep. How different Clare is, Isabella thought. Everything is changed because I am changed. Only this huge old house is the same as when I was eighteen and acted in that play with Kate and I thought everything here so beautiful. Like paradise.

A log in the fireplace fell in a shower of sparks. The Earl stirred.

"He won't wake for another half hour," Clare said.

Isabella looked at her.

"Your father must not blame himself for Denys going, Clare. He went because of me. He couldn't bear to be with me. He chose to go as far away as possible. To the other side of the world."

Clare looked into the fire.

Her face, with that big ugly nose, that odd look of a daring boy, was somber. She sighed.

"If somebody I loved hurt me, *I* wouldn't run," she said. "Nor would Robert. Carteret was never very brave."

Clare didn't seem to find anything curious about the conversation, though the suffering had sprung, full-armed, from her own action. If I am changed, Isabella thought, so is she. I suppose, because she won, she forgave me. Yet I lost, and I don't hate her. Isabella wondered if it was Denys whose wounded spirit altered everything. But he wasn't here yet: she couldn't tell.

Clare picked up her sewing. As she pulled the silk through the taut fabric it made a snapping sound.

"It was good of you to come here. I am sure Carteret will need you. I remember when Freddy was born he said you were brave. He told Papa so. I hope it's true. Because you're going to need to be again."

In the days that followed Isabella resumed the pattern of living she'd known all through her marriage and which the Bagots had set hundreds of years ago. She remembered it as an actress might recall a role she had played years before. The family had formal meals together. In the mornings or the afternoons they rode out or walked in the park despite the bitter weather. They visited the nursery. The children, exquisitely dressed, were brought in by their nurse for tea. In the evenings the family often played backgammon, a favorite of the Earl's. They always played cards in the Music Room, where Kate had acted in *The Welsh Girl* so long ago, and where the marble Venus stood in its unchanging place.

Isabella and Clare didn't speak again of anything that mattered. Clare and the Earl behaved to her with a marked courtesy. They felt in her debt.

Freddy and Betsy took her presence with the marvelous lack of surprise of people under six years old, merely asking when they could snowball and would *she* please read to them, she was so much better than Nurse.

The snow didn't melt. It fell again, freshly white on the top of the old frozen snow, thickening along the window sills, its surface starred with the tiny feet of birds. One day colder than the rest there was the sound that everybody in the house, from the Earl to the youngest servant, was waiting for. Wheels in the drive, a carriage with four tired horses at the doors.

A weary old man, gray-bearded and in Army uniform, alighted from the carriage with Robert, and together they supervised carrying the stretcher into the house.

Clare and Isabella had been in the drawing room, and when they heard the carriage wheels they stared at each other with an identical expression of dread. Clare didn't move. But Isabella ran to the door and opened it in time to see two footmen, Robert and the unfamiliar figure of the doctor going by with a kind of pallet, which was slowly carried up the main staircase. All Isabella could see was a motionless figure covered in blankets.

She watched the procession disappear up the staircase.

Coming back into the room, she said in a low voice, "Clare. Ought I to have—"

"Of course not."

"What must we do? Wait?"

"We will do a great deal of that," Clare said, picking up her sewing. Her hand shook.

Isabella went to the window and watched the horses steaming in the cold air and the grooms running to blanket them and leading each horse away with a sweet coaxing whistle. In her mind Denys had a mystery about him now that he was ill. Everything about him was mysterious, his sickness, his nearness to death, the long journey on the sea, the far-off places he had come from, the battles he had witnessed. He no longer seemed either the indolent nobleman who had married and loved her or the stony stranger who had made her suffer. But someone else, frightening and unfamiliar in whose presence soon—today—she must go as if to face the Day of Judgment.

The door opened, and Robert came in. He still wore his long coat trimmed with fur, and mud-splashed boots.

"When he has rested you may see him."

They said nothing until Clare remarked severely, "You look exhausted."

"The ship didn't dock until two. I was up and about quite early."

"All night, you mean."

He smiled slightly and then, to Isabella in the window seat, "I see Denys is in his own room."

"I have moved next door. If it troubles him that I am close I shall move to the nursery wing."

"I did not mean that."

"Robert, you cannot seriously imagine he would wish me to share his room."

Denys's presence, Denys's sick presence, came into the house like the snow from outside. Neither his wife nor his sister were allowed to see him for the rest of the day. The nurse engaged by the doctor, a tall elderly woman with narrow eyes like a Russian, sat beside him, cared for him expertly, was quiet and confident. Servants came and went. The house was quiet. The Earl sat for a while by his son's bed while Denys slept, then sidled out in silence.

When Clare and Isabella had dressed for dinner and were together in the drawing room, Robert came to them. He had slept during the afternoon and looked more like himself. He was also in evening dress. Its black and white had always suited him, Isabella thought. He is so like Denys. It is something about his eyes, I think.

"Clare. If you'll forgive me, I will take Bella up first."

Robert walked beside her up the great marble staircase and along the corridor to the room Denys and Isabella used to share, where both Freddy and Betsy had been born. Robert opened the door.

Only two candles burned. The room was as quiet as a church at night. Denys lay in the big double bed with heaped pillows arranged to support him. His eyes were shut and he was very pale but when she saw him she lost the feeling, at once, that this was a stranger. It was dear, familiar, sleeping, stricken Denys. His nightshirt was open at the throat and she could see the dark hairs on his chest. His hands on the counterpane were whiter than the sheets. They were very beautiful.

The nurse stood up and said in a low voice, "I think his Lordship is awake."

"Thank you, Nurse. You may leave us for a while."

She went quietly out, and Robert drew a chair for Isabella. She sat down, took the pale hand in her own and pressed it against her cheek. She did as she used to do, rubbing his hand backward and forward against her face. He opened his eyes.

Faintly, through the luminous haze of the candles, he saw a girlish oval face, a small straight nose like a child's. He sighed.

"Ah. My dearest," he said.

Isabella moved not to the nursery wing to be away from him but into the sickroom. She slept in a bed at the foot of his own. Always afraid of sickness and the prison of suffering, she stayed with him all day long, slept in the room at night, would scarcely stir from his side. She learned nursing from the old woman with the slanting eyes. She was often alone with the patient for long hours and sat holding his hand until her own became so numb Robert had to chafe it back to feeling.

Sometimes Clare or Robert came in and forced her to go out for a walk in the snow or ride round the park or spend an hour with the children or have tea with the Earl. But Isabella was always fretted, impatient, and ran back up the staircase to Denys's room like a dog to its master.

Denys was often in pain and glad to take the chloral, which made him sleep and relieved his suffering. He drifted like a soul aswoon but followed her with his eyes when he was awake. Sometimes when she put her cheek against his hand he somehow managed to move his other hand and touch her.

Young, sanguine, healthy, hopeful, how could she help believing she could make him better?

"Robert, he *must* live, I shall *make* him!"

She was in the hall, having just come in from impatiently walking up and down the snow-covered terrace. Her fur-edged cloak was sprinkled with snow. She looked up the staircase, about to hurry back to the sickroom that she could not bear to leave.

Robert said slowly, "Dear Bella. Don't hope."

He took her hand.

"But I must! I shall!"

She wrenched away her hand and ran up the stairs two at a time. She slipped through the door into the room where Denys lay. The room was full of love and suffering. It smelled of flowers and chloral, it was airless and very still. She could hear a dying fall of music there but she blocked her ears against it.

Denys died a week later. He had seen the children, but Isabella knew he had scarcely known them although he tried to smile. Once or twice he had seen his father, he had pressed his sister's hand, spoken to Robert. But it was Isabella, jealous, tender, passionate and calm, whose figure he looked for with his dying eyes. She was alone with him when, so quietly, his breathing grew slower and slower and then stopped.

Isabella had been the solitary center of Denys's dying; she carried the whole weight of his illness and death, never letting go of an ounce of the burden. But when he was dead the center shifted to Clare. Isabella did not become ill. She was always about the house, pale and collected in her black dress. But she knew nothing about such a thing as a Bagot funeral. The Earl was ailing, and Robert and Clare took over the house and organized the coming funeral as if it were for a Royal prince. It would be a huge affair. People would come not only from all over the county but from London, every room in every mansion would be crowded with distinguished visitors, Bagot Park would be full, not a bedroom of the seventy or more unoccupied.

Fanny's child was due soon, and her doctors would not allow her to travel from Cumberland, to her deep grief. But every other relation and friend in the great world would be there. Everything was arranged with formality, and Isabella listened in silence as they decided on the invitations, chose the music and the flowers. There was a letter from Her Majesty and one from the Duke of Wellington. There was mourning to be arranged for the children. Isabella thought Freddy and Betsy's little figures pathetic, head to foot in black serge.

On the day of the funeral there was no sign of a thaw. The air was clear and bitter, with a hint of winter sunshine cold as the snow.

Isabella, with the Earl, Clare and Robert, traveled to the church in the huge old-fashioned Georgian carriage brought out for Bagot state occasions. Isabella had last sat in it for Betsy's christening and she remembered how she and Denys had laughed because the carriage was so huge and solemn, the baby so tiny in her yards of cambric and lace.

The Earl said nothing during the drive; Clare looked at him now and again. Once she said, "Papa. Would you like some air? Shall I open the window?"

"Don't be a fool, girl. Do you want to freeze us to death?"

The small old church was crammed with black-clad sad-faced people, only half of whom Isabella recognized. She and Clare were shown with reverence into the high-backed Bagot pew, and the Earl collapsed beside them, bent and pale. The music began. The choir of children, some scarcely older than Freddy, sang with a piercing sweetness as the coffin, covered with white flowers, was carried in.

Isabella's heart ached just then. What was all this, so mournful and austere, so comforting because of prayers, so comfortless because of the silence of death, to do with Denys?

It is my fault he is dead, she thought. It is my fault that lazy, sweet man had his life ruined. For Buckley. For Buckley and something I wanted and can't remember. The voices of the children rose higher and she remembered Denys exactly as he had been when they were happy. He moved again in her imagination. She heard the lazy tones of his voice, saw him stretch out his long legs and stare idly at his polished boots. She saw him laugh, smelled his eau-de-cologne, felt his gentle passionate kisses.

Then, with a swish of black silk skirts and the sound of feet on cold stone, everybody rose and went out of the church into the icy graveyard.

Some of the guests who had come for the funeral stayed on for a while. Most were elderly relations whose presence Isabella found comforting. Denys's grandmother, old Lady Bagot, now in her eighties, was kind to her for the first time since they had met. She took her grandson's death with more steadiness than the Earl, who spent his time either shut up in his study with Robert or riding on the frozen roads round the estates.

When Isabella returned to the house on the afternoon of

the funeral her husband's sickroom was completely transformed. The bed in which he had died was gone, a small
eighteenth-century four-poster was in its place. Curtains and
covers were changed. There were pots of winter-flowering
camellias from the hothouse, fresh-covered cushions on a
chaise longue. The altered room banished the days she had
spent beside him. She said nothing.

A week later she went into the library one dark afternoon
and found Clare sitting wearily at a desk, brightly lit with two
branched candlesticks, answering letters.

Clare looked up.

"I am trying to answer some of them. Papa has taken the
most important, but there are five hundred still to do. I want
to do thirty a day."

"I will do thirty as well."

"Would you? Are you sure?"

"I will be glad to."

Clare gave a brief smile.

"I know they must write and we must answer. I accept it
with my mind. But every time I read a letter and every time I
write one, it still makes me cry."

Isabella suddenly leaned forward and kissed her.

They were both startled by the embrace. Clare said in an
uneven voice, "I never apologized to you. For that terrible
thing."

"Perhaps I deserved it."

"But Carteret didn't. I can't forgive myself for that."

"You mustn't be like your father. Denys would hate you to
be unhappy, wouldn't he? Clare. I want Denys's bed back in
my room."

"But I thought—"

"Oh, I know. You were right. I couldn't have slept in it, not
the very next night or even after a week. But now I want to."

It was Clare whose eyes filled with tears.

The desk was wide, and Isabella pulled up a chair beside
her. With the candles lighting both of them, she picked up
one of the letters and began to read.

* * *

It seemed to everybody at Bagot Park that their lives forevermore would be spent surrounded by snow, or slipping on the icy terrace, or studying a sky turned a threatening mauvish gray, foretelling new snow falls.

The thaw came suddenly. One morning when Rivers pulled the bedroom curtains Isabella knew that something had changed. Then she saw there was no longer a six-inch white bar along the window ledge. The air was full of the sound of dripping water. She heard children laughing on the terrace and the sound of the puppy barking.

It was like the transformation scene in a pantomime, she thought, as she came down the staircase to breakfast. The park was already turning green. The sun was shining. When she went into the breakfast room her father-in-law looked up from his newspaper and nodded at her. Robert smiled. Swayne served her with coffee and looked disappointed when she refused any of the five hot dishes on the sideboard.

Robert glanced at her during the meal. How silent she was these days. In the past she was a girl who was never quiet, it had been one of the things about her Denys had liked when they first met, her friendly, frivolous chat. Now she sat, upright and graceful in her deep black clothes, like a figure in a mourning ring. She had altered so often. She seemed to take on the color of life around her, to become a part of it. Was it the actress in her? Robert asked himself what her future would be, whether she intended to take up again with that actor, her sister's husband. The dignified black-robed figure seemed to him an infinity away from such a thought.

The Earl shuffled with the documents which had arrived from London that morning. He cleared his throat.

"Isabella. I have something to say to you."

She looked up. It drifted into her mind that perhaps he no longer wished her to be here.

"Whitfield has written to me. In short—about that damned thing."

She saw that he was upset, and genuinely wishing to save him pain, said, "Would you rather we did not speak of it?"

At this strange sentence, proof of her own strength and indifference, he stared.

"Of course I wish to speak of it. To finish with it. Whitfield says, *I* say, that it's to be forgotten. Never a word of truth in it."

He blew his nose fiercely.

"So Freddy is still—"

"For God's sake!"

He stood up, muttered, "Kiss me," gave her a peck on the cheek and sidled out of the room.

"He is more glad than he wishes to show," said Robert, who had been watching in silence.

"Then I am glad, too."

He looked at her, somehow forcing her to meet his eyes, and gave a smile.

"Do you suppose you could wake up? It is very unsatisfactory being with you nowadays. Like being with the Sleeping Beauty."

"I am quite awake, Robert."

"Then you must be relieved that the miserable thing is finally over."

"Yes. For Freddy's sake. But Denys is gone. And then, you know, one gets used to having no reputation."

"All that will be mended now," he said vigorously. He spoke, she thought, as if planning to repair a farmer's damaged roof.

"There's more news. It's a day for news. First the thaw. Then Lord Whitfield. And now Clare. She told my uncle last night that when the mourning time is over she wishes to be married. He knew about the offer, of course, but not whether she would accept. He's very pleased."

"Oh, I'm so glad!"

It was the first time she had shown any vitality. It was ironic, he thought, that her reaction to the sister-in-law who had hated her was warmer than that about her own good fortune.

"The Duke of Blackwell's heir," he said and laughed. "Clare will be a duchess one day. Fan is already jealous."

"Clare will make a fine duchess."

"She'd agree to that."

There was a pause. In his usual way Robert was walking about, now standing at the long window watching the children romping on the terrace, now coming back to collect the papers which the Earl had left scattered on the table.

"May one ask what your plans are, Bella?"

"To go back to my house quite soon."

"This is your house."

She shook her head.

"No, it is not. It is the Earl's. Clare's. Yours. Freddy's one day. It is nothing to do with me."

"You proved the contrary when Deno was brought home."

"Yes. I was glad to be here. Glad you brought me—forced me to come. I think it *was* mine for a little. But not any more. Everything is changing. I can feel it, and so can you."

"Perhaps."

"So I must go back to Twickenham and have the covers taken off my poor furniture and make the house live, and see my family, and the children shall be with me when it's spring. I must make something of my little life."

"I hope I shall be part of it."

"Well. I daresay a cousin is a small part," she said with her tired smile.

Chapter Twenty

SEEING HIM EVERY NIGHT OF HER LIFE, Kate visited Davenant's house only on Sundays. It was the only day of the week when they were not at the theater. Davenant gave his servants the day off, and he and Kate spent the day alone.

She had arrived for luncheon, one early spring Sunday. He had said the previous evening that he would show her the costume designs for a new production of *Love's Labour's Lost.* Something sly in his manner made her immediately guess that his costumes might outshine her own.

Davenant lived in a rambling old house in Chelsea, on part of the site of what had once been Henry VIII's Tudor palace. Along the riverside were beached boats and willow trees, and in Davenant's garden were ancient brick walls and traces—a mulberry tree, a stone plinth—of lost Tudor glory.

She waited for him in the upstairs drawing room. A visitor would have wanted to spend an hour staring round the room, which was full of the treasures heaped upon a great actor. Portraits of Davenant as Hamlet and Shylock, framed programs printed on satin, silver engraved snuffboxes. In a glass-topped table was an embroidered slipper which had belonged to Garrick.

The room's romance left Kate untouched. Artists also painted her, distinguished visitors brought her offerings. She spread out her velvet skirts and stared into the fire. She was waiting, tensed, expectant, for Davenant. Kate had, at last, found a master. He had taught her some of the subtlest of the acting arts, and every single one of those arts of sexual love. He found her ignorance infinitely exciting, and never tired of the things he could teach her, that they could do to give each other pleasure. This passionate beauty had had no climax until *he* gave her one, had never been kissed between her legs until *his* mouth gave her ecstatic pleasure. Her body was a kingdom he explored, claimed, and ruled like a despot. Kate, strong-willed, ambitious, until now utterly self-possessed, was as helpless with him as a slave. And that, he knew, was what she needed, a sensual bondage which he stimulated, enjoyed and satisfied. "Beautiful woman," he had said once as he took her, "do as you are bid!"

She looked up quickly when Davenant came into the room. He walked over to kiss both her hands.

"A glass of madeira, Kate?"

She gave him the radiant smile which was, perhaps, the most potent of her spells.

"Nothing, thank you."

"I shall," he said. "You are always assuring me that even small quantities of wine dull the artistic perceptions. Why do you suppose you will need your *artistic* perceptions today?"

"I wonder," she said, laughing.

He walked with her across the room to a table under the window, and arranged for her inspection the designs for the new production of *Love's Labour's Lost*. Sitting in a pose she had often seen him take onstage, back straight, arms spread out, hands grasping the edge of the table, he talked of work. He made her laugh, mimicking the designer and some of the actors. He picked up a copy of the play and read a passage aloud. He made her eyes fill. He could always do that.

"So you like the designs. Excellent," he finished, putting them away without hearing her opinion.

"Some of my costumes may have to be changed a little," she said mildly.

He met her eyes, and they both laughed.

When they went back to the fire and sat down he asked, "Did you see *The Times* yesterday?"

"No."

He looked at her sceptically.

"But you know the news. That your sister has lost her husband."

"Yes. Gwynyth told me. I shall write to her."

He was not impressed, still looking at her with his brilliant eyes slightly narrowed.

"You're a hard little creature on occasions. You remind me of a peach. Your sister, from what I've gathered, was an egg. Well-shaped. Smooth. Firm shell. Perfect. But if you close your hand upon it, what happens? Now a peach is a very different thing. Juicy and soft, beautiful and luscious. But if you bite too deeply, by God, you crack your teeth on the stone."

"You think me hardhearted," she said, despising her own weakness in asking the question.

"Not for some," he replied coolly. "Not for your audience. You are all melting womanhood and virtue to *them*. And I like my peach, juice and flesh, even its danger to my teeth."

She said nothing. When would he take her in his arms? She was hungry for him.

But he remained silent, leaning back in his high-backed chair and reflecting.

"It is time you saw that sister of yours again," he said suddenly.

She was very taken aback.

"But I have refused to see her for two years. She knows very well why."

Davenant raised his eyebrows.

"Kate, Kate."

Meeting his glance, she blushed. He perfectly understood her. Understood her prejudices, her sometime lack of heart.

And knew just how much she was wanting him.

"You must write to your sister today," he said. "It is your cue, as you are very well aware. Do you love me? Good. Then come here and show me."

Isabella decided not to take her children back to Twickenham when she left Bagot Park. The thaw had come, and the children were riding out with their friends every day, looking comic and rosy-faced on their shaggy ponies.

Robert and Clare were both relieved when Isabella told them that the children could stay.

"Freddy is such a comfort to his grandfather," said Clare.

"Betsy's rather a comfort to Clare," added Robert, smiling.

The family came out on the terrace to bid her good-bye. Swayne fussed over her. Mrs. Judge had packed a traveling basket of food and wine for her—Isabella might have been journeying to Scotland. The groom wrapped her round with a sable-covered rug, tucking it under her feet. Every member of the family, every servant, treated her like that. It moved and oppressed her.

It was late and dark when the carriage galloped through Twickenham, took the quiet road near the river and turned into her own drive. The brougham which followed with the servants pulled up and there were voices, stamping hooves and figures scurrying with boxes. Isabella, who had been asleep, woke up and shivered. She walked into the ice-cold house with the servants round her, like a queen among courtiers.

Kindly fussed over by Rivers, who brushed her hair and wrapped her shoulders in a filmy shawl, Isabella went to bed and blew out the candle. The new-lit fire burned, but scarcely warmed the icy room. She felt so sad. She lay back on the pillows, which like her thoughts were damply cold. She had a feeling of yearning loneliness.

But next morning the sun was an orange disc above the trees, and she woke to Rivers's cheerful face and a tray with a pot of hot chocolate.

"A letter, my Lady. Delivered very early."

Rivers pulled and looped the curtains, lit the fire, muttered, "Come on, Chloe, my girl," and left with the spaniel at her heels.

Isabella picked up the letter. It would be another among the hundreds of condolences which she and Clare had painfully answered. But when she looked at the envelope she knew the rounded writing.

"My dear Isabella,

"I was grieved to hear of the Viscount's death. He was a wonderful man and so kind to our parents. It is sad for your children to be fatherless. Our lives have been much severed and perhaps it is time to try and mend this before we grow older and it is too late. I am quite willing, at least, to attempt to do so. If you would like to see me, come to the theater on any afternoon about four o'clock if that suits you. I do not work at that hour."

Exactly as Denys's letters used to do, in the same abbreviated, meaningless way, the letter ended, "Affectionately. K."

During the morning, Isabella took her dog for a walk along the towpath under the leafless willows. The letter had made her nervous. She knew she must accept the hand coldly offered to her, just as she'd had to go to Bagot Park when the family needed her. It would please Ellen if she and Kate met, if it did nothing else.

"Robert would be pleased, too," she thought. Had Robert become her conscience? She hoped not.

She was walking homeward, picking her way along the muddy path, when she heard a rider behind her. She stood to one side and a voice said, "Hello!"

Reining in his horse, grinning down at her, was Buckley. He dismounted and pressed her gloved hand.

"Do you know I've ridden over from Richmond every morning for a week? How is that for devotion? It is good to see you. I've so much to tell you."

He walked beside her, leading the horse, telling her all that had happened to him since she had been "spirited off" to the country. He had refused the Irish engagement but "they still keep begging, you know." He was to start on the Kent circuit soon, but there was talk of a possible engagement at Covent Garden. "*That* would make Davenant look stupid, wouldn't it!" He did not ask how she was. If he found her subdued he did not say so.

Isabella asked him to luncheon, and he accepted with scarcely the usual politeness of manner. He was perfectly at home with her, she thought with wonder. He might have been her husband for years.

Buckley did indeed find her changed. The deep mourning had a distancing effect. She wore a black braided gown, a tiny black lace cap suited to a woman of fifty, a great mourning ring on her finger. Nothing sparkled in the room but the silver on the table, the fire in the grate and a jet necklace on her bosom. He was accustomed to mourning onstage or in lodging houses, or to seeing it worn by strangers in the street, or at other people's funerals. But actresses tried to avoid it and soon struggled out of its dark confines because they needed engagements and it might spoil their chances. Isabella's mourning was a barrier which Buckley wished to overleap.

When the meal was over and they were alone he pushed back his chair and refilled his glass with the excellent burgundy. He gave her the smile which made women feel beautiful. Isabella was not immune to it.

"Have you thought about me, Bella?"

"I have thought about you since I returned."

"Only since then?"

That was a mistake. He went on quickly, "We must be together, you know."

"Don't ask me yet," she said quite kindly. "It is too soon. And then the children are coming home. There are so many things to think about. It isn't as it was when there was only myself."

"I don't see how it's changed except that you are a widow. For which I'm very sorry, Bella, if you are upset. You always had a soft heart. But otherwise things are the same. Kate and I are living apart, of course. That is over for good. There is only one woman for me. Now. Always. You know who that is," he finished with heavy roguishness.

She rather admired his vulgar egotistic confidence. She showed him Kate's letter, and he burst out laughing. How exactly like Kate it was. So sniffy. He'd wager Bella intended to go and patch it up.

"Why don't we go today?" he said. "I ought to see her, too, as a matter of fact. I want to take the children to the Zoological Gardens. They are all the rage, you know. They have some snow leopards from Southern Asia; I've always liked looking at wild beasts. Let me go with you to the Royalty. It will give you courage."

"But that is impossible."

She was shocked. A lot of things about him shocked her: some pleasurably.

"I didn't mean we would waltz into Kate's dressing room together, you ninny. I will drive with you to the theater and call on old Laurie Spindle for a pint of wine. You can make peace with Kate. Then you can sit, like the lady you are, in the Bagot carriage and wait for me and I'll toddle along and arrange about the leopards. What could be more simple?" Isabella consented doubtfully, but during their journey together to London she had a flash of her old common sense. Of course Kate wouldn't care a straw if she knew Buckley was with her . . . why hadn't she thought of that?

The gaslamps were lit, the evening was foggy. Isabella asked her coachman to wait, Buckley winked at him and was ignored. Isabella's servants disliked Buckley and discussed together how long it would be before my Lady gave him the cold shoulder.

"Off you go and see the Tragedy Queen and I'll wend my way to Laurie Spindle," Buckley said.

Isabella waited at the stage door, having sent up her card. Almost immediately a little woman with dyed hair came to her.

"Lady Carteret? Kate said would I fetch you. I'm her dresser."

Gwynyth took her into an enormous room so filled with flowers that it was like walking into the hothouse at Bagot Park. The air was scented and heavy, the room more gilded and fussy than those Isabella was used to.

Kate, in costume, was at her dressing table. She wore a blueish-green silk robe with huge sleeves and a four-inch gold sash round her waist. Her feet were bare, her coppery hair strangely dressed and threaded with pearls. She wore full stage makeup, her freckled skin white as alabaster, her lips reddened. Her sister's black-robed figure startled her. She had forgotten the mourning.

She stood up and walked over, saying kindly, "Do sit down. Would you like tea? Gwynyth always makes me some at this time."

"Thank you. That would be nice."

They could have been strangers.

When the old woman came in with a tray and Kate absently thanked her, she was given a look of adoration. Isabella had never seen such a look on the face of any servant of the Bagots, even those who had worked for the family all their lives.

There was an embarrassed pause as Kate poured the tea.

She's changed, each sister thought. To Isabella her sister had become curiously larger. Physically she was still a little thing, but there seemed an invisible aureole about her. Perhaps it was fame. She moved and smiled as the Queen might do. I know nothing about her any more, Isabella thought. And her face is masked with paint.

But although Isabella felt separated from her sister by Kate's unfamiliar look and manner, Kate was far more affected. With the sharp eye of an artist she noticed infinitely more. She could scarcely recognize this woman with her delicate pale face and mournful eyes, her repose which had a kind of aristocratic detachment.

Could this really be her sister, who had embraced Buckley,

perhaps mothered his child, been through a disgraceful scandal and was now a widow?

They talked banalities for a while. Kate made her smile once, and the sallow face changed a little. That horrible black, thought Kate. I suppose as she is a Viscountess she will wear it for months, years, even. It's like putting her in prison.

There was a knock at the door.

"Ten minutes, Miss Winter! Ten minutes!"

"Bother," said Kate. Then, taking it at a run because otherwise it would not be said, "Isabella. About Buckley. I have finally decided I shall divorce him."

"I didn't know."

"Neither did I," said Kate, her manner natural for the first time. "I was afraid there would be a sca—I mean Davanent has persuaded me it can be done when one is established, you see. Audiences are willing to forgive you if they love you. That's what he says."

She stood up, arranging the peacock robe which dragged behind her. She walked barefoot to her sister and touched Isabella's arm.

"Bella. If you want to be with Buckley, feel that it can be. I think perhaps you love him. As we are sisters you cannot marry him, but he could be *with* you. I want you to know that."

Isabella said nothing for a moment. Then she said, "It's very soon. I'll think about it. Thank you."

"I'm glad to see you," Kate said suddenly. "But I won't kiss you or you'll get covered in paint."

Isabella left the dressing room. As she walked away along the passage she had a curious feeling, a kind of wave of memory. It was full of lost friends and clapping hands, of tawdry finery and dusty theaters half-asleep. Dressing room doors stood open, actors called to one another. Somebody began to sing in a voice of perfect pitch which its owner knew was beautiful. A further door stood ajar, and as she walked nearer she heard a voice she knew very well. Buckley. She was about to look in at the door when she heard him say caressingly, "Have you thought about me, Dolly? We *must* be together, you know."

Isabella stopped for a moment in sheer surprise. Then quietly walked past the door. His back was turned to her, his arms were round a fair-haired girl who was delightedly giggling.

Isabella went swiftly out of the theater to the carriage and told the coachman to leave at once.

Buckley rode over to Twickenham the following morning. The butler announced him in the colorless voice he reserved for the one visitor he disliked: "Mr. Vernon has called, my Lady."

Isabella, who knew every nuance in the voice of her servants, said pleasantly, "Thank you, True. You may ask Mr. Vernon to come in."

"Will the gentleman stay for luncheon, my Lady?"

"No, True. I will be alone."

The butler retired to make what he could of the news.

Buckley had been furiously angry at being left flat the previous afternoon, and had ridden over to pick a quarrel. But when he was shown into the drawing room he changed his mind. The room had a fresh, formal look, and so had she. Wearing black silk, she was sitting on the window seat.

"Good morning, Buckley. I was not expecting you," said Isabella untruthfully.

"Why not? I always come to you."

He went close to her, instinctively knowing that he was strongest with women when he was near them.

"Isabella. You hurt me very much yesterday. Why did you leave like that? I simply couldn't believe you had gone."

"I am so sorry. I had something urgent to attend to."

He wanted to go on reproaching her but saw by her manner that it would be a waste of time. Besides, he disliked being the offended person in any encounter. It was a role he never played. He must be the one sought after, the one convinced of his welcome.

"Sit down, Buckley. May I ring for a glass of madeira?"

"Yes. I would like that," he said, willing to be wooed.

The wine was brought. The butler placed the decanter on a silver tray in front of Buckley, together with a gleaming glass engraved with the Bagot crest. When he was waited on by the Bagot servants Buckley always felt both important and at ease. That was how *he* should live.

He asked how the interview with Kate had gone and laughed when he heard that the sisters were reconciled. He told her about Laurie Spindle, recounting a conversation in which Laurie looked foolish and he—Buckley—shone. Isabella politely smiled. Then she said, "I'm afraid I must hurry you away now. The Bagots are arriving. It would not do for you to be seen here."

"I quite understand. Specially with you dressed in your Hamlet rig," he said impudently. "I've heard from the Irish manager again, Bella. You'll have to say yes. We *must* be together."

She stood up and he came to her and stood close, his hand on hers. She took her hand away.

"I'm afraid, Buckley, I have to disagree."

"What do you mean?"

"I don't think we should be together at all. I think this is good-bye."

He stared at her, at first appalled, then beginning to get angry.

"It's Kate—what has she been telling you, the vixen—"

"Be quiet, Buckley, it is nothing to do with Kate," she interrupted in a low voice. "When I went out of the theater yesterday afternoon I saw you with a woman."

"But that was nothing—just some little—"

"Buckley," she said, scarcely raising her voice but fixing him with a look of such disdain that he stopped speaking. "Until that minute I never really knew you. Do you think I would sacrifice my life, my children, my name, everything Denys stood for, for *you?* You're not worth bothering about. Please go."

For one incredible moment she thought he would strike her, but he gave a kind of gasp and rushed out of the room before she could ring. She heard the front door give a shuddering slam.

Kate wrote to invite Isabella to luncheon in Kensington for the following Sunday. Driving along the country roads from Twickenham, Isabella thought how green the trees and fields were now. Denys had been dead for nearly five months. When she thought of him, as she did many times a day, her deep and honest sorrow remained. Her heart ached, yet it did so tenderly. He had held her hand, called her "my dearest."

Separation between Kate and herself had done curious things to the past, she thought. There must always be great gaps now, things which had happened to each of them the other could never know. She was not even sure how Kate felt about her.

Kate's house, which she had never visited although Kate had lived there more than a year, was spacious, almost grand. There was a handsome entrance gate, high wrought-iron railings and in the front garden of the house a bronze statue of Neptune. The laburnams were in flower.

"Bella!"

Kate kissed her and took her to the upstairs drawing room. It was long and spacious, with windows overlooking the bronze Neptune at the front of the house, and more windows framing a vista of lawns, rose beds and a line of yew hedges. It might, thought Isabella, be a setting for *Much Ado*.

As if to make her sister feel at home, Kate rang for the nurse to bring in the children. When Matilda and Billy came shyly into the room, Isabella clasped her hands.

"Oh, Kate, how they've changed!"

Matilda, pretty and self-conscious, was startlingly like Buckley, with the same mouth, the same melting eyes. Billy had Kate's red hair and freckles; he was plump and timid. When Kate encouraged him to kiss his aunt, he looked as if he might cry. What touched Isabella was how much they had grown. As with her own children when they had been away from her for many weeks, they seemed strangely tall: they reminded her of flowers with long stems.

When they had gone she said, "They're lovely. Matilda is going to be a beauty, and Billy is a darling, too. Poor man, he was frightened of my black. You wouldn't recognize my Freddy and Betsy, they look pathetic all done up in black serge. But Robert and Clare say they will be allowed to come out of it in a month or two."

"And how long shall you be in mourning, Bella?" asked Kate. The laws of the nobility, like those of Royalty, were unknown to her.

"Maybe a year. Then I shall be in half-mourning, which is lilac and white. I shall wear Denys's amethysts. He always liked me to wear them. Of course I must not go about, you know, although Robert says he will. He told me women always mourn longer than men," Isabella said drily.

"Do you mind? Black for so long, I mean?"

"Oh, no. I prefer it."

Conversation during luncheon was pleasant but constrained. After the meal Kate took her sister round the house, showed her the nurseries, the garden room, a small paneled library where two full-length portraits of Kate hung, one as Beatrice, the other as Rosalind. They went into the conservatory full of exotic flowering plants.

When they were back in the upstairs drawing room Isabella said, "It's a lovely house. You must be happy here."

"I think Mama enjoys it more than I do," Kate said. "She goes round seeing whether the plants are being looked after, and suggesting improvements to every room. She does enjoy spending money."

"And Pa?"

"He likes being with the children best. He's teaching Matilda to speak verse. Do you know, she is quite gifted? The other day when I went into the nursery, can you guess what I heard being recited?"

"*Not* the Ten Dramatic Passions!"

"You are right."

There was a pause. Isabella, looking at her sister's pale freckled face, thought how young she still seemed. There was a kind of veil of innocence wrapped round her. How did she keep it?

"I've something to tell you, Kate. I've sent Buckley away."

Kate looked astonished, but before she could speak Isabella exclaimed, "Oh, Kate, how could we possibly have loved him! How did you? How did I? He is *ridiculous*, isn't he? When I came to see you at the theater the other day I went down the passageway between the dressing rooms and I passed by one room and there he was. Hugging and kissing some ballet girl or other. And do you know, he was saying *exactly* the things he'd said to me that very morning!"

She began to laugh. It was a sound Kate once knew very well and had heard every day when they were children, a low giggle, impossibly infectious.

"Poor Buckley," said Isabella, mopping her eyes, which watered with laughter. "He just has to have everybody worshiping him and nobody must say a word, not a single word of criticism or he snarls like a dog. So there he was, with that voice and handsome face, and it was so *funny*, Kate. Using the same words. Do you think he said the same things to you and me as well?"

She was still laughing, and Kate couldn't help joining her. They giggled weakly.

"So I told him to go, just as you did," said Isabella, dabbing her eyes again. "Do you think he will ever forgive us?"

"I am sure he won't."

Everything could be talked about after that. Kate spoke of Davenant and confessed that she was in love with him.

"Oh, Bella. So madly."

Her sister pressed her hand, and Kate sighed.

"I am to marry him, he says, when the divorce—which I truly dread—is over. He knows I am afraid of what people

think. Do you know what he said? 'We are the makers of
manners, Kate.' You know . . . Henry the Fifth and his
Queen . . . oh, Bella, when he is near me I feel—"

"How?"

"Helpless," Kate said.

There was a pause.

"You are very brave to take on such a fierce fellow."

"That is what he tells me," Kate said. Then she leaned forward impulsively.

"But what about you? What are your plans?"

"You sound just like my cousin Robert. Must one have
plans?"

"It won't do for you to be lonely."

"I cannot imagine I shall marry again."

"But you talk of your cousin Robert, as you call him, a
good deal," said Kate teasingly.

"Goodness, Kate, Robert would never look at me. Even
when I first met him years ago in Newcastle, I know he always saw me as an actress. But he has done so much for me. I
suppose one would say he is chivalrous. Yet . . . he has not
the aristocratic virtues, as Denys had. He is quick and clever
and impatient. Very strong. Worldly, too. Quite hard. He
would never look at me after what I have done. After my
past."

"But *you* look at him."

Isabella smiled. It was true. She thought so often of him.
His thin tall figure, dark thick hair, something strong and autocratic about him, haunted her.

"Kate, I see you are still sentimental. It is a great comfort."

Kate murmured that it was getting dark, and she must ring
for the lamps to be lit. It had begun to rain, and they could
hear the sound of rain falling on the summer leaves outside.

But they stayed in the dusk, talking of the past. Of their
childhood, and the coaches jolting them through so many
nights. Of the North Street theater and the winter evening
when they had played *The Welsh Girl* at Bagot Park. Of the

fire and the snow. Of Newcastle, the corn riots. Of Davenant. Of Denys. They had not talked together like this since they had shared an attic bedroom together.

Suddenly Kate lifted her head.

"Bella, you didn't order your carriage early, did you? I hoped that you would stay to dine."

"I hoped so, too. I told the carriage to return by eleven o'clock. But why?"

"Listen!"

Both the girls, at the same time, heard the familiar noise of impatient hooves, the slam of a carriage door. As if on cue, they both stood up, and went to the front windows. They stood together, looking down.

The rain was heavy now, and it fell steadily upon a yellow and black carriage which stood at the door. It made the carriage glitter under the light from a lamp in the drive. Everything about the carriage shone, from its brass fittings to the wet, glossy coats of the chestnut horses.

A man had descended from the carriage and was walking to the front door. It was Robert Bagot.